SHE RAISED HER ARMS TOWARD THE SKY AS IF TO TOUCH THE STARS. . . .

It was as if she had become part of the music. She moved closer to the fire, feeling its warmth. Her eyes met Rafael's, and she danced now only for him. No one else existed. Only Rafael. The rhythm quickened. Faster and faster she danced, caught up in her passion, whirling, spinning, gyrating until, at last, the lingering notes died away. She whipped her head around, her mass of dark hair in wild disarray, and bowed as the hypnotized watchers chanted her name: "Alicia! Alicia!"

Rafael, too, called to her. "Alicia!"

She fell to the ground exhausted. It was as if she'd been in a trance, as if some spell in the music had driven her, urging her to say with her movements what no words could ever say: that she chose him, wanted him. . . . How could she deny what was in her heart?

Also by Kathryn Kramer:

DESIRE'S MASQUERADE

UNDER GYPSY SKIES

Kathryn Kramer

A DELL BOOK

Published by
Dell Publishing
A division of
The Bantam Doubleday Dell Publishing Group, Inc.
1 Dag Hammarskjold Plaza
New York, New York 10017

Dell ® TM 681510, Dell Publishing, a division of the Bantam
Dell Doubleday Publishing Group, Inc.

ISBN: 0-440-20008-3

Printed in the United States of America
Published simultaneously in Canada

May 1988

10 9 8 7 6 5 4 3 2 1

KRI

This book is dedicated in loving memory to my stepfather, Wesley Hockett. You are gone, Daddy, but not forgotten.

Again, I would like to thank my mother, Marcia Hockett, for her aid in research for *this* work. I could not have done it without you. And to my editor, Marilyn Wright, whose advice and expertise is so greatly appreciated. I look forward to working with you again.

Overhead the stars were shining candles,
    flooding all the earth with gentle light.
Your arms reached out to bring my body closer,
    all strength and tenderness, you held me tight.
Violins around the Gypsy campfires,
    played their haunting melody.
Under Gypsy skies, I loved you
    and changed forever my destiny. . . .

Kathryn Kramer

Author's Note

Gypsy. The very word brings forth a feeling of freedom, like the flowing rivers or the whispering wind. Gypsies have for centuries rejected city life to live in open spaces. Unconfined. Free. Wanderer. Nomad. The men are handsome and the women beautiful, bedecked in colorful garments, traveling in their caravans.

The Gypsies told a romantic story of their flight from Egypt to escape the marauding Saracens and the name "Gypsy" was derived from "Egypt," their supposed land of origin. The Gypsies wandered through Europe for hundreds of years, thus no one is certain just where they truly came from, but most scholars agree that rather than Egypt, they originated in India. Their language, called "Romany," is similar to those of northwestern India, with words from the Persian and Armenian languages. They call themselves "Rom," which in their language means "man." Mysterious and interesting, their name brings to mind fortune-telling—tarot cards, crystal balls, and palm reading—though in fact these skills were more often than not used as ploys against "gorgios," or non-Gypsies.

In Russia, Hungary, and Poland many are musicians. Gypsy legend tells of Mara, whose love for a gorgio brought forth the first violin. Many composers, Liszt and Brahms particularly, have used Gypsy tunes in their work. The women were accomplished herbalists, the men skilled with animal healing—nature's people.

Unfortunately, the unsettled way of living of the Gypsy has created prejudice against them in many countries. People often fear what they do not understand. Thus they were accused of witchcraft, child-stealing, and thievery. The fact, instead, was that major crimes were rare among Gypsies.

The Gypsies were a persecuted people, driven out of many countries of Europe. Many were also killed. King Ferdinand and Queen Isabella of Spain were among those persecuting the Gypsies. In the edict of 1492 the Jews were expelled from the country and the Gypsies as well.

This, then, is the setting for my story of a young Gypsy girl and her love for a Spanish nobleman. *Under Gypsy Skies* they find a love far stronger than any earthly law, as timeless as eternity.

UNDER GYPSY SKIES

One

A THOUSAND EYES
Castile 1491

The night has a thousand eyes,
And the day but one;
Yet the light of the bright world dies
With the dying sun.

The mind has a thousand eyes,
And the heart but one;
Yet the light of a whole life dies
When love is done.
—F. W. Bourdillon, *Light*

1

Illuminated only by the light of the moon, the gaudy wooden wagons rumbled along the narrow, winding road toward the forest beyond the City of Toledo. At the head of the caravan, the Gypsy named Rudolpho rode upon the back of a midnight-black stallion, a powerful animal managed by a most formidable man. The years had lined Rudolpho's face, but he was still an imposing sight, with broad shoulders, a strong chin, challenging dark eyes, and a drooping black mustache. Wiping his sweaty face with his bright green scarf, he raised his arm in signal that they would make their camp here at the edge of the woods near the river.

Acknowledging his leadership, the other men of the tribe began forming their wagons and horses into a circle, unrolling tents, and freeing horses to roam and graze upon the woodland grass. Women and children gathered wood for the fires that would be built on this night, as they were every other night, to celebrate the freedom that was the Gypsies' joyous heritage.

A warm breeze whispered through the branches of the trees, blowing the unruly mane of rich dark-brown hair that cascaded nearly to the knees of the young woman who jumped down from the first of the wagons. It was bad luck for any Gypsy woman to cut her hair thus, as tradition declared, and Alicia had never shorn a single lock of her tresses. Now she laughed as she let the wind whip her hair about her, throwing her head back with the gesture of ultimate freedom.

A beautiful girl of seventeen summers, Alicia was tall and animated, her green eyes sparkling like stars in the moonlight. More than one Gypsy's eyes were swept in her direction, bewitched by her haunting beauty.

"Alicia!" Rudolpho's voice was caressing and soft as he spoke his daughter's name, with none of the fierce thunder that so often frightened some of the others. "Alicia!"

She swept toward him with an all-embracing smile, her many skirts rustling as she walked. Her low-cut white blouse was stitched with threads as beautiful and colorful as the wings of a butterfly; her gold and silver earrings bobbled as she moved, in rhythm with her graceful motion.

"What is it, Papa?" she asked, her eyes gentle as they met his.

"I just wanted to see your sweet face," he said, dismounting from his horse with the agility of a man half his size and age. "This long ride has jiggled my bones until I feel as if I might fall apart, but your smile always soothes me."

Looking at him with concern, Alicia noticed a grimace of pain etched around his mouth as he stretched his arms and legs. He was growing old, his face pale and lined. How she wished that another would take his place as leader of the tribe and ease the burden from his shoulders, but to that she knew Rudolpho would never consent. Until he died he would be the Gypsy lord of their small band of wanderers. There was nothing she could do or say to change his mind.

As he tugged at a stray curl of her hair in a gesture of affection, Rudolpho's expression brightened, changing from misery to pride as he recalled the lovely child who had been brought to him so long ago by a heartless woman whose face was now forgotten. Even at a very early age Alicia had very delicate features and large expressive eyes. "Ah, what a lovely woman you have become," he whispered. "But then I knew you would outshine the stars themselves. Only a prince is good enough for you."

"A prince!" She reached out to touch his shoulder. "No prince, Papa. I will marry a Gypsy just like myself. Perhaps Vito, Stivo, Ramón, or Xenos with his dark, brooding eyes, eh?"

He did not answer, only looked at her with great sadness, as if there were something he wanted to tell her. She wondered at his sudden change of mood, the worried expression that had molded his features many times of late.

Alicia put her curiosity into words. "Is something wrong, Papa?" Tugging at the sleeves of Rudolpho's bright green shirt, she maneuvered him toward a grove of trees, leaving the others behind to set up camp. Perhaps if he were away from the noise and confusion, he would relax and confide his anxieties to her, she reasoned.

The trunks of the massive giants of the forest swept upward toward the sky, their thick foliage blocking out the moonlight. Beneath these trees they sat upon the damp grass, listening as the din of voices from the camp blended with the woodland sounds—the chorus of night birds serenading them with song, the contented hoot of an owl far away, the chirp of the crickets in syncopated rhythm. Comforting sounds.

Neither Alicia nor her father spoke a word for several minutes, then Alicia broke the silence by asking Rudolpho once again what was troubling him.

He wanted to answer her; needed to confide in her, yet the words would not come. How could he tell her she was not one of them? How could he break her heart that way? He couldn't tell this happy, beautiful child of his heart that she was not truly his daughter, nor of the woman who had brought her to his camp nearly fourteen years ago.

The child was a gorgio, a non-Gypsy, yet one look at her had touched his heart; and despite all that he had been taught, Rudolpho had claimed the child as his own. But the laws of the tribe to keep the Romany blood pure were strict. Alicia could never marry among them. Could he tell her that now, while she curved her mouth in a smile? She was so happy and proud to be a Gypsy. No, he could not tell her.

"Papa?"

"I am no longer young," he said, taking her hand. "I worry about what will happen to you when I am gone from this earth."

"Gone? I won't let you leave me, Papa." How like the young to want to combat death, he mused. "I can't imagine life without you. We've always been together." Or so it seemed. Yet there were times when she was bothered by dreams, haunting memories of another place, another time. She seemed to remember walking, reaching up to take the hand of an unknown woman, only to have her clinging hands pushed roughly away. She had imagined that the woman had been her mother, but Rudolpho had insisted that her mother had died when she was born. Questions of her childhood and about her mother always seemed to furrow his brow, and so she had let him keep his silence. It didn't really matter as long as she had her father's love.

"Always?" Rudolpho smiled. "You have been with me a long time, and every day of my life I have given thanks for that day when you came into my life. You have brought me much happiness."

Alicia felt the strength in his fingers as he squeezed her hand. Despite his years he was more than a match for most men, she thought. Someday she wanted to marry such a man. "I love you, Papa."

"And I love you." He smiled. "You are easy to love, child. Beautiful, wild, and spirited, like the wild colts we seek to tame."

"I am Gypsy!" she said, sitting up tall and thrusting up her chin. She was content with the life she led, wandering with the wagons, camping out beneath the stars. Never would she want to be *gorgio*. Thinking about the non-Gypsies made her scowl. Those whey-faced fools who always crossed themselves against the Gypsies and the *evil eye,* staring at the wagons as if they had come straight from hell. There were many stories of where her people had originated long ago. Some said they were from exotic Egypt, thus the name *Gypsy,* that they had fled the Saracens, moving westward and southward. But Alicia knew differently: They were Romany, from the Indus River Valley, traveling from there many years ago. Of her people she was very proud.

"Alicia . . ." Again Rudolpho had that look, as if there were something he must say, as if he were troubled.

"Yes?" She cocked her head and smiled, waiting for his words.

If only he could find a man of her own kind, a man for her to wed who would love Alicia and care for her when he was no longer with her. If he could find such a man, perhaps all would be well after all and Alicia would never have to know. "Nothing." He shook his head, reaching out to touch the tip of her nose with his finger. "You *are* a Gypsy with all the passion and fire of the Romany." He was not yet ready to die. He still had time.

A voice, like a chant, rose in the air. "Rudolpho!" The men were calling to him as the soft strains of music sounded and the pungent smell of burning wood wafted through the air. Already the others had set up the camp and were about to begin their dancing and playing while the evening meal cooked over the open fires on caldron and spit.

Usually Alicia was one of the first to start the rhythmic clapping of hands that accompanied the guitar and the stamping of heels. Sometimes she let the music have its way with her and swayed to the melodies, or threw her hair about and moved her hips and feet in wild abandon, but tonight she was not in the mood. It was so peaceful in the woods that she longed to stay for just a little while longer.

"Come, Alicia, we will go back." Rudolpho stood up from his soft seat on the grass. "We will be missed."

"You go on, Papa. I'll be there in a little while. The birds are singing my favorite song." Her laugh was as melodious as the brook that bubbled nearby.

He kissed her cheek. "I understand, child. But be careful. One never knows what these woods are hiding, what manner of beast."

"I will be careful." She knew of whom he spoke, of those who hated Gypsies. There was danger in these times. One called Torquemada had said that the Gypsies were not capable of being Christians because of their wild, free ways. "Sorcerers, blasphemers, astrologers, observers of rites contrary to Christianity, abstainers from the sacraments, and givers of love potions, he had called them. She didn't know what many of those words meant, but she did know that he was the one responsible for killing Jews and those called *Marranos*, converts to the faith of the gentle Christ who were said to practice the Jewish faith in secret. Alicia felt for the small knife hidden in her belt. "I will let no harm come to me, Papa."

Looking up at the shrouded glow of the moon, she felt a surge of primitive magic, the same enchantment that her ancestors must have felt, she thought. She was not aware of the precise moment her bare feet took flight, but suddenly she was running swiftly over the wild grass and soft moss of the forest.

Wandering in and out among the shimmery curtains of trees that sheltered her from the danger of any unfriendly eyes, she gave herself up to the quiet splendor of the night. The stars were like tiny campfires hovering high above the earth, and she paused just long enough to throw her head back and gaze at their light, which pulsated in rhythm to the crickets' lovelorn song.

Suddenly a sharp sound intruded upon her ears, one not made by a creature, bird, or insect of the night. Owls and nightbirds did not shriek so, nor did animals curse in anger. It was a human voice she heard! Alicia stilled her breath to listen. Voices. Men's voices, speaking not in Romany but in Spanish.

She felt the urge to run away; knew that if she were wise she would leave, yet her curiosity got the better of her. Who had intruded on this soft, gentle night? Were these men any danger to her people? Creeping forward, careful to hide in the shadows, she was determined to find out.

"Cristo! You have killed him, Manuel," said one of the figures standing near the river's edge. What devil's business were they about? Should she run and get the others?

"Shut up, José! We had to hit him hard. Were we just supposed to ask him politely for his jewels and finery?"

"No, but did we have to kill him? What if someone comes by . . . ?" A soft moan escaped the lips of the figure lying on the ground. "He is not dead!"

"Throw him into the river. Quick, before he comes to!" The order was shouted in a voice as cold as the snows of the high country.

"Throw him in?"

"Yes. Now, or by all that is holy you will join him!"

Alicia watched as the two men picked their victim up and flung him into the swirling waters, then took to their heels and ran. They were robbers. Thieves. They had *killed* a man! Left him to drown! Gorgio thieves. And they had the nerve to criticize the Gypsies and call them such names. Ha! A Gypsy would not stoop to such a treacherous act, Alicia thought angrily. She wondered if the man in the river was gorgio or if by chance he was Gypsy from a different tribe. Did it really matter? A man would die, would surely drown, if she did not act quickly. What else could she do but try to save him?

Without another thought she jumped into the icy waters, gasping as the cold depths engulfed her. Although she was used to swimming, the turbulent waters tugged her under, burning her lungs with want of air as she held her breath.

Her ears were filled with a roar; her heavy skirts threatened to drag her even deeper.

"O Del. O Del," she cried, calling to God for aid. Would she join this stranger in death? No. She would survive. She was strong. She was Gypsy!

Fighting her fear, she kicked her legs furiously to propel her body upward, gulping in the sweet nectar of air, of life, as she reached the surface. Several feet away she saw the body of the stranger, and with surprisingly strong strokes approached his sinking form. It was as if God were answering her.

From childhood Alicia had known how to swim; it was as natural to her as breathing, but always before, it had been in summer when the waters were warm, not in autumn's chilly rivers. Still, as she fought the currents, she knew that she would be the victor, not the river.

The watery prison had seemed endless at first as she paddled her arms and kicked her feet. Now, grabbing the arm of the man, then fastening her fingers in his hair, she pulled him to the surface. Having swallowed some of the water, he choked, and she once again called upon *o Del*, this time for his life. He had no chance if she could not get him to the riverbank. As if in answer to her prayers, the currents rose to aid her, and she found that she and the stranger were drifting toward the shore.

With all her strength Alicia dragged the stranger out of the water, exhilarated by the feel of the rocks beneath her feet. Hovering over the man, she felt for a pulse. It was weak, but there was a sign of life.

How am I to get the water out of his lungs? she wondered, then remembered a time when a child had fallen victim to the river's currents and Rudolpho had pulled him out. Her father had sucked the water out of the child's body and had pushed upon the boy's back. She would do the same now with this stranger.

"Live!" she cried aloud, working her hands upon his

body, listening to his groan. "Live." He could not die. Not now. No, not now. His existence had become a driving force within her. Be he gorgio or Gypsy, it did not matter. He had to live.

Turning him over on his back, she pressed her mouth to his, breathing the air of life into his lungs, feeling her spark of life descending into him as their breath mingled. He was a large man, muscular, with long, thick dark hair that fell across his forehead. Alicia was shocked by the depth of feeling that overwhelmed her at the touch of his mouth. Pulling violently away from him, she was frightened, though of what, she could not say. She would have left him, but his voice drew her back.

"No . . . don't go . . . who . . . ?" he rasped. He was staring at her in surprise and confusion, trying to sit up as if he intended to follow her if she didn't comply with his wishes. Alicia was startled by the intensity of his gaze. It was as if he had cast a spell upon her. Only by the greatest effort was she able to draw her eyes away.

"Lie back. Save your strength," she whispered in Spanish. He was shivering from the chill of the night and she covered his body with her own to still his quaking. Looking into his face, she was mesmerized by the strength and beauty she found there. His eyes were fringed by dark lashes, and she found herself wondering what color they would be in the light. He had not the coloring of the Romany line but was fairer of skin, hair, and eyes. This man was not Gypsy. Still, she admired him. It had taken two to overwhelm him. Two cowards.

As their eyes met again for just a moment in time, Alicia thought of what the old grandmother, the *phuri dai* of the tribe, used to say, that if one saved another's life, their souls would be joined for eternity. Was it true? A tidal wave of sensation flooded over her and she knew the answer. This man was somehow part of her destiny.

2

The flickering candle flames illuminated the face of the man lying on the rough bed of linen and straw in the Gypsy wagon. Alicia's eyes swept over him as she gently wiped the blood from his head with a cloth moistened with healing herbs.

"Who are you?" she wondered aloud, knowing she would get no answer from the sleeping stranger. She had never been so close to a gorgio before, and his looks fascinated her. He had not the swarthy complexion or the facial hair of the Gypsy men. His face was smooth and his hair fell to his shoulders in the Spanish fashion. His eyebrows were thick, his cheekbones high and strong, his nose finely formed as if by a sculptor's hand. The eyelashes that shadowed his cheekbones were long and curling, a dark brown. Such a strikingly handsome man.

Alicia had kept a constant vigil over him, wiping the blood from his face and washing the gash on his head with a mixture of goldenseal, water, and myrrh. When he moaned in his sleep she reached out to him, her hand and gentle words soothing his tortured murmurings.

It had been a struggle to get the semiconscious man back to camp, but somehow she had managed, only to face another obstacle. The Gypsy men, always suspicious of any outsider, had argued that a gorgio should not have been brought into camp, that his presence was a bad omen, that he would bring evil and bad luck upon them all. But Alicia had stood firm in her determination to care for him. All of them knew that she could be a wildcat when crossed, and so in the end the other Gypsies had reneged, though their dour looks had followed her as she and Rudolpho had taken him into Alicia's own wagon. There had been angry murmurings, whisperings that she did not understand, as the elders of the tribe had looked her way. It was as if the older Gypsies of the tribe shared some secret. Usually Alicia would have been curious, but her concern for the wounded gorgio soon pushed the curiosity from her mind.

While removing the gorgio's wet doublet with its many lacings, the silk shirt gathered at the neck and wrists, edged with beautiful Spanish blackwork embroidery in red, gold, and black silk threads, Alicia marveled at the beauty of the man's garments. Such finery was not practical wear but to her eyes fascinating nonetheless. Rudolpho and Alicia had laughed at the funny pants the gorgio wore, which clung to his legs like a second skin. Her father called them *hosen,* scoffing at the manner of dress these gorgios adopted, "like strutting birds arrayed in brightly colored feathers."

Toweling the man dry and changing her own garments, Alicia let her eyes roam over his naked body. His smooth skin was golden where it had been exposed to the sun, but where the sunlight had not touched he was several shades lighter. A dusting of hair covered his broad chest and trailed in a thin, straight line down to his navel; his arms were well muscled, his waist thin, his legs straight and strong, and his manhood—the part of him that marked him as male—was well defined. Just looking at him was strangely exciting, stirring her blood with a languid heat, bringing forth a longing that shamed her. A virgin should not think such thoughts.

As if sensing her searching eyes, the man stirred in his sleep, a moan escaping from his mouth, and Alicia hurried to calm him. "You are safe here; there is no one who will harm you. I will see to that." She meant to keep her promise. In his defenseless slumber he brought out all the protective instincts within her, and she vowed to do everything in her power to see that he would be safe. So thinking, she reached for a linen blanket and pulled it over his nude form to shield him from the chill of the night, then sat down upon the floor beside him to watch and to wait.

For a long while it was peaceful in the wagon as Alicia kept vigil, so tranquil that she nearly nodded off to sleep once or twice; but the stillness was suddenly shattered as the stranger cried out, "No! No! Don't kill me." Thrashing about, he seemed to be struggling with his assailants once again. "Don't kill me! For the love of God! You are cowards. Two against one. Damn bastards!"

Jumping to her feet, bending over him, she sought to calm him, only to find herself looking into the deep, dark depths of his eyes as his eyelids fluttered open. Dark eyes, eyes of a rich dark brown met her own, eyes as dark as any Gypsy's and just as wild. "Who . . . ?" he whispered, reaching up his hand to entwine the soft silken strands of her hair, pulling her closer.

"Alicia!" she answered quickly, trying to draw away from his stare. His hold on her hair kept her captive. "Please, let me go. It was not I who sought to harm you."

"Those men?"

"Gone. They threw you in the river, then took to their heels like the dogs that they are. I pulled you out."

"You?" His eyes were penetrating, looking deep into her very soul, then he smiled. "Beautiful witch." Loosening his hand from her hair, he closed his eyes again.

"Witch?" The word wounded her, and she fought against her despair. She had saved his life, and he had called her a *witch*, this beautiful man with eyes like the rich brown earth. "Ungrateful gorgio," she rasped, turning her back on him in anger. Only the knowledge of his head wound kept her from leaving him and going out into the night. Instead she knelt beside him once again. Let him call her what he might, he would soon learn the truth. She was not witch, but healer.

The hours passed by slowly, the candles burned themselves out, and still Alicia kept watch over him. Lost once again to a haze of dreams, the gorgio tossed and turned in the throes of sleep, mumbling beneath his breath, "Marranos. They called her Marranos. Jew. Condemned to the fires and I could not save her. I never knew." He reached out his hand as if he were drowning again, and once again Alicia offered him comfort, wondering who it was he was mourning. Lover? Wife? Scolding herself, she fought against her jealousy. She had no claim on this man no matter how he stirred her senses. He was gorgio born and she of Gypsy blood.

Pressing her hand against his brow, making certain that his thrashing about was not caused by fever, she could see that he was in that state of consciousness halfway between reality and dream, again mumbling beneath his breath. She leaned closer to hear what he was saying and winced as she again heard the words: "Witch. Lovely, lovely witch."

She started to protest, to tell him once again that she was not one of those evil crones, but before the words were out she felt the warm, soft touch of his fingers upon her breast, sending a shiver of desire coursing through her blood. His hand cupped the tender flesh, caressing the peak through the thin material of her blouse with infinite tenderness, the sensation so stirring that, though she caught his hand with the intention of removing his fingers, she did not stop him.

He does not even know what he is doing, she thought, looking down at his face, the eyes closed in sleep. Remorse pricked her heart that perhaps it was of another he was dreaming. She wanted him to desire *her*, foolish though that wish might be. A violent longing shot through her that when he awoke he would reach out to touch her, that he would find her beautiful.

As if in answer to her wish, his exploring hand moved

lower, sliding over her small waist, resting on the full curve
of her hip. How could she ever have imagined that a man's
caress could cause such a fire in the blood? Even her dancing
did not cause her heart to race at such a furious pace. Over
and over she remembered what the old grandmother had
told her about the act of mating, and could not help wondering what it would be like to be with this man. Was that a
wicked thought? Somehow it did not seem so. It seemed
instead to be as natural as breathing. Seeking the warmth of
his body, she lay down beside him and nestled into the
security of his arms, closing her eyelids to await the dawn.

3

The sound of neighing horses, chirping birds, barking dogs, and laughing children awakened Rafael de Villasandro from his sound sleep. Opening his eyes slowly, expecting to find himself within the familiar confines of his bedchamber, he was startled as his eyes wandered over the enclosure of some sort of wagon. His pulse quickened as he stiffened, eyes opening wide to take in these surroundings—the small windows, the wooden walls, the canvas hanging at the far end to act as a door. Mother of God, where was he?

He started to get up, nervous in his confusion, and it was then he saw her, the young woman who lay beside him. He was mesmerized by the most beautiful face he had ever beheld. So he had not been dreaming, she was real. As he stretched his sore muscles the hard planes of his chest caressed her breasts and his strong thighs touched hers with an intimacy that sparked his desires.

His eyes appraised her—the dark hair spread out around her like a cloak of darkest velvet (never had he seen such hair), the flawless complexion the color of dark cream, the long, thick lashes. Her lips were full and meant to be kissed. But it was her body that made him tingle—long legs; firm, full breasts that he ached to touch; a waist he could encircle with his hands; and hips that had just the right amount of flesh. Even fully clothed she had the kind of curves that caused the minstrels to languish and turned men into love-sick fools.

Asleep, she looked angelic, yet he had the feeling that once awake she would be full of the devil's own fire. She was Gypsy, by the looks of the wagon. Gypsy. The women were known for their beauty, but in all his days he had never seen one like this. Gypsy. The name evoked scorn and fear as he remembered stories he had heard since his child-hood, yet he could not help but feel differently toward this young woman. He seemed to recall that she had saved his life.

All the memories of the night before and of the men who had assaulted him swirled about his mind. His head throbbed as he reached up to touch the swelling above his temple. "Bastards!" he swore aloud, startling the Gypsy girl beside him out of her slumber.

Alicia awoke to find penetrating dark eyes appraising her, and flushed as she recalled the way he had touched her dur-ing the night. She wondered if he, too, remembered. Open-ing her mouth to speak, she was too flustered to say a word. The gorgio was not shy, however.

"Green eyes. Such lovely eyes. Like the sea," he said softly, his gaze raking over her. "Am I right in remembering your face hovering above me like a sea nymph?"

Still stung by his words of the night before, she turned hastily away, managing to whisper, "You called me witch."

He sensed her hurt and, cupping her face in his hand, forced her to look at him. "I merely meant that you be-witched me with your beauty. I meant no insult." For a long, timeless moment they stared into each other's eyes, speak-ing a silent language, then he tried to sit up. "I'm still as weak as a newborn colt," he said as a wave of dizziness engulfed him.

"You will gain back your strength. I know of healing herbs that will work like magic." She smiled, showing the perfection of her pearl-white teeth.

"Gypsy magic," he gasped, wary of her for just a moment as he thought of the whisperings bantered about of poisonings by their ragged bands, child stealing, witchcraft, and thievery.

His raised eyebrows angered Alicia as all the old resentments, the memory of gorgio crowds calling them names, came flooding over her. Sitting up on the bed, thrusting her shoulders back, she tilted her head with pride, her eyes flashing fire. "Healing magic, Gorgio! Take it or be damned!"

He threw back his head and laughed, a deep rumbling sound like the stroke on a guitar, melodious and rippling. "You *are* full of fire! I was right about you." His laughter caused her ire, and in a fit of temper she struck her fists against his chest, forgetting for the moment his injury and her concern.

"How dare you laugh at me! I should have let the river have you. Gorgio devil! *O Beng!*" she swore.

His laughter ceased, his eyes became gentle, dark pools that seemed to engulf her in their warmth. "I am not laughing at you, lovely Gypsy, but this situation." Giving in to the impulse to touch her, he stroked her hair, wincing suddenly in pain as he moved. "Damn, but my head feels as if all the soldiers of Castile were marching through my brain!"

His wince of pain stilled her anger, and she reached out to him with the intention of examining his wound. Before she could touch him, however, he had grasped her extended hand, taking it in his large one and kissing the palm with lips that were hauntingly gentle for one so masculine and strong. The feel of his mouth upon her skin sent shivers of liquid fire coursing through her. "Are you sorry that you saved me?" he asked softly.

In startled confusion she pulled away, looking at him with wide dark-fringed green eyes. "Perhaps I am glad after all that I did not let you drown." He smiled at her then, and her heart leapt in response. *It is he who is the witch,* she thought, *to so weave a spell over me.* Never before had she felt like this. She tingled all over if he even looked at her; trembled at his touch. Being near him brought a sweet ache to the pit of her stomach. No other man had made her feel so strange. Teasing the Gypsy boys with laughing eyes and swaying hips, she had held herself aloof and kept away from their grasping hands and hungry eyes, determined not to give herself to any of them; but now . . . somehow she wanted to be crushed against his hard chest, held by the strength of his arms.

"God, you are beautiful. So beautiful." As if some hidden force were urging him on, he reached for her, gathering her into his arms in the embrace they both so wanted.

Alicia's pulse quickened at the passion she read in his eyes. Knowing that he wanted her, too, was as potent as any Gypsy love-potion. Closing her arms around his neck, she offered her lips, wanting him to kiss her. She waited breathlessly as his mouth descended upon hers, kissing her like a man with a deep thirst to assuage, drinking in the sweetness of her lips, reaching for her, stroking her. She gave herself up to the fierce emotions that raced through her, answering his kiss with a hunger of her own, entranced by this her first taste of a man's lips.

"Oh, Gorgio!" she murmured when at last he pulled away. Entranced by emotions and sensations she had never experienced before, she was oblivious of anything but the man who had kissed her—at least until she looked down at the thin linen covering his nakedness. She could see the pulsating hardness of his manhood and flushed with embarrassment as she tore herself from his arms. Her eyes were filled with fear, not of him but of herself.

"No, don't touch me!" Quickly she bolted from the bed to stand looking down at him.

He tried to rise to his feet, longing to capture her in his arms again, but dizziness rendered him helpless to do anything but look at her. Her eyes held as much apprehension as if she were facing a bull in the ring. Nothing could have extinguished his ardor more quickly than the sight of those eyes.

"I'm sorry. I should not have acted so, sweet Gypsy," he apologized, shaking his head to clear it of its whirling. Was it his injury or her nearness that made him so damned dizzy? he wondered.

She didn't answer, merely averted her eyes, and the crimson blush that colored her face made him realize the reason for her fear. Drawing a blanket from beneath his feet, he covered himself. So she was an innocent, he thought in disappointment. He had heard of how fiercely the Gypsies guarded their virgins. He would have to put any lustful thoughts out of his mind. Yet that was easier said than done. Here he was with a woman as beautiful as Eve herself, while he was as naked as Adam. How could he help but think of making love to her?

There was tension in the air, a silence broken only by the beating of their hearts; but at last Alicia spoke. "Your garments will be dry now. I put them before the fire." She started to leave the wagon to retrieve them but heard him cry out to her.

"Your name. I do not remember . . ."

"Alicia," she answered, tossing back her dark mane of hair. "And you, Gorgio?"

"Rafael Córdoba de Villasandro." He grinned at her, his eyes smoldering as they gazed at her with mischief. "I would stand up and bow as polite custom dictates, but I fear you have me at a loss without my clothes." His eyes danced merrily. "Or would you prefer that I greet you as a noble Spanish gentleman should?"

"No. No." She blushed again. It was one thing to see him naked when he was asleep and unaware of her gaze—then he had been her patient—but to view the muscular strength of him now only reminded her that he was a man. A strong, handsome man. One she must not allow to touch her. "I will get your garments and return, Gorgio . . . Rafael."

Running from the wagon, her eyes caught sight of a band
of men gathered by one of the trees for the ritual of knife
throwing, while others busied themselves with the horses.
All heads turned when she walked by, and she could read
their resentment in their eyes. Gathering up the scattered
remnants of the garments, she returned before any of the
men could wound her with their words. She was not
ashamed of taking in another human being, or of saving a
life. Let them be damned if they did not approve. Rudolpho
had given his consent. He was the leader, not any of them!

By the time she returned to the wagon the gorgio had
managed to get out of bed and was standing, his head and
shoulders stooped over slightly as he tried to keep his balance.

"Your clothes, Gorgio!" she said, dropping them on the
floor, frantically emphasizing the word *gorgio*. They were different, he and she. Their worlds were far apart. No matter
how sweet his kisses, there was no future in his arms.

He was stung by the icy tone of her words. "Gorgio? You
call me Gorgio. No. I told you my name is Rafael. I want to
hear you call me that, Alicia. See, I am not afraid to speak
your name."

Her head snapped up, her shoulders stiffened. "I am not
afraid to call you by *your* name. I am Gypsy. I am brave. I
merely forgot, that is all." She turned her back while he
dressed, knowing that now he would leave her and travel
back to his people while she stayed behind with hers. Why
was the thought so very painful? It was the way it should
be. It was fate.

"When I get my hands upon the two who split my head
open, they will wish they had never been born," she heard
him mumble under his breath. "Damn, I'm still dizzy."

She whirled around, reaching out to steady him. Her
hands touched the strength of his arms, and in that moment
all her resolve was swept away. Just once more she wanted

to taste the fire of his lips, just once more. A yearning passion clamored in her veins.

"Alicia. How I hate to leave you, but I must. Let this be
my thank you and my good-bye." His mouth claimed hers
just as she had wanted, in a kiss that devastated her senses.
Engulfed in a whirlpool of fiery sensations, she reached her
slim arms up to draw him closer as his mouth plundered
hers. She was lost to the flush of sensations that swept over
her, aware only of her body, which ached for the touch of
his hands.

Rafael had meant this to be a farewell kiss, but he was
caught up in his desire, a desire that consumed him. Never
before had he wanted a woman so desperately. If only this
magic could go on forever, but he knew that it could not.
Only by the greatest self-control was he able to break away,
shaken by the passion that had passed between them. He
could see that she was just as dazed as he, and this pleased
him. Perhaps someday . . .

"I must go, though I think I would nearly sell my soul to
stay," he said softly.

She turned her face away to hide the tears that threatened
to spill from her eyes, determined not to call him back. The
soft leather of his boots echoed her heartbeats as he left the
wagon.

"I will not cry, I will not. I am Gypsy," she whispered,
wiping her hand across her cheeks, feeling the wetness,
damp as the early-morning dew. Only the loud shouts from
beyond the wagon cut through the fog of her misery.

"You! Gorgio. You are not going anywhere. Not yet," she
heard a deep voice shout. Stivo. Stivo could be dangerous.
Hurrying to the entrance of the wagon, she looked in horror
upon the scene outside. The gorgio, her gorgio, was lying on
his back on the grass with a knife pressed to his throat.
With their dark eyes glittering as brightly as the flames of
the morning fire, several men of the tribe were hovering
above Rafael de Villasandro.

4

"No, Stivo!" Alicia screamed, throwing herself at the Gypsy, her long fingernails scratching and clawing him as they wrestled for the knife. Not caring that he was three times her size, her only thought was to save the gorgio.

"Get off me. Leave me be, you she-devil!" Stivo raged. Knowing that Rudolpho was far across the camp repairing an axle on a wagon and could not come to Alicia's aid, he gave her a push that sent her sprawling. "Dionisio! Todero! Ramón!" He motioned to the others to tighten their grip on the stranger.

"Leave him alone!" Alicia demanded, raising herself from the ground. She was not so easily beaten. Hadn't she wrestled with Todero and Ramón when they were but children and easily won? Only when their bodies grew to manhood, when their size and strength outgrew her own, did she reluctantly admit that the days of playful sparring were over. Now she fought them as she had in those early years, with teeth, hands, and kicking feet. "I will scratch your eyes out! Todero, take care. And you, Stivo, I will rip off your ears and throw them to the fish."

"We don't want to harm you, Alicia," Todero, the gentlest of the four cried out. "We just want to keep your friend, the gorgio, from leaving us. We cannot trust him. He will give our camp away and bring us into danger."

"Have you forgotten Torquemada, that *Beng* himself?"

Stivo cried. Alicia was not entirely calmed; she stood with feet apart, arms up, as if ready to fight again. "Gorgios are our enemies."

"Not this gorgio. I do not want you to harm him. I did not save his life to see him torn apart by wolves like you!" She hovered over Rafael as if daring them to strike her first.

"I will not be kept prisoner!" Rafael shouted, coming to his own defense. "Nor will I let a woman fight my battles." With hostile defiance he eyed Stivo, his gaze unwavering. Stivo was tall, strongly muscled, with dark, swarthy skin and hair as black as the wing of a raven. The set of his jaw showed his arrogance, but Rafael did not cower. He would go down fighting.

Stivo stepped forward with a mock gesture of politeness, his even white teeth gleaming as he smiled. He was handsome, with flashing dark Romany eyes. Dressed in pantaloons and jacket, the large whip he carried over his shoulder made him look formidable, and Rafael cursed beneath his breath at the injury to his head that had taken away his own strength.

"You will not be our prisoner but our guest," Stivo was saying. "For three days, Gorgio. Until we leave camp."

"No. I must go now!" Rafael argued, infuriated by the situation. "Is my word not good enough for you? I will not tell anyone about your camp. One of you," his eyes swept over Alicia, "saved my life. I am grateful. Why would I seek to betray you?"

"Money, Gorgio!" Dionisio spat. "We have been betrayed before by your kind."

Todero nodded. "I would not like to feel the flames of the fire. There are many who hate the Gypsies even more than they hate the Jews. No, you will stay until the last wagon in our caravan is well out of sight." He looked toward Alicia as if to assure her. "We will not harm him unless he gives us cause. It is for you to keep your gorgio friend in line. You are the one who brought him here."

Alicia knew that she should do all in her power to persuade them otherwise, but the thought of having the handsome young Spaniard with her for three more days stilled her tongue. What harm would there be? They would release him unharmed when they abandoned camp.

"Three days," she whispered under her breath, watching as Stivo and the others took Rafael away with them to be carefully guarded night and day. Had he left camp, she would not have been able to speak with him, to touch him. Now he would be nearby. "If only we Gypsies really could weave spells," she thought, "I would give him a love potion that would bind his heart to mine forever." She visualized the face of the old grandmother, the matriarch of the caravan, the *phuri dai,* and felt a great sadness. She would have helped her. It was said that the old woman had been gifted in the arts of magic and in foretelling the future. But she was dead now and another had taken her place, a woman who hated Alicia with a jealous fury.

"You are attracted to that one you pulled from the river," a low voice said behind her. Turning, she found Rudolpho's kind eyes appraising her.

She could not lie to him, never to him. "Yes. He is like no man I have ever met before. Strong, yet gentle and so handsome. It is as if fate cast him into my arms, as if it was meant to be."

"Alicia . . ."

She could see the pain in his eyes and mistook its meaning. "I know that it is forbidden for one of the tribe to marry with a gorgio. I know also that I must come to my marriage bed a virgin. I cannot let the gorgio touch me in that way; it is so written, I understand."

"But still you long for him. I can read it in your eyes, Alicia." He wanted to tell her all then, that she, too, was gorgio, not Gypsy, but his adopted daughter and therefore free to join with the stranger if she so desired. But was now the time? If he just let nature take its course, perhaps these two would fall in love. Just the thought made him feel as if a burden had been lifted from his heart. All these years he had felt her loneliness like a knife to his throat, wondering how he would ever tell her that she could never marry into the tribe. "Alicia, this gorgio . . ." he began, but she reached out to him, covering his lips with her fingers, misunderstanding his intentions.

"I know what you are going to say, Papa. I will never disgrace you, no matter how the gorgio fires my blood. Above all I am Gypsy and proud of the Romany blood that flows in my veins. When he leaves in three days I will have a pleasant memory to carry forever in my heart and I will feel that *o Del* has smiled upon me."

"Alicia . . ."

"I will not be like Mara of the legend," she whispered, remembering the tale. "I will not sell my soul to the Devil, to *O Beng*, for the gorgio's love." It was a sad story, which now came vividly to her mind. A beautiful Gypsy girl named Mara had fallen in love with a gorgio who was immune to her many charms. In her longing, she sold the souls of her family to *O Beng* in exchange for his help. But the Devil was cunning. He turned her father into a sound box, her four brothers into strings, and her mother into a bow. They became a violin, which Mara learned to play with such haunting beauty that the gorgio fell in love with her; but *O Beng*, wanting to claim his own, took them both off with him to hell. The violin was left lying on the ground, to be found by a poor Gypsy boy. From then on, the violin and Gypsy music became inseparable.

"No, you could never be like Mara. You are strong, Alicia. In time perhaps . . ." Was it possible this stranger might eventually feel the same? Again he had that look in his eyes, and Alicia wondered at the cause. Did he regret that she was not born a male child? Is that what it meant? If she had been his son, she would have followed in his footsteps.

"We must accept things as they are, Papa." She led him

toward the communal fire, where the leaping flames shone
with orange and blue light. As always the women cast lots
to see who would prepare the morning meal and who would
be free to enjoy the beauty of the day. To her annoyance
Alicia was assigned to fix the meat for the spit, a job she
hated. The blood stained her skirts, and she pitied the poor
slaughtered animal. But a Gypsy must never refuse her duty
to the tribe, and so she went about her tasks with firm resolve.

As she worked with the other women Alicia tried to forget the smoldering dark eyes and the dark hair of the
stranger, but his face loomed before her; the memory of his
lips upon her own was branded on her soul. Sitting before
the heat of the fire, she thought of him, hardly tasting the
food she had helped prepare, barely hearing the words of
those who spoke with her.

"You saved a gorgio?" asked Vashti, her face alight with
awe.

"He is handsome." Solis, with dark eyes and full bosom,
smiled as if to challenge Alicia. It was well known among
the women that Solis was a lusty woman. Her husband was
one of the older men, frail and past the age of being able to
satisfy her desires. That she had not been punished for her
wanton nature by her husband was a matter of concern to
the others. Was it because he did not want to believe the
truth? Or was it that she was more cunning than he, using
her sharp tongue as a Gypsy wields a knife?

Alicia felt a spark of jealousy and flashed the other
woman a look that said more than words. "He is mine."

"You pulled him from the river?" Zuba's voice was tinged
with fright, being one who was terrified of the flowing water.

Alicia told the tale quickly, anxious to be gone from their
presence and return to Rafael. Was he still angry? Was he
comfortable? He would be hungry. She must take him some
food. Some goat meat, perhaps, and a bit of chicken. Both

had been stolen from one of the villages the caravan had passed through, and Rudolpho had been furious. "We do not want it said that Gypsies steal and bring on Torquemada's wrath," he said. But the deed was done.

Waiting until the other Gypsies had eaten their fill, Alicia approached the communal pot and was pleased to find it was not empty. There was more than enough for the gorgio. Using her own dish, for there were no extras, she scooped freely, overfilling the plate, then added some wild berries and mushrooms to give color and variety to the fare, thinking it was a shame that there was no hedgehog to eat this morning, such a delicacy among the Gypsies.

Searching among the tents and wagons, she at last found where Stivo had taken him, to Dionisio's tent. Opening the flap, she knew well what she would find; but even so, the sight of the poor gorgio, tied up like some animal, made her gasp. His hands were bound behind his back, one leg was securely fastened with ropes so that he could walk only a short distance from the pole in the center of the tent. All in all he looked a great deal like a bear Rudolpho had kept imprisoned once in the hopes of taming the beast. Stivo was a cruel jailer.

"I brought you some food, Rafael," she said softly.

The only answer he gave to acknowledge that he had heard her was a nod of his head.

"Are you not hungry? You will need your strength."

"Am I to eat with my hands tied behind my back? Or perchance, pretty Gypsy, will you feed me like a helpless old man?" His dark eyes glowed with suppressed anger, and she had no doubt that in his present mood he would be more than a match for Ramón and the others.

"I will untie you, but only if you give me your solemn oath not to try to run away."

"So, at least *you* think that I can be trusted," was his scathing answer. He paced up and down the length of his rope, saying at last, "I swear by the blessed Virgin Mary that

I will not give you cause for alarm. I will be as tame as a kitten." His eyes looked into hers, and seeing that she was truly sorry for his bondage, he resolved that he would keep his word. Besides, he was ravenous.

Without another word Alicia put the plate of food down upon the ground and bent to untie him, her hands lingering over the heat of his strong hands, remembering his touch. Catching her by one of her wrists, he pulled her close to him, bringing her face only inches from his own. "You do not like seeing me bound. I can read it in your eyes. Does that mean you have a fondness for me, my Gypsy?"

Her eyes were deep green pools, shadowed by the dark fringe of her lashes. "I do not like to see anything, animal or man, confined, Gorgio. Gypsies value their freedom. It is precious. How could I enjoy the sight of yours being taken from you?"

"Then let me leave here. Free me, Alicia. Help me escape." His breath whispered in her ear, stirring the silken strands of her hair as the night wind stirs the trees. Being so close to him wreaked havoc on her senses, like partaking of the nightshade plant. She was nearly ready to promise him anything.

"No. No. I cannot. I could never betray my people." Even for you, she thought. Wrenching free, she picked up the plate of food and held it toward him, a bridge between them. "Eat. It will grow cold."

He took it from her hands. "I will need a fork."

"A fork?" She had heard of the foolish gorgio's fancy utensil, imported from the East. "We have no forks, Rafael."

"A spoon, then."

She laughed. "We use no spoons, Gorgio. How foolish. The fingers are all that one needs."

Shrugging his shoulders, he resolved that he was too hungry to argue table manners with her. The meat was spicy and tough, but to his hungry mouth it tasted delicious. Devouring it, eating freely, he soon cleaned his plate.

"You like? It is good, no?" she asked. "Do you want more?"

"What is it? Beef?"

"Goat."

"Goat?" He had never eaten goat meat before. The very idea made him wince. Only peasants would eat such a thing, or Gypsies.

"I am only sorry that we have no hedgehogs. They are difficult to skin, so many needles, but oh so tasty."

"Hedgehogs!" He shuddered. Surely there was even more of a gulf between them than he had realized. Yet when he looked into her eyes, saw her smile, somehow the differences didn't matter. Was it true, what they said about these Gypsies? Could they weave spells? Surely this one had enchanted him.

Alicia, too, realized they were worlds apart. As far as he was concerned, she might as well have come from one of the stars. What was his world like? she wondered. Other Gypsies had whispered that the gorgios' church held power over the people from cradle to grave, offering heavenly rewards for virtue and hellish horror for those who did not follow their supreme authority. How different the Gypsies' lives were with only Rudolpho and the *phuri dai*'s authority to obey.

In his world she would not feel so free and happy, she reasoned, remembering the stories she had heard from Rudolpho. If his world was as wonderful as he supposed, then why did the people look so sad? There was hunger in the streets of Castile, León, and Aragón, poverty and selfish greed. Among the Gypsies there was none of that. They were family. Tribe. No one would starve.

As they stood staring at each other for the longest time, trying to fathom their differences, trying to understand this attraction that pulled them, each to the other, they did not notice the intruder.

"Alicia! Foolish woman!" She did not have to turn around

to know who had entered their lovers' sanctuary. Stivo. "You untied him. He could have escaped!"

"He gave me his word, Stivo."

"Ha! What good is that? He is not one of us. His word is nothing!" Quickly he tied the ropes again, pushing his prisoner down upon the floor when he was finished.

"You are cruel, Stivo. Cruel and stubborn. I had to untie him so that he could eat. Would you have him eat like a dog, like a *jukel*?" Standing with her hands upon her hips, she stared him down.

"Next time I will guard him while he eats. It is too plain upon your face, the soft spot you have in your heart for this one. I warn you again. He can cause the death of us all. In the town I have heard rumblings. They say it is only a matter of time before Queen Isabella and her consort, Ferdinand, expel all the Jews from the country again, and with them will be the Gypsies. Do you want to be forced to leave this land of your birth? No. And neither do I." Taking her gently by the arm, he propelled her toward the opening. Alicia looked back at Rafael and was stunned by the overwhelming sense of loss she felt upon leaving. But she would return to him. No one, least of all Stivo, could keep her away. Walking across the encampment, she spotted a white horse, a good omen, and felt that *o Del* had given her a sign.

5

Rafael paced his prison tent like a caged animal, growing angrier and angrier by the minute. Gypsy dogs! Heathens, that's what they were, he thought to himself. The one named Stivo who strutted about like a rooster particularly raised his ire. Rafael had not missed the look Stivo had given Alicia, a look that had nearly devoured her.

The Gypsies said that they would let him go at the end of three days. Rafael did not believe them. They did not trust him, and neither did he trust any of them.

The time passed slowly as Rafael hobbled about the confines of his prison. He had been given a rope about eight feet in length so that he could attend to his personal needs, a difficult thing to manage with both hands tied behind his back. It was humiliating and degrading to call out for help whenever he had the need to make water. With each moment that passed, with every step he took, his rage increased tenfold. They clearly had no intention of setting him free.

They will slit my throat and leave me to the vultures when they leave camp, he thought as bitterness washed over him. He grew more and more certain that they had only promised Alicia that he would be freed so that she would not untie him, but the one named Stivo had murder in his eyes. They were nothing but thieving Gypsies. How, he wondered, could such a lovely, gentle creature like Alicia be one of these people? He could not imagine her stealing or giving the evil eye. She did not belong here. If only he could take her with him when he left—if he left alive, that is. But he knew that it would be impossible. How could he bring a *Gypsy* beauty home with him? He would be disowned and scorned.

Gypsies never lived in towns or cities; they were a secretive people, practicing sun worship, astrology, and magic, or so he had heard. Just the very sight of them brought forth violent outcries. Take her with him, what a foolish thought!

Escape. Would he ever escape? Was it possible to get free with so many eyes always watching him? Even now he could hear the voices of Todero, Ramón, and Dionisio outside the tent. If by some means he could slip out of these ropes that bound him, he would still have to deal with those knife-wielding heathens.

Alicia, he thought, was his only hope of survival, of gaining freedom. He had already asked her to help him, and she had told him she would not betray her people; but what if she were tricked into helping him? The idea made him feel lower than a snake; but when an animal was cornered, he reasoned, it would use every means of defense at its disposal, even chicanery. Alicia. He would use her attraction to him for his own purposes and hope that someday she would understand what force drove him on. Self-preservation.

But how? What could he do? He would have to be cunning and ready to take advantage when the moment presented itself. What would she do if he promised to take her with him? With a sigh he sat down on the hard dirt floor of the tent, his mind searching out a plan.

6

Alicia looked upward toward the immense sky, where thousands of stars blinked like watching eyes. As a child she had thought them to be God's eyes looking down at her, for Rudolpho had told her that God was the sky, the Supreme Being. *O Del,* the one God, *O Del.* Did *O Del* see her now? Could he read into her heart and mind? Did he know her feelings for the gorgio? Could he feel her emotions, know how she was torn between her duty to her people and their laws and her blossoming love for Rafael? How many times she had been tempted to free him only to hear Rudolpho's words echoing in her thoughts, repeating the laws of the tribe.

Rafael was not one of them, it was true, but it was still not right to treat him so. At first she had been secretly elated that he would be with them for three more days, selfishly happy that she could see him now and again. But now she felt shame for those thoughts when she realized the humiliation he was enduring. Still, she could not free him. Among people who lived so close together, traveled such distances, had a language and customs so different from others in the land, were so disliked because of their dissimilarity, the laws of the tribe were a deep bond; and though her heart ached every time she glanced in the direction of the prison tent, she would not falter in her resolve.

If only he were a Gypsy, she thought, feeling the wind's

caress and remembering the way she had shivered at his touch. With Rafael beside her she would have gladly traveled to the end of the world and back if only he were Gypsy. But he was not. She had to put away her childish dreams.

"Dreaming about the gorgio?" Putting a hand upon her shoulder, Stivo spun her around, his eyes dark and piercing.

"No!" she lied. "Though if I was thinking about him, you could hardly blame me. I would have to have a heart as hard as stone not to feel sympathy for him and the way you are treating him."

His laugh was harsh and far from genuine. "What would you have us do? Should we give him the very best wagon? Perhaps a bed of furs to lie upon? Shall we . . ."

"You could at least treat him with respect so that he could face his fate with dignity!" she snapped. "He has been cooped up in that tent all day. How can you decry how the gorgios treat us when we are just as bad?"

"He is a prisoner, a gorgio prisoner. At least he is not in some dungeon below ground with only rats for company."

"Our prisoner? And what was his crime? Did he try to steal from us? No. Did he harm one of us? No. His only crime is to be different from us."

"All gorgios are our enemies, as we are theirs. They made those rules, not us. All we seek is to be left alone." He clenched his jaw tightly as if fearing that his temper might well lead him into saying something that he would soon regret.

"He did not come into our camp; I brought him. He was attacked by two of his own, thieves. Why can you not set him free?" This one last time she would plead for him.

"No. Not until we leave! You are a *woman*!" He said the words with scorn. "You know nothing of such matters. Your place is cooking before the fire or warming your man's bed." Whirling, he left her to seek the warmth of the pulsating fires. But when Alicia looked toward the campsite a short

time later, she could see that Stivo had listened to at least
some of her words. Rafael sat in front of one fire, his feet
untied, though he was surrounded by Stivo, Todero, Ramón,
and Dionisio, whose flashing dark eyes dared him to make
any attempt at escape. Meeting the gorgio's eyes, she read
his gratitude and saw his whispered *thank you.*

Alicia took her place by the women's fire to eat with the
women and children, but her eyes were constantly drawn to
where Rafael sat, so tall and golden. Before the caravan left
in two days time, she knew that she had to feel the touch of
his kiss again, one last time, to recall when the cold winds of
the winter blew from the north.

The thought made her pulse quicken. Tonight. She would
come to the tent. What could it hurt? One kiss. One last
kiss.

A piercing cry, long and sustained, shattered the calm of
the night, like the chant of a Moslem from a high minaret
calling the faithful to prayer. From her perch by the fire
Alicia could see the gorgio jump as if he expected the very
demons of hell to fall upon him, but it was only the signal
for the dancing to begin. Usually one who watched the
dancing, accompanying the others with clapping hands, Alicia felt a sudden urge to sway and move to the rhythms as if
some primitive hand were leading her on. Rising, her body
moved with liquid heat as she took her place with two other
women. The guitar echoed a haunting beauty, sweet yet
sensual, as Alicia swayed from side to side, letting her
waist-long tresses swirl about her shoulders. She raised her
arms toward the sky as if wishing to touch every star. It was
as if she had become a part of the music, moving like the
clouds across the heavens.

From his seat before the fire Rafael watched her with
burning eyes, feeling in his heart that she was dancing only
for him. Impassioned by her dance, he could not take his
eyes away from the graceful beauty whose curves he ached
to touch. His blood surged wildly in his veins, his heart

seemed to beat in rhythm with the steps of her dance. She was a glory to behold. If he lived to the age of ninety, he would never forget the sight of her.

Alicia moved closer to the fire, feeling its warmth. Her eyes met Rafael's and she danced now *only* for him, imagining herself being loved by him, giving herself up to feelings as old as time itself. It was as if she had forgotten that anyone else existed. There was only Rafael. The rhythm quickened, and now it was the flamenco, that Andalusian dance of stamping heels and wild guitars. Faster and faster she danced, caught up in her passion. Whirling, spinning, gyrating, she was all energy and fire until at last the lingering notes died away and the dance came to an end. Throwing her head down, her mass of dark brown hair cascading in wild disarray, Alicia took her bow as the hypnotized watchers chanted her name.

"Alicia. Alicia."

Rafael too called to her. "Alicia!" It was all that he could do not to reach out for her, drag her into the forest, and give vent to the heated longing he felt; but the flashing eyes of Stivo gave him warning. One false move and he would regret it. And yet perhaps there was a chance. . . .

Alicia fell to a heap on the ground, as exhausted as she had been after saving the gorgio from drowning. Licking her lips, she smiled. It was as if she had been in a trance, as if some spell in the music had driven her on, urging her to say by her movements what no words could ever say. That she chose him, wanted him. How could she deny what was in her heart?

From across the campfire Rudolpho smiled in approval. His daughter's blood burned for the gorgio. It was as if *o Del* had answered all his prayers. That the elders of the tribe knew the secret of Alicia's birth would make it a simple matter. Marriage. He would marry his daughter to the one named Rafael and adopt the gorgio into the tribe as Alicia had been taken in. It was possible. All the years of worry seemed about to melt away like frost in the early-morning sun. His eyes swept over the gorgio with approval. He was strong, that one, manly yet handsome. One of Alicia's own kind. They would make a perfect pair. He could not have chosen a better husband for her himself. "The heart speaks and the inner self listens," he whispered.

Only one matter caused him worry. What if the gorgio was not content to live with the tribe as a Gypsy? Could he abide the thought of Alicia being taken from him?

"No!" he groaned, that could not be. She was his sun and moon. But that would not happen. *O Del* would not bring this gorgio here, this mate for Alicia, and then steal *her* away. No, no. It was meant to be that the gorgio live with the Gypsies. Rudolpho would have a son as well as a daughter. Alicia had saved the life of this man to be reborn, to live among the tribe. It was the gorgio's destiny and fate to be a member of the caravan. He must talk with the gorgio, make him see so that he would not go back to his people when he was set free. He would live in peace and contentment at Alicia's side. It had to be.

"Stivo, untie the gorgio. Bring him to me. I must speak with him!" Rudolpho was intent on settling the matter as quickly as possible.

"Untie the gorgio?" Stivo glowered.

"Do as I say!" Rudolpho's voice was like thunder.

Reluctantly obeying the command of the man who had been his tribal leader for as long as he could remember, Stivo cut the bonds and gave Rafael a shove, mumbling beneath his breath. As Rudolpho motioned for Stivo to bring Rafael to him, as the two men fought a silent battle with their eyes, Rafael had just the distraction he needed. Alicia swept by him, her heart filled with love, only to feel the gorgio's arms reach out to her, grasping her.

"Forgive me, Alicia, this is my only chance." Reaching into the deep folds of her skirt for the knife he had seen her conceal there, Rafael brandished the weapon. Knowing in his heart that he could never bear to use it, Rafael hurled threats as he edged away from the campfire, holding Alicia as a shield. The ploy might work, he thought. How were the Gypsies to see into his heart and know he would never harm Alicia?

"No, Gorgio. No!" The Gypsies' outcry proved that he was right. They did fear for her safety.

Alicia was too stunned to offer resistance. Like a puppet she felt herself dragged along as Rafael fled his captors. Only when she was thrown upon a horse to sit astride the beast with Rafael's arms locked around her, his hostage, did she let out a piercing scream.

7

Rafael rode at a furious pace, which was no easy trick, considering the struggling, cursing, angry Gypsy girl astride the horse with him. Several times her kicking and wiggling threatened to send them both toppling to the ground. All the while she raged at him.

"You son of a *jukel*! Bastard. I curse you, Rafael de Villasandro! May worms eat your flesh. May you lose all your gold! May the crops in your field shrivel and die! May your manhood wither!" This last oath hurt him to the quick, and he tightened his arms about her.

"Hush, Alicia! Don't you know how I hated to use you to escape? You saved my life. Twice. But I could not stay a prisoner. No *man* would. I will not ask you to forgive me, only to understand!"

She did. Deep in her heart she knew that he was telling her the truth. Was he not only echoing the words she herself had said to Stivo before the dancing began? Yet her wild temper urged her on.

"You tricked me, Gorgio! I will never forget that. You are *O Beng* incarnate." But her cries soon ceased. She would never have admitted it, but this kidnapping was very romantic and in its way exciting. What woman had not dreamed of being carried off by the man she loved?

But where were they going and for how long? She did not want to leave the Gypsies and her father. She wanted to stay with Rudolpho. Her father would be frantic! "Gorgio! Gorgio! Where are you going?" At last she put her curiosity into words.

"To Toledo. I must find those men who robbed me! As I remember from their clothing and accent, they were from that area. I will show them how to treat a nobleman."

Rafael looked behind him, watching for any sign that he was being followed, and thankfully saw none. They were not being pursued, at least for the time being. But he would keep the Gypsy girl with him just in case.

Alicia began to struggle again. She had to go back. Who would take care of her father if she did not? She was his only child, the only member of his family. He needed her. "Take me back! You son of a dog, take me back! I will not go with you!" Fear of the gorgio world intensified her swearing. She had been to Toledo once. The gorgios were not kind. They had thrown rotten apples at the caravan and told them to move on. And the solemn-faced black-garbed leaders had been frightening, cursing them as spawns of the Devil, threatening to punish them with everlasting fire. "No. I—I cannot go to this Toledo. I cannot go!"

Rafael had no intention of taking Alicia that far, just far enough to ensure his own safety, yet the thought of her beauty, of her body opening itself like a flower to him, tempted him. From the first moment he had opened his eyes and seen her hovering over him, he had been drawn to her with a current as fierce as the tide. He wanted to kiss her, touch her, drown all his pain and sorrow in her sweetness and fire. Desire flamed within him as hotly as the Gypsies' fires, fanned by the brush of her breasts grazing his arms as she thrashed about. The farther they rode, the greater was her allurement, weaving about him like a spell.

"Gorgio . . ." Alicia's wail was lost in the wind as Rafael bent close to the churning muscles of the horse, seeking a firm grip on the reins as he guided the horse onward. He did not even want to think about what would happen to him if the Gypsies caught up with him. Stealing the tribal leader's daughter, a horse, a knife, leaving the camp as he had, would surely cause them to seek vengeance. Still, he would do it again.

Rafael's heart was beating like a drum in his chest and yet he smiled, whispering a name to the wind. Alicia. Her hair smelled of summer flowers, blowing all about them as they rode, like a silken mantle. That she was no longer cursing him was a blessed relief. Now he could concentrate upon the road.

How long they traveled he did not know. He knew only that at last his aching backside urged restraint. He had been pushing the horse at a savage pace. Now when he sensed that Alicia could stand no more, when he feared that she would be exhausted beyond endurance, he pulled at the reins to urge the horse to a halt. The stubborn beast refused to comply.

"Whoa! Whoa!" The animal had a mind of its own and ignored his command.

"He does not know your gorgio language." Alicia laughed. "Nor does he respond to restraint upon the reins. *Grai! Grai!*" she shouted, touching the animal upon his head. Instantly the animal obeyed. "You see, Rafael, he is a Gypsy horse. Only a Gypsy can tame him."

"Like you, Gypsy beauty!" he said, helping her down. "Can you be tamed?" He held her in his arms, their breath mingling as he gently kissed her. For the moment he nearly forgot the danger as he looked into her eyes. "Alicia. Do you forgive me?"

She tossed her thick dark hair. "I may and then I may not, Gorgio," she teased. Already she had done so. Would she not have done the same thing if their places had been reversed? She knew that she would. And he had taken her with him. Did that not prove that he was attracted to her as deeply as she was attracted to him? Perhaps if she were patient and clever, she might at last convince him to go back

with her to stay among the Gypsies. Were he to return on
his own, it would give proof of his intentions. How could
the others do less than to forgive him? Alicia let her dreams
overpower her reason. She knew only that she could not
bear to leave Rafael just yet.

"Forgive me, Alicia."

Again she tossed her hair about her shoulders, but this
time she smiled. "We will see, eh?"

Rafael knew at that moment that it was more than her
forgiveness he wanted, he wanted her love. Alicia stirred
him with deep longing as no other woman ever had. She
was like a dream, a fascinating blending of softness and
wildfire. How could he deny his heart? If only things were
different, he thought, I would keep her by my side forever;
yet he could not fight reality, no matter how lovely the
dream. He was attracted to her, yet she would be totally
unacceptable in his world. When he rode to Toledo he
would have to leave her behind, and that very thought tore
at his soul. No matter how much he desired her, she was
forbidden fruit. Yet the knowing did not make the wanting
go away.

It was growing cold, darkness was falling fast over the
earth. Rafael decided to spend the night in this place where
they had stopped. In the shelter of an old gnarled tree he
gathered together leaves and small twigs to make a bed for
them, resigning himself to leave Alicia untouched. It was a
vow that grew weaker with each moment that passed.

The night was filled with the cries of night birds, the air
crisp with the blowing wind. Now that Alicia and Rafael
were together, alone, they were both suddenly shy and silent as the current of anticipation crackled between them
like the tension before a storm. Alicia broke the silence.
"Am I now your prisoner, Gorgio?"

He reached out and brushed her hair from her eyes. "No.
You could never be any man's prisoner, Alicia." He pulled

her to him. "God, you are beautiful. Have you any idea how I've longed for you?"

She backed away slightly, a frightened virgin, trembling at the thought of the unknown. Only a fool could not have known what he wanted, and deep in the depths of her soul she wanted it too, but the laws of her people forbade this passion that flamed between them. Someday when she married, her husband would demand proof of her virginity by her blood on the bed linen. What would she do when that moment arrived if she gave herself now to this gorgio? She could not. She *must* not. "No, Rafael. Please do not touch me."

"I won't. Not if you don't want me to, Alicia. I would never harm you." He gestured toward the pile of leaves. "But come. You must get some sleep."

She sat down beside him, her eyes looking upward. "Do you see all the stars?" she asked, her voice without guile.

He laughed. "I would have to be a blindman not to." What an exotic blend of woman she was. So full of fire one moment, kicking and cursing; so soft and womanly the next, then dancing like some primitive being; but now childlike as she gazed at the stars.

"They are all people."

"What?"

"Not people, actually, but . . . well . . . we Gypsies believe that each man and woman on earth belongs to a star. Thousands of stars. So many. And so many people."

He reached up to point at one of them, and she quickly grabbed for his hand. "But it was a falling star."

"No. Do not point your finger at him. It is a thief trying to escape here on earth. You will cause him to be caught." She broke out into gales of laughter at the thought. "Poor man. You have hastened his fate, eh?"

Her laughter was so melodious, her eyes sparkling as brightly as the stars. Without thinking, forgetting about his promise, he put his hands on her shoulders, sliding the material of her blouse aside so that he was touching her bare skin.

"Alicia!" He let one of his hands drop, reaching for her hand. Lifting it up, he kissed the palm, his tongue lingering on the soft center where her lifelines spoke of her destiny. His touch made her heart nearly skip a beat, but she did not pull away. It was so easy to forget everything out here alone with him. "I want you, Alicia. Please don't deny me, my little Gypsy love." He could not fight his desire any longer.

He bent forward, his lips claiming hers again with a gentleness that stirred her heart. She gave him her trust, wholly and completely. He loved her, just as she loved him. Everything would be all right. He would never hurt her. Never. Maybe Rudolpho would let them marry. He would if he knew what was in her heart.

"Please let me love you, Alicia." This time his kiss was one of hunger, his tongue warm as it pushed past her lips to explore the moist darkness of her mouth. Never had she thought a kiss could so fire her blood. Even her dancing had not made her feel like this.

Caught up in a spell, she felt reality vanish as he tugged her blouse down around her waist, baring her breasts to his sight. She made no effort to hide her body from him. Gone was her modesty. This was her fate, her destiny. To belong to this man.

Bending his head, he gently kissed the peaks of her breasts until she gasped, her hands clutching at the dark strands of his hair as a shudder took her. With light, teasing strokes he explored the full mounds as swirls of pleasure swept over her. Rafael was an accomplished lover, showing her the full depth of his love.

He left her for just a moment, removing his own clothing, then slowly stripping away the last barriers she had against him. She wore seven skirts in all and, like the petals of a flower, he pulled them away.

"Beautiful. More beautiful than I could ever have imagined." And she was. Long legs, full breasts, a waist that could be spanned by a man's hands. She was made to be loved. Her skin was dark where it had been exposed to the sun, dark and golden, but that part of her that had been hidden was a pale gold. Moving his hand across the softness of her belly, he worshipped her. She was as smooth as silk. A cool breeze touched the peaks of her breasts, swelling them into succulent buds that beckoned his touch, and he gave in to his longing to do so once again.

Alicia could feel his eyes touch her skin as if they were branding her, and she felt an inner glow to think that her body pleased him. It was as it should be. He was her man. His voice was husky with desire, sending shivers up her spine.

Reaching out to touch him, her hands slid over the hard smoothness of his shoulders, touching the crisp hair of his chest. His skin was warm.

"I love to have you touch me!" he groaned, closing his eyes. If only it could always be like this. If only he never had to leave her. She was everything a man could ever hope to find in a woman. Everything.

His mouth closed over hers in fierce possession, and feeling her shiver, he knew that she felt the same ecstasy, a rapture that seemed to entwine their very souls.

He pulled her down beside him, their bodies writhing together in the slow, sensuous dance, as primitive as time itself. It was a dance similar to the one Alicia had done in the camp, but this time she had a partner. Her senses were reeling as she felt the fire of his lips, exploring her, seeking out the tastes and textures of her body.

"I swear to you, Alicia, I've never felt like this," he whispered, and he did not lie.

His mouth strayed to seek out the secrets of her womanhood and she opened up to him like a blossoming flower, moaning with her pleasure, overwhelmed by the fiery need she felt. Her body responded with a will of its own. Any

fears or misgivings she might have had were now forgotten
as her passion was ignited. She returned his touches, exploring his body as he had hers, feeling joy when he moaned
with desire.

Stroking the velvety flesh, he made her ready for him,
then when she was moist and willing, he entered her ever so
gently. Alicia gave one sharp cry of pain as he passed
through her unbroken maidenhead.

"Do you want me to stop?" he asked, aching at the sound
of her pain.

"No," she breathed. "I want you. . . ." Surely she would
die if he left her now, or so it seemed. Her trust was complete.

In answer he soothed her with his kisses, cradling the soft
curves of her hips with his hands, sheathing himself in her
softness with gentle movements as he whispered her name.
"Alicia!" Slowly he began to thrust, and all the hurt was
gone, to be replaced with a fire that seemed to inflame them
both. Their bodies blended; became one, as if each of them
had waited their lifetimes to find each other.

Ripples of pleasure washed over Alicia as she clutched
him to her, her eyes mirroring the wonder of this ecstasy
they were sharing. She had never imagined that it would be
like this. She gave herself to him and found a love that
seemed to shatter the very stars with fire.

"Ah, Rafael!" she cried out, closing her eyes, declaring her
love there beneath the stars. Even *o Del* himself must have
smiled, she thought. Surely God had sent this wonder, this
man she loved.

In the quiet aftermath of their passion they lay together,
reluctant to move and break the spell. At last they both
dozed off in a contented slumber.

8

The distant mountains were purple against the light of the dawn as Rafael de Villasandro gazed out at them, his brow creased in a frown. Alicia. He could not take her with him, not where he was going. There was a mission that he must complete, and it meant going alone. "Alicia." Even her name seemed to be magic as it tugged at his heart. She was beautiful, this Gypsy girl sleeping beside him, trusting and innocent, and he knew that he was going to hurt her. He felt lower than a dog as he turned his gaze to look upon her face, so peaceful in sleep.

I have asked you to forgive me once already, sweet Alicia, he thought, gently stroking her hair. She stirred in her sleep at his touch but did not waken.

Why had he let their passion flame so brightly last night? What kind of a devil was he to take advantage of her love, knowing he must leave her when the morning light came? She had called the devil *o Beng.* Surely he was that being now. If only he had kept his resolve and had not touched her, but it was as if a powerful force had driven him on. It had not been lust. It had been even more powerful than that, and it was frightening to think that he had lost his heart and soul to a *Gypsy,* but it was true. God help them both. They were from two different worlds. Did their love have a chance? No. He could not, nor would not, want to join her Gypsy caravan and wander about the land. Nor would she be happy in his world, she who was as free as the stars.

Oh, God, Alicia, he thought, *I'm sorry.* It would have been better for both of us if you had left me to drown! She had saved his life, had given him her virtue, and now, like a dog, like the *jukel* she had called him, he was leaving her; but he had no other choice. He could not let anything stand between him and the mission he had vowed to take. Even his love for this Gypsy girl.

Fear of the power of attraction he felt for her caused him to tremble. Was it love? Had she bewitched him, cast a Gypsy spell? She looked more angel than witch, although he had called her witch that first night he had looked into her green eyes.

She would be better off with her people and he with his. He must seek retribution on those two thieves who robbed him and then seek to help those whose destiny and his own were tied together because of his mother's blood. Perhaps someday they would meet again if fate was kind. Reaching down, he picked up the largest of her seven skirts to drape over her naked body and shield it from the morning sun. There was no place for her beside him, beautiful though she might be. He did not want to waken her, knowing that if he did, he would have to witness the pain and anger in her eyes at the thought that he would desert her.

Casting one last glance at her, his heart aching, guilt plucking at it like the strings of a guitar, he knew well what she would think when she woke to find him gone. He had heard her curses before, now the very forest would ring with her outrage, but it could not be helped. He was "gorgio," as she had called him, and she was Gypsy. Their fate was sealed.

Throwing down the knife that belonged to her, he said one last good-bye. She would find her way back through the trees to the encampment. He would go on foot and leave the horse for her. It was the least he could do.

"Good-bye, Alicia," he whispered, shading his eyes against the early-morning sun. Then he was gone, vanishing as silently and as quickly as the wind.

9

Warmth, blessed warmth, engulfed Alicia and she stirred, opening her eyes to the heat and light of the sun. Breathing deeply of the fresh fragrant smells of early morning, she smiled as she remembered the night she had spent in Rafael's arms. She had never known such happiness existed but had found it in the arms of a gorgio. Sighing, she whispered his name.

"Rafael." Craving the warmth of his body, she reached for him, only to find herself alone. In disappointment she turned over on her side, her eyes searching for him. Had he gone to see about his personal morning needs? she wondered. Perhaps he was looking about for signs that her people had followed them. She could see the horse, Grai, grazing only a few feet away from her, and she smiled as she remembered how she had bested Rafael and proved her skill with the animal. She should have told him that this was the horse she had helped Rudolpho train, taking delight in that secret command to make the animal stop. Even Stivo was afraid to ride him.

Her stomach rumbled and she thought how surprised Rafael would be when he came back to freshly picked berries. Bright red ones that were tangy and not too sweet. Rising to her feet, brushing the tangles out of her long dark-brown hair, she picked up her scattered garments—blouse, chemise, and skirts—and quickly donned them. Her eyes were drawn to the bloodstains on her underskirt, the cloth she had lain upon while Rafael made passionate love to her. Proof of her virginity. Rafael would know beyond a doubt that he had been her first love.

My only love, she mused. Had last night been their wedding night, the stain would have been shed on the bed linens and hung up the very next morning for all to see that Rafael de Villasandro had taken a virgin bride. So, the wedding night came before the wedding, she thought to herself. All would be set to rights. Rafael loved her. He could not have been so gentle and so loving if he did not.

Going in search of the berries, she picked two handfuls, holding them in the folds of her outer skirt. It took some time to gather them, and all the while she kept a lookout for Rafael. Where was he? What was he doing? Her bare feet stumbled upon the knife, and picking it up, she tucked it safely in the band at her waist. So he had not gone hunting. Fishing perhaps. He could accomplish that with a sharp-pointed branch.

Fish and berries were delicious together. She would start a fire so that when he brought back the food it would be prepared so much the quicker. Wrapping the berries in one of her scarves, she set about rubbing two sticks together and soon had a blazing fire going. Now she began to worry. Rafael had been gone a long while. What if something had happened to him? Had those men come back and killed him?

No. Pressing her hands to her temples, she refused to think of such a thing. Pacing up and down, she wore a path through the wild forest grass, and still there was no sign of him.

"Rafael!" she shouted, cupping her hands to her mouth. "Rafael!" Her only answer was the wild, sweet song of the birds. Alicia felt suddenly all alone, frightened, not for herself but for him. But she was Gypsy. Throwing her head back, she cursed her stupidity in not searching for him

sooner. He was gorgio. He would not know the ways of the
forest as she did. He might have stumbled and fallen into a
hole, or injured his ankle. Even Stivo had done that once.

Again she called to him. Her cries frightened a family of
squirrels gathering their morning meal. Scampering up a
large tree, they scolded her with their chattering.

Bending low, Alicia scanned the ground as she had been
taught since childhood. It was easy to follow a human trail
if one knew what to look for. A bent twig, a rock pressed
deeply into the ground, grass swept to one side—all were
like arrows pointing the way. Thus it was that she found
Rafael's tracks, leading farther and farther away from where
they had made love. Where was he going? Why had he not
come back?

She refused to listen to the voice in her head that whispered that he had left her. No. No. He would never do that.
Not after he had taken her virtue. No honorable man, no
Gypsy, would do such a thing. "But he is gorgio," argued
the voice.

He loved her. Rafael loved her. He would come back. He
would! Yet the heartbreaking evidence was clear as she
walked farther and farther along. Looking up toward the
sky, toward that place where *o Del* lived, she asked for his
wisdom.

"Del, please help me," she cried, lifting her arms toward
the heavens. As if in answer, a feeling of warmth swept over
her. Was it just the sun? No. *O Del* was with her. He knew of
her pain. She had to face the truth. Rafael had deserted her
to walk alone back to the people of his own kind.

Tears streamed down her cheeks and she lifted her face so
that the sun's warmth would dry them. A Gypsy must not
cry over a gorgio. She was brave. She was a Rom. Yet the
knowledge that she had been left behind nearly destroyed
her, her sorrow turning to anger, a burning rage as hot as the
flames of desire.

"Gorgio bastard!" she shrieked. He had used her. Used

her kindness and love to escape. The others had warned her but she had not wanted to listen. Instead, she had been in awe of his manly beauty, his touch, his smile. Now she understood Stivo's hate. She had seen at first hand how treacherous gorgios could be.

"He thinks Gypsies are as the dirt beneath his heels," she cried aloud. "I spit on him and all his kind!" And yet when he had kissed her . . . No! No! No! She could not think about that ever again. He had shamed her. To her people she would be a disgrace. A woman's virtue was her treasure, and Alicia had been left impoverished by the ecstasy of a man's kiss.

Closing her eyes, sinking to her knees, beating her chest as one who mourned another's passing, Alicia poured forth her sorrow, mingling her tears with the blessed dust of Mother Earth.

How long she lay there she did not know. Her only sense of awareness came with the sound of pounding hooves, the feel of powerful arms lifting her up, the low voice of her papa calling her name.

"Alicia. Alicia, come, don't cry." Rudolpho brushed away her tears. "Tell me what has happened."

Her words were mumbled, spoken through the choking sobs of her sorrow. "I have been foolish, Papa. I thought he loved me. I told you that I would not, but I . . . I did."

His eyes swept over her and without seeing the proof of her lost virginity, the blood on her skirt, he guessed the cause of her weeping. He had seen the looks between the two; had seen her dance for the gorgio. "Where is he?" he asked in anger.

"Gone."

"Gone?"

"He has left me behind." Burying her face against the firm muscles of his chest, she gave vent to her anguish at last, asking, "Can you ever forgive me?"

"Forgive you? Oh, Alicia. You have been hurt by this far

more than I." He stroked her hair as he had done when she
was but a child. At last she quieted her sobs and looked at
him with her tear-sparkled green eyes.

"I have brought shame upon you. The others . . ."

"The others? Bah. You are my daughter. Let them scorn *me*
if they must. I will always give you my love." He set her
gently down upon the ground. "We will go home now. I will
find this gorgio someday, I swear it. He will right this wrong
he has done you, Alicia. He will marry you. . . ."

"No!" Her anger mingled with her sadness. "I will have
no part of him though I be shamed forever. He betrayed me.
I saved his life, gave him my love, and he threw it all away
because I am Gypsy and not good enough for him." Her
anger melted away, leaving only the sorrow. Reaching up,
she gently brushed Rudolpho's weathered face. "Oh, that I
could undo what has been done. . . ."

His eyes met hers, and she was stirred by the love and
kindness she saw there. Despite what she had done he did
forgive her. "Trying to change the past is like trying to jump
over your own shadow, *Chavi*. Ah, child . . ."

Chavi. The word for little one. He had not called her that
in many years. Somehow at this moment she felt like a child
as his wise words echoed in her mind.

Numbed by her grief, Alicia had not noticed the other
men who had followed her father in his pursuit. Now they
urged their horses closer, and Alicia could see Stivo's eyes
impale her with their scorn. Hastily she turned her back on
him, repeating her father's words over and over again. She
could not change what had happened, but she would remember, with each breath she would remember. Mounting
her horse, urging Grai onward, she followed the others back
to camp.

10

The sun shone overhead like a torchlight as Rafael walked along the pathway. The sky was a brilliant blue without a sign of clouds. Fields of gold and red flowers stretched before him, tall trees loomed high above. Nature's beauty surrounded him. Alicia's world. He winced at the thought, remembering how lovely she had looked asleep under the tree. Now her world had reached out to punish him. He was lost. Fool that he was, he did not know where he was.

How could he have lost his way? The answer was clear. He was not used to the forest. Walking along with his head aswim with thoughts of her, of Alicia, he had been roaming about in circles, retracing his own steps. Before, it had been those two men who led the way. "Leading me into a trap. Bastards!" He would find them, and when he did . . .

Sitting down upon the stump of an old tree to rest for a moment, Rafael put his face in his hands, remembering. Would he ever be able to forget all that his father had revealed to him on that fateful night when they had quarreled so bitterly? Rafael had wanted to leave, to seek his own way in the world. He was tired of being the second son of Pedro Ortega de Villasandro. The constant warfare against the Moors had given him his desired chance to become a caballero, a knight, to fight for King Ferdinand and Queen Isabella.

"Please understand, Father," he had said, but his father's eyes had been cold.

"And so you leave me as she left me," he had said, so quietly that Rafael had barely heard him. "Your mother."

Rafael had been confused. His mother had died of a fever when he was just a small boy. All his life he had been told the story over and over. "What are you saying?"

Anger blazed in his father's eyes. "She left me to join her people. Left me! It was the fires of the Inquisition, not the fever, that took her. And now you will desert me too!"

"No. It is not true." Rafael had been consumed by a turmoil of emotions that threatened to unman him, but he fought against his tears and took refuge in anger. "You lying old man." Reaching out, he came perilously close to striking his father and severing the thin thread that held them together, the last semblance of love. But something in his father's eyes told him that he was speaking the truth, and so he withdrew his fist and demanded, "Tell me."

The story had poured forth with the old man's tears. He, Pedro Ortega de Villasandro, had fallen madly in love with a physician's daughter, a young Jewess from Navarre. On the night she was to wed another, one of her own faith, he had brazenly abducted her from the arms of her waiting bridegroom, taken her back with him to his own lands in Castile, and there married her himself.

"It was a madness. A madness. An obsession to make her love me as much as I loved her." As he threw back his shoulders, holding his head erect, it was as if the years had melted away, and Rafael could see a vision of the man his father had been in those days. "And in time she did love me. She bore me two sons and we were happy."

Rafael's father was a man of power, a *prócer*, an independent noble, fiercely loyal to his new Queen Isabella. It was at his insistence that the nobles had denied the potency of Henry IV, *Enrique el Impotente*, refused to acknowledge his claim of fathering a daughter, Juana, and instead named Henry's sister, Isabella, as his successor.

"And so we were safe and very, very happy, my Sarita and I," Pedro had whispered, closing his eyes as if again envisioning those days, but just as quickly he had opened them. "But it was not meant to be. They killed her. Oh, if only she had stayed with me, I would have protected her. But she left me. She left me. She wanted to be with her people."

"You said she died by the fires. When? Why?"

From his father's lips the story had unfolded, a sorrowful tale. In 1480 there were those in power who thought it a necessity to remedy the evils arising from the mingling of Jews and Christians. It became an obsession to some, whose fanaticism stirred ripples of discontent in the calm waters. A storm was brewing, and Rafael's parents were caught in its gales.

It was decreed that the old laws concerning the Jews should be reinstated, that all Jews should wear the circle of red cloth on their shoulder to mark them, that they should be kept in *juderías*, their own section of the city, always returning to these sections by night. Walls were erected around this *judería*, and no Jew was allowed to practice as a physician, surgeon, apothecary, or innkeeper.

The sovereigns delegated the Cardinal of Spain, Pedro González de Mendoza, and Frey Tomás de Torquemada as inquisitors in Castile. They began at once to carry out their mission to proceed *por vía del fuego* (by way of the fire).

"They could do nothing to those Jews who had converted to Christianity unless they offended against the faith by returning to Jewish practice or sheltered one who did," Rafael's father had explained. "Much as an army deals with deserting soldiers, these church officials dealt harshly with any Christians who reverted to former religions and practices. Public feeling against Judaizers and apostatizing *Moriscos . . . .*"

"Moriscos?"

"Baptized Moors . . . became hostile. The word *Jew* became equated with *Judas,* with cruelty to man and beast. *Don't be a Jew* became the cry." Pedro Ortega de Villasandro had become so enmeshed in his grief that he had buried his face in his hands, but at his son's urgings he continued the tale. "Bigotry filled the people's minds and destroyed all sense of reality. They called the Jews *Christ killers,* my Sarita's people!"

"And was my mother then a Jew?"

"She had been baptized into Christianity, but her father had not. He could no longer practice medicine and had to move to the *juderías,* taking his wife with him. Sarita loved her parents very much and frequently went to see them. She was doing nothing wrong, but they accused her of returning to the Jewish faith because she had been at their home on several Jewish feast days and on their Sabbath." Pedro Ortega de Villasandro closed his eyes and shook his head. "One was the Feast of Purim, a ritual practiced from the time of the Babylonian captivity, before the birth of Jesus. They said it was intended as a mockery of the Passion of the Redeemer. Rumors were spread to inflame the public mind against the Jews, and your mother, too, was a victim."

The story had taken a great deal out of Rafael's father, and for a long moment he had quieted as he seemed to be transported back into the past. Only Rafael's questioning had prompted the older man's continuation of the story.

Fanatical monks led by Mendoza and Torquemada went throughout Castile, ignoring the papal injunctions of forbearance and tolerance toward the Children of Israel, preaching that God's wrath would fall upon any land that gave them a home. They commanded the faithful to arise and destroy the Jews. Massacres were the result of their wagging tongues. Massacres that took place in Castile, Aragón, and Navarre.

"And my mother . . ." Rafael had felt anger rise up in his throat to choke him.

"Your mother and her family were afraid. They hid. I did not know where she was. She did not want to bring harm to me or her sons . . . did not want to bring us into danger and so . . ." Anguish had strangled his father then, so much so that Pedro Ortega de Villasandro, a man who had always held himself proud, let his tears run down his cheeks unchecked. "They burned her. Burned her at the stake, all those who were not fit to kiss the hem of her gown. They seared her lovely flesh, my Sarita. Made her meet the fires as a heretic!"

"God be merciful!" Rafael had crossed himself, praying for her soul.

"But she was not!"

"And my mother's father?"

"He and your grandmother escaped to Rome. You were so young then, only a boy of twelve. I could not tell you. You would not have understood. And so I told you that she had died of a fever. That was eleven years ago. Eleven years ago. They called her *Reversa* and *Marrana*. My lovely Sarita."

"Marrana?"

"At first converts were called New Christians by Spaniards, *Marranos* by those of their own race who had remained faithful to the Jewish ways. It meant the Lord is coming— Maran-atha—but it came into misuse by the Christians, who thought it meant accursed and so used it as an insult." His eyes blazed again as he pointed a finger at Rafael. "And you, too, will be in danger if you leave here. They will burn you, too, if they learn of your Jewish blood. You must stay here with me or seek safety with your brother. I was too late to save your mother, but if I had known, I would have done so. But I am not too late to warn you. You must remember that Torquemada is dangerous!"

Rafael had listened to his father's story with deadly calm, but now, having learned of his mother's fate, he was more determined than ever to leave his father. Pedro Ortega de Villasandro's words had not frightened Rafael, only left him with fury and a desire to help those who, like his mother, were in danger of the fires. And so he had left.

Raising his head, Rafael looked around him again. The past quickly vanished at the sight of the lush green forest. His father had dared to love someone different from himself and it had brought tragedy. Remembering the fate of his mother only reinforced his decision to leave Alicia behind. His love would only lead her into danger.

And so, Alicia, if you knew the truth, he thought, *knew that I am not free to live my life fully until I have accomplished my mission, perhaps you would forgive me. But you are free. As free as the wind. And for a moment I, too, was like the wind.*

Rising to his feet, he again sought his way out of the forest, and this time, as if he had been forgiven, he found the way. It was a grueling journey, and he scolded himself for being so generous as to give Alicia back her horse. His shoes were worn through, his legs ached, and his feet were blistered. And yet he could not have done otherwise. The horse was hers. How could he have taken it? He had taken enough from her, he thought in self-condemnation. Would he do the same again if he could relive that moment? Yes. He could not lie to himself. That one taste of ecstasy had been the happiest and most beautiful experience of his life.

Rafael uttered a groan as he walked up the long, rocky road. He was hungry, his back and feet ached, and he was tired. Yet the memory of Alicia's beauty acted as a balm to soothe him.

For the first time he truly understood the madness his father must have felt for his mother, the total all-consuming love that had transcended all earthly laws, and yet that love had been doomed. *"And just like their love, ours, too, was doomed, Alicia,"* he whispered. Bidding the forest good-bye, he turned his back upon any further thoughts of the enchanting Gypsy girl and continued on his way to Toledo.

11

The wind smelled of smoke from the wood fires as Rudolpho, Alicia, Stivo, and Ramón rode back into camp. Alicia was in a haze of unhappiness, barely noticing the black eyes of Stivo boring into her, studying her now with newfound interest. She was only aware of the ache in her heart, the dream that had been shattered beyond repair, a dream that had been as bright as the dawn sky but that was now only a storm.

Already it was mid-afternoon, and Alicia could see several of the men beneath the trees taking their siestas. She was thankful that they at least had not been among the staring throng who watched her arrival back into camp. It was enough to have to suffer the eyes of the women, who asked each other the unspoken questions.

"Where is the gorgio?"

"Did he have his way with her?"

"Is Alicia's virtue still intact?"

Did they really wonder about these things, or was it merely Alicia's guilty conscience conjuring up such thoughts? She did not know, but their whispering threatened to drive her mad. Looking behind her, seeking comfort from Rudolpho, she caught sight of Stivo instead and shuddered at the leer he boldly gave her. He grinned, as if amused by her discomfort.

Oh, why did Stivo have to accompany Rudolpho in his

search for me? she thought frantically. Stivo knew of her shame, and it would not be long before he told the others. Both he and his mother were like that. Malicious, spiteful, and vain. Of all the men, Stivo was the only one who was clean-shaven. It was as Rudolpho said, that he "did not want to hide his perfect face with the dark thatch of mustache that was a Gypsy man's pride." Dressing in bright colors, Stivo sought to be the center of attention, and Alicia thought in her heart that he resented Rudolpho's authority. But as Rudolpho would say, "Clothing oneself in feathers does not make a duckling a rooster."

"Alicia!" The high-pitched feminine voice was Zuba's. She at least had a look of kindness in her eyes when she looked Alicia's way. But then Zuba was like that. Small and fragile, she always reminded Alicia of a sparrow. "Are you all right? Did he harm you?"

"I am all right," Alicia answered tonelessly, fighting to keep her chin up and not give in to her tears before the others.

Zuba took her hand, her large brown eyes filled with concern and affection. "When I saw him carry you off I feared . . ."

"He did not harm me," Alicia whispered, knowing it to be a lie. He had bruised and broken her heart until it ceased to be a living thing.

"He was so handsome. . . ." Zuba intoned with a sheepish smile, as if to say that she wished she had been the one he had carried away with him.

Solis pushed her way through the crowd that was now gathering around Alicia. Her full lips curved in a smile. "Yes, he was handsome. It makes one wonder just what went on beneath the Gypsy skies." The woman's dark, searching eyes seemed to be seeking the answer.

Usually more than a match for the voluptuous woman, Alicia could not utter a word. She felt beaten and no longer had the will to fight, at least for the moment. She had promised Rudolpho and had just as easily broken that promise, and though she knew he loved her and would protect her, still she suffered with her private shame. Only Rudolpho's booming voice saved her as he strode through the crowd, waving the women aside like gnats.

"Enough of your chatter," he scolded. "Your cackling is as unnerving as a gorgio's flock of chickens." The women quickly grew silent, recognizing Rudolpho's authority at once, parting to allow him a pathway to his daughter. "Come," he said to Alicia, giving her that smile that always touched her heart.

Following in the footsteps of her father's large stride, Alicia walked in silence, gazing about her at the beauty of the forest. There was such a sense of peace that came with walking amid such serene loveliness that at last the pain in her heart diminished. Breathing in the fresh scent of pine, she paused for a moment and closed her eyes.

"Dear Papa," she thought. He had known the remedy for her sorrow.

"Such beauty," he said at last, gently touching her arm. "You know, Alicia, in Gypsy legend the earth, *De Develeski,* is the Divine Mother of all existence. Looking at this beauty, I well believe it."

Alicia remembered that at one time *De Develeski* had been the supreme Gypsy deity, more important even than *o Del,* who the Gypsies said came into being when the earth had already been formed. "As do I," she whispered.

"Living so close to nature, it is not surprising that we hold the trees, river, grass, and earth so dear. And freedom." He looked at her searchingly beneath his dark brows. "Never let anyone, Gypsy or gorgio, take away that freedom. It is like the soul, the very essence of life."

"But what if I am put into bondage, prison? I have heard some of the others talk about Torquemada. . . ."

Rudolpho jabbed at his chest with his index finger. "The heart. That is where freedom lies. As long as we are free in our hearts, no one can imprison us or harm us in any way. It is, I think, our link with *o Del.*" Taking her chin in his hand, he looked deep into her eyes. "And freedom is also the courage to face ridicule and wagging tongues with our head held up, knowing only sorrow for the frailty of mankind. I am not perfect. You are not perfect. Only *o Del,* only God, is perfect, and though we try to do what is right and live with honor, we may not always succeed. But take pride in being *you,* Alicia." For a moment his eyes filled with tears. "You will never know the joy you have brought into my life. Leaving you will be my only regret when I die."

She gasped. "Do not talk of dying, Papa. I could not bear to lose you."

"Death is a part of life, Alicia. Someday I must leave you, but let us not speak of such a thing now. I want you only to remember all that I have said this day."

"Freedom is in the heart and in the mind too, I suppose." She smiled then, and it was as if the clouds had suddenly vanished, to be replaced by the sun. Alicia's old fire returned. "I will not let the others and their gossip harm me. I am Gypsy. I am free. Solis is no match for me!"

Rudolpho threw back his head and laughed, delighted to glimpse the return of his daughter's spirit. "Come. We go back to the others, my little flame. One of the horses is ailing and you will help me, no?"

"I will help you, Papa."

They walked back to the Gypsy camp at a faster pace, filled with the joy of life, thinking themselves alone in their forest hideaway. They did not see the eyes watching them. Gorgio eyes. Eyes filled with loathing.

"Gypsies, Manuel."

"Gypsies."

"There are those who would reward us to know just where these heretic bastards keep their camp. Shall we follow them?"

"You read my mind exactly, José. We may not have found

de Villasandro's body, but perhaps we have found something more valuable. Besides, we feared that if de Villasandro was found we would be in danger, and I say to you now that we need only blame his death upon these black-eyed dogs." The hush of the forest was shattered by the sound of laughter.

12

As Alicia had supposed, Stivo's wagging tongue alerted the entire camp, and her lost virginity became the topic of conversation around the campfires. Rudolpho's words to her, however, gave her the courage to hold her head up, and soon other matters began to occupy the Gypsies' time. Casting an occasional sideways glance or a frown, the others went about their business and left Alicia alone. Except for Stivo.

It was as if *o Beng* himself were goading that one on. His taunts were as bitter as gall, his hands reached out to grasp at her with fingers that bruised her tender flesh when no one else was around. Alicia began to hate him, fighting against the loathsome emotion he evoked. She tried to evade him, but somehow he always managed to find her.

"Gorgio's whore!" he would hiss at her when they were near each other. He stared at her with a look that seemed to scorch her, and it took all of Alicia's self-control not to scratch his eyes out.

"Leave me alone, Stivo!" she would warn, returning his fiery glance with icy disdain, but always it was the same. He ignored her words, watching her. Always watching!

Late one afternoon as she scoured out the caldron that would be used to prepare the evening meal, Stivo approached. He smiled at her, his lips curling. "Good afternoon, *rawnie,* " he greeted, using the Gypsy word for lady but making it sound like an insult by his tone of voice.

"Good afternoon, Stivo," she answered in a chilly tone, continuing her job of cleansing the utensil with sand to dislodge the dried food from the night before, hoping that if she ignored him he would go away. Instead, it only goaded him into seething anger. Stivo did not like being ignored.

"You seem to have recovered from your amorous escapade," he exclaimed, coming closer.

"I am feeling fine, Stivo. Thank you for your concern."

"My concern. Ha! It is not you I am worried about but what you have done. You may soon have reason to regret giving your body to that gorgio. He will be the death of us all. You will see. The gorgios despise us!" The rasp of his breathing proved how angry he was, and Alicia stiffened, preparing herself for the argument that she knew was to come. Why could he not let the matter rest? What was done was done. Why was Stivo so hateful?

"Whether I regret it or not, it is not for you to judge me, Stivo. What I do is none of your concern! Rudolpho is our leader and not you."

His laugh was scornful. "Rudolpho. Ha! He may have been strong once, but he is quickly becoming an old man. An old *fool.* "

Alicia could not control her anger this time. Let him say what he would about her; she would hear no insults toward her father. Throwing a fistful of scouring sand into his smirking face, she stood back, her hands on her hips.

"Old or young, he is twice the man that you will ever be!" Turning her back, she reached for a jug of water with which to rinse the caldron, gasping out in pain as Stivo roughly grabbed her from behind.

"You bitch. I will show you who is a man!" he growled, wrenching her arm behind her back until tears came to her eyes.

"I curse you!" she breathed, closing her eyes to fight

against her torment. No matter how he was hurting her, she was determined that she would not beg him to release her. That was what he wanted, to humiliate her. Let him do his worst, she would not humble herself before him. Although she was trembling, Alicia held her head up with pride.

Just as quickly as he had reached for her, Stivo released his hold and hastened away. Opening her eyes, Alicia saw Todero and Zuba coming up the pathway hand in hand. No wonder Stivo had fled. He would not want witnesses to his cruelty. But it was not the last time he would torment her. Alicia knew for certain now that she and Stivo would always be bitter enemies.

"Do you need some help?" Zuba asked cheerfully, unaware of Alicia's turmoil. Shyly she pulled free of Todero's grasp.

"You can tip the caldron while I pour the water if you would like." Alicia picked up the jug, fighting to still her trembling hands.

"Here, let me help you, Zuba." Todero was quick to offer aid. "The caldron is so large." Even he had difficulty managing its bulk, but when the task was done and the caldron left to dry in the late afternoon sun, he stood back grinning, his eyes soft as they looked on Zuba.

Love, Alicia thought, *it can be so beautiful.* She wondered if there would be a wedding between these two soon. They were a perfect pair, both with hearts as big as the sky above them. Neither Todero nor Zuba had shown anything but kindness to Alicia, and with all her heart she wished them well.

Todero sensed Alicia's eyes upon him and suddenly became flustered. "I . . . I had best go now and leave you women to your . . . your chores," he stammered.

"Don't go, Todero!" Alicia pleaded, regretting that her thoughtful gaze had embarrassed him.

"There is much to be done," he answered softly, though his eyes looking in Zuba's direction told her he wanted to stay. "Tomorrow at dawn we will leave this place and go in search of another campsite. There is much that I must do." Bowing slightly, he turned and left.

"I'm happy for you, Zuba," Alicia whispered. "Todero is a fine man, a *rai*. He will make you a fine husband."

Zuba blushed. "Fate has smiled upon me. I love him with all my heart." Reaching down to pluck several of the white and yellow wildflowers that grew in abundance and placing two of the white flowers in her hair, one on each side, she smiled sadly. "I only wish that fate had been as kind to you, Alicia. How I wish that you were happy and with your gorgio."

Alicia shook her head. "It was not meant to be. He did not love me." Her calm manner belied the tumult she felt inside. Even now, after what had happened, she had the overwhelming longing to go in search of him, to follow him to the end of the earth if need be, to walk in his footsteps, share his dreams, to be his shadow if necessary. But it wasn't possible, and so she fought against this desire. Foolish. It would be insanity. "I thought that loving him as much as I did, he would find it in his heart to love me back. But he left. I will never see him again." Even now, that truth brought an ache to her heart.

"Oh, Alicia!" Zuba ran to her friend and threw her arms about her, hugging her tightly. "He must be a fool not to want you. You are so beautiful and brave. How could he have betrayed you so? What kind of a man was he to bring you so much pain?"

"An apparition, a dream, but the man who stole my heart and even now holds it in the palm of his hand." Alicia had fought her tears, holding them back with fierce determination, but now they burst forth, rolling down her cheeks like the currents of the river. She hadn't realized the aching void the gorgio's leaving would bring. Nothing could have prepared her for this heartache, this bitter wound that would not heal.

Zuba tried to comfort Alicia, holding her hand and wiping away the tears, murmuring over and over again, "It will be all right. You will see. You will see. You will forget him." But it didn't stop Alicia's tears. In a torrent of sorrow she unleashed all the pain she had held inside. Then just as quickly as she had let herself be engulfed by her emotions, she brushed away her tears to become the proud Alicia again.

Pulling away from Zuba's comforting arms, Alicia said merely, "Come. We must help the others." Gathering branches and pine cones, they started the large fire, then dragged the caldron through the grass to place it upon the crackling flames. No more was spoken of the gorgio, nor would there be, Alicia vowed.

It was a tedious chore to cut up the vegetables, the wild carrots and crisp green peppers and the onions that stung their eyes, yet one that needed to be done. From somewhere Todero had procured another chicken, and Zuba sneezed and coughed as she plucked its feathers.

Later, as they sat around the campfire, the last portions of their food eaten, Alicia bade farewell to this place of both her joy and her sorrow. The men were sitting or reclining on one elbow around the fire, and she could hear snatches of their conversation as well as their uproarious laughter. It was obvious that they were exuberant about the morrow's move. South, they would be going south, to a part of the country that Alicia had never seen before. She heard the word *Granada* once or twice and remembered that it was ruled by the Moors, dark-skinned people like the Gypsies, only even darker, nearly black.

Always before, Alicia had shared her people's enthusiasm, but tonight she could not find happiness in the thought of leaving. There were so many horses and wagons in the *kumpania*, the large group of Gypsies, many families—men, women, and children. It would be a tedious journey to go so far, a journey spent hiding from those who might not be friendly. Why could they not just stay here in the safety of the forest? What if a horse went lame or if they encountered rain and had to struggle to pull the wagons from the mud? And what of the Moors? How could they be certain they would be peaceful? What if they sold the Gypsies into slavery?

Stop it, she scolded silently to herself. She sounded like a frightened gorgio. She was Gypsy. Wandering was their way of life. Rising from her perch beside the fire, feeling the sudden need to be alone with her thoughts, Alicia fled to the quiet of her wagon. Stripping off her clothes, she buried herself amid the soft feather quilts of her bed, but sleep would not come.

Long into the night she tossed and turned, assailed by a feeling of apprehension. Even the soft, sweet sound of Todero's singing did not soothe her.

"What is wrong with me?" she fretted. Why did she feel as if something terrible was about to happen? Long after the others had gone to bed and the camp was hushed, she received her answer. A noise. She was certain that she heard something.

The hoot of an owl, nothing more, she reasoned, yet it had sounded more like the outraged cry of a man. The beat of her heart drummed in her ears as she listened. Then she heard the sound again.

Slipping from her bed, Alicia crept forward to explore. Carefully pulling aside the canvas that guarded the wagon's entrance, she peered out and shrieked in terror as she saw, illuminated in the moonlight, the figures astride their horses. The shattering sound of hoofbeats and angry shouts assaulted her ears, and she had only one thought. Danger! It was not in friendship that these midnight riders had come.

Slipping her blouse and one skirt on in a hurried frenzy, she rushed outside. The entire camp was in an uproar. Children's cries, women's high-pitched screams, and men's angry voices filled the night.

"Papa! Papa!" she shouted, searching the shadows for his

beloved form. "Papa!" She saw him, his large frame looming in the distance as he sought to defend his people from the violence he knew was to come. The approaching horses sounded like the roll of thunder. Alicia sensed that many would be killed by the shouting horsemen, and in that moment she remembered Stivo's warning that the gorgio would bring death, that he would give their campsite away.

"I curse you, Rafael de Villasandro!" she swore, raising her fist toward heaven in impotent fury. How could he have done this to them? The question tore at her heart, and though she wanted to believe him innocent, the men riding toward the wagons gave proof of his betrayal. Alicia had no time to lament. Fleeing back into her wagon for her knife, she prepared to do battle.

13

Alicia held her knife poised to strike, horrified as she saw that the enemy were as thick as the trees that rose from the forest. Although the horsemen had come first, others followed behind, armed with sticks, stones, and clubs. A rabble. A mob.

The night birds screeched and shrieked, fluttering their wings in a frenzy as they darted from tree to tree, protesting the intrusion. Their angry voices blended with the other cries as women and children sought places to hide. The women cried and the children wailed. Such a pitiful sound, Alicia thought as she watched a small group of Gypsies run toward the trees. Peering from the shelter of the foliage, they wept. Others stood their ground to fight, like Alicia and Rudolpho, determined to stand their ground.

"Gorgios!" Alicia spat the word. What kind of men would sneak up on others in the night while they were sleeping? "Cowards! *Jukela!*" She cursed the day she had pulled the gorgio from the river. Stivo was right. Rafael *had* brought her people to a sorry plight. Had he been rewarded for his treachery? In anger at the thought, she cursed him again.

The horsemen thundered down upon the caravan, brandishing their swords. The others, farmers and villagers, came at a slower pace, but they, too, were armed. Alicia could hear the Gypsy women's cries for mercy and knew that they would have none this night.

The clatter of swords, the grunts of those prepared to fight, and the moans of those already wounded sounded in Alicia's ears. Gripping her knife, she waited for *them* to come closer, those gorgio devils.

A bloodcurdling scream! Vashti was struck down and killed before Alicia's eyes, and there was nothing Alicia could do except to mourn her. "Poor Vashti!" Nor would she be the only victim.

There was hatred written on the faces of the villagers as they pushed aside the curtains of the wagons, crying, "Death to the heretics. Death to the spawn of Cain. Death to all Gypsies." Others shouted out that it was Gypsies who had refused to help the Virgin Mary during her flight from Egypt. Just as God had punished them by making them wander the world, so must they punish them. Alicia had heard such foolish accusations before. These gorgios were fools as well as killers. How could the worshipers of the gentle Christ bring such violence even if they did have such fanciful illusions about her people?

Already blood was flowing as tents and wagons were ransacked, then put to the torch. Alicia could stand no more. She would not wait for the gorgios to come to her; she would go to them and avenge this brutality. She could not stand by while her people were being killed. She would die with them! So thinking, she rushed to the center of the camp.

"Look at this!" a stout peasant shouted, clutching at Alicia as she ran by. "A Gypsy wench. Shall I kill her as I did the other?"

"No! We'll take her back with us and make her our slave. She's too pretty to kill." With deadly menace they surrounded her, but she fought valiantly. Slashing out at her attackers, she was accurate in her aim; and finding flesh, drew blood from one of the rampaging men.

"Cristo! Damn Gypsy bitch!" swore the man who was stung by Alicia's blade. Kicking out his foot, he sent her knife flying from her hand, and she winced in pain, holding her injured wrist.

"We'll see how fiery she is without her knife!" shouted one of the other men, seizing her by the hair and yanking her backward. Kicking and cursing, Alicia refused to be subdued. She fought against her attackers, biting and clawing those who held her. With a strength born of fear and desperation, she lunged free of her captors and took to her heels.

She could see the tall figure of Rudolpho fighting to fend off his attackers, and ran in that direction. Her papa. He had always been a haven of comfort. "Papa! Papa?" Seeing a horseman move forward, she yelled, "Look behind you!" Her warning saved his life.

"Get back, Alicia!" he screamed at her. "Flee while you can, I will join you later."

"Flee? No. I could never leave without you."

"You must. That is an order!"

Her instinct warned her to do as he asked, yet her sense of loyalty kept her hovering near. This time his voice was a loud boom of thunder as he repeated his command. Heeding his wishes, she ran into the cover of sheltering trees and there watched the destruction of the Gypsy band. Carnage. Death. Before her was a tangle of dead bodies and broken weapons, gorgio as well as Gypsy. The Gypsies had been outnumbered. They had put up a fierce fight, but the strength and pride of her people were draining out with their blood.

Alicia heard a scream, one among so many, yet this one came from Zuba. Three men were dragging the Gypsy girl from beneath a wagon, where she had taken refuge. They were holding her down, sweet, gentle Zuba who had never done a living creature any harm. Alicia heard Zuba scream again and saw a large-boned peasant tugging at her skirts. In that moment all thought of her own safety fled Alicia's mind. She had to save Zuba!

"Leave her alone, *jukel*!" Alicia screamed like a wild woman as she ran forward. She was not Zuba's only rescuer. From the opposite side of the camp Todero ran to save the woman he loved.

"Zuba!" As Alicia watched, fighting one of the gorgios herself, Todero struck one of the villagers in the chest with his knife, but as he turned to attack another, he was surrounded by horsemen, crying out for his death.

"Todero!" Alicia's warning came too late. Everything seemed to move in slow motion as she saw Zuba's gentle love ruthlessly run through with a sword. "No!" Determined to help, Alicia threw herself into the fracas of horses and men, fighting with curses and claws like a wildcat.

"Alicia, get back!" She heard Rudolpho's impassioned scream; it was the last thing she heard. A searing pain tore through her head, and she fought in desperation to swim through the blackness swarming before her eyes. Her efforts were in vain.

"Damn you, Rafael. Damn you, Gorgio," she moaned as she fell to the hard ground.

14

"Alicia. *Chavi*. Please open your eyes!"

Alicia heard the voice from far away and reached out her hand. "Papa. Papa." She felt him grasp her hand, felt the soft strokes of his fingers brush back her hair. Though she struggled to sit up, he gently pushed her down.

"You have been hit on the head, *Chavi*. A gorgio's club struck you down. That gorgio is not now among the living."

She opened her eyes wide, remembering. Where was she? In her wagon. But how could that be? She had seen them setting the wagons afire.

"How . . . ?" Her voice was hoarse, filled with pain as she thought about Todero. Poor Zuba, how heartbroken she must be.

"We were outnumbered, Alicia, but we fought bravely. I curse them! Intolerance always brings on persecution, but we Gypsies have the right to trial instead of being murdered in our beds. The Inquisitors have decreed that heretics when so condemned by the church be delivered over to the secular authority to be punished. They think that fear of death will inspire a return to the faith. Fear! It seems their whole way of thinking is based on fear. It was their hatred and babblings that sparked the fires of the violence and caused the death of our people."

"Papa, what happened after . . . after I was struck down?"

"Several of our people were killed, victims of the frenzy. Those villagers were led on by a thirst for blood." His voice was gruff with his anger.

"And the wagons?" Her eyes scanned the confines of the wagon in confusion. "They were burning."

Rudolpho smiled and raised his eyes upward as if in benediction. *'O Del* sent his rain. These Christians believe in miracles, but I tell you that I have seen one this night. It saved our lives and our caravans, and seemed to cleanse away the gorgios' hatred. They left as quickly as they had come."

"The rains!" It *was* a miracle. In all the time that they had camped in this spot over the years, there had been hardly a trace of a cloud. "Oh, Papa!" This time he did not stop her when she tried to sit up. Her head was spinning yet she managed to cling to his shoulders. "What of Todero? I saw him fall. Is he . . . is he dead?"

"No. At least not yet. If he survives, it will be yet another miracle. Zuba is at his side carefully tending him."

Alicia had held her breath and now she let it out in a sigh of relief. "He will not die. I know it. I feel it. Zuba will be his reason to live." There was a long period of silence, and then she asked, "And the others? Who among us has died?"

Rudolpho's face was ravaged with grief. "Too many! Dionisio. Ramón. Vashti. Truffeni. Bazena. Keje. Many others are wounded."

Forgetting the pain in her temple where the club had struck her, Alicia threw back her head in anger. "A curse on those gorgios. A curse on Rafael de Villasandro! He brought this evil upon us. I shall hate him until the day I die."

"No, Alicia. Hatred destroys." Rudolpho grasped her by the shoulders, his eyes demanding that she heed him. "You do not know that it *was* your gorgio. Things are not always as they seem, *Chavi.*"

"But who else knew about our camp in these woods? Who but the gorgio?"

He shook his head. "I do not know." Somehow he had

not judged the one named Rafael to be the kind of man who would seek to harm others. Despite the fact that he had taken Alicia's virtue and left, he had seemed noble, one who would not stoop to such treachery. But who, then? "Perhaps we will never know."

"It was him! Stivo was right! Gorgios. I hate them all!" Alicia met her father's eyes and wondered why he had that look on his face again, as if there were something he wanted to tell her. "Papa, what is it?"

He would have told her then if she had not had such an innocent expression on her face, so open, so trusting. It was not right that she should hate her own kind. He should tell her that. But now was not the time. She had fought as well as any Gypsy, perhaps even more valiantly. He could not reveal to her that those who brought such destruction were those to whom she belonged.

"Papa, what is wrong?"

He rose from his knees by the side of the bed and turned his back so that she could not read the truth in his eyes. "There is nothing wrong." He walked toward the opening of the wagon, pushing the canvas aside.

"Papa, don't go. Not yet. Not until you have told me . . ."

"I must see to the others. We cannot stay here. It is much easier to kill a cow that stands still."

"But the rain . . . the mud. It will be difficult to move the wagons. . . ."

"Nevertheless we must move on. We will separate the caravan into three parts so it will not be so easy to follow us." Alicia knew that eventually the three caravans would meet again. It was always so when danger threatened; like quicksilver they would divide and merge, then divide and merge again. They would keep in touch with each other through secret contacts and by leaving signs along the way, such as a scrap of a scarf or perhaps an earring.

"Yes, Papa. We must move on. We are like the wind

through the branches or a river ever flowing, eh?" She stood up, swaying for a moment on her feet, then steadying herself. "I must help the others." He nodded, eyeing her warily. Then, seeing that she was able to walk, he left her.

Rushing outside, Alicia helped Solis and some of the other women gather up the bedding of those who had been sleeping beneath the wagons when the attack occurred. Soft quilts and blankets were piled inside wagons haphazardly, along with dishes and food. The heavy iron caldrons were lifted up, food and all, and suspended from hooks underneath the wagons. Later they would dry the rain-soaked bedding and clean the caldrons, but for now, haste was of the greatest importance.

As for the dead, Gypsy law required them to be burned with their possessions to ensure a comfortable existence beyond the grave. Thus Alicia watched sadly as each of the bodies of those she had known and loved was put inside a wagon with all that they had valued in life. If there was not proper time to mourn them, well, that would come later. For now, each Gypsy had to be content with a brief show of sorrow before the wagon was burned. It was no easy task, for the rain had wet the wood; but at last the wagons of the dead blazed forth in bright flames, and each whispered the prayer "I leave you now to *Del*, to God."

Weeping, Alicia said her last good-bye to Vashti, remembering her friend's wide smile, her mischievous black eyes. She remembered the time they had danced as children for coins in the marketplace, how Vashti had laughed because she had been given more coins than Alicia. They had shared their dreams, their laughter, but now Vashti was gone.

"Forgive me, Vashti," Alicia cried. "Forgive me." Could she ever forget the look of awe on Vashti's face as they sat around the fire. "You saved a gorgio?" Vashti had asked. If only Alicia had known then what the future would bring. But Rudolpho would tell her not to look back. Live for today, that was the Gypsy way, without regrets about the past nor too many thoughts about the future. With a last look at the burning wagon, Alicia walked on.

The wounded were placed in wagons and made as comfortable as possible. One woman was assigned to tend the needs of the wounded for each caravan. Alicia shared her wagon with two young children who had lost their parents in the carnage; a boy, Palo, and a girl, Mala. They brought their little black dog with them, which whined in fear as if sensing that something terrible had happened. Alicia quieted the dog and tucked the children into bed under one of the quilts, whispering words of comfort. As if not fully understanding, Mala kept asking for her mother and stopped crying only after Alicia had rocked her to sleep.

Looking out the opening of the wagon, Alicia watched as the men rounded up the horses, hitching them to the wagons, or climbing upon their backs to ride at the head of the caravans. Rudolpho was to lead one, Balo another, and Nano the third.

She heard Rudolpho's booming voice: "Mountains do not meet, but men do. We will see you soon. Travel in safety." Going their separate ways, they rode out of the forest.

The rain had stopped, but as the wagons rolled along one would occasionally get stuck in the mud, and all the men would work feverishly to free it. Using stones, branches, or just brute force, they soon had it out of the mud, and with a violent lurch the wagon would travel on.

Alicia lay back upon her bed, cradling the two children on either side of her. At last, rocked to sleep by the swaying of the wagon, knowing the reins were in Todero's strong hands, Alicia succumbed to her dreams as the caravan moved on toward the ever-changing horizon.

15

It was hot in Rafael de Villasandro's bedchamber. The blazing orange sun hurt his eyes, and lifting his hand, he sought to shade his face.

"I must get up!" he exclaimed, but his body did not react to his words, and so he lay there listening to the songs of the morning birds that flitted about the gardens.

He had spent a restless night. Again he had dreamed of Alicia. He had hoped that once he was in Toledo, away from the forest, he would forget her, but he could not. Not even his thirst to avenge himself on the men who had tried to kill him could chase away her memory.

"She is gone now, you fool. Her caravan will have departed those woods, traveling to God knows where. She is happy and safe with her people. Forget her! Even if you wanted to find her, you could not!"

Rising from his bed, he walked to the terrace and looked out on the landscape. Toledo rose steeply from the river, a stairstep of stone, wood, and clay houses dominated by the Gothic cathedral, which raised its towers to the sky as if to put itself high above earthly things.

Rafael was staying for the moment with his brother, Carlos, and his family in a house right outside Toledo, a two-story dwelling of elegant simplicity. His plans were to move on to León after he had found the two named José and Manuel. So far they had vanished as if into thin air.

"I will find them," he mused with a scowl. "I will recover my coins and soon deter them from their thieving ways!" He was so entranced with his thoughts that he barely heard the knock upon his door.

"Rafael. Rafael. Are you up, my brother?" came a soft voice from beyond. It was María, his brother's wife.

"Just a moment, María!" he called out, making a dive for his clothes. It had been so hot that he had slept in the nude, a custom that was not unusual for him. Pulling on his garments, lacing up his doublet, he answered the door to find the plump figure of his sister-in-law waiting patiently. She was a jewel, this one. Short and round-faced, she had the face of an innocent angel and the temperament of one as well. Her eyes were brown pools, her hair a blue-black, always pulled back in a knot. She had given his brother three sons and a great deal of devotion and love, and Rafael could not help but love her too.

"I thought you would be hungry, Rafael, so I have prepared breakfast. I have pleased you, have I not?"

"Yes, you have pleased me, María. I *am* hungry, as ravenous as a wolf!" He followed her downstairs to the dining room and found a lavish display of dishes awaiting him. Now he knew why both his brother and his wife were so plump. All they did was eat, eat, eat. But they were happy. "If I stay here much longer, I will look just like Carlos," he thought with a laugh.

"Ah, brother, come join me," Carlos invited. He had the same dark hair that Rafael had, but his skin was much darker, his eyes were hazel, and his facial features were less well defined. "María has outdone herself today. Eggs with peppers, onions, and tomatoes; fresh fruit and cream; and sliced beef seasoned with garlic." As if to show his brother how tasty it was, he raised a portion to his lips, smacking them loudly in appreciation.

Rafael sat down at the table, trying to find room for his long legs and at last succeeding by putting them out in front of him. Taking a taste of the eggs, he had to agree with his brother.

"Excellent. María is not only beautiful but a fine cook as well. You are a lucky man," Rafael intoned, delighting in María's blush.

"She could have ten cooks if she wanted," Carlos said proudly, "but she insists on doing it all herself. I have been successful in more ways than one." Besides being heir to their father's estates in southwestern Castile, Carlos owned rolling estates of his own, covered with olive trees.

Rafael ate quickly, anxious to get to Toledo. There was a man he was to meet there, a nobleman like himself who was anxious to help the *Conversos* escape from Spain. Already this man was hiding fugitives on his land, though if he were caught, he would be in great danger not only of punishment but of excommunication. And so will I be, Rafael thought. Persons under ban of the church could not hold office nor claim citizenship. To be excommunicated was for one to cease to exist. Even should such a person be ill or distressed, none were allowed to show him charity under penalty of incurring the same fate. Nor would his body be given a Christian burial after death. But the Inquisition was unpopular with the people who were educated, particularly the nobility, who were being doubly taxed to support Torquemada's vengeance, as if the war in Granada weren't monetary burden enough. Rafael knew that even if he had not been told by his father of his Jewish blood or of his mother's death, he would have wanted to help these poor unfortunate Christians of Jewish ancestry.

"How was Father when you left him?" Carlos asked, his mouth full of food, his eyes studying Rafael as if wondering why he had come.

"Angry. He told me about our mother, Carlos." Carlos nearly choked on his food, and it was obvious that he was afraid for María to hear. He gestured to her to leave them, and like an obedient wife she retired to her bedchamber upstairs.

"Are you mad to speak so freely? Do you want to meet your death at the stake, brother!" Carlos scolded when they were alone.

"I am what I am, Carlos. I am not ashamed of my blood and never of my mother. She died bravely. I hope to God that I will have such courage!"

"I suppose the next thing you will be telling me is that you want to revert to the Jewish faith. Is that what you will say?"

Rafael shook his head. "No. I know almost nothing about the Jewish religion. I have heard that they read from the book called 'Torah.' I have heard about their dietary laws. I merely want to help them, not to join them."

"You are still a good Catholic, then." Carlos eyed him warily as if facing his own conscience.

"I am not a *Converso*, Carlos, have no fear. I am a Christian, but I am also a realist, allowing myself no sentimentality. I ask myself how a God of either Christian or Jew could allow people to be so cruel to one another. How can he not listen to the voices of those who cry out from the fires? How could a just God allow a man like Torquemada to have his way?"

"It is not for you to question! Torquemada has said . . ."

"Torquemada is a madman, obsessed with power. He uses this issue of the Jews to further his own career and to put money in the Queen's coffers. But I will save as many as I can, this I tell you!" Rafael's voice had risen in his anger, and now he read the caution in his brother's eyes and bowed to his wisdom in this matter. One could not be foolhardy. Listening ears and wagging tongues could well mean a man's death, and though he trusted his brother and María, one never knew about servants. There was money for any who turned in a suspected heretic to the officers of the Inquisition. "Somehow I feel that I have been chosen to save them," he said in a softer tone of voice.

Carlos lowered his voice, too, but that did not hide his anger. "I suppose the next thing you will be telling me is that you also want to save those ragged Gypsies who imprisoned you from Torquemada. Is that what you will tell me?"

"They weren't ragged." He remembered Alicia and her father, Rudolpho. "I think they have been misunderstood by us because they are different."

"They are thieves! Heretics! Mark my word that Isabella will one day exile the lot of them from Spain."

"They are no more thieves than those who stole my purse and tried to murder me. And as to being heretics, that they cannot be called, since they have never been converted to Christianity in the first place."

"Heathens, then." Carlos shrugged his shoulders, wiping his mouth with his napkin and rising from his chair. "But come, let us not argue. Besides, it does not matter. The Gypsies will not bother us any longer."

Rafael did not like his brother's tone of voice. "What do you mean by such a statement, Carlos?"

"They are gone. A group of villagers swept down upon them and chased them away, though I regret to say they might have killed a few. They burned their wagons and . . ."

Rafael's face turned white, and he felt the sudden urge to vomit up his breakfast. Grabbing his brother none too gently by the shoulders of his doublet, he growled, "What did you say?"

Carlos eyes him with frightened eyes. He had never seen Rafael quite so outraged before. "I said that a group of villagers chased them away."

"By burning their wagons and killing them?" He shook his brother, his eyes filled with fire. "Did you have anything to do with this, Carlos? Did you? If you did, I swear I will not be responsible for my actions. I should never have told you what happened to me. I gave them my word that I would not tell anyone. But I trusted you. I trusted you. We are brothers."

Carlos's voice was choked with terror. "No. No! I swear by the Blessed Virgin. It was two men. Two men from the village who saw the caravan in the forest."

"What were their names?"

"I can't remember." Carlos was shaking in fright, never one to like violence. He was a peaceful man. Seeing his brother's ashen face, Rafael released his hold.

"I'm sorry. But you see, there was a woman . . . and not all of the Gypsies were as we have been told. I must find them. I must know what happened. Please try to remember."

Carlos brushed at his garments in indignation, but after a time he gave the matter serious thought. "I believe they were named Manuel and Juan . . . no . . . José."

"Manuel? José?" He remembered those names all too well. Suddenly the truth of the matter struck him. "They came back for me, to make certain that I was dead, and it must have been then that they saw the Gypsies. Like the dogs that they were, they brought others back with them to pillage and kill." He remembered the word Alicia had used, *"jukel."* Surely this Manuel and José were just that, *jukela,* dogs. Now Rafael had another reason for vengeance against the two, but first he had to find Alicia. It was an all-consuming need, to find her. Running to his brother's stable, he sought the fastest horse and rode in the direction of the forest.

16

⁓

Rafael entered the forest, praying all the while that his brother had been wrong. Perhaps the Gypsies had escaped. Remembering his encounter with the Gypsy named Stivo and the two others, he knew they were men who could put up a fight.

His hopes were dashed as he came upon the spot that had once been the campsite. There was no laughter or singing now; instead, all was ominously still. Even the song of the birds had quieted.

"Cristo!" He was horrified at the sight that met his eyes. Death and destruction, the skeletal remains of wagons and men smoldering into embers and ashes. About him was a tangle of dead bodies and broken weapons that the Gypsies had obviously tried to burn but could not because of the dampness.

Dismounting from his horse, Rafael walked in and out among the bodies, searching frantically for any sign of Alicia. His eyes were nearly blinded by his tears at such a senseless carnage. How? Why? Kicking at the body of one villager in anger, Rafael vented his scorn. "See what your hatred brought you, fool! Your death! And all for what? Because these people were different from you?" He remembered all too well his first impression of the Gypsies, that they were thieves. And Alicia. He had called her *witch*, and though fascinated by her beauty, he had left her behind.

Sorrow coiled in Rafael's belly and, sinking to his knees, he gave vent to his anguish. Was Alicia among the dead? Had her glorious body been consumed by the flames? Or had she escaped? Did he dare hope? She had called God *o Del* and now Rafael prayed with his heart and soul that this deity had heard her cries and reached down his mighty hand to help her.

Counting the number of burned wagons, Rafael assessed how many were left. Only a few of the wagons had been burned. The rest of the Gypsies would have fled through the forest, but where? Alicia had not spoken of where they were headed next. He searched for wagon tracks and found none. The heavy rains had washed them away. At last he gave up and would have left the forest if not for the sound of jeering laughter wafted on the wind. Ducking quickly out of sight, Rafael peered through the foliage to view the intruders and gave a start of anger and surprise to see the very men he was searching for.

"Ha, I told you that if we were but patient we would be able to profit from all this."

"I know, Manuel, but stealing from the dead has never appealed to me." He gestured with his arms to the charred wagons. "And the Gypsies. You said there would be gold, but I see only ashes."

The one named Manuel ran forward, searching through the ruins of the nearest wagon. "No gold! No gold! Those bastard Gypsies, they took it with them!"

"Perhaps there was no gold. They did not look rich to me. I have seen the baubles that their women wear, the gold at their ears, but perhaps that is all there was?"

Manuel did not have time to answer, for like an avenging fury Rafael flew from his hiding place. "You murdering swine. You caused the destruction of these people just for your own greed!" The one named José stared at him aghast, his face as white as the ghost he thought he was seeing.

"Manuel! Manuel! It is *him*. Back from the dead. May the

saints preserve me." Quickly he made the sign of the cross, whimpering as Rafael reached out to grab him. "No! No! Don't kill me! It was not me who did the deed but him. Him!" He jabbed a finger in Manuel's direction.

Too caught up in his anger, Rafael did not listen. Together the two men rolled upon the ground as the thief tried desperately to pull away.

"He is not back from the dead," Manuel said scornfully. "But he will soon be among them." Reaching for his sword, Manuel fell upon Rafael. Rafael ducked just in time as the weapon swished through the air and the blade found a tree trunk instead of his neck. Turning José loose, he centered his attentions on the more dangerous of the two. Seeing himself free, José took to his heels, fleeing the woods.

Reaching for his own sword, Rafael blocked another of his opponent's sword thrusts. "You will not overcome me this time. I know you for what you are. I will not be your hapless victim a second time!"

"We shall see. I am not the coward that my friend is. I will not run from you, I will kill you!"

Again and again he swung his sword like one possessed, and each time Rafael managed to elude him, the last time by only a hairbreadth.

"You see. The next time I will spill your blood!" Manuel growled, throwing himself at Rafael. His act of reckless daring gave Rafael the advantage. Lashing out, Rafael felt his sword hit flesh; saw the red blood oozing from his enemy's shoulder.

"I should kill you for what you have done, but that would make me no better than you. Put down your sword and I will take you back with me to be punished for your thievery."

"Put down my sword? I would rather die than face being imprisoned in the living hell of those jails. If the heat and disease did not kill me, the food would." Ignoring the pain in his shoulder, he struck out again, but the blow was parried and his own sword knocked from his hand by Rafael's expert swordsmanship. Before he had time to pick it up again, Rafael was upon him, his fist aiming a deadly blow to his stomach, which made the man curl up as if inside his mother's womb.

"How does it feel to be facing death?" Rafael taunted, pointing his sword at the man's heart. The thief's eyes blazed hatred. "At least I do not strike you down from behind. Now, get to your feet!" They walked in the direction of Rafael's horse. "You will walk behind me like the dog that you are." Reaching for a length of rope from the saddle, Rafael tied the man's hands behind his back.

"I will not go back to that stinking prison!" Manuel spat. "On my mother's grave I swore I would not go there again." With the speed of a striking reptile he aimed a kick that caught Rafael in the chest, then ran through the foliage. Struggling against his pain, Rafael followed. He would not come so close to catching the snake only to let him slither away. Pursuing his quarry with the keen instincts of a hunter, Rafael found him on the banks of the very river that had nearly claimed his own life.

"You cannot escape me, thief, murderer!" Rafael cried, taking a step closer. The other man was pulling frantically at the ropes that bound him in an attempt to be free.

"I will escape and I will kill *you!*" Manuel threatened. The roar of the river accompanied his words. As in a ritual dance he swayed on his feet, retreating as Rafael took him closer to the riverbank. Standing upon the edge of the bank, he pulled one last time at his ropes before the ground gave way beneath him. His eyes widened in disbelief and his mouth opened in a horrified scream as he fell into the raging waters.

Rafael rushed to the bank, helpless as he watched the waters claim another victim. Unlike Alicia, Rafael could not swim.

"May God have mercy on his soul," he intoned, watching

the river pull Manuel under. The rains had added ferocity to
the river's currents, and Rafael doubted that even Alicia
could have saved this man. It was as if God had issued his
judgment. Was it not written "an eye for an eye"? Or perhaps it was *o Del* who had sought vengeance? Rafael could
only shake his head in wonder. His thirst for blood was
quenched as was his anger. Justice had been done.

Rafael stood watching the swirling waters for a long time
before he turned his back and walked in search of his horse.
He would ride back to his brother's house and from there to
the city. It was as if a chapter had been closed in his life.
Alicia was gone. His would-be murderer had been punished.
Let José keep his miserable life. Like the coward that he was
he would soon be punished by his own fears. Rafael had
many lives to save and an appointment with destiny.

17

It was late morning when Rafael arrived in Toledo. The sun was high in the sky, blistering the earth with its heat. In a few hours it would be time for siesta and there was still much to be done.

Quickening his footsteps, Rafael walked over the rough stones of the street. He could hear the women singing as they washed their family's clothing in the wooden troughs in the city square, the rhythm of their rocks keeping time as they beat at the dirt. Soap was a luxury only for the rich.

It was the poorer section that he came to now, where the small one-story huts were made of wood and sun-baked clay. Dogs, chickens, and pigs wandered about freely, and Rafael wrinkled his nose as the strong animal odor wafted to his nostrils. Here and there a small naked child ran about getting underfoot, and Rafael reached out to tousle the hair of several of the oldest ones. Someday when this horror of the Inquisition was over, he wanted to have many children of his own.

"I wish I could stay and watch you at your play," he said to a boy pretending to be El Cid. "I, too, used to delight in conquering the Moors, but I must hurry." He was on his way to the tavern and a meeting that could well change his life. The man's name echoed in his mind. Fernando de Torga.

Half Italian and half Spanish, de Torga was reported by

those who disfavored Torquemada's policies to have been responsible for finding ships for hundreds of *Conversos* and taking them out of Spain. A mapmaker and navigator himself, he could help Rafael make contact with those who would be useful in this matter of the "Marranos."

The tolling sound of the church bells told Rafael that he was late, and he cursed under his breath. Time. There never seemed to be enough time. But he was getting closer to the area of town he sought. He could smell the savory aroma from the kitchens, could hear the strumming of the minstrels' lutes as they roamed about serenading the beautiful town ladies, as well as note the chatter of gossip.

At last the whitewashed walls of the tavern loomed before him. It looked like an oasis, surrounded as it was by tall trees offering refuge from the scorching sun. Resting for a moment beneath the largest one, he was suddenly accosted by a man who stepped out from a narrow alley.

"Pssst. You." Motioning Rafael to come closer, the man looked warily behind him as if fearful that he would be seen. Cautiously Rafael approached, preparing to defend himself lest this one, too, prove to be an enemy. Thieves were as plentiful as flies in Toledo.

"Who are you?" Rafael demanded, studying the man. Strong and bull-necked, he looked to be the son of a peasant. His brown eyes were deep-set and bored into Rafael's own as if he, too, were seeking to make certain that he was not about to be betrayed.

"I might ask the same, *amigo.*"

"I am looking for one called de Torga. Have you heard of him?" Rafael's voice was barely more than a whisper, and he kept his eyes on the man, who moved closer.

"Why do you seek him?" The brown eyes narrowed.

"I have need of information. I want to help and he holds the key." This time the man's face broke into a smile.

"Then I will tell you that I am the man you seek."

"You are de Torga?"

"Do I surprise you? I *am* from Castile, and you?" When meeting a stranger, the most important thing to learn was the region that one was from. It was at times even more important than status.

"I also am from Castile. Shall we go inside?"

"No! Everywhere there are eyes and ears, spying for Torquemada. One cannot be too careful. We will discuss our business out here in the open, Señor, if that is agreeable to you." He pointed to a rock as if it were the softest of chairs. "Please, be seated." The spot afforded a view of all who came upon the tavern and also a quick retreat, if one became necessary, down the narrow winding alleyways of the town.

Rafael immediately came to the point. "I have heard about your brave efforts on behalf of the *Conversos* and I seek your aid in my own efforts. I have land on which I could shelter fugitives and money to see that they are eventually taken to Rome or Constantinople."

"And just why do you offer these services? A young nobleman like you must have many ways to spend his money."

Rafael shot him a murderous glance. "Like women and wine?" he asked derisively. "I am not that kind. Many educated men in this country are against the methods of the Inquisition. I have already talked with Don Francisco. It was he who sent me to you."

De Torga laughed. "Calm yourself, *amigo*. I, too, have talked with Don Francisco. That is why I was expecting you. One cannot be too careful. We have great need of men like yourself, men who are brave and dedicated to the cause of justice."

"Time is of the utmost importance. I fear that soon Torquemada's fanaticism will spread from the *Conversos* to the Jews themselves. Perhaps then it will be impossible to save them."

"Torquemada is incensed that some heretics are fleeing the country. He has imposed a fine on any shipmaster who conveys *Conversos*. Any person of Jewish descent is strictly forbidden to leave Spain."

"Then I am too late."

De Torga shook his head. "No. It is never too late. It only means that we will have to exercise the greatest caution. Despite the fine, there are still those who will help us." He looked at Rafael slowly and thoroughly, then seemed to make a decision. "I know that you came here to seek my help, but it is I who need *you*."

"You need me? Why?"

"Because together I think we can save more lives than by working separately. I can find fishing boats to take the fugitives to the ship, I can commission the ship, I can gather together the provisions that are necessary and chart a course for the ship to sail. What I cannot do is gather the necessary information, information that only a nobleman would be privy to."

"Information? What information?"

De Torga's voice was little more than a whisper. "We need to know which families are in danger, where Torquemada is going to strike next, so that we can whisk those very people right out from under his nose. We need someone who can get close to Torquemada himself. We need you."

"How can I get close? I do not even know him."

"There is a priest, Juan Dorado. He is the stepson of one of the most influential men in the province of León. You must seek him out and become his friend. Not only is the priest the favorite of Torquemada, but his father is an adviser to the Queen herself."

"And in the meantime, while I am trying to cultivate this friendship, what can I be doing to help? I will not be content until I have done something."

"You spoke of your lands. Don Francisco tells me they are to the north, bordering León. It is there that we will shelter our *Conversos* until a ship is available. Does that meet with your approval?"

Rafael nodded. "Yes. I will be content with that. But tell me. Just where is this Juan Dorado?"

"He is here in Toledo with Torquemada. As to gaining his friendship and confidence, I will leave that up to you." He was about to say more, but the sight of three Spanish soldiers approaching stopped him. "I can say no more. If you have further need of me, I will be nearby. Do not seek me out. I will keep my eyes and ears open and come to you." With that he was gone, leaving Rafael to face the soldiers alone.

"You there," said one. "What are you doing loitering about?"

"He is no peasant by the look of him," said another, eyeing Rafael's black doublet and hose and the jeweled ring upon his finger.

Rafael thought quickly. Although it was no crime to be sitting on a rock in front of a tavern in the center of town, he did not want to call attention to himself in any way. Not now. "I am waiting for a lovely señorita," he lied, winking amiably at the soldier.

"Ah, a señorita," said the first soldier.

"But she is late. So like a woman, no?" said the second.

"Is she beautiful?" asked the third.

Rafael thought of Alicia. "Yes, she is very beautiful. Spirited. Her eyes are as green as the leaves of the trees, her skin soft as velvet."

"And her hair?" asked the first soldier.

"Dark brown, with a touch of red when she is in the sun."

"Perhaps we will stay and see this woman," said the third soldier, returning Rafael's wink with one of his own.

"No. Leave the lovers alone," scolded the second. "My throat is dry. Come. I did not come to the tavern to stand outside. I don't care how beautiful a woman is when I am thirsty." He walked away, followed by the others, and Rafael was left alone.

18

The sun was a stinging hot ball of fire burning Alicia's skin as she sat on the wide board at the front of the wagon, holding the reins in her hands. The mud-covered earth had dried into a dull cracked surface, and she shaded her eyes in an effort to see Rudolpho, who had ridden on ahead in an effort to find the safest pathway. Fear ruled the caravan now, fear of another attack or capture by those of the Inquisition.

The lump on Alicia's head had healed, and she was able to drive her own wagon again. It calmed her to be independent, for she relished the thought of being strong. Hearing the bark of the children's dog, she glanced back to see to their safety. Mala's face peeked through the opening in the canvas, followed by the mischievous black snout of Moor, who was yipping at the rocks that bounced up from the road as the wagon rolled along.

"Be careful, Mala. Don't fall out," Alicia cautioned, turning again to the road before her, but not soon enough. The wagon lurched as it rolled over a large stone, hurling Alicia about and nearly causing her to lose her grip on the reins.

"Are you all right?" she heard Todero's voice yell from his wagon right behind hers. Though his wound still pained him, he had insisted upon guiding the horses himself, a difficult feat for a man with one arm in a sling.

"I'm fine," Alicia called back. "But I must remember to

keep my eyes on the road." She thanked *o Del* every day that
Todero had survived. In spite of his own wounds, he had
looked after her. Had there ever been a better friend?
Todero, Zuba, and Rudolpho seemed to be the only ones
whom Alicia could call her allies. The others shunned her.
No doubt Stivo's accusations were still on their mind. The
Rom strongly believed that an unchaste woman knowingly
tolerated in their midst brought bad luck, so it had not been
difficult for Stivo to plant more seeds of distrust. Still, they
could not cast out the leader's daughter even though her
transgression could not be rectified in marrying the man
who had defiled her. All they could do was glower.

Let them frown, Alicia thought, though she alone knew
how much her foolishness had cost her.

The countryside was beautiful in a rugged way. They
were out of the forest now, coming to the bare plateau. Hiding would be difficult now, so extra caution would have to
be taken.

Such beauty in the world, she thought as she looked at
the jagged stone of the distant mountains and at the rich
green of the low foliage. And yet there was such ugliness
too, mankind's evil and hatred. How could people do to
others what they did? The question brought sorrow to her
heart. Once again Rafael came to mind. No matter how she
tried to forget him, she could not. She could only remember
that she had saved his life and by so doing had entwined
their destinies.

As the wheels churned along, Alicia choked on the dust.
How good it would be to stop, to fill her stomach, wash the
dirt of the road from her body, and sleep once again on the
soft bed in her wagon.

The sound of giggles behind her startled her out of her
reverie and, looking once more behind her, she was horrified
to see Palo hanging from one of the wooden beams beneath
the wagon, swinging along from beam to beam as if playing
some sort of game.

"Palo! What are you doing?" she shrieked.

"Playing," he called back cheerfully. "I want to see how long I can stay under here without falling."

She couldn't tell him to let go or he might be trampled by the horses of Todero's wagons, nor did she want to frighten him. But he was clearly in danger. Alicia thought quickly.

"That's fine, Palo, fine. You are a strong boy. Strong enough to help me drive the wagon. I need your help. Give me your hand and I'll help you onto the front board."

"No!" He laughed fiendishly, as if to mock her, innocently unaware of his peril.

"Please, Palo." Alicia tried to keep her fear out of her voice. The caravan was traveling at a faster pace. With fewer wagons and people, they were less encumbered. She had to give the signal to halt the wagons or take the risk that she could pull the boy to safety.

With one last effort, fighting against her terror for the child, she reached out her hand to him. "I cannot hold these reins much longer, Palo. I need you. Please. Won't you help me?" This time he reached for her outstretched hand, grasping it firmly. With a strength born of desperation, Alicia pulled the boy up on the wagon, but in saving the boy, lost her firm hold on the reins. The wagon swerved, narrowly missing a large boulder as Alicia fought for control. Behind her she could hear angry shouts and the screeching sound of wagon wheels as they ground to a halt.

"What are you doing, Alicia?"

"Fool woman!"

Pulling with all her might, shouting at the top of her lungs, Alicia finally managed to bring her wagon to a stop, but not before she heard the crack of wood.

"The axle!" She did not have to look beneath the wagon to know the damage that had been done. It was not an unusual problem, but one that would slow the caravan down at a time when every moment counted.

"I helped you," Palo said, smiling, unaware of the trouble his mischief had created. "I stopped the horses."

"Yes, you helped me," Alicia said grimly. "I should have stopped the wagon."

Todero ran from one direction, Stivo from another. "What are you doing, you fool?" Stivo shouted. "Women. They have always been the scourge of man."

Todero's words were kinder, for his main concern was Alicia. "What happened, Alicia? Did you lose control of the horses?"

"She should let a man drive the wagon. A woman is too soft to handle a man's job!" Stivo sneered.

"Palo . . ." Alicia breathed. "He was playing underneath the wagon. I couldn't take the chance of his being hurt."

"Palo! Bah! Children. They are worse than women!" Stivo cursed, making a threatening gesture as if to hit the boy. Alicia quickly stepped in front of the child. She was angry with the boy too, but violence would not solve anything.

"Leave him alone! If there is anyone to blame, it is me. The boy is my responsibility."

"He should be punished!" There was malice in Stivo's eyes.

"If it is to be done, I shall do it," Alicia answered, meeting his eyes without a sign of backing down. In anger Stivo stalked away.

"Someday his temper will be the death of us all!" Todero swore beneath his breath. His face was etched with pain, and Alicia could see that his own struggle to control his wagon had cost him dearly. Fresh blood was seeping through the white linen of his bandage.

"Todero, you are hurt!"

"It is nothing. I am only glad that you are unharmed."

"The axle on the wagon is broken."

Todero smiled. "Better the axle than your neck. You are a brave one, Alicia. If not for your quick thinking perhaps something far worse might have happened."

Alicia looked up as she heard the sound of horses' hooves and saw the approaching figure of Rudolpho. "What is it? What has happened?"

"A broken axle. We will have to make camp here for the night," Todero answered. "With the light of morn we will fix it."

"We might just as well. At least there is some foliage here to shelter us, and a small lake that will furnish us fresh water." His eyes took in the wagon, Alicia's expression, and Palo's wide eyes, and he grunted with a knowing nod. "The boy, eh?"

Alicia nodded. "He was unaware of the danger he was in. Perhaps you had best take him aside and explain the necessity for obedience."

"Obedience. Yes, Palo. It is one of the most important Gypsy codes. You must listen to Alicia because she is older and wiser. That, too, is the Gypsy way. Now you have caused a delay by your stubborn foolishness. You shame the name Gypsy." Rudolpho shook his finger at the boy.

If Stivo had taken a hand to the child, it could not have made him cry harder, for he worshipped Rudolpho, as did all the children.

Alicia gathered the child to her breast. "It will be all right, Palo. It will be all right. Don't cry. Come, you can help me gather wood for the fire." Glancing back at the wagon, once again Alicia trembled at the thought of Palo's small body beneath the wheels.

Later that night around the fires one would hardly have known that this was a forced encampment. The men talked, the women laughed. All of them were glad to be away from the villagers' hatred, yet still Alicia saw the eyes of the others watching her, damning her, as if to say that yet again she had brought danger upon them. There was another look in their eyes as well. One that Alicia did not clearly understand. Was it admiration? Alicia wanted to believe that it was.

Stivo's eyes watched her too. He stared at her hungrily, causing a shiver to creep down her back. There was a dark shadow to his smile that made Alicia look quickly away. Would he never let her forget what had passed between the gorgio and herself? In frustration and unhappiness, she withdrew from the others to find a spot outside the fires. There she ate and drank in solitude until Zuba sought her out.

"What are you doing out here all alone?" the girl asked her softly.

"They blame me for what happened. I can see it in their eyes." Alicia sighed. "I could not have brought any worse luck to them if I were gorgio."

Zuba sat beside her on the ground. "They are foolish. You are blameless. I know it, Todero knows it, and so do the others deep in their hearts. Give them time. They will forget and gossip about some other matter tomorrow."

"I hope you are right, Zuba. How I hope you are right. Being Gypsy is so important to me. It is my very life. I cannot stand the thought of my own people being angry with me. To think that they have banished some from their midst. The idea makes me shudder!"

Zuba sought to lighten the mood. "I have shown Todero a token of my love."

"You have filled a cake with coins and thrown it over a bush to him, no?" Alicia's eyes were filled with tenderness for this young couple. "Next will be the scarves."

Zuba laughed, bringing forth a red handkerchief from the sleeve of her dress. "I have already taken Todero's kerchief. We are betrothed!"

"Betrothed!" Alicia forgot about her own unhappiness and flung her arms about her friend. "I am so happy for you. I knew that it would be so. My heart nearly died for you when I thought Todero killed. But all is well. Oh, Zuba, Zuba."

They laughed and cried together as Zuba hastily confided

how Todero had spoken of his love for her while she nursed him back to health.

"When is the wedding?"

"When we join my father and brothers, who went in the other caravan. I insisted on staying with Todero. But when we are all together again, our fathers will make up the marriage contract." She beamed in pride. "Todero thinks I will bring a high bridal price, and his father is rich enough to pay it. But I would come to Todero though he were a pauper with not a horse to his name. I love him, Alicia."

"I know that you do."

The soft strains of a song trilled through the night air, like the song of a night bird, and the two women stopped their talk to listen. It was Todero, strumming his guitar and singing love songs to his Zuba. In melody and words he begged her to come to him, to walk with him in the moonlight.

"I hate to leave you here all alone," Zuba said softly, tugging at Alicia's hand. "Come. Join us."

Alicia shook her head. "No. It is a night for lovers. I would only be in the way. Go to your Todero. I will join the others in a moment." She waved her hand frantically as if shooing a chicken. "Away with you, now. Your betrothed awaits."

Zuba floated off with all the grace of a woman in love, walking on air, her head filled with dreams, and Alicia was once more left alone.

It was a hot, breezeless night. Palo and Mala were safely asleep. The others were immersed in their tales and legends. Even now Jana was telling the story of how the moon had once been dragged down to earth by the witchery of the Romany tongue. Alicia would not be missed. Walking toward the lake, she relished the thought of the cool water.

The lake was an oasis amid the mud and sand, surrounded by tall grass and low bushes that fed upon its moisture. Breathing deeply, Alicia bent down to splash some water on her face. It soothed her parched skin and she sighed in pure rapture.

At a sound behind her Alicia turned her head, trying to see who was coming. Suddenly hands gripped her, holding her so tightly that she cried out in pain. She heard the sound of laughter and knew at once who her attacker was.

19

"Stivo!"

He whirled her around to face him. "I knew there would be a time when I would find you alone without your watchdog, Rudolpho, or those chattering children. And Zuba and Todero are occupied elsewhere."

Alicia fought her terror. "Let me go, Stivo!"

"No!" His hand groped for her breast, leaving no doubt as to his intentions. "Just as I like them, ripe and firm."

Alicia screamed in outrage. "Let me go, or I swear to you, Stivo, I will—will—" She reached in her belt for her knife, but he had guessed her intent, and pulling it free, threw it several feet away. "So the little bee is without her sting?"

"You are an animal!" she hissed. "Your touch repels me."

He grinned insolently. "An animal I may be; but animal or not, I'll make you moan with pleasure." He leered as his lips descended upon hers. "Now I shall taste of the honey the gorgio sampled." Alicia felt his strong arms imprison her; felt the cool air on her skin as he tore away her blouse and forced her down upon the ground. She kicked wildly, shouting oaths at him. When his mouth claimed hers, she bit down with her teeth, tasting the blood of his lips. Reaching up, she raked her nails across his cheek, tearing the flesh of his treasured face, his prideful vanity.

"You bitch. You will scar me!" he growled, pinioning her

arms above her head. If he had been rough before, he was brutal now.

Alicia knew that she could not let this happen. She had to escape. Never would she allow him to take her body. It belonged to her. All the while she remembered Rafael. *He* had not forced her. *He* had been gentle. Closing her eyes, she screamed her outrage only to find, when her eyes opened again, that she was suddenly free. A bellowing Rudolpho stood above her, holding Stivo by the hair, pulling his head backward. He had heard her cries and come to her rescue.

"You are lower than a snake," he thundered, striking out at Stivo. "If I ever see you anywhere near my daughter again, I will kill you. This I swear."

Glaring at him, Stivo rose slowly to his feet. "I will leave her for now, but there will come a day, old man. There will come a day." His voice was filled with menace, and Alicia knew that if ever Rudolpho was not there to protect her, Stivo would keep his word. With the strut of a young fighting cock, he walked away.

Rudolpho took her in his arms, stroking her long dark hair. *"Chavi. Chavi.* I feared that such a thing might happen. Stivo! He is a bad one. Long have I known it. His lust would crush you, take away your spirit."

Alicia reached out to him just as Rudolpho's arms went limp. The excitement had been too much for him. Grasping his chest, he gasped for air.

"Papa! Papa! What is it?" Alicia cried, kneeling down beside him as he slumped to the ground. His face had taken on a deathly pallor in the moonlight.

"My heart," he rasped, closing his eyes. Curling up like a child in its mother's womb, he fought against the pain that tore through him as Alicia hovered over him.

"What can I do to help you, Papa? What?" she whispered, running her gentle hands over the muscles of his back in an effort to relax him.

"It will pass. It always does," he croaked. "I am strong as

an ox. It will pass. It will pass." He thought about Alicia and knew at that moment that he must find the gorgio again. Only when his Alicia was safely wed to one of her own kind could he die in peace. And he *was* dying. Eventually this thing of the heart would kill him, this he knew.

20

Alicia lay in her bed, wide-eyed, unable to sleep. Across from her on the bed lay Mala, hugging Moor in her arms, and next to her, looking all innocence, was Palo. Watching the young boy now, one would shake one's head in disbelief if told that the child's mischief had so disrupted the caravan, Alicia thought, caressing the children with her eyes. The soft sighs of the sleeping children were soothing, and she thought how someday she would like to have two small ones such as these, but until then she would be content with caring for the boy and his sister.

Closing her eyes, Alicia tried once more to get to sleep, but too much had happened on this day to allow her that sweet slumber. She had sensed before that Rudolpho was ill, now she knew it for certain, and this deeply troubled her. Rudolpho, who had always comforted her, now needed her, though he insisted that what had happened was nothing. Alicia could not believe him, knowing as she did that he would have said that just to spare her any worry.

"Something I ate," he had said at last when he had conquered the pain sufficiently to rise to his feet. "We will speak no more about it, Alicia." She had helped him to his sleeping place beneath the wagon, spreading the quilts with care and then giving him a hot drink of borage tea from the store of medicinal herbs in her wagon. No matter how Rudolpho had argued, she had stayed firm and insisted he

drink the tea to the very last drop, knowing the herb helped
strengthen the heart.

"What would I do without you, Papa?" she thought, feeling tears sting her eyes. She could not remember a moment
when he had not been by her side, and yet her dreams were
often haunted by the memory of other faces, a man's, and a
woman's as well, frowning, always frowning. Quickly Alicia
banished them from her mind, as if conjuring them up were
in some way disloyal to Rudolpho.

"He will get well. He must get well!" she whispered. She
would give him the tea every night; would plead with him
again to let another man lead the caravan for a while. He
needed rest. She would even relinquish her wagon so that he
could sleep inside on her soft bed. Then, when he was
strong again, he could ride at the front of the caravan astride
his big black horse.

Hearing Palo's frightened whimper, Alicia jumped up
from the bed. Was he also ill? The boy thrashed about in his
sleep, and Alicia reached out a hand to comfort him, whispering to him until at last he quieted once again. It was a
nightmare. He seemed to be afraid of someone striking out
at him, and Alicia cursed Stivo under her breath. Not only
had he sought to harm her, but he had frightened the boy as
well. Stivo had a temper. It was as if *o Beng* had control of
him sometimes. Alicia shook her head. So not only was it
gorgios they had to fear, but a Gypsy in their midst as well.
She remembered the way Stivo had looked at Rudolpho,
and shuddered. Stivo was jealous. Did he think that just
because he was son to the *phuri dai* he would be next in line?

O Del, *help us if that one is ever our leader,* she thought.

Seeing that Palo was sleeping peacefully, she started to
make her way to her own side of the bed when a noise
outside the wagon startled her. Remembering Stivo's lustful
eyes, she reached for her knife. He would not find her un-
guarded tonight. Anger coiled in her stomach as she gripped
the handle. Never would she let Stivo touch her like that

again. Inching her way to the canvas opening, she waited, listening.

"I bid you, Manolo, to find him. I would go myself but I cannot leave the caravan, as you well know. While you are gone I promise to look after your wife and little ones as if they were my own." It was Rudolpho's voice.

"It must be important to you, or you would not ask this of me. I do not understand your reasoning, but I will do as you ask, Rudolpho. How can I ever forget the time you saved my life?"

"I will be most grateful to you. I do what must be done. Only then can I die in peace."

"Do not talk of dying. You will be with us a long while yet."

"We all must go when our time comes." There was a long silence, and Alicia strained her ears to hear. Who was Rudolpho searching for?

"I will take Gyuri with me. We will have him in front of your eyes before the sun sets again." The voices lowered to a whisper, but she heard Rudolpho's warning.

"Take care. Remember the treachery of those who fell upon us. I would not forgive myself if I sent you to your death."

"We will move as quietly as the night and just as invisibly. We will steal him from his bed if need be."

Alicia peeked out and could see the shadowed figure of the man she knew to be Manolo take leave of her father, then watched as Rudolpho once again took his place beneath the wagon. She wanted to go to him, but this was men's business. Rudolpho was wise. He would never knowingly do anything that would bring harm to his people.

I will let him sleep and think no more about this matter, she thought. There was much to be done on the morrow. A strong tree would have to be found so that another axle could be fashioned; there was the washing to be done while they were near a body of water, bedding to be aired, food to be prepared. Still her curiosity was piqued, and it was all she could do not to run to Rudolpho as she had when just a child.

Curling up in her blanket, Alicia closed her eyes. It was a long time before sleep claimed her, and when it did she dreamed of the gorgio, that she held him in her arms, that he kissed her, caressed her, whispered words of love. Together they rolled about the soft earth, locked in an embrace, and once again Alicia was engulfed by the aching swirl of pleasure. But the pleasure turned to shame and heartbreak when she opened her eyes. It had all seemed so real. She had yielded again to him in her dreams, had wanted him to make love to her, and had dreamed that he had.

"Weakness. Such a weakness. What can I do?" she sobbed. "Will I never be free of you, gorgio? Will I never be free?" Covering her face with her hands, she gave vent to her tears.

Nor was Alicia the only one troubled. Rudolpho, too, was unable to sleep. Lying awake beneath the wagon, he remembered the day the dark-cloaked woman had brought Alicia to him. Cold gray eyes had met Rudolpho's flashing brown ones as the woman had gathered up her courage to say what was on her mind.

"I have come to bring you this child!" she had said, pushing Alicia forward. "I have heard that you often steal children from the town and have made it easy for you."

Rudolpho remembered vividly how he had clenched his jaw in anger and replied, "We do not steal anything, especially young ones!" His dislike of the woman still boiled in his blood. "Gypsies are honorable people." He should have sent the woman away right then, but something about the child had tugged at his heart. As he bent down to get a closer look at the dark-haired, green-eyed little girl who was showing no fear, Rudolpho's anger had evaporated like the early-morning mist. "What is your name, little one?" he had asked.

"Alicia." Reaching out, she had touched one of the glittering bangles he wore in his ear and she had giggled, her expression clearly showing Rudolpho that she liked him.

"The girl has no family," the woman had said. "If you do not buy her, I will be forced to turn her out upon the streets to starve. She can no longer depend upon my charity to feed and clothe her."

Alicia had looked up at him with such a trusting look in her eyes that Rudolpho had known he would keep her. She would be his child, his daughter, the one he might have had with his wife if that sweet woman had not died so young.

"Well, do you want her or not?" the gray-eyed woman had snapped, giving the child a push so that she stumbled and fell. Rudolpho had reached out to pull Alicia to her feet, gently patting her soft brown curls. She was a beauty even then, with delicate features and large eyes that seemed to hold a great deal of wisdom for her tender age.

"I will take her. From this day forward Alicia will be mine." Taking the child by the hand, he had turned his back on the woman only to hear her shrieks of outrage.

"Wait! I want money for her. Coins."

"Money?" Striding toward the woman, he had picked her up as if she were no more than a doll, dangling her up in the air. "No money! The child is now mine."

He had put the sputtering, pinch-featured bundle back down upon her feet and stood answering her glare with one that was even more fierce. Though he knew the woman was afraid of him, she tried to mask her fear.

"All right! All right!" she answered at last, turning her back on him and mumbling beneath her breath. Then she had stalked away, leaving Rudolpho with his new daughter.

"Come, little one. You are far better off without such a one as that. I will take care of you." Clinging to his hand, toddling along beside him on short chubby legs, Alicia had gone with him to the campsite.

Thick clouds had swirled around the moon like smoke,

the pungent scent of the campfires filling the air, as Rudolpho walked slowly to the ring of Gypsy wagons. Inside one of those wagons he and the child had come before a woman whose face was leathery and wrinkled, showing her many years—Rudolpho's grandmother. The thick mat of her gray hair was tucked up in a scarf with strands peeking out; her shawl was decorated with designs in green, red, and black, a swirling print; and her gnarled fingers were thick with jewels.

"Who is this child, this green-eyed little one? She is not one of our kind, she is gorgio. Why have you brought her to me?" asked the *phuri dai*. She was the spiritual leader and hers was a position of great importance, which she would not let Rudolpho forget now.

"A woman brought her to us. The child has no parents, nowhere else to go." Knowing of her wisdom, Rudolpho had been eager for her advice.

"If she stays with us, she will never be able to marry into the tribe; you know the law. It will be a lonely life for this child when she becomes a woman." Her squinting eyes had scrutinized the child, yet Alicia had not shown any fear. It amazed Rudolpho that even though others trembled before the wise woman, the child showed no such emotion.

"I know the law, but she will be better here than living with a woman such as the one who brought her to me. She hates this child and would harm her if we did not take her in. I do not have to be *phuri dai* to know this to be true." Bending down upon one knee, showing his grandmother the respect due to her, Rudolpho had pleaded to keep the child. "I will raise her as my own. We can try to find a husband for the girl among her own kind when she is grown."

The old woman had finally nodded her head in assent. A single candle lit the wagon, and as a night breeze caused it to flicker, it was as if *o Del* himself had given a sign.

"And so, you will live with the Gypsies now, Alicia. Now our lives and fates will be intertwined." And so it had been for these many years. How he loved Alicia. How he hated the thought of leaving her, and yet he must; it was the one thing over which he had no control. Stivo's lust and resentment raged within his heart. She would not be safe from that one when he was gone. "I vow that as long as I live there will be no one to harm you," he had promised. Now he had to find another to protect her. It was Alicia's destiny to belong to the gorgio she had saved from the river.

"It is her destiny. Her destiny." Closing his eyes, Rudolpho at last welcomed sleep, knowing in his heart that he had made the right decision.

21

Rafael de Villasandro walked across the stone courtyard that led to the Church of San Miguel, wondering what he was going to say to the priest Juan Dorado to ingratiate himself. What would they have in common? In truth there were times when Rafael questioned the church in his heart. So many had died for refusing to accept the blessed Christ—Moors, Moslems, Jews, *Conversos,* and how many others? How could a loving God condone such bloodshed?

Again the thought of his mother's death evoked his bitterness. She had not even been a *Converso.* Her only crime was to have loved and comforted her Jewish parents. And what of Alicia? What had been her fate? Had hatred and bigotry taken her life too?

Oh, Alicia, he thought, *I must go on believing that you still live or I will surely go mad.* He had to concentrate on doing all he could to help those who were as innocent as his mother . . . and Alicia. He must go to visit Juan Dorado and hope that the priest could not look into his heart or read his mind.

Rafael passed through the large stone archway and entered the church, taking the steps two at a time. It was crowded, and he took his place at the back of the sanctuary, keeping his distance from the other worshippers.

The light of the candles seemed to be dancing, the flames casting their glow upon the face of the priest, who raised his arms toward the heavens, uttering the words always spoken at the beginning of a mass.

"Dominus vobiscum."

"Et cum spiritu," Rafael answered with the others. "The Lord be with you and with you the spirit." Rafael said his own quiet prayer, that God would truly be with him this day and help him do what must be done.

Immersed in his own thoughts, Rafael barely heard the words of the mass, but instead watched in fascination at the flowing motions of the priest's hands, like a dancer's. Rafael studied the face, trying to judge the man. It was a plain face, pinched of feature. The cheeks were pale, the lips thin and colorless, yet it was the eyes that showed the man to be the fanatic he was said to be. Here were the cold, gleaming eyes of a zealot, an officer of the Inquisition. Looking out at the multitude, scanning the crowd, it was as if, even now, he were straining to see into men's souls, to strip away their masks and read their secrets. Rafael felt a quiver of revulsion, a sudden urge to abandon this quest and seek to free the *Conversos* in his own way, but he had given his word. Once again he wondered what he could say to gain Juan Dorado's trust.

The candles shed light on the altar of the Holy Virgin to the left of the high altar; the priest's eyes seemed drawn to the statue. Juan Dorado gazed upon her with worshipful eyes, as if that exquisite, serene face were alive, and in that moment Rafael had his answer. The man's reverence, his love of beauty and art, would be the key.

Several years ago Rafael's father had gone to Italy and acquired three paintings by an artist named Leonardo da Vinci. He had kept one; the other two he had given to his sons. Rafael's gift had been a portrait of the Virgin Mary with the Holy Child in the hollow of her arm. He had marveled at her look of love, at her beauty, at the wisdom portrayed on the Christ Child's face. He treasured that painting, but now he would give it up in the hope that it could work a miracle.

"A miracle," he sighed. The mass had ended, and as the people filed past him on their way out of the church, looking at him out of the corners of their eyes as if he were demented, he regretted his muttering. Then they were gone, and at long last he was alone with Torquemada's priest, this one of the Dominican order *fratres predicatores*, the terrible tribunal. Very slowly Rafael walked toward the kneeling figure in black, this grave judge of the Holy Inquisition. It was as if Juan Dorado were in a trance; he rocked to and fro, oblivious to anyone else's presence.

"Cursed Jews. Blasphemous heretics. All those who have known the glory of baptism only to revert to Judaism again. I will not rest until I have watched every one burn. I will stomp out this pestilence before it can spread to endanger other souls. Death to heretics is your will, O God. I am but Thy minister."

Rafael clenched his fists, longing to strike out at this raving monster, to rid the world of such hatred; but he kept himself in check, managing a half smile as the priest crossed himself and turned his eyes in Rafael's direction.

"Who are you?" The voice showed that he was annoyed to find himself observed.

"My name is Rafael Cordoba de Villasandro, Holy Father," Rafael answered. "I am a nobleman of Castile. My brother owns the olive groves outside Toledo."

"A nobleman." His eyes swept over Rafael, taking in his apparel, the black hose, red doublet, the purse that hung from his waist. His eyes softened and he returned Rafael's smile. "From Castile?" He rose from his knees. "And what brings you to my humble church?"

"I have heard of the simple beauty of this church and of its devoted priest. I have come to see for myself and I have not been disappointed."

"It is a humble dwelling only. I have need of much wealth

to adorn it so that it can be as magnificent as it was meant to be." Again his eyes swept over Rafael as if to judge the contents of his purse. To maintain the church, tithes, a portion of every man's wealth, were taken. Already nobles and merchants gave generously in return for prayers, but the war had been costly; and though no one dared challenge the church's demands, it was still difficult for Dorado to amass as much as he would have liked.

"You have need of wealth?"

The priest's obsequious smile faltered. "We in Castile have been so busy fighting the Moors that we have not given proper attention to God and His needs. But all that will change, I will see to that."

"And I will help you." Rafael could see from the narrowing of the priest's eyes that he had spoken the right words. He had judged the man accurately after all.

"You will help me? And just how will you do that?"

Rafael reached out to touch the statue of Mary. "She is beautiful, is she not?"

"Yes, I would give my life for her."

"I have a painting that you must see. Da Vinci's 'Virgin and Child.' I will give it to you to hang upon the walls of your church."

"A painting of the Virgin and Holy Christ Child? Where did you get it?"

"Florence. Never have I seen anything quite so magnificent. Oh, that I could work such wonder." He nodded his head. "But it is only for me to appreciate art, not to work its magic." Rafael bowed his head slightly in a gesture of humility.

"And you would give this to me?"

"As a gesture of friendship. There is something about you that strikes a chord in my soul. We are alike, you and I. We both share a passion. I sensed it as I watched you. Your devotion and love of all that is beautiful impressed me, Holy Father."

"You did see into my soul." He touched Rafael's arm. "I, too, am a lover of art. Would you believe that before I took the vows I thought to be an artist? But God had other plans for me." Pushing Rafael ahead of him, he guided them out of the church.

They walked along to the priest's apartments at the back of the church as Juan Dorado talked on and on about himself. He was the youngest stepson of Philip Navarro of León. For five years he had been a priest, but the look in his eyes spoke of his fervent desire to rise much higher in power. Bishop. Archbishop. His ambition had made him seek out the likes of Torquemada.

"And what of you?" he asked Rafael. Something in his tone of voice warned of danger. This was the kind of man who would always be alert to the least hint of heresy. Rafael would always have to beware lest by a slip of tongue, a look, an expression, he gave himself away.

"I, too, am a second son. I thought to fight the Moors but have settled my sights upon other enemies of Spain." Rafael spoke in double meaning, baiting the other man into talk of important matters.

"Conversos!" Juan Dorado hissed. "Jews. So we are two of a kind, you and I."

Rafael was not used to such deception, such chicanery. It made him ill. How could he continue this mockery when with every fiber of his being he wanted to shout out the truth, to strike out at this foul rodent and put an end to all the evil he had done, all that he was about to do? Instead he calmly answered, "Yes, we are two of a kind."

When they reached the priest's apartments Rafael took his leave with a promise to bring the painting to the church the next day. He was not aware of the eyes that watched him nor of the two men who followed him as he hurried away.

22

The eyes of the Virgin Mary looked down upon Rafael. She smiled demurely from the painting on the wall as if giving him her blessing. Reaching up, he lifted the heavy gilt frame from its hooks and laid it gently down in front of him to look once again upon her lovely face.

"Leonardo da Vinci is a genius," he said aloud. The painting looked so lifelike that he hated to part with it, but he had given his word.

It was so quiet in the chapel of his brother's home. Peaceful. It was difficult to believe that only miles from where he now stood there were those who faced the terror and torture of Torquemada's zealots, priests of the Dominican Order like Juan Dorado, the Archbishop of Toledo, and Cardinal Jiménez. All were under the direction of the lawyers of the Supreme Council of Castile, the Council of the Inquisition, those graduated doctors of canon law so proud of their pure blood.

"Rafael?" María stood behind him, no doubt noticing his contemplative gaze. "Is there something wrong?"

He turned around to face her, soothed by her concern. "No, I was just thinking."

Seeing the painting on the floor, she rushed forward, thinking that it had fallen from its lofty perch; but Rafael stepped in front of her to block her way. "Rafael, what is it?"

"I took it down. I am going to give the painting away."

"No!"

"Yes. I would try to tell you why, but you might not understand. All I ask is that you believe that it is a thing that I must do."

Her soft brown eyes swept over him. "If you say that it is imperative that you do this, then I know you speak the truth. I will say no more about it."

"But I will!" Carlos de Villasandro stood in the doorway, his hands folded across his chest. "That painting was given to you by our father. It is to be handed down from generation to generation. Because you have no home of your own you have placed it within my keeping, and it is here it will stay. It is not your right to dispose of it!"

"I do not intend to 'dispose of it,' as you put it. What I do I do for others." Quickly he told his brother of his meeting with Juan Dorado, expecting understanding but receiving none. On the subject of helping the *Conversos*, Carlos stood firm.

"You are a fool. You will not only impoverish us but bring the family to ruin. Do you know the penalty for aiding these heretic Jews? It will be your death, I say."

Rafael's eyes flashed anger. "*You* say? It is none of your concern, Carlos. If you choose to turn your back on your mother's people, to spend your days getting richer and fatter, then I will not dissuade you. But I have chosen another path!"

"Your mother's people?" María's eyes opened wide. "What does he mean, Carlos?" Too late Rafael realized that his temper had made him careless. He had forgotten María's presence in the room.

Carlos's eyes flashed a warning, but Rafael had gone too far to keep silent now. María must be told. "Our mother was Jewish, María. She was a convert to the Christian faith. She died at the hands of the officers of the Inquisition. It is something you have a right to know."

"Jewish? A *Conversa?*"

Carlos reached out to take his wife's hand. "It is of no importance. I was raised by my father after she died. I am, like you, a good Christian. And Rafael is too, despite his foolish notions. Put it out of your head, little bird."

"But our sons . . ."

"No one need ever know. No one."

Rafael turned his back on his brother in disgust. He did not remember his mother, but he was proud to be her son. It was men such as Carlos, who lived in comfort and chose to ignore the horror around them, that were as much to blame as Torquemada himself. If one chose to ignore evil, it only multiplied until it was an all-consuming hell.

Seeking to cool his temper, Rafael left the house, wandering far from the hacienda to a secluded spot overlooking the olive groves. Squinting at the light of the fading sun, he gazed over the countryside.

I am so tired of Carlos and his fears, he thought. The way he had looked at María, as if he even feared what she might do now that she had found out their secret, disturbed him. He and Carlos were still the same men they had been before. Having a converted Jewish mother did not change them. Didn't Carlos realize that? And yet, Rafael reflected, perhaps Carlos had reason to be cautious. Perhaps he had been over-zealous. He should not have tried to change his brother's mind any more than Carlos should have tried to control *his* fate. They were separate souls. Each had a duty to fulfill his own destiny.

The barking of one of his brother's dogs alerted him to the fact that he was not alone. Turning, he saw two men on horseback riding toward him. His first thought was that somehow, someone had learned of his plans.

"My sword!" he lamented. He was unarmed, but he *would* *fight*! Once again it seemed that it was going to be two against one. This time, however, he would not be attacked from behind.

But as the riders approached, Rafael saw to his amazement that they were Gypsies. The bright green and yellow scarves they wore around their necks attested to that.

Gypsies? What were they doing here? Alicia! Had she sent them? If so, then she *was* still alive. But was she in danger? He forgot about combat as he ran toward the horsemen, recognizing one of them as Rudolpho's right-hand man. So intent was he on thoughts of Alicia that it did not occur to him to be afraid.

Eagerly Rafael raised his right hand in the greeting he had seen the Gypsies use, but neither of the riders replied in kind. Suddenly the larger of the Gypsies lunged forward on his horse, cutting off Rafael's line of retreat while the other Gypsy guided his horse to block Rafael's advance.

"Rudolpho told us not to harm him," the large Gypsy said.

"We will not harm a hair on his head," answered the other with a grin. Throwing the rope that he held in his hand in such a manner that Rafael found himself bound and helpless, the Gypsy laughed.

Angered now, Rafael fought savagely, but it was too late. He was as powerless as a poor bull after a bullfight, and all he could do was to shriek his rage as he was overtaken and pulled to the ground.

"Let me go! I have done you no harm," he grated between clenched teeth. "Turn me loose. I have done nothing."

"No, you have not harmed us, but it is another who beckons you," the large Gypsy answered. Rafael felt himself pulled upward and thrown across the horse's back like a sack of grain.

23

With Palo sitting safely beside her, Alicia held the reins firmly as her wagon rolled along. She would make certain that the boy did not have another chance to do mischief. It had taken the men most of the morning to find a tree strong enough to use for a new axle, to carve it to just the right dimensions, and to attach it to the wheels.

Todero had taken his place behind Alicia, riding about a wagon's length behind, followed by the two-wheeled carts filled with supplies. Riding at the end of the caravan was humiliating, yet the fact that Todero had willingly taken a place behind her soothed Alicia's wounded pride. Perhaps it would be safer for the children, she reasoned, and this thought, too, consoled her and made her forget the smug smile upon Stivo's face.

It was proving to be a rough and tiresome journey. Now they had come once again to a plateau, crisscrossed by deep ravines. Fearful of becoming caught up in the impending war in Granada, Rudolpho's tribe had decided upon a northern route as they now traveled from Toledo toward León, rather than to Granada, as had once been planned. They had kept in touch with the other members of the tribe through a web of secret contacts and would join them in a month's time near León.

The caravan rode all day in the hot sun, stopping only once to rest the horses and to let them drink from the waters of a cool stream. Alicia took advantage of the pause in the journey to splash herself with refreshing stream water, relishing its healing moisture. Her backside ached from sitting on the hard wooden seat; her fingers were stiff and sore from holding the reins. She was hot and tired and filled with the overwhelming longing to unhitch her wagon, mount her horse, and ride with the wind at her back.

Seeing Rudolpho sitting ramrod-straight, she marveled at his strength and discipline. No one would ever have questioned his authority, or have associated him with the man who had writhed in pain only the night before. Now he looked vigorous, though Alicia suspected he was but hiding his agony for the sake of the others. How could she help but admire his courage?

Alicia could not miss Rudolpho's backward glances. He seemed agitated. Was he watching for some of the other wagons that had taken another route to catch up with their caravan? No, that could not be. It had been decided to come together only when they reached León. Who, then, or what was Rudolpho looking for?

Perhaps he feels the same urge that I feel, she thought, *to ride on ahead, to savor the feeling of ultimate freedom.* With a sigh she dried herself off and climbed back up into the wagon to start the horses moving down the road. This time she let the reins hang loose and allowed the horses to drift on their own for a while. The terrain was flat and monotonous, the landscape dull and colorless. Alicia missed the greenery of the forest, but there was no turning back.

The creaking of the wagon and the grinding of the wheels seemed to grow louder and louder. All her life she had heard that sound. Why was she suddenly bothered by the noise?

It is because I am anxious to reach camp again, she thought. Palo was also restless, squirming around in his seat. After a time his dark head nodded and he started to drift off to sleep. Fearful that he might fall off the wagon, Alicia gently tapped him on the shoulder to awaken him. Mala was fast asleep inside the wagon, and Alicia could not resist saying, "You see, Palo, if you had not been so unruly the other day, you, too, could be fast asleep in bed instead of sitting on this hard wood." Laughing, she reached over to tousle the boy's hair. She couldn't really be angry with him, for hadn't it been said that boys were meant to be active and mischievous?

"I'm sorry, Alicia." The child's dark eyes looked up at her in innocence. "I will never be bad again, Alicia. I am a good boy. Someday I will be like Rudolpho, a Gypsy leader!" He looked so exhausted that she took pity on him, knowing that he was too tired to get into any trouble.

"Go on, then, into the wagon, Palo. Join your sister in sleep, eh?" She stopped the wagon just long enough for the boy to crawl through the canvas opening and to see that he was safe before she signaled the horses to start up again. Even the horses were tired and were not as quick in their step. Once or twice they even stopped of their own volition along the side of the road.

Then, at last sensing that everyone had been pushed beyond endurance, Rudolpho made the sign for the wagons to stop, forming them into the usual circle. The Gypsies prepared for night even though darkness had not descended upon the horizon. Climbing down from the wagon, Alicia hurried to join her father.

"Papa, are you feeling better?" she asked, studying every line and plane of his face. He was pale, but somehow the lines of pain around his eyes were no longer visible.

"Much better," he answered, trying to smile. But as he reached out to touch her hair, there was a look of sadness about him that troubled her.

"I will give you more of the tea tonight, eh?"

He nodded. "Yes, more of the tea." His mind seemed elsewhere, and Alicia noticed that he was again scanning the horizon.

"Papa, who are you watching for?" Gently she touched his arm.

Cupping her face in his hand, he looked into her eyes. "You will see, Alicia. You will see. What I do, I do for you."

"For me?" She wanted to question him further, but there was work to be done and she could not shirk her duty. While gathering wood for the fire she resolved to take the matter up with him again after dinner.

As darkness descended, blotting out the world beyond the camp, several fires were started and their dancing flames lit up the night. The flickering, crackling fire illuminated the faces of the exhausted, silent Gypsies as they sat upon the ground, relishing the rabbit stew the women had prepared. From across the fire Stivo watched Alicia, the touch of mocking irony in his eyes telling her that she was not as safe as she supposed. Did he sense Rudolpho's illness? Was he waiting like a vulture to pounce? Alicia returned his look with one of scorn.

I must remember not to go out alone, she thought. Stivo would not take her unaware again. If he dared to touch her, she would brand him with her fingernails and put a deep gash upon his other cheek.

"Someday, Alicia," Stivo whispered from across the fire. "Someday."

She had started to answer him, to tell him that he would never possess her, when the sound of hoofbeats shattered the stillness of the night. Like the other Gypsies, Alicia reached for her knife to prepare herself in case the intruders meant harm, but it was not a band of soldiers or farmers, only two Gypsies, Manolo and Gyuri. Alicia was unconcerned until she suddenly realized that the two Roms were not alone. Who was that in their grasp?

"Rafael!" she gasped. What was he doing here? That he was a prisoner again she could have no doubt. His arms and legs were securely bound, and despite all her pent-up anger at what he had done, she pitied him. Is this what Rudolpho had meant in saying that what he had done he had done for her? Was he seeking revenge for her lost chastity? That was not her father's way. He was not a cruel nor a vindictive man. Why then was Rafael de Villasandro now standing before her trussed up like some stolen chicken?

"Rafael!" she whispered, stifling a sob with the back of her hand. The very sight of him stirred her. Feeling as if the entire world were spinning about, she reached out to steady herself. She had thought never to see him again.

He stood with his back to her, and Alicia let her eyes roam over him. She had forgotten how wide his shoulders were, how trim his waist. As if sensing her gaze, Rafael turned his head in her direction. For a long, timeless moment their eyes locked and held. She wanted to reach out to him, but he seemed so distant, so far away, like a phantom or a dream.

Seeing Alicia again, Rafael momentarily forgot his outrage. She was so lovely standing there, so very beautiful. "Alicia," he whispered, but just as the dawn brings a new day he suddenly remembered that he was here again as a prisoner. His hands were tied; he could not even raise his hand in greeting. It was not by accident that they had been reunited. He thought of Juan Dorado. What would the priest think when he failed to bring the painting? How could he save lives from *this* place? Why had these Gypsies again taken him captive?

Alicia saw Rafael's body stiffen, his face grimace in anger, and the spell was broken for her too. The memory of all that had happened rose up like a wall between them. He had taken her virtue, then callously left her without a second thought. She was not good enough for him. He scorned all Gypsies, and not being content with leaving her, had given away the Gypsy camp. Vashti's face swam before her eyes and her heart grew cold. She opened her mouth to speak, but before she could utter a word Rudolpho stepped between them, raising his hand to quiet the angry murmurings of the Gypsies, who, like Alicia, remembered the attack upon the Gypsy camp and thought the gorgio to blame.

"What is *he* doing here?" shouted Stivo. His words were instantly taken up by others who had finally found their voices.

"I had him brought here," Rudolpho answered, holding his head up, his eyes sweeping over the throng, the expression on his face clearly reminding them that he was their leader.

"Had him brought here? Why?" Todero's voice was filled with an anger that was rare for the gentle Gypsy. Not only did he remember the tragedy of the attack upon the camp but also Alicia's betrayal. This gorgio was *o Beng* personified, and now Rudolpho had brought him *here!*

"We do not want him!" shouted the women in unison. "He will bring misfortune upon us again."

"Make him pay for what he did," shouted another woman, who had lost her husband in the raid.

"Cast him out! Send him far away from here," Jana, the *phuri dai,* hissed, raising her hand to point in Rafael's direction. "He is evil!" In the light of the moonlight she looked frightening, her unblinking eyes staring at Rafael, her deeply lined face contorted with anger.

"Silence!" Rudolpho's rumbling voice shattered the night. "This man took the virtue of my daughter, Alicia. It is my right as her father to seek retribution upon his head or to see that my daughter's honor is restored. I seek to do the latter."

Alicia forced her trembling legs to support her. He was going to force Rafael to marry her! "No!"

Her voice was lost in the rumbling of the crowd. Again Rudolpho raised his arm. "By my father's hand I swear that it is my right!" His eyes met those of Rafael and he said, "You will marry my daughter on the morrow, gorgio. Thus have I spoken."

24

The fire crackled in the tense silence as Alicia gazed up at her father, her voice quivering as she pleaded with him. "Don't do this, Papa! Don't!"

Wanting privacy between himself and his daughter, Rudolpho motioned the others away. They were slow to disperse, curious as to what would be said now between father and daughter. "Go!" Rudolpho thundered in impatience, frowning as the stragglers moved slowly away, still looking back over their shoulders. It was a custom among Gypsies, living as they did in such close contact, to respect another's privacy when asked to do so, and in true Gypsy fashion they would close their ears and eyes to what Rudolpho had to say to his daughter no matter how curious they might be.

Alicia's eyes followed Rafael as he was led away to Manolo's wagon, and again she whispered, "Don't do this, Papa!" She was confused. Marriage between a Gypsy and a non-Gypsy was disapproved of by the tribes. How could Rudolpho sanction such a thing, even if she had given herself to the gorgio? "I will not marry him!"

"You must. I have decided. It is for your own good." Although his voice was gruff, his eyes were kind.

"No, it is not possible." The thought tormented her that now she would be exiled from the tribe, held in contempt, made to wander far from the caravan, as if she, too, were a gorgio. Yet would it be so terrible a punishment if she were to be with Rafael? Her heart whispered that it would be her fondest dream to follow the man she loved to the ends of the earth if need be, but her mind rebelled against the idea. She was Gypsy. It wasn't possible. She would never fit in Rafael's world. Besides, his deceit had destroyed her love. And what of Rudolpho?

"It *is* possible," Rudolpho said stubbornly. "I have spoken and it will be so. It is not for you to question me."

Alicia looked at him through her tears. "I could not stand being banished from the tribe. It would be worse than death."

Rudolpho gathered her into his arms. "No, *Chavi*. No. You will not be banished. You are my daughter and I love you. How could you think that I would ever allow that? Alicia." He stroked her hair. "The gorgio will live among us, I will see to that. How could you have doubted me? Always I think of you. I want your happiness."

"Then let the gorgio go. This marriage between us is a thing that must not be. I do not love the gorgio, nor does he love me."

Rudolpho held her at arm's length from him, looking into her eyes. "Lie to yourself, Alicia, but not to me. You love him; I can read it in your eyes and I believe that he loves you too, though perhaps he does not know that yet. I knew from the first that he was your destiny." He turned his back upon her. "Now, go. I will speak no more about it. As your father and as leader of this tribe, I tell you that the gorgio shall be your husband." With that he walked away, and Alicia fought the impulse to follow, to beg. Instead she moved listlessly to her wagon and climbed inside. She was lost. Lost. Her father was right, she *did* love the gorgio, though she would never admit it.

She had trusted the gorgio once, but never again. With every fiber of her being she would fight against this weakness she had for him. She would fight. She would *fight*. He

would never know the power he had over her. Never!
Climbing into bed between Mala and Palo, she buried her
face in her hands and burst into a storm of tears.

Rafael de Villasandro, bound hand and foot, was also unable to sleep, knowing now why those two oafs had brought
him here. Not only was he uncomfortable, but he had to
swallow hard against the bitter bile arising in his throat
when he thought about his forthcoming marriage. Alicia
was beautiful. He had almost gone mad when he thought
she might be dead. But to be forced into a Gypsy wedding
made him seethe inside. He had never been a man who liked
being forced into anything. His helplessness was like a can-
kerous sore that was eating away at his heart.

If he had sought Alicia out, things might have been different, but his anger poisoned his mind. He would not marry
her. Let her father do what he might. "Damn!" He was not
some sheep or goat that could be tamed and made to do as
some Gypsy dictated. No, he was not a dancing bear, he was
a man with a will of his own. He was a nobleman, not some
peasant. The Gypsy had no right, he thought. Yet a small
voice nagged at him that the man had every right. Rafael
had abducted his daughter, made love to her, and then left
her alone in the forest. Surely any father would react as this
Rudolpho had.

"If he had come to me, talked man to man, all might be
different," Rafael mumbled aloud. He was an honorable
man, a reasonable man. Again he struggled with the ropes
that held him. Was his brother even now searching for him?
Was there any chance that he would be rescued? No. He was
trapped once again. Or was he? Hadn't he dreamed of Alicia
these last days? Longed to see her again? When he had
turned around and seen her looking at him, could he deny
the way his heart had lurched in his breast? The sight of her,
the knowledge that she had not been among those killed,
had turned his insides to a quivering mass and he had been

overwhelmed by the urge to touch her. Even his hurt and
anger had not done away with those feelings.

Your wife, Alicia will be your wife, a voice whispered. He remembered how he had nearly been lost in the dark pools of
her eyes. Was it such a tragic fate? Could he truthfully say
that the thought of never seeing her again, or hearing her
voice, or touching her had not filled him with sadness? His
warring thoughts brought an ache to his head. "A Gypsy
bride." He remembered his father and the pain his love for a
woman of a different faith had brought. Just as there had
been a chasm separating their two worlds, so there was one
between Rafael and Alicia. Whatever kind of ceremony
might be performed between them, it would not be recognized by his world. He had heard talk of the pagan ceremonies of these Gypsies, their belief in demons and forest spirits, and had believed such stories until he met Alicia. She
was everything a woman should be: beautiful, brave, kind,
and loving. He longed for her now as much as he had before. Yet marriage? No. The love he felt for her was a thing
that must not be.

And what of his promise to de Torga to help him in his
efforts to aid the Conversos? What kind of man would Rafael be if he let the seduction of fiery green eyes and soft lips
keep him from his duty? There was so much at stake. Many
lives depended on the mission he had undertaken.

Let her father do what he would, he thought, stubborn in
his frustration. But as he lay there in the darkness, reason
took hold of him. Why risk the Gypsy leader's anger? Without a priest, the marriage would not be valid; why, then,
was he fighting it so? Was it because he feared his own
emotions? One look into Alicia's eyes and all reason fled. He
thought only of loving her. But this was a real world, a
world in which many innocent people were dying. Even
now Torquemada was planning his next strike.

He must escape, but he would be cunning. He would not
fight the marriage; he would come meekly before Alicia and

do what must be done. They could not keep him tied up forever. He had escaped once before and he would do so again. Once again he would be free.

The words should have made him happy, but they made him strangely sad. To again betray Alicia's trust was loathsome to him and caused a fiery ache in his heart. Was he a fool to think there could be any future for a nobleman and a Gypsy girl? Yes, he was. At the back of his mind was the hope that somehow, someway, he and Alicia would find happiness.

25

After having spent a sleepless night tossing and turning on her bed, dreading the morning, Alicia was up and about before the sun's rays had touched the earth. Her wedding day. This was her *wedding day*! It should have been the most wonderful day of her life, and instead she felt empty. Seeing *him* again had made her realize how vulnerable she was. She had always prided herself upon being strong, upon being Gypsy, and yet last night she had weakened. Had he beckoned her to him, she would have melted in his arms.

"But this morning I will be strong," she said, so loudly that she awakened the children. They looked at her with wide brown eyes, trying hard to understand what was troubling her.

"You look sad," Mala exclaimed, cocking her head to one side as if to look into Alicia's heart. "Why?"

"Little one, you would not understand," Alicia whispered, reaching out to tousle the girl's hair. How could she make the child understand the agony of broken dreams?

"But you should be happy," Mala exclaimed, taking Alicia's hand and squeezing it with the deepest affection, trying to cheer the beautiful woman standing before her. "I do not understand your frown. Is it that you did not bring a high bridal price?"

Alicia shrank from the child's innocent words. How could this little Gypsy girl ever understand her humiliation? There would be no bridal price set for her, no haggling between the bride's father and the papa of the groom. She was being foisted upon a man who did not want her, a man who was being forced to marry her, a man she had every reason to hate, yet one whose very nearness tortured her with memories of a star-filled night and with dreams and visions of what-might-have-been.

"Yes . . . yes, it is the bridal price." Her voice was barely more than a whisper. Fleeing from the child's searching eyes, she quickly donned her clothing and stepped outside the wagon.

There was a festive mood among the others, as if the Gypsy band had forgiven the gorgio, at least for the moment. They even seemed to be welcoming the chance for a celebration. *They do not understand,* Alicia thought, averting her eyes from the stares of the curious, who undoubtedly wondered at her obstinate reaction to her father's command, she who always obeyed Rudolpho in everything. "She brought this on herself," their eyes seemed to say. Alicia's Gypsy pride sustained her, allowing her the courage to walk about with her head held high, belying her desire to flee the camp and ride her horse to the far ends of the earth. All the while she was in a daze of confusion. Why was her papa insisting she marry this man? She was not with child. It was so unlike Rudolpho to go against her wishes.

Never before had a Gypsy girl married a gorgio. Alicia wondered why the older members of the tribe had not argued with her father. So many questions tugging at her brain made her uneasy. Odd visions and dreams haunted her at times, but she had always pushed them out of her mind. She *was* Gypsy. It was because he took her virtue, because she had given herself to the gorgio, that she must now obey her father's wishes. Still, a streak of stubborn pride raged in her. She would marry the gorgio, but she would never again let him claim her body, husband or not. If she ever let the gorgio near her in that way again, she knew that she would be lost. His willing slave, that is what she would become. No longer free, no longer Gypsy, she thought, clenching her fists. She made a silent vow of celibacy, a vow that quieted her fears.

He will leave us at the first opportunity, she reasoned, walking about the encampment. Yet, unbidden, a tear came to her eye. If only Rafael had wanted to marry her, things would have been so different. She would have given him a love that would have been unequaled by the light of the sun.

"Alicia?" Zuba's gentle hand on her shoulder brought Alicia from her musing, and she turned around to look into the girl's smiling eyes. "Do not look so sad, my friend. All will be well. Just wait and see." Somehow the words calmed Alicia's fears, at least for a time.

Wandering amid the throng, hand in hand in the friendship she had come to treasure, Alicia and Zuba viewed the preparation for the wedding. Several makeshift tables were set up and heavily laden with all kinds of food. Rations were usually tight when they were traveling. Where had it all come from? There was a side of pork cooking on the spit, flavored with aniseed; a roast fowl, a chicken Alicia suspected had been pilfered from a distant farmhouse, seasoned with sage, thyme, and marjoram and stuffed with apples. There were large plates of vegetables—beans red from the paprika seasoning, chick-peas in vinegar and oil, and bowls of steaming lentils. There were black olives, onions, and eggplant. From some hidden stock, no doubt Rudolpho's, came a keg of wine that had been watered down to serve the many "guests."

"You see, Alicia. Your people do love you, no matter their harsh words." The display of foodstuffs lent truth to her statement, and Alicia's heart was touched. In their own way the Gypsies were wishing her well. Only Solis eyed her with malice.

"Just where is your groom?" she asked, coming up behind

Alicia and Zuba, her fingers perched upon her hips like cat's claws primed to strike.

"I don't know," Alicia replied truthfully, determined not to let this one spoil her day.

"Perhaps he is tied like a dog in the prison wagon," she hissed, her face stamped with envy. Alicia reasoned that, prisoner or not, this woman would not hesitate to take the gorgio for her husband, and the knowledge spurred a sudden surge of possessiveness. Rafael was to be her groom. Hers!

"So . . . look to him well so that he does not escape you." Her words clearly meant that she would be watching and waiting for any chance to get the gorgio into her bed.

"He will be *my* husband. Remember that, you she-wolf." Alicia stepped forward with the intention of giving the buxom woman a push, but Zuba came between them, giving Alicia time to cool her anger.

"Leave us, Solis," Zuba shrieked, in a rare display of anger. "Or I will tell the others what you are about. Would you like to have your head shaved? Eh?" With a toss of her dark hair, Solis hurried off, not one to tempt fate.

"That woman. She shames the name Gypsy," Alicia stormed.

"Yes, she does. If you ask me, she and Stivo would make a fine pair." Zuba tugged at Alicia's hand. "Let me help you dress." Reaching into her pocket, she pulled forth a string of gold pieces and slipped them around Alicia's neck. The necklace would symbolize a warning to other men that Alicia was now to be a bride.

"I can't take this, Zuba. It belongs to you." Alicia began to take it off, but Zuba stayed her.

"I will get another. Please. It is my gift to you. A token of our friendship." Green eyes met brown ones in deepest understanding. For a moment there was silence, and then Zuba whispered, "You love him, Alicia. Whether or not you know it, I feel it in my heart. Your words to Solis . . ."

". . . were but words of anger. The gorgio means nothing to me. Any love I had for him died the day he deserted me." She sought to turn away, but Zuba's small hands held her shoulders, forcing her to look again into the gentle girl's eyes.

"Lie to yourself, but not to me, Alicia. You love him, and all the words of denial you might utter are as useless as wings on a cow. Don't let your bitterness spoil what happiness you might have. A cloudy morning often changes to a fine day. A Gypsy never knows his tomorrows."

Alicia started to protest, but the firm hand of Zuba pushed her along and into the wagon. "A Gypsy never knows his tomorrows," she whispered, closing her eyes and offering up a silent prayer to *o Del* that her tomorrows would be tranquil.

26

A large throng was gathered to watch the wedding. From the youngest child to the eldest, all were bedecked in their finery of brightest colored scarves, shirts, and skirts, many with golden coins at neck and ears. Above the commotion rose the trill of gay songs and peals of laughter as the Gypsies pushed and shoved at each other in an attempt to be the first to view the bride. It had been a long time since there had been a wedding.

On a long pole a white handkerchief was tied, fluttering in the breeze as an emblem of the bride's purity. It seemed that for the moment the Gypsy band had forgotten the reason for this hasty ceremony. If Alicia was not completely pure, well, it did not matter. Soon all would be set to rights. A yellow furze was nailed over the caravan where the bridal couple was to stand, the spiny yellow flowers the only flowers visible. This was tradition, but any other cut flowers were forbidden. Cut flowers were a symbol of premature death, and this feast marked the beginning of a new life.

"There she is! Alicia!" a small child yelled out as Alicia stepped from her tent.

"She is beautiful!" Palo exclaimed, waving at her from the crowd with childish exuberance.

Alicia was beautiful. Dressed in a richly embroidered blouse of white, the contours of her breasts outlined by the sheer cloth, her many skirts billowing in the breeze, she

looked like some pagan goddess. Like a rainbow of colors
her skirts were visible: white underneath, then yellow, pink,
and red—like the petals of blossoming flowers. Emphasizing
her small waist was a tight belt of black, decorated with
multicolored beads. Large gold earrings drooped from her
ears, and her arms flashed with the gold of her many bracelets. Around her neck were many strings of beads of black
and red for good luck. like a rippling waterfall her long
tresses fell to well below her waist, and the bridal crown of
leaves laced with many colored ribbons that fell to either
side of her face looked somewhat like the bridal veil that
Christian women always wore. As he stepped out of another
wagon to join her, Rafael could not help the gasp of surprise
that escaped his lips. She was even more beautiful than he
could have imagined.

Alicia felt Rafael's eyes upon her, sensed his presence
with every fiber of her body, heard the sound of his footsteps as he approached her, but did not dare to look at him.
They stood side by side in front of Rudolpho, who would
act as the priest for this ceremony, his right as leader of the
tribe.

One by one the elder leaders of the tribe gave speeches,
wishing the couple the best in their new life, telling stories
about their own wedding ceremonies; and it was only while
they were speaking that Alicia dared to look in Rafael's direction. He was wearing a Gypsy outfit, and she could not
help but think what a handsome Gypsy he would make.
The thin material of his white shirt nearly burst at the
seams, so broad were his shoulders. She recognized the shirt
as one belonging to Stivo and thought of the irony of it all.
Stivo hated the gorgio, but had been asked to part with his
shirt, being the only Gypsy muscular enough to lend Rafael
his garments.

Although Alicia stood in her bare feet, feeling the warmth
of the earth, Rafael wore hempen sandals with a ribbon tied
around his leg at the calf. Unlike the Gypsies, he wore no

woolen stockings, and Alicia could not help but notice how well formed his legs were. His pantaloons were of dark wool, a bit too small for him and doing little to hide the cool strength of his hips, buttocks, and thighs. Around his neck he wore a kerchief of bright blue with a golden crucifix dangling at his chest as if to taunt them all and mock this pagan ceremony.

As if feeling her eyes upon him, Rafael turned his head, and for a moment their eyes were locked in silence, the intensity of their gaze tingling with currents of emotion.

"Alicia . . . I . . ." Rudolpho's chastising grunt stilled Rafael's words.

Rudolpho motioned to Todero, who brought forth an armful of small branches, holding them forth for the leader's hand. "These come from seven different kinds of trees and represent our many tribes," he said in a booming voice. Mumbling an incantation, he broke the branches one by one and gave them up to the winds. "Like these branches you, too, will be as free as the winds, but you must not break your pledge to one another until either one of you shall die!" Alicia trembled at his words, awed by the finality of such a vow. Rafael would be her husband until death parted them.

Again Rudolpho motioned to Todero, who brought forth a jug of water, a crystal of salt, and a small loaf of freshly baked bread. Rudolpho took them one by one, holding forth the jug first to Rafael, then to Alicia. With trembling hands Alicia raised it to her lips, feeling the cool water trickle down her throat as she drank from the spot Rafael's lips had touched. Rafael watched, moved by the dignity she displayed. To her this ceremony was as real as any spoken before a priest. Touched, he damned himself silently; he must remember it meant nothing to him. Nothing. And yet he longed to reach out, touch her, comfort her. Whisper that all would be right, that he loved her.

A crash startled him. The earthenware jug lay scattered in

pieces at his feet. For a moment Rafael thought it an accident, but Rudolpho's triumphant grin told him his notion
was false.

"These many scattered pieces represent the years of happiness you will have together." Picking up two pieces,
Rudolpho held one out to each of them. "Keep these and
take care. If you lose them, misery and loneliness will surely
come upon you."

Rafael reached out his hand slowly. It was unnerving to
be told such a thing. It sparked of superstition. Heresy. And
yet he was suddenly loath to part with the earthenware
shard, tucking it into the belt of his pants to keep it safe.

"Hold forth your hands."

Both Alicia and Rafael obeyed. Alicia's hands were cold,
Rafael's as warm as the sunshine that shone down upon
them. In an effort to warm her hands, Rafael grasped them
firmly, his touch possessive and caressing, sparking a fire in
her blood.

Oh, why does his very touch have such power? she wondered,
resolving once again to keep her vow. Was Zuba right? Did
she love him? Yes. The answer was shattering. No matter
what he had done, no matter that he did not want her, she
loved him with every beat of her heart.

Rudolpho bound their wrists together with three knots, to
symbolize unity, fertility, and a long life. "For as long as
time rules us, you can never be divided." He held forth a
piece of bread and a lump of salt crystal for them to eat as a
cheer from the throng rent the air.

Untying the rope that bound them together, Rudolpho
took from around his neck a string of gold coins and thrust
them into Alicia's right hand and Rafael's left. "From me a
little gold, but may *o Del* give you plenty."

From out of the crowd Zuba stepped forward, tugging at
the leaves and ribbons that Alicia wore upon her head and
replacing the bridal wreath with a red kerchief, tying it

around Alicia's head. The badge of a married woman of the tribe.

"May you have a lifetime of good fortune and love," Zuba whispered.

Alicia's face was flushed with excitement and fear. Married. She was married to the gorgio. Rafael de Villasandro was now her husband! Moving as if in a trance, she barely felt the hugs and kisses of all who wished her well.

Fires were started as the Gypsies began to sing and dance in celebration. It was an unruly throng that shouted and jumped about as the guitar and violin began to play. By tradition the festival should have lasted three days. Since they were on the road, it would last only one night but would be three times as lusty.

Although there was plenty of food, Alicia could not force a bite past her lips. She watched wide-eyed as the mob of people she had grown up with celebrated, gorging themselves, drinking to her health, knocking over flagons, upsetting dishes in their joyous celebration.

At last, as the sun sank below the horizon the festivities waned. The women linked arms to escort Alicia to the bridal wagon, the floor of which was strewn with sweetmeats and the ribbons that Alicia had worn in her hair. Standing still as a statue, Alicia felt their hands undress her and shivered. Was it from the cool breeze that swept through the opening or from fear? She did not know.

She only knew she would not let him touch her. Husband or not, she would be firm in this. Never bending. Standing in a gown as thin as the wings of a butterfly, Alicia awaited the man who was now her husband.

27

The crackling flames of the campfires cast eerie shadows on Rudolpho's face as he stood scrutinizing his new son-in-law. His eyes glittered dangerously; his expression gave clear warning: there would be no attempt to escape. There was a long silence as the two men dueled with their eyes. At last Rudolpho spoke.

"Alicia has been a good daughter to me. I would not have wanted any other. Her happiness is all I ask in this life. To harm her is to do harm to me. Do you understand, Gorgio?"

Rafael nodded grimly. "Yes, I understand." He wanted to tell this Gypsy giant that he, too, wanted Alicia's happiness, that what he must do eventually tore at his heart. Instead he held his tongue, saying only, "But you do not ensure her future by forcing me to take her as my wife." The words were out before Rafael could silence himself. "I can never be a Gypsy!"

Rudolpho raised one eyebrow, pacing back and forth in front of the fire, deep in thought. From time to time he would tug at the ends of his long drooping mustache, casting a glance first at Rafael, then at the other Gypsy men who were lingering about, drinking and singing their songs. It was as if with every look he was measuring Rafael as a man, wondering silently just what he must do now.

At last when Rafael thought he could stand the man's

pacing no longer, Rudolpho stopped in his tracks and once again eyed the younger man up and down.

"And if Alicia were to go with you to your world, what then, Gorgio? Would you make her happy? Could you love her as deeply as I believe she loves you?"

"You would allow her to go?" Rafael had long ago given up any thought of taking Alicia with him.

"I would sacrifice my very heart if it would make her happy. Gypsy ways are the only kind of life my daughter understands. The others would shun her, those of *your* kind." He kicked at a large stone by the fire in his frustration. "You gorgios can be cruel in your treatment of those who are different from yourselves. Never would I want Alicia wounded by the sharp barbs of such prejudice." He shook his head violently, making his decision. "No. *You* must join *us.* Become Gypsy. It is a good life. A life of freedom."

"Freedom?" Rafael could not hide his bitterness. "Twice now your people have taken me captive and held me against my will. How can you speak of freedom?"

The Gypsy avoided his eyes. "For that I am sorry. It was unavoidable. Perhaps I have been wrong in many things." Again he began his pacing, talking more to himself than to Rafael. "It is not a wise thing to say that you have been wrong. If you allow you have been wrong, people will say that you may be a very honest fellow but that you certainly are a very great fool."

"I do not think you a fool. But you are wrong to hold me prisoner."

"I only sought in my own way to hasten this joining between you and my daughter." Taking Rafael by the arms in a gesture meant to show friendship, he looked deep into his eyes. Rafael saw a great sadness there and wondered at the cause. "It is right that you be together."

Rafael started to speak, to ask the questions that plagued

him, but the Gypsy leader silenced him. "We will say no more about it this night. Your bride awaits you."

Bride. The word filled Rafael with a myriad of feelings. He remembered how lovely Alicia had looked bedecked in her bridal garments. He longed to rush to her, to hold her in his arms, yet his pride, his longing for freedom, filled his heart with resentment. When he had first been taken captive his fury had been overwhelming. He had vowed to revenge himself upon these Gypsy scoundrels. Then, seeing Alicia again, knowing that she was alive, had completely unnerved him, and any thought of avenging himself had disappeared. What kind of power did this Gypsy girl have over him?

I should try to escape right now, he thought, eyeing a large wooden log in the fire that offered a weapon. One well-aimed blow would obliterate this giant from his path. Why, then, did he not act? The Gypsies were in their cups and unprepared for violence. Chanting and singing, they hardly seemed fearsome. Why, then, did Rafael *not* run? There were horses about the camp. Why did he not go? Tonight? Why?

Because I cannot bear to leave Alicia without touching her, without telling her good-bye, without making love to her. He could envision her that night beneath the stars and knew that he wanted to feel her passion for him burn again, wanted her naked beneath him. He thought about the priceless gift she had given him that night and knew that he could not leave her yet. She belonged to him by Gypsy law, if not his own. She was his Gypsy bride, at least for this night.

"Come. Let me lead you to her," Rudolpho said softly, reading Rafael's emotions in his eyes. "She is your destiny."

A full moon hung like a pendulum in the sky, shedding its glow as the procession walked along to Alicia's wagon. Rafael walked behind Rudolpho, followed by several Gypsy men who had put aside their anger at having an outsider in their midst and now looked forward to the "abduction" that was to come. The groom would have to fight for his bride.

Only Stivo clung to his anger, hissing in Rafael's ear, "Beware, outsider! You have no rights here."

Hurried along, Rafael had no time to answer the threat, but knew the handsome Gypsy was his deadly enemy, that one day Stivo would try to take his life.

Gathering in the open space between the wagons, the men chased the women away with clucking tongues and shooing hands. In one voice they called out, "Alicia!" Even though Rudolpho had given his daughter in marriage, though the wedding had been celebrated with eating and drinking, still the bride must *surrender* to her new husband and the groom *fight* for what he now claimed as his own.

"What is going on?" Rafael asked, bewildered and apprehensive to see his "enemies" line up before him as if preparing for battle.

Rudolpho's answer was a deep laugh, which rumbled forth like thunder. "Why, only that you must take that which is yours, my son. You must kidnap Alicia. Take her from the arms of those who seek to keep her from you. It is Gypsy custom."

"Kidnap her?" It did not make sense to Rafael. What sort of a game were they playing? He watched warily as the Gypsy men linked arms and stood as if in a protective wall in front of Alicia. "How am I going to take her from so many men? I am clearly outnumbered."

Again Rudolpho laughed. "By trickery. But do not fear. It is for me to aid you in this as father to the bride. Come."

While Alicia pretended fright, weeping and thrashing from side to side, as was the custom for the bride, Rudolpho lunged forward, breaking through the human chain by the sheer force of his brute strength. Taking advantage of the confusion Rudolpho's sudden movement caused, Rafael reached for Alicia's hand, tugging her through the throng of outstretched hands. Together they ran toward the outskirts of the camp, looking behind them from time to time. Rafael was reminded of that other time he had taken Alicia from her people and was filled with the overwhelming urge to carry her off again. His eyes scanned the distance for sight of a horse, only to be disappointed. The Gypsies were not as trusting of him as he had supposed. All horses were hidden out of his sight.

"You will not escape this time, gorgio," Alicia snarled, clearly reading his mind. "Though I wish you would leave me and never return again."

Her words stung him. He had not been prepared for such hatred, though perhaps he had earned it. "I deserve your scorn, Alicia," was all he could think to say. "I'm sorry for any hurt I caused you."

"Sorry? Sorry?" Alicia forced her trembling legs to support her. Fearful of her weakness, she cast him a look of pure hatred. "I will never forgive you for what you did. Never."

Rafael was shaken. Had he known the reason, he might have told her of his innocence in the raid on the Gypsy camp, but he took her anger to be solely the reaction to his desertion.

"It was a thing that I had to do. Can you not see that?" He reached to take her hand again, but she pulled away from him as if he were holding forth fire.

"I will remember what you have done until the day I die," she breathed. "You are as poison. Never will I believe the honeyed words of a gorgio again. Never!" She whirled, with the intention of running from him, but the sight of Stivo coming upon them prevented her from taking one more step. She loathed Stivo, but as much as she feared him, she stood her ground. As dangerous as he was to her, he was even more so to Rafael. His hatred of the gorgio ran deep.

"You did not fight for her, gorgio," Stivo growled. With the grace of a cat he reached for the whip that was the mark of Gypsy manhood, snapping it so hard that it sounded like a crack of gunpowder.

"I abducted her fairly. Alicia is now mine."

"Yours, gorgio? She will never be yours, though the secret of her birth be known by many. You do not want her. I do. Give her to me. I will claim your husbandly rights in your place and let you go free." He toyed with the whip, making it wriggle about like a snake at Rafael's feet.

All of Rafael's protective instincts bubbled forth. Never would he give Alicia to this man. If there truly was a devil, *o Beng,* it was this one. He was evil. Rafael could sense that it was lust that drove him to desire Alicia, not love.

"No! You will never touch her. Not while I live."

Stivo lunged forward, slashing the whip through the air, striking Rafael a painful blow to the arm. "Then you will die." Springing forward, Stivo lashed out at his quarry just as Alicia screamed.

"Stivo, no! No!" Seeking to stop him, heedless of her own safety, she stepped between the two men only to feel the taste of the lash herself as it wrapped itself about her waist. With piercing laughter the Gypsy devil used the whip like a rope to draw her into his arms.

"Leave her alone. If you be not coward, then fight *me,* not her." Rafael's voice clearly issued a challenge.

"I *will* fight you." Loosening the whip from Alicia's waist, he stood scrutinizing Rafael, daring him to take one more step.

"He is unarmed, Stivo. You fight him unfairly. That is not the Gypsy way." Alicia's breasts heaved with indignation, her eyes blazed anger as she looked about wildly for any kind of weapon. If only she had her knife. In helpless frustration she could only watch as the two men came together. "Rafael is no match for Stivo," she whispered, closing her eyes to say a silent prayer. Stivo was well known to be a treacherous fighter. Even from childhood he had fought unfairly. Didn't she know that? Hadn't she the scars to prove it?

A violent oath rent the air like thunder. "What is this? Stivo! What are you doing here?" Rudolpho bellowed.

"Go away, old man." Snarling like a wolf after a bear, Stivo turned, aiming his whip at Rudolpho's head, missing only by inches as Rudolpho ducked.

"Jukel! You are no Gypsy to act this way." Ignoring the lashing whip, Rudolpho moved forward. "Stop this moment, or I will banish you from the tribe. I swear by my father's hand that I will do so."

Like a dash of cold water on a fire, his words quenched the flames of Stivo's reckless fury. To be banished from the tribe, to roam forever alone, was the worst possible punishment any Gypsy could face. Even greater than death.

"You would not do such a thing. My mother is *phuri dai.* She is seventh daughter of seven. I am ninth son of her loins."

"I am tribal leader; it is my right." Rudolpho spat on the ground, aiming at Stivo's feet. "You are a disgrace to all we hold high. Now go; the sight of you sickens me." Clenching his fist, he brought his hand up to his chest as if to control his rage. Without saying another word Stivo slunk away, but the gleam in his eye promised that this was not to be the end. Rudolpho's voice was choked. "Alicia. Gorgio. Go to the wagon. Quickly. Tonight is your wedding night and I will let nothing stand in the way. Go!"

Obeying his command, Alicia hurried off, followed by Rafael. Only when they had gone did Rudolpho give in to his pain, clutching at his chest.

"Nothing will keep you from your gorgio," he whispered. "He must take care of you when I die." Sinking to the ground, he fought against his anguish and pain. He must not die. Not yet. Not until Alicia's happiness was assured.

28

They stood side by side in the small wagon, gasping from the exertion of their haste. It was silent in the safety of the canvas and wood shelter except for the whisper of their breathing. Each of them was achingly aware of the other, of the rippling current of expectancy.

Alicia felt an aching longing to touch Rafael. She wanted to call out to him, to have him put his arms around her, to love her as he had that night beneath the stars, but her pride silenced her. She must never forget what he had done.

"Are you all right? Alicia. Did he hurt you?" Rafael's voice broke the silence.

She turned around slowly, avoiding his eyes. "No. The whip did not touch my flesh."

"Good. Good." He was tongue-tied, remembering her words of hatred only moments before. He wanted her to love him again, to forget all the bitterness in her heart, but he didn't know what words he could say to her. Instead he reached out to trace the curve of her cheek, forcing her to look at him. "Alicia. Sweet, sweet Alicia."

A warmth deep inside her flowered at the sound of his voice. His presence drew her like the currents of the river. She could feel the heat of his body, and her head spun at the memory of his caresses, his lovemaking. The overpowering desire to let him take her, to love her, nearly overcame her reason.

If time existed, she was hardly aware of it as she stood there before him. Her heart was beating so wildly in her chest that she feared he would hear it. "Did Stivo harm you?" she asked, her voice barely more than a whisper.

"No. Your father came between us before he could manage to draw blood." Reaching up again, he buried his hand in the silk of her hair. "Were you worried about me, little Gypsy? Perhaps your hatred of me does not run as deep as you say."

Pulling violently away from him, she sought to still her trembling. "I . . . I . . . would not want harm to come to any living thing, Gorgio," she stammered.

"Gorgio. Always you call me that. Rafael. My name is Rafael, and well you know it. Say it. Say my name."

"I do not answer to your commands, Gorgio."

"I am your husband now, Alicia, by *your* laws and customs. You are to obey me, is that not so?"

She nodded, shivering but not from the cold.

"Say it. Rafael."

Her voice was barely a whisper. "Rafael."

"I like the sound of my name on your lips."

Alicia could read the desire in his eyes and quickly stepped away. "No, do not touch me, Gorgio. Never again!"

"Never? Never is a long time, Alicia." Before she could step away, he pulled her into his arms. "Sweet Alicia. It has been so long."

Alicia breathed in the virile scent of him; tasted the wine on his tongue as he kissed her. She wanted to protest against the lips claiming her own, but the sweetness of his kiss silenced her.

Against Alicia's will, her body responded to his touch. A warm tingling swept over her and she trembled at his touch, her own body betraying her.

"No. No." Loving him would destroy her. He would quench his lust for her, then callously throw her away again as he had done once before. She could not trust him, not someone who had brought such destruction to those she loved. Vashti. She must remember Vashti. This man would destroy her too.

Her fear gave her the needed strength to push away from him. "It is lust, not love, that guides your hand," she spat out at him.

He shook his head. "No. Stivo is filled with lust; I am filled with love."

"Love. Ha! You expect me to believe that? You lied to me once."

"I did not lie to you about my feelings, Alicia. There was nothing false in my kisses. My hands never lied when they touched you. I longed for you then and I long for you now."

"You longed for me? Why, then, did you leave me?"

"I had to. Perhaps you will never understand, never forgive me." His eyes swept over her in a caress. "I should never have made love to you that night. I should have left you alone. But you were so incredibly beautiful, I could not bear to leave, never having loved you. And I am *not* sorry. I will never forget that night."

She was mesmerized by the depth of emotion in his face. Was he telling her the truth? Did he feel something for her? She wanted to believe so, yet what of her vow? What of Vashti and the others? The memory of the attack on the Gypsy camp hardened her heart. He was to blame. Rafael.

"If you are sorry. If you truly have any affection for me, you will leave me alone." Her voice was cold, belying the warmth in her heart. "For some reason I do not understand, my father chose to marry me to you."

"He thinks you love me. Do you, Alicia?"

"No. Once, perhaps. But your treachery has killed whatever affection I felt for you, Rafael. You will never again have my heart."

He took an sudden step forward, the pulse pounding erratically in the hollow of his throat, his eyes glowing with an inner flame. "You belong to me, Alicia. By the word of your father you are mine. I will have you this night."

Feeling like a trapped animal, Alicia threw herself upon him, beating at him with her fists. "I hate you. I hate you. I will fight you with every ounce of strength I have. You can take me, force yourself upon me, but you will never have my love."

Rafael caught her up in his arms, pulling her to him, plundering her mouth with his. Alicia couldn't think as his hands traveled over her with consummate skill, his fingers brushing the peaks of her breasts. Now the hands that had fought him, her hands, were pulling him nearer, digging into his flesh, bringing him closer. Reaching up to him, she wound her arms around his neck, shamelessly pressing against him, wanting him as much as he wanted her.

His voice was soft as he drew his lips from hers. "You see, you don't hate me, Alicia. I think I proved that just now."

Burying her face in her hands, Alicia gave vent to her tears. It was true. At that moment she hated herself and this body of hers, which always flamed with his touch. *He* was not her enemy. No, it was *herself* that she must fight. Herself.

Seeing her tears, Rafael forgot his desire and longed only to comfort her, to gather her into his arms and never let her go. "Alicia."

"Please leave me. Please." Her green eyes sparkled with her tears. She had to be alone, safe from these emotions that fired her. She was confused, afraid. How could he ever understand?

"I will leave you alone, Alicia. At least for this night. Sleep in your lonely bed. But remember this. I love you, and one day I will make you mine again."

29

Alicia awoke with a start at the first light of dawn. She had tossed and turned all night and now her head ached miserably from lack of sleep. The cool early-morning air hurt her temples.

"What am I to do? What am I to do?" she moaned. Sitting up too quickly, she found that the sudden movement made her head ache all the more. Too much wine from the wedding feast? No. She had drunk sparingly. It was tension and worry that had caused her malady. She would have to fix an herbal remedy for herself. Catnip, perhaps, or peppermint.

Outside the wagon she could hear the giggles of the children. Mala. Palo. She missed seeing their smiling faces this morning, but since it was her wedding night, they had been taken to another wagon to sleep. Rudolpho had thought of everything.

"But there is no reason for them not to stay with me. I do not intend to be Rafael's wife in anything but name." Why did the words sound so sad? Why could she not forget the softness in his eyes when he had looked upon her last night?

Had theirs been a normal Gypsy wedding, Alicia would be displaying her bridal bed-linen this morning, to prove her purity. All the camp knew she was no virgin bride. Yet she could not allow herself to feel shamed. Rafael's words came back to haunt her.

". . . I could not bear to leave, never having loved you.

And I am not sorry. I will never forget that night." Wasn't that how she felt too? If she were honest with herself, she would have to admit that she would give herself to him again, even with all the pain, all the scorn, she had suffered from her people. Why, then, had she hurled such hateful words at him? Fear. Pride. Anger. She had told him that she wished he would leave and never return, but she knew those words to be untrue. Rising from her bed, she suddenly feared that he had believed her. Had he escaped during the night after all? Could she blame him?

"Rafael. Rafael." Forgetting that she was wearing nothing more than her gown, she went in search of him only to have her fears realized. He was not with the others. He was gone, and it was she who had driven him away with her sharp tongue! Tears rose to her eyes as she returned to her wagon. All she could do now was to get dressed and search for him.

"I've not gone, Alicia," a voice called gently. Rafael emerged from his sleeping place beneath the wagon. "I would not leave you. We have not yet finished what we have begun." Their eyes met and he smiled.

He had understood her thoughts. Embarrassed, Alicia threw back her head, thrust her shoulders back, and maintained her pride. "We shall see, Gorgio. We shall see." Climbing up, thrusting aside the canvas curtain, she sought the privacy of the wagon before he could read in her eyes her joy at seeing him. Dressing in her many skirts and white blouse, she would have been the last to admit the care she took with her appearance, brushing her hair at least a hundred strokes so that it would shine in the sunlight, darkening her eyes with just a touch of kohl, putting berry juice upon her lips so that they would glisten with a pink glow. From now on, as a married woman she could not be without her head scarf, but she tied it about her head with pride, feeling a strange sense of contentment. If she had to belong to any man, she was glad it was to Rafael.

She loved him, why could she not admit that, to herself at

least? Through the opening of the wagon it seemed that the sun was just a little brighter, the air just a little more fragrant. Her eyes searched out Rafael and found him with the other men, pulling down the tents and rolling them up for travel. Was he really so much taller, so much more handsome than the others? Yes. To her eyes at least. Despite the fact that he had been brought here against his will, he seemed to be laughing with the others and working just as hard to break up camp. What a Gypsy he would make, she thought, feeling a sudden surge of happiness and pride. If the others could forgive him, why couldn't she? It was a question she asked herself over and over as she helped the other women prepare breakfast.

"He is handsome, that one," Zuba said in her ear. "Nearly as handsome as my Todero." Zuba's eyes asked many questions. Hastily Alicia looked away, seeming to take particular interest in the potato she was peeling.

At last Zuba could stand it no longer, and taking Alicia's hand, she pulled her away from the others. "Alicia. Tell me. Did he make you happy last night? Were his arms strong, did he make you moan with pleasure, did he . . . ?"

"No."

"No? What does that mean?"

Alicia turned away from those large brown eyes that seemed to be probing into her very heart. "I . . . I would not let him touch me last night."

"You would not let him touch you?" Zuba threw up her arms in frustration. "Why?"

"Because he . . . he . . . the raid on the camp . . . I . . . I . . ."

"You are afraid of him. Admit it, Alicia. I am your friend, we grew up together you and I. Admit it to yourself if not to me. That *is* the reason. You are afraid to give your heart."

"Of course I am afraid; can you blame me?" Alicia clutched nervously at the folds of her skirt. "Do you think I want to be hurt again?"

Taking her by the shoulders, Zuba looked deep into Alicia's eyes. "You will be hurt again if you do not learn to trust and to forgive. But it will be you who will do the hurting."

"But Rafael . . ."

"He loves you. Why else has he not tried to run away? Perhaps even he does not know the depth of his feeling for you, but I do. Give him a chance to make you happy, Alicia. I do not believe he was the one who brought the others upon us; and if you ask yourself, you will have to answer the same."

"I do not know what to think anymore. Once everything was so simple, but no more. No more."

There was no more time to talk for the other women gestured frantically for Zuba and Alicia to join them. No time for idle chatter, even for a bride. Much needed to be done this morning to prepare to abandon camp. Alicia joined the others, but Zuba's words rang in her ears as she went about her duties. Her eyes sought out Rafael again, and as he looked in her direction she smiled.

At last all the blankets, tents, and cooking utensils had been loaded in the wagons, the horses tethered, and the journey begun. Rafael sat beside Alicia at the front of the wagon, his hands firmly upon the reins.

"I can guide the horses, Gorgio," she said stiffly, trying desperately to hide her feelings from him. She was painfully aware of his nearness and was careful not to touch him lest his touch ignite the fire within her breast that she remembered so well. She remembered Zuba's words again and for just a moment wondered if perhaps Rafael could be innocent. Was it possible? With all her heart she wanted to trust him. Casting him a glance, she found him looking at her and hastily turned away.

"Don't turn away, Alicia. What is wrong? What are you thinking?" He reached out with his free hand and to take the reins, and this time she did not resist him. "There is something more than my leaving you in the forest that is troubling you. What is it?"

She wanted to speak but couldn't form the words and said instead, "We are different, you and I. We come from two separate worlds. Papa must have been touched with moon madness to ever join us together. It will never work. Never."

He pulled tighter on the reins. "I used to think so too; that is why I left you that day, but now I am not so certain."

"Papa should never have forced you to come here. He was wrong."

"He had his reasons."

They rode on in silence for a long while, each struggling to understand his own feelings. Rafael was still angry about having been abducted so ruthlessly, but now that anger was softened by the knowledge that it was for his daughter's happiness that Rudolpho had done such a thing. He liked the Gypsy leader and respected him, yet he could not stay among these people much longer. Could he make Alicia understand why he must leave her again? He would have to try. Her anger was too much of a torture to endure forever.

"Yet despite all that I need to do, all that my reason tells me, I don't want to go," he whispered, jerking at the heavy leather wagon-reins as if to restrain his own heart.

30

The caravan traveled all day, stopping only to rest the horses. At last dusk came upon the land with a vivid swirl of pink and lavender. Like a huge fiery globe the sun sank on the horizon, and Alicia knew that once again she would find herself alone with Rafael.

All the long day, though she was silent and brooding, she had nevertheless been conscious of his strong masculine presence beside her. The sound of his voice, the musky, fragrant smell of his body, the strong yet smooth feel of his hand whenever he had touched her, all drew her as did the very sight of him. Would she ever really tire of looking at Rafael? No. She liked the way his muscles rippled as he pulled at the reins, the finely chiseled lines of his profile, the way his dark hair whipped about his face as they rode along.

With him beside her the world was more vibrant, as if she were seeing it for the first time. Throwing back her head, she rejoiced in the feel of the wind blowing her long unbound hair.

Rafael turned to look at Alicia, and the sight of her tugged once again at his heart. How could the love he felt for her be wrong? Turning his gaze to meet her eyes, the depth of his feelings shone in his eyes, mesmerizing Alicia with the emotions she read there.

"I love you, Alicia, beyond all reason or thought. Somehow a voice inside my head tells me I am foolish, that we are too different, you and I, but my heart argues the point. I want to listen to my *heart.*" As Rafael spoke he pulled the horses to a halt, guiding the wagon into its resting place with a skill that belied the fact that he was gorgio, and again Alicia thought of what a handsome Gypsy he could become.

Alicia's hand was taken in long, strong fingers as Rafael helped her down from the wagon, and once again she was at a loss for words. She thought he had said "I love you." Had she heard him correctly?

"Rafael . . . Rafael . . . did you . . . did you . . ." She had to ask him the question. She had to know the answer before there could be any hope of love between them.

"Did I what? What are you trying to ask me, Alicia?"

She started to speak, but before the words were out Mala and Palo were upon her, hugging her with childish exuberance. Laughing and tugging at her long hair, they demanded her full attention.

"We missed you, Alicia. Why could we not sleep with you last night?" Palo eyed the stranger in their midst with a frown, knowing that it was because of him they had been cast out.

Alicia blushed. "It was my wedding night, Palo."

"We would not have bothered you. Mala and I would have been as quiet as two lambs, wouldn't we, Mala?"

Giggling, the little Gypsy girl nodded her head. As she looked shyly up at Rafael, it was clear to see that she adored him. "Can we sleep with you tonight?"

Rafael had other things on his mind, but he was at a loss as to what to say. "We shall see." As he spoke he tightened his arm about Alicia's waist, and for the first time since he had come to the Gypsy camp, Alicia welcomed his embrace. "I want you all to myself tonight," he whispered in her ear.

Only the nightly chores could separate them, yet even then Alicia could sense Rafael's piercing gaze upon her wherever she went and knew that his eyes followed her. She fought hard against the love in her heart, but she was powerless. Zuba was right. If she turned her back on Rafael again, she would only be hurting herself. As she huddled with the women, the sultry eyes of Solis seemed to issue a challenge, and Alicia answered with a look that bespoke a warning.

He is *my* husband. *Mine.*

It seemed an eternity before the cooking was done, the food eaten, the wagons unloaded, and the cooking pots cleaned. But at last Alicia heard the deep, soft rumble of Rafael's voice speak her name as he came up beside her.

"It is time for the others to go to sleep, but you will have no time for slumber, my lovely Gypsy bride." His breath stirred her hair, and she felt a quiver run down her spine. Still Alicia would not let him know the true depth of her feelings.

"I am tired, Rafael. There is a long journey ahead of us tomorrow."

He reached out to touch her, and she felt his strong hand on the curve of her hip. "Ah, still you fight me, Alicia. What must I do?" Tightening his arm about her, he moved against her, the heat of his body enveloping her. They moved like partners in a dance as they walked together. Gently he kissed her, offering a promise of things to come.

"Alicia. There you are." Palo broke the silence with his childish innocence. "Tell us a story. You always do at this time of night."

Rafael was helpless for the moment and could only watch as Alicia took the children's hands and led them over to an old tree stump. Sitting with the children at her feet, she promised to tell them the story of the first man and woman.

"Do you believe in Adam and Eve?" Rafael asked, taking a seat beside Alicia on the stump.

She looked at him in mock horror. "Adam and Eve? No. I am Gypsy and we know the truth." Smiling, she threw back the long tendrils of her hair.

"The truth?" he asked, raising one eyebrow. "And just what is that?" Her brown hair glowed with red highlights in the firelight, and he feasted his eyes upon her beauty. His fiery Gypsy, that was what she was.

"*O Del* made the first man out of chalk and put him in the fire to bake. But he was so busy with creating the desert sands and river valleys that he forgot to take him out in time. Alas. Poor overcooked man."

"The Moors," Palo piped up.

"The Moors? I see. Interesting. The first man was a Moor." Rafael looked at her askance, but let her continue. "What happened then?"

Alicia was aware of his firm muscles as his thigh moved against hers, and she fought to keep her mind on the story. Moving away from him, she answered, "*O Del* made another man. This one he took from the oven too soon."

"The first Spaniard," Mala said proudly, anxious to show the stranger her knowledge.

Rafael flinched, wondering what would happen if Torquemada should hear this story. He would say it sparked of heresy. Did it? Were these Gypsies heretics? Heathens? No. He could not believe them to be. It was such a charming story.

"The first Spaniard?"

"The first of the white race," Mala and Palo echoed.

Rafael thought the story had ended, but Alicia silenced him with a wink of her green eyes. "The third attempt was the successful one. Once more *O Del* made a man of chalk, but this time he timed it just right. Not too long in the oven, not too short a time. He created a nicely browned man. The first Gypsy!" She laughed triumphantly, and he joined her in her merriment.

"And then he made a woman for each," Palo said above the laughter, the seriousness on his face plain to see.

Mala shook her head in disagreement. "I think that *o Del*

made the women first and then the men. Just like at birth.
Man comes from woman, not the other way around."

Palo was quick to challenge her. "Man came first. It is
man who is tribal leader."

"But woman who is *phuri dai.*" Mala was not one to admit
defeat. For a moment it appeared that they might come to
blows.

Rafael picked one child up in each arm, carrying them to
Zuba's wagon. "I believe he created them at the same time.
Man and woman. Now, go to bed, you two." Gently he set
them down before the wagon entrance, ignoring their indig-
nant protests and pleas to stay with Alicia. Tonight he
wanted the lovely Gypsy all to himself.

"Rafael. The children. What will they think?" Alicia
started toward them, but Rafael blocked her way.

"They will know that we want to be *alone.* It is time they
understood such things." Before she could issue another
word of protest, he swept her up in his arms and carried her
to the wagon. Pushing aside the curtains, he entered, laying
her down on the bed with a devilish smile. "You will not say
no to me again, Alicia." The sight and smell and touch of
her was intoxicating as his eyes feasted on her beauty. The
dark, silken strands of her hair tumbled about her, a glorious
shawl covering her shoulders as she stared up at him with
blazing green eyes.

"I have told you, Rafael . . ."

"And I have told *you.* You belong to me, Alicia, and I will
have you tonight." He met her heated gaze with his own
eyes steady. "I would have preferred that you not fight me,
that you would desire me as much as I desire you. But I will
not leave the wagon to sleep alone *tonight.*" His face had a
look of hunger, like a man relishing a feast, and she knew
that the time beneath the stars he had *not* made love to her
just so he could escape.

Still, remembering her vow, Alicia frantically sought her
escape. She was Gypsy. She was brave and yet she trembled

in fright, more afraid of her love for him than she had been of Stivo's whip.

"How can I let you touch me after what you did?" she breathed. "Death and destruction is what you brought to my people." Her eyes dared him to deny it.

"Death? Destruction?" It was as if she had reached out to slap him as the realization of her accusation struck him.

"The villagers and the others who swept down upon the caravan, killing so many . . . so many. Vashti. Poor Vashti." Closing her eyes, she seemed to be reliving that terrifying night.

"And you believe that I . . . My God! No wonder you said that you hated me." Turning his back on her, he shook his head. "It was not I, Alicia. Never would I do such a thing."

She wanted to believe him, yet her stubborn pride refused to let the matter rest so easily. "Then who did? How did the gorgios find us?"

"The two men who tried to kill me. They came back to find my body and must have spied your camp." Lashing out, he struck at the wooden wall as if at them. "The greedy bastards! I heard them talking when I came back to find you that night. Had I known what evil they would have brought, I would have killed them the moment I first saw them."

"You came back to find me?" Her voice was little more than a whisper. When he turned to face her she could see the truth of his words written in his eyes. "You came back?" she asked again.

"Yes, I came back. I was sick with grief and outrage. I feared you dead, and the thought nearly destroyed me." Slowly he moved toward her. "Oh, Alicia, Alicia. I would never have betrayed you in such a way. You must believe me."

She did believe him. No one at that moment could have doubted him. Swallowing convulsively, trying to keep from crying aloud, she opened her arms to him, her heart aching with love. Now it was she who offered comfort, comfort from the great wrong she had done in thinking the worst of him.

"I believe you, Rafael," she gasped, aware of the surge of desire that overtook her at the feel of her arms holding him so tightly. His body was strong, exuding a virility that drew her to him like the currents of a raging river. She could never hate him, even if he *had* been responsible for the tragedy. "Oh, Rafael, my love."

They clung to each other then as the full fury of their desire unleashed itself. She could feel his arousal beneath the tight-fitting pants that he wore, but this time his passion did not frighten her; instead, it stirred a sweet ache.

Slowly his hand cupped her breast, the thumb moving slowly, spreading fire with his touch. The peaks tingled, hardening at his feather-light caress. It was so wonderful to have him touch her again like this.

"Rafael."

His face was flushed, his eyes riveted to the soft mounds of her flesh. His breath was a gasp. How could he ever forget how very beautiful she was? How could he ever have thought of living his life without her? Letting his hands drift over the thin fabric of her blouse, he pushed it down, baring her breasts to his sight.

"My God," he swore hoarsely. At that moment all else in his life was forgotten. Juan, the painting, his mission. All. He wanted only to make love to her. To stay by her side forever.

Rafael's lips trapped Alicia's in a hungry, demanding kiss as she surrendered to him. This was what she wanted. She loved him. He had come back to find her after the raid on the camp. He had come back! As she returned his kiss her defenses crumbled and she succumbed to her own cravings, her own desires. His mouth kept hers a willing captive. The warmth and heat of his lips and tongue made her aware of how much she wanted him, hungered for him. There was no question of stopping him now, no thought of trying to escape the inevitable. She would worry no more about her pride. Tonight was for loving.

Worshipping her with his hands, Rafael slowly stripped off her blouse and outer skirt. There was a languid quality to his movements, as if he wanted to savor this magical moment. The inner skirts followed and lastly Alicia's undergarments. When she was completely naked, he let his eyes roam over her, caressing the flat stomach and rounded hips, the graceful curve of her waist that he remembered so well, the full softness of her breasts.

"You are beautiful, Alicia," he whispered.

Proudly she stood before him like some pagan goddess basking in the warmth of his heated gaze. When he reached out to touch her again, she could feel the tremor of his hands. Nervous. The gorgio was nervous? Why? Her eyes questioned him, knowing the answer long before he spoke.

"You have unleashed emotions in me I did not know I had. I'm a strong man and yet I am trembling like a child." He drew back his hand, staring at it in fascination. "You have put a spell on me, my beautiful sorceress."

"It is *o Del* who has worked the magic," Alicia whispered, longing for his touch again.

"I want this night to be beautiful for you, Alicia. I want you never to forget." Pulling her gently down upon the bed, he explored Alicia's body with the moist fire of his lips, intoxicating her with sensuous tenderness until she was writhing against him, wanting him with a blazing longing. For just a moment he left her to divest himself of his shirt and pants, and she watched him silhouetted by moonlight. His manhood stood erect and proud. What a magnificent man he was, all grace and strength, she thought. Her Rafael. Hers. Sleek and powerful with wide shoulders that tapered down to narrow hips, and long, powerful legs; the very sight of him stirred her.

Rafael was not unaware of her eyes caressing him, and it pleased him. Joining her on the bed, he took her hand and guided it to the strength of his manhood.

"Do you want to feel me inside you as much as I long to be there? Do you, Alicia?"

"Yes. Oh, yes." Her body arched up to his, seeking closer contact with his strength. Reaching out with impatient hands, she let her fingers explore him, the broad shoulders, the hard planes of his chest, and then down again to his manhood. "Love me. Love me now." The frantic desire for him was nearly unbearable as he covered her body with his own, stroking her, kissing her. His bare chest brushed the tips of her breasts, searing her with the heat of his passion. Warm, damp, and inviting, she welcomed him and he entered gently. Alicia locked her long, slender thighs about him, arching and surging against his thrust.

"Alicia!" His cry was like a benediction as he buried himself deep within her. She was tight and hot, like a sheath about his manhood, and he closed his eyes as delirious bursts of pleasure rippled through him. It was heaven here in her arms, as if she had been sent just for him. Their bodies were like a fusion of two stars, and he smiled as he thought about that time when she had told him that each Gypsy belonged to a star. She was all things to him at this moment—a nymph, a temptress, an angel—as fragile as a flower with the fire of that star.

Alicia moved with him, her body surging up against his sensuous rhythms, possessing him as he possessed her. There was nothing in the world but this man filling her, loving her. She wanted time to stand still, the earth to stop its spinning so that they could be entwined like this forever.

Like a sweet shaft of fire, pleasure streaked through them as green eyes met brown ones. Clinging to him, Alicia called out his name, burying her face in the warmth of his chest, breathing in the manly scent of him. How could she ever have thought to deny this ecstasy?

"You will never leave me now," she said softly, welcoming his lips as he kissed her gently.

Rafael gazed down upon her face, gently brushing back the tangled dark hair from her eyes. From this moment on she was his. How could he leave her? "And yet I must. I must." The thought was a torment to him, and for the moment he put it out of his mind. Gathering Alicia into his arms, he held her close as they drifted off into a deep and delicious sleep.

31

Rafael awoke as the first rays of the sun shone through the cracks of the canvas wagon-covering. He let his eyes feast on the beauty cradled in his arms. Her long lashes fanned out from her heavy closed eyelids, her thick mane of hair spread like a dark silken cloak over his chest and shoulders. He felt an aching tenderness. She looked so much younger, snuggling up against him in her sleep, and he wished with all his heart not to hurt her.

Leave. Always I am leaving you, little one. But it is a thing that cannot be helped. Until Spain is rid of Torquemada's treacherous power, I must do all that I can. . . .

As if sensing his thoughts, Alicia reached out in her sleep to touch him, smiling with contentment as her soft hand met the firmness of his chest.

What could he say to her? How could he find the words to make her understand what he must do? Memories of the passion they had shared quickened his pulse and he felt himself tighten with anger at himself and the world. He longed to shelter Alicia from every heartache, yet once again he was to be the instrument of her torment. And Stivo, what of him? His obsessive lust for Alicia would surely bring pain. How could he leave her alone with him? Rudolpho would watch over her, guarding her as he had before.

He should have been comforted, but instead he felt a sense of foreboding. A voice urged him to stay, to stay with the woman he loved. Reaching out, he stroked her hair, closing his eyes. He loved her; there could be no denying that now. Never had he realized that love could be like this, a shattering ecstasy that was almost pain. He wanted to stay with her, to protect her from every harm, but he could not. There would be no peace for them until his mission was completed, nor any rest for his soul.

"I love you, Alicia," he whispered. There was no denying that. Now he understood his father's all-consuming passion for a woman different from himself. Gypsy or Castilian, he would have loved Alicia. He did not care now that she was one of these wanderers, nor that her beliefs and customs were different from his own. How could he have been so foolish as to think any of that would matter where the heart was concerned?

Alicia shivered in her sleep, and he gathered her into his arms, the heat of his body warming hers until her trembling subsided. What would happen to her now, now that he had sparked this all-consuming flame? Would she be safe until he could return to her? Would she understand what he must do? Somehow he had to find the right words.

If only life were simpler, my love, he thought, *I would be content to roam the world as your Gypsy lover, your mate.* His eyes roamed the confines of the wagon, at the brightly colored blankets folded so neatly beside the bed, at the pans and casks that hung from the walls, proof of a nomadic way of life. The Gypsies had very few possessions, and yet somehow they were happier than many of the richest Spaniards. Without large haciendas, without riches or great wealth, they seemed less encumbered, free to be happy without the worry of losing that which tied a man down. Riches. Things. Inanimate objects. Perhaps they were far richer than the Spaniards realized. The very sky was their ceiling, the entire earth their bed, and laughter was the music that they sang.

He had been so wrong about them. Hadn't he, too, thought of them as thieves? Yet the Gypsies had a strict code of honor. Rafael had seen it firsthand as he traveled with them these past two days. They only took from the land to meet their most basic needs. Never were they greedy and never did they take anything that had not been given them by *o Del. O Del.* These were no heretics. *O Del* was just another name for God.

Alicia sensed the eyes looking down upon her, heard the steady breathing of the man lying next to her, and opened her eyes. So it had not been a dream after all.

"Rafael," she whispered, reaching up to touch his cheek, to assure herself that he was real and not some fabrication of her imagination.

"Good morning." Rafael's voice was husky, and Alicia flushed to remember the night they had spent making love. He knew every inch of her body, he had explored her with his hands and lips, and now she truly belonged to him.

"Rafael, I love you. I am happy to be your wife."

"Alicia . . ." He had to tell her now. To prolong the truth would only hurt her more.

Quickly she covered his lips with her fingers. "No. Just hold me. Love me." She wanted only to feel his hard, warm flesh against her, to love him again as she had last night. "I like your hands on my body, your lips on mine. Let us not waste precious time with words."

Pulling her to him, nuzzling the soft flesh of her throat, his hands moving over her body, he ignited the same sweet fires, enveloping her with his love.

"Rafael." She sighed and then there was only his caress, his kiss, flesh melting into flesh as lightning flashes of desire poured through their every vein.

When at last their passion was spent, they both drifted off to sleep, oblivious of the sounds of the stirring camp.

He will never leave me now. He loves me, Alicia thought, smiling as she closed her eyes. Snuggling into the warmth of his arms, she was content.

32

Rafael awoke later that morning to find himself alone. Hurrying to dress, he peered out of the wagon opening to see Alicia already about her chores, gathering wood for the breakfast fires. It had surprised Rafael that these people, who were accused of stealing chickens from time to time, did not eat eggs. They seemed to abhor them for some reason he did not understand, so he well knew there would be no eggs with green peppers this morning.

Ah, well. María's cooking had threatened to make him fat. He would make do. He smiled. If his culinary appetites were not being satisfied, his carnal appetites were. He was a contented man. Jumping down from the wagon, he made his way toward the horses with the intention of feeding them. Rudolpho had given him this task, and he suspected it was to test him. So far Rafael had not given in to the temptation to leave. He did not have to ask himself why. It was because of Alicia.

"So, you are still here," Stivo taunted. Stepping from behind a tree, the handsome dark-eyed Gypsy stared at Rafael as if memorizing his every feature.

"Of course I am still here. Did you think I would leave, knowing of your lust for Alicia?" Standing with his hands on his hips, Rafael stared the Gypsy down.

Stivo's snort of laughter was derisive. "It is only a matter of time." He sniffed the air disdainfully. "Gorgios are just like fish. After three days they *smell* bad." Clutching his nose with his fingers, he laughed again and walked off.

"Arrogant bastard!" Rafael swore. "Vain and self-centered ruffian. One would think you King of the Gypsies the way you strut around." Stivo ignored his words but someone else heard.

"My feelings exactly, Gorgio," purred a voice that Rafael recognized as belonging to Solis. Emerging from the bushes, she walked toward him with swaying hips and a provocative smile. Bending over as if to pick up some object from the ground, she offered him a good view of her full bosom.

Rafael smiled uneasily. Her feline manner and smoldering eyes might once have stirred him, but now that he had found Alicia he could never even think of bedding another, no matter how voluptuous her charms.

Reaching up to tug at the shoulder of her blouse, she looked coyly up at him. "There is a small pond nearby. Not as refreshing as the river, perhaps, but still it offers cool and clean water. Would you like to join me there for a swim?"

Shaking his head "no," Rafael sought to put as much distance between this vixen and himself as possible. He had heard whispers of her wantonness around the camp and knew that someday such a woman would bring her lover a knife between the shoulder blades. Her husband could not close his eyes to her behavior much longer.

Stumbling through the trees, Rafael had only one thought: to get away from this she-wolf before one of the Gypsies saw them together and came to the wrong conclusion. Now that he had won Alicia's heart again, he did not want a woman like Solis to come between them. Dodging in and out of the bushes, he heard the sound of horses' hooves and ran in that direction. If it was Todero out for his early-morning ride, he would seek his help in cooling this woman's ardor. Waving his arms about, he sought to get the riders' attention only to stand aghast as his eyes took in the details of the approaching horsemen. They were not Gypsies.

"Carlos. I do not believe it!" he whispered, torn between joy and alarm. Now he would be able to leave the Gypsy camp, and yet at this moment it was the last thing he wanted to do. He could not leave without talking to Alicia, promising her that he would return for her as soon as his mission was completed. Fool that he was, he should have said so many things to her this morning, but it was too late for regrets.

As the horses thundered down upon him Rafael saw to his alarm that the riders were well armed with swords and even a musket or two, that new weapon that brought death in its wake. Aiming their weapons at him, they rode forward, and Rafael suddenly remembered his Gypsy garb. Like the four horsemen of the apocalypse they came bringing death.

"Carlos! Carlos! It is I, Rafael!" His voice was lost in the echo of the hoofbeats. *My God, my own brother is going to kill me!* It was the last thought Rafael had before he felt the slicing pain of a blade and fell to the ground.

33

Rafael looked up with pain-glazed eyes. "Carlos!" The horror of recognition struck the attacking man.

"Merciful Cristo, my brother!" Pulling on the reins so violently that he was nearly thrown from his horse, Carlos waved his arms about frantically. "Stop! You fools, stop. This is no Gypsy, it is Rafael." Dismounting, he ran to his brother's side. "How badly are you wounded?"

"Just a flesh wound," Rafael gasped. "Yet painful nonetheless. I think God that you have never been an excellent swordsman, brother, or I should now be dead." Clinging to his arm, Rafael sought to stop the flow of blood. Only a few inches to the right would have meant his death.

Reaching out to tear the scarf from around his brother's neck to use as a tourniquet, Carlos eyed him skeptically. "What are you doing dressed like that?"

Rafael smiled despite his pain. "When traveling as a Gypsy one always dresses as a Gypsy. These are my wedding clothes, brother."

"Wedding clothes? Have you gone mad?" Touching his brother's head, he felt for a wound but found none. "What are you saying? This is no time for jests. We must get you out of here before we are discovered and are forced to fight."

"Fight? No. There will be no fight. Please, Carlos. Leave these people alone."

"Leave them alone? The thieving bastards, they abducted you; took you from my lands. Mine. Had I been able to raise more men, I would have shown them God's retribution!"

Rising up from where he lay on the ground, Rafael clutched at Carlos's shoulders. "No! No! Promise me that you will do them no harm. These are honorable people. If I was taken captive, it was partially my own fault."

"Your own fault? Now I know you must have hit your head. How could it be your fault? They tied you up like an animal. When Pepe told me, I swore vengeance. To think that a Spaniard, a Castilian, is not safe upon his own property!" Shrugging free from his brother's grasp, Carlos looked at Rafael in irritation. "You know what I think about Gypsies."

"You are wrong. We have both been wrong in judging them so harshly. I know. These last few days I have come to know them at least a little."

"Fine, fine, so you have misjudged them. I still say that they should be taught a lesson, but I will bow to your wishes." Pulling his brother to a standing position, Carlos gestured to one of the other men to bring the riderless horse for Rafael's use. "I brought Diablo."

Rafael hesitated. "Wait. I cannot leave yet, Carlos. There is someone I must see. I must say good-bye."

"Good-bye? You must say good-bye to a Gypsy?" At his brother's expression he suddenly understood. "A woman?"

"My Gypsy bride. It was to avenge her honor that I was abducted, and now I am a married man, brother. Could I leave without seeing her one last time?" Rafael winced in pain as he pushed past his brother's arms, but Carlos sought to block his way.

"I have come to take you home, and it is home I will take you now. Now! There is no time for amorous adventures. Do not blame me if my foul temper shows its wrath on these vagabonds you esteem so highly. It will be on your head if my men break a few heads. They have had a long, hard ride trying to track you down. I cannot tell them to calmly stand by while my brother tells some little Gypsy witch good-bye."

"My Gypsy wife."

"Bah! There were no words spoken before a priest. You and I both know that whatever ceremony they forced you to endure is not valid. The woman is your concubine, nothing more. Now, hurry. My patience is wearing thin." Mounting his horse, Carlos flashed a warning with his eyes.

"I cannot leave her without telling her why I go. I only ask you for a few moments, brother." Rafael eyed his brother warily, knowing firsthand the cruelty Carlos was capable of when crossed. Pride, it had always been Carlos's downfall. Before his men he would spit in the devil's eye to maintain his men's respect. "Please."

Before Carlos could reply, a rustle in the bushes caught his eye. Motioning for one of the others to investigate the noise, Carlos watched as the Spaniard beat the foliage with his sword, unleashing the screams of a terrified Solis, who ran from her hiding place and threw herself down upon the ground, groveling for mercy.

"Is this *your* Gypsy, Rafael?" Carlos asked with a snarl.

"No."

"Then she was eavesdropping. Yes?" Carlos's eyes met those of the terrified woman. "We will take her with us. She is a beauty, Pepe. You can take her for yourself."

"Leave her alone, Carlos. I will go with you." Reaching out to take Solis's hand, Rafael helped her to her feet. "Have no fear, I will not let them harm you."

"I . . . I . . . was just trying to find you. . . . am sorry . . . sorry. . . ."

"You have done nothing wrong, but you can do something very right. You can carry a message to Alicia for me. Will you do that, Solis? Please."

Solis's eyes were dilated with fear. Too recent in her mind was the raid on the Gypsy camp, the sight of Vashti cut down before her eyes. She would have promised this Castilian the moon had he asked for it.

"Yes . . . yes . . . I will do anything you ask."

Rafael searched her eyes, wondering if he could trust her. No matter that she had flirted with him, sought to bed him, she was one of Alicia's people and his only hope of getting a message to the woman he loved.

"Tell Alicia that I must go. I do not want any bloodshed on my conscience." He nodded with his head toward the horsemen. "I must leave and leave quickly. Tell her what has happened and that I will find her again. I will come back for her, do you understand?"

"Yes. Yes. I understand. You are leaving now but you will be back. I will tell her." She eyed his wound, wondering why he would leave with the very men who sought to strike him down. Gorgios were a strange lot. Turning, she began to walk away when Rafael reached out to touch her shoulder.

"Wait." As she turned around Rafael slipped a ring from his finger, a ring that had belonged to his mother, his most treasured possession. "Give this to Alicia. I want her to know that I *will* come back." Dropping it into Solis's hand, Rafael fought against his unmanly tears. *Alicia would wait for him. He would find her again. He must.*

Closing her fingers around the ring, Solis smiled. "I will give it to Alicia, on that you have my word." She watched as Rafael struggled to mount his horse, clutching his wounded arm. Only after they had ridden from sight did she return to the Gypsy camp. "So you want me to give this ring to your precious bride, do you, Gorgio?" Looking down at the golden ring, she spat upon it in anger. "You run from me as if my touch were poison, yet your eyes fill with tears at the thought of that skinny girl." Resentment and jealousy flooded through her as she remembered the look of disgust on his face in the forest. "High and mighty gorgio."

Solis's laughter rang through the air. *Alicia acts as if I were the dust beneath her feet, as if my need for a man's flesh were a disease. She*

walks about with her nose in the air as if she were a Gypsy queen while I
have heard whispers that she is not even a true Gypsy. Well, we shall see
about her pride when I am through with her. Solis thought.

Clutching at the ring, she paused for a moment, tempted to keep such a thing of beauty for herself, but another thought made her smile. "I will give your Alicia the ring, Gorgio," she whispered softly. "I have given a promise and it shall be kept." Picking up her long skirts, Solis ran to join the others.

34

The cackling of the hen and Alicia's swearing caused many an eye to turn in that direction. What on earth was Rudolpho's daughter trying to do?

"Fool hen, *o Beng*'s daughter!" The feathers tickled Alicia's hand. How did the gorgios get these stubborn fowls to cooperate? Perhaps pleading would help. "Please, chicka, please. Already it is time for breakfast and I must hurry." This time, when she put her hand beneath the hen, as if by a miracle she felt the warmth of a newly laid egg and held it aloft with pride.

It was thought that eggs, milk, and other slippery substances weakened one, so no Gypsy ever ate eggs. But Rafael had talked with such longing last night of an egg for breakfast, had spoken so glowingly of his brother's wife and her cooking skills, that Alicia was determined to prepare eggs for him. If it pleased him to have eggs, then eggs he would have. It would be her surprise.

Waiting patiently for the hen to lay another egg, Alicia gathered together onions, a slab of dried pork, and a clove of garlic. There were no green peppers in the camp and so these would have to do.

"I am glad that Keja stole you, chicka," Alicia said with a laugh as the hen produced yet another egg and she scooped it up in her hand. "Perhaps as your reward I will see that you do not find yourself in the cooking pot, eh?" Laughing, she shooed the chicken away to safety, then set about her task of preparing the eggs. So engrossed was she in her cooking that she did not hear Rudolpho come up behind her.

"Eggs, *Chavi*? Eggs?" he asked, throwing up his hands in mock horror.

"For my husband, Papa. These gorgios have strange eating habits, but I intend to humor him if it will make him happy. I only hope that it will not take away his strength, at least at night." Blushing, she smiled up at him, and he was soothed by the happiness he read in her eyes.

"Your husband has been good to you. I can read it in your face and I am pleased, Alicia."

"He is all that I ever hoped and dreamed for, Papa. I am the happiest of women. I love and am loved in turn." Stirring the eggs carefully, she cast him a loving glance. "I think you for bringing him to me, Papa. It is as always. You were most wise. What a Gypsy he will make."

For just a moment Rudolpho's smile faded as he remembered the gorgio's words, but the serenity in his daughter's face eased his fears. "A fine Gypsy. Yes. Yes. He seems to have a Gypsy's touch with the horses. I would not doubt that I will soon have him helping me with the healing." Looking about him, Rudolpho wondered just where his new son-in-law was. Surely he was finished with feeding and watering the horses by this time. Shrugging his shoulders, he supposed that Rafael was with Todero.

"Yes, Papa, soon," Alicia answered, warily taking a taste of the concoction she had prepared. She found it a rather tasty mixture and took another bite, laughing at the stern frown on Rudolpho's face. "Don't worry, Papa. It is Rafael who will become Gypsy, not I who will become gorgio, though I want to learn about my husband's customs and strange ways."

Rudolpho reached out to stroke her hair, remembering the first time he had set eyes upon the small green-eyed child.

Would she be happy among her own people? he wondered, tempted to tell her the truth now that she had found her love. He clucked his tongue, saying only, "You must not try to live between two worlds, *Chavi*. With one bottom you can not sit astride two horses."

Alicia tossed her thick mane of hair out of her eyes, squaring her shoulders with pride. "I am Gypsy, Papa. Always I will *be* Gypsy." Scraping the eggs into a wooden plate to rest beside thick slices of red apples, she smiled again. "Don't worry." With Rudolpho trailing along behind her she started toward the outskirts of the Gypsy camp in search of Rafael just as Solis ran between two wagons, nearly stumbling in her hurry to get back to camp. Alicia eyed her with curiosity and a bit of jealousy, knowing well what Solis was doing coming from the woods. Like a cat in heat, she had been after Rafael. Well, she would have no luck with him, she would see to that.

Balancing the plate of food in her hands, careful to avoid colliding with the Gypsy woman, Alicia scanned the horses anxiously for any sign of Rafael. Had he gone back to camp?

"You will not find him," purred a voice behind her. "He is gone."

"Gone?" Whirling around, Alicia nearly spilled the contents of the plate upon the ground.

"Yes. Gone." Solis toyed with the ring in her palm. It felt hard and hot between her fingers, and again she was tempted to keep it for herself but realized that it might be recognized by one of the others, that she might be accused of thievery and perhaps banished. Instead she held it forth. "He left this behind."

Before Alicia could utter a word, Rudolpho thrust forward. "Woman, what are you saying?" he demanded, his eyes blazing a warning.

Solis's voice was mocking. "The gorgio has left his Gypsy bride; gone off with those of his own kind."

"No!" Alicia's cry was a wail. "You are lying! He would

not leave me, not again. No." Dropping the plate to the ground, she was upon Solis in an instant, shaking her by the shoulders as her eyes pleaded with the other woman to deny the words she had just spoken. "Take back your words. Take them back. Your lies are as serpents to my ears." Only Rudolpho's intervention could separate the two.

"Silence!" His voice reverberated through the early-morning air. As the two women calmed themselves he nodded toward Solis. "You. First, you speak."

"The gorgio has left the camp. I was on my way to the pond for a bath when I saw the four men ride up and gesture to him. The gorgio was excited to see them, waving his arms about like a man possessed by demons." Solis licked her lips nervously. She was not actually telling a lie, she reasoned to herself.

"Perhaps they were his enemies," Alicia gasped, refusing to believe that after their night of love Rafael could once again abandon her. "Please, Papa. We must go after them. They might kill him."

"Kill him? I think not. Even gorgios do not kill their own brothers." Like a cat with a bird, Solis's eyes gleamed mischief. Once again she held forth the ring, smiling as she saw the look of pain that flitted across Alicia's face. "He left this . . . in payment for your, ah, favors. It is a gorgio custom, I am told, to pay for their women." As Alicia stared with horror, Solis held the ring forth, pulling it out of reach as Alicia reached out to touch it. "It is of purest gold and worth much money, so you have not come away empty-handed."

This time not even Rudolpho could hold back Alicia's fury. With a violent cry of outrage she sprang on Solis, pulling her hair, scratching her face, biting and kicking, as the Gypsy woman returned blow for blow.

"You liar. You wanted him for yourself and he shunned you. You stole his ring. And now you seek to taunt me." The two women rolled over and over on the ground as Rudolpho watched silently. Perhaps it was better to let them expel their bitterness and hatred, like poison. Alicia was a fighter; he had no doubt that she would be the victor. In this he was right. With her breasts heaving, her fingers trembling, Alicia held Solis to the ground. "Take back your lies, witch! Tell me the truth or I swear I will cut all the hair from your lying head. By my father's hand, I swear it!"

Knowing that Alicia might very well carry out her threat, Solis could not prove herself to be a liar now. "It is true. I swear he left, that he gave me the ring to give to you. On my father's grave I so swear!" Tears of pain filled her eyes as Alicia pulled at her hair. "I swear it, I swear it."

"Leave her be, Alicia. To swear upon one's father's grave is most serious. No Gypsy would so lie. Not even this one." Pulling Alicia to her feet, he cradled her in his arms. "He has left, *Chavi*. He has left. May *o Del* forgive him, for I cannot." Raising her hand, he motioned to Solis to get up. "Leave us, woman. What I have to say to my daughter is not for others' ears."

Rising to her feet, shaking off the dirt from her skirts, Solis trembled in anger and humiliation. Throwing the ring upon the ground, she stalked away, looking back only once, her eyes blazing hatred. "Mourn for your gorgio, Alicia. You will not see him again."

Oblivious of everything but her pain, Alicia sobbed her tears upon Rudolpho's strong chest, feeling as if the life-force within her had just died. "I loved him, Papa. I loved him. So much. Why did he leave me? Why? Why?"

"I do not know, *Chavi*, I do not know." Clenching his jaw in anger, Rudolpho vowed to soon find out. Rocking back and forth with Alicia in his arms, he was infinitely gentle as she vented her grief. Her wail was like a cry for one dead, and it broke his heart to see Alicia's pain. Anger at the gorgio rose up to choke him as he reached out for the ring, squeezing it in his fingers until it nearly bent with the pressure. "I will find him and learn the truth, of this I give you my word," he whispered, picking Alicia up in his arms. With long, slow strides he carried his daughter back to the Gypsy camp.

35

Like a wounded butterfly taking refuge in its cocoon, Alicia hid among the quilts in her wagon, shutting her eyes tightly to keep from crying. Burrowing her face into the softness of the blankets, Alicia fought against the thoughts that tortured her, only to be reminded of Rafael by the musky male scent of him that still lingered on the pillow. There was even more pain at Rafael's second betrayal, more heartache, because this time she had been so certain of his love. She had opened her heart so completely. The vivid memory of his caress, his passion, was forever branded on her heart and in her soul. Why had she been so trusting? Why had she believed that he would stay by her side and eventually become adopted into the tribe? "Oh, Rafael," she gasped, stifling her sobs with the pillow.

The brutality of Solis's words came back to haunt her. She knew the scheming Gypsy woman capable of any misdeed, any lie. But no Gypsy would swear by his father's grave unless what he said was true. No Gypsy, not even Solis. And Rafael *was* gone.

And the ring! To think that he had given it to Solis to give to her. Had she not seen it with her very own eyes, she would never have believed it. It was not Rafael's way to be so unfeeling, to deliberately break her heart. She did not want to believe that he had left the ring "in payment for her favors," as Solis had so crudely stated. Perhaps he had left the ring in an effort to atone for leaving her, yet even that thought could not comfort her. Did he pity her, knowing he could not return her love with the same intensity? Had he felt obligated to leave her a token of their time together? Pity! How dare that gorgio feel pity for her. Anger coiled within her like a viper at the very thought of such an insult. She was a Gypsy, she was a Rom, Rudolpho's daughter, not some creature to feel sorry for! She could accept any emotion, even hatred, but never pity.

Bolting out of the bed, clenching her fists so tightly that her fingernails cut into her flesh, Alicia stalked out of the wagon. She ignored the stares of the other Gypsies who looked at her curiously, wondering at Rudolpho's rage when he had ridden out of camp with Todero beside him. Let them wag their tongues with their suppositions.

With her nose tilted in the air, Alicia vowed to maintain her pride. They would never know that the gorgio had torn her heart out and taken it with him. To her dying day she would insist that she was glad that he was gone, this husband who had been forced upon her. Splashing cold water from a jug upon her tear-streaked face, she forced a smile upon her lips and went about her daily chores. Life would go on without him; she would soon prove that to the other Gypsies and to herself as well.

Scouring the cooking pots to make ready for the midday meal, Alicia was distracted by the sounds of childish laughter and looked up to find Mala and Palo playing in the tall grass. Mala was strong for her age, a tomboy much as Alicia had been at the same age. Alicia watched in interest as the two children wrestled, but when Palo pinned his sister beneath him, demanding that she cry out and admit him the winner, Alicia interceded, knowing that Mala would never admit defeat and might be injured.

"Let her up, Nanosh! Now," Alicia demanded, managing to look very stern and reproachful as she towered over the two, her green eyes flashing a warning. As she reached down to help Mala up, Palo scampered away.

"I should have beat him. I should have, Alicia," Mala confided with a pout. "I am quicker than he and much smarter. It is just that he is stronger than I am. Oh, how I wish for just one day I could be a boy. I would show him. I would show them all. I get so tired of all their airs, so superior just because they are males."

In spite of her grief Alicia smiled. It was as if she were seeing herself again in this child. Drawing the girl into her arms, she hugged her tightly. "It is just that we women are playing a game, Mala. A game that you will soon learn. You see, we only let the men and boys think they are stronger because we know the truth, that we are not only stronger but wiser as well. They need our guidance, but their pride would forbid their admitting it. So for the good of the tribe we pretend. You have heard Rudolpho say 'A wagon will hold more people when there is peace among us.' It is true, Mala. It is true."

The child's eyes widened in surprise. "A game?"

"A game. We would not want to injure their manly egos, now, would we? Instead we just wink at each other, we women, and know the truth in our hearts."

"And Rudolpho. Is he not wise?"

Alicia thought hard for a moment. It was important that the child respect the leader of the tribe. "Rudolpho is different. He is leader and therefore wiser than all of us. He is the wisest human being I have ever known and the strongest."

"And Rafael?" The child's eyes swept the camp as if to search for him.

"We will speak no more of the gorgio!" Alicia said sharply, bitterness suddenly sweeping over her. "He is gone. Never to return."

"Gone?" Mala's eyes darted to and fro as if to put to lie Alicia's words. "But I liked him. Why has he gone?"

"Rafael gone?" Palo's voice echoed his sister's as he crept up behind them.

"Yes, gone. He has returned to his own kind." There was a long moment of silence as each child digested this unexpected news. At last Palo, who was more than just a little jealous of the gorgio, tugged at Alicia's hand.

"Does that mean, then, that we may sleep in your wagon again?" At Alicia's nod a smile curled his lips. "Then I am glad he has gone."

Thrusting back her small shoulders, standing tall, nearly eye to eye with her brother, Mala's eyes flashed anger. "Well, I'm not. I liked him. And that . . . that is a terrible thing to say." For just a moment the two children glared at each other as another fight threatened to break out; but before another word could be spoken, Alicia heard a wailing sound and the thud of horses' hooves. Turning around, she gave a shriek of alarm as she saw Todero riding into camp, pulling behind him Rudolpho's horse with the Gypsy leader's body slung over its back. The keening wail of the women rose again, like a tide in its intensity as the horses passed by them.

"Rudolpho! Papa! My Papa!" Ignoring the others, Alicia threw herself on the still form of her father.

36

"What happened, Todero?" Alicia asked at last as she raised her tear-streaked face to the Gypsy man who was her friend. "Is . . . is he dead?"

"He is *not* dead. Not yet," Todero answered gently. "We did not even meet your husband. Before we were far from camp Rudolpho collapsed. I fear it is his heart, Alicia. He was so angry, so anxious to find your gorgio. He . . . he . . . just clutched at his chest and . . . and doubled over in pain. Then he spoke to me no more."

"Get him to the wagon. Quickly." Four Gypsy men hastened to do as she asked, carrying Rudolpho to Alicia's wagon and depositing him gently on the bed. Bowing their heads in reverence, they left Alicia alone with her father. "You will not die, Papa. You will not. You will not!" she whispered frantically, fighting against her fear. He had recovered before and he would again. And yet his face was so pale, his hands so still. Taking his wrist in her hand, she felt his pulse, so faint, as if he already were half dead.

Tearing open the wagon canvas, Alicia shouted out for Zuba to bring her some cayenne, some red pepper. Rudolpho needed a stimulant to start his heart beating strongly again. Administering to him gently, fighting her fear, Alicia closed her eyes to prayer. She couldn't lose Rudolpho. *O Del* would never be so cruel.

"I will do anything you ask of me, only spare my papa,"

she whispered, trembling as she took Rudolpho's hand in
hers.

Alicia was by her father's side all through the day and
into the night as he struggled to live. She soothed him as
best she could, administering her herbs and stroking his face
with her fingers, all the while torturing herself with blame
for what had happened. If only she had never given her
virtue to the gorgio, then Rudolpho would not have gone
out riding to bring Rafael back and all would have been
well.

"Always you think of my happiness, Papa. Always. I love
you so." Outside the wagon she could hear the weeping,
rising and falling like a stormy sea. Already they were
mourning him. Alicia froze as a terrible sense of inevitability
swept over her, but she fought against such feelings with
fierce determination. "No. No. You will not die, Papa, you
will not die." Taking his large hand between her two smaller
ones, she looked down at his face as if willing him to live.
"Please, Papa."

"Alicia." The word was barely more than a whisper, yet,
as if hearing her words, Rudolpho opened his eyes, eyes
mirrored by pain. "Must . . . must . . . tell you . . . before . . . I . . . before . . . I die."

"You will not die!"

"Yes. Already . . . soul . . . bidding me good-bye."
Wincing with pain, he reached out to her. "But . . . must
. . . must tell you . . . before I leave this earth. You . . .
you must know."

"Don't try to talk, Papa. You must save your strength."

"No . . . must tell you. You are not . . . not . . ." A
spasm of coughing interrupted him, and Alicia hurried to
force an herbal drink to his lips. The warmth of the brew
stilled his coughing and seemed to give him strength. "I
could not have . . . loved you more if you . . . you were
the child of my loins."

His words struck Alicia like a fist. "What are you saying, Papa?"

He struggled to sit up but fell back down, writhing in pain. "You are not . . . not who you think you are, Alicia."

Closing her eyes, Alicia knew deep in the fiber of her being what he was trying to tell her. Hadn't she somehow sensed that she was different from the others by the way they looked at her at times? Was that why they had allowed her to marry the gorgio? "No. No. I am Gypsy." And yet that dream. Who was the woman in her dreams? Bending down, only inches away from Rudolpho, she asked, "Are you . . . are you trying to tell me that I am not your flesh-and-blood child?" Before he could answer she went on. "If so, let me tell you that if love binds the heart, then you and I are tied together more surely than if I were truly the fruit of your seed."

He reached out again for her, cradling her small hand between his two large callused ones, fighting against the agony that stabbed through him. "You make it easy for me, child. I have dreaded this day for so long. But now that I am dying it is not right that I keep it from you. When I am gone . . ."

"You will not die!" Alicia's voice was a wail as she fought against her tears. She must be strong, for Rudolpho.

"We all die. I, sooner than I had wanted. No one lives forever, Alicia. I go to meet my maker." He paused for a moment, collecting his strength, then blurted it out. "You are not Gypsy."

"Not Gypsy?" Her voice had a mournful sound as pain exploded in her heart. "Not Gypsy?" The truth she had always feared had been spoken.

He related as best he could the story of how she had come to him then, leaving out only the details of the hatred in the cold gray eyes of the woman who had sought to rid herself of a wide-eyed child. He spoke of the prediction his grandmother had foreseen, that the dark-haired girl would one day save them from a grave danger, clutching her hand as he spoke.

"I should have told you, but . . . but I feared losing you, Alicia. I should have let you go away with your gorgio to join your own people, but I . . . I . . . am a selfish old man and I could not . . . could not bear losing you. Forgive me."

"Forgive you? There is nothing to forgive." Alicia's eyes misted with tears, tears that she could fight against no longer. "You gave me all the love in the world, Papa. I was proud to be your daughter. I am still proud. I *am* your child. I am Gypsy. Here, Papa. Here." Touching her heart with her hand, she emphasized her words.

Rudolpho smiled. "Yes. In your heart you *are* Gypsy. All passion and fire. But you must acknowledge in your mind that you are gorgio, Alicia. León. Remember that word. It is there that I found you and there that you must return someday."

"Gorgio!" Alicia spat the word out as if it were poison. "I am Gypsy and will be one until the day that I die."

"No . . . no . . . remember. I tell you this . . . not . . . not to hurt you, but so that one day you may try to find your people. León. Remember, Alicia. León. It is there that your roots lie."

Too stunned to speak, remembering all the vows within the tribe to keep the Romany blood pure, Alicia was silent, mourning in her heart the death of her dreams.

"Take me outside," Rudolpho said after a long silence, bringing her back to reality again.

"What?"

"Take me outside. I am dying now. Please." Rudolpho's face was as white as the linen he lay upon. Clearly the strain of the moment had taken a toll on his heart, draining what little energy he had possessed. Now it was obvious that he was indeed dying. Alicia could hide the truth from herself no longer.

"I will have the others take you outside, Papa." Opening the canvas once again, she motioned for Todero and two others. "My father . . . my father wishes to be taken out into the open." It was Gypsy custom to avoid meeting death in an enclosed space, and she would not go against such custom now. Though her heart ached to believe that Rudolpho was *not* dying, she knew the truth.

Bowing her head, she led the small procession that took Rudolpho to his final resting place as the others wailed their grief. Howling and tearing at their hair, gnashing their teeth in a show of sorrow, the Gypsies paid their last respects to the man they had come to love and respect. Parading past their tribal leader as he lay nearly motionless on a thick quilt beneath a gnarled old tree, they begged his forgiveness in true Gypsy fashion for any wrong they might have done him, and he in turn whispered that he forgave them.

"May *o Del* forgive you too." As they squatted beside him, he asked them to forgive him any wrongdoing, for it was not good for a Rom to leave this world and go to the next without having settled his debts and unburdened his conscience.

Long into the night the ceremony continued. They drank wine and told stories of Rudolpho's courage and wise leadership as they shared their grief. The night was endless, but no one slept, and then shortly before daybreak, uttering one last word, "Alicia," Rudolpho died, leaving one world to enter yet another beyond earthly understanding.

Bereaved, more lonely than she had ever been in her life, Alicia bade him a final good-bye. No more would she hear Rudolpho call her *Chavi*, nor warm to his smile. He was gone. Gone. Throwing herself upon his lifeless body, she sobbed out his name, clinging to him fiercely as if somehow to keep him in *this* world, until strong hands lifted her away.

37

Rudolpho's funeral had all the dignity that befitted a Gypsy leader. Dressed in all his finery, he looked much as he had in life. His eyes were closed as if now he were only peacefully asleep; his hands were covered with his rings, and bracelets adorned his arms. The whip, symbol of Gypsy manhood, was near him, as well as all his earthly possessions. Like his body, they would be burned. The Gypsies did not believe in keeping anything that had belonged to the dead.

The open coffin, built by Todero, now rested in Rudolpho's wagon. The canvas covering had been torn off so that all could view the body. Alicia, who had used the wagon as her own these past few years, now found herself homeless. It was to be Rudolpho's funeral pyre. As the mourners filed by, moaning and saying their final good-byes, the flames of the seven tall candles around the body fluttered in the breeze as if reflecting Rudolpho's final breath before he left the world of the living forever.

Alicia sat at her father's feet, weeping softly and rocking back and forth as she mourned. She had lived through the days following his death lost to the realities around her, numb to the words of others, knowing only her own pain, intoxicated by her sorrow.

"Oh, Papa. Papa," she gasped, finally opening her eyes to watch the mourners show their respect. The Gypsies circled the coffin, clinging to each other for strength and comfort. They had all loved this gentle giant who had led them with wisdom and love. Now he was gone.

"Rudolpho, we leave you to *o Del,* to God," they intoned, throwing gold coins onto the body as a final offering. They were a haggard group, for strict rules of mourning declared that the men not shave, the women not comb their hair, and many a garment had been shred to show the depths of their sorrow.

The soft, mournful melody of a violin and guitar sounded through the early morning mist, merging with the voices of Rudolpho's people. Faces shone wet with tears, and now and again the stillness was shattered by the wail of an uninhibited mourner.

For three days Alicia had neither slept nor eaten as she kept vigil over Rudolpho's body. Only a few swallows of water had passed her lips, and now she felt weak and lightheaded. As if sensing her weakness, Todero reached out an arm to comfort her, whispering words of solace. Alicia tried to smile at him, but her face felt frozen in a perpetual grimace of grief, and she wondered if she would ever smile again.

"Thank you for all you have done, Todero," she finally managed to say.

"Take this. It will bring you good luck," he answered, pressing into her hands a piece of the ribbon he had used to measure the coffin. Cut into short pieces and tied in a knot, the ribbon was thought to have magical properties and was called *mulengi dori,* or deadman's string. Carried on a person at all times, it could be used, but only once, to give aid to one who had been imprisoned or was in danger. As she took his gift, Alicia was unaware that one day she would call upon its magic to save another's life. "When you have used it, dispose of it. Fling it into flowing water."

"Yes. Yes, I will," she whispered quickly, joining in the chants and lamentation before Stivo stepped forward with a lighted torch. At the sight of the flames, Alicia's eyes grew crazed. "No! No! They will hurt him, burn him!" Only Todero's strong arm kept her from rushing forward.

"Rudolpho is dead, Alicia. You must accept that. You cannot keep him from leaving this world now. He belongs to *o Del.* You are Gypsy. You must be strong."

"Gypsy." Hanging her head she gave vent to her tears. Gypsy. No, she was not. She was not a Rom after all. What was she then? Not gorgio. Not Gypsy. Nothing. She was nothing at all. It was as if the flames that consumed Rudolpho consumed her as well. "Good-bye, Papa. I will never forget you. Never."

Tightening his hold on her, Todero sought to draw her away, but Alicia stood firm. "Come away, Alicia."

"No. I must stay," she sobbed, looking into his eyes. Like her own, they were bloodshot from constant crying, and she reached out to brush a tear from the corner of his left eye. "But thank you for your kindness. You have always been my friend, Todero, you and Zuba. I thank you for that."

The heat of the flames seared her skin, the smoke made her lungs feel as if they would surely burst, and yet Alicia stood watching the burning pyre, saying her final farewell to her father. At last there was nothing left but ashes. Nothing remained of Rudolpho except the memory of his kindness and his love. Only then did Alicia turn around to find that she was alone. The others had returned to the campsite, where a feast for the dead would be prepared. For the next several days no drinking, singing, or rejoicing would be allowed. All mirrors had been covered, all vessels containing water had been emptied and would now be filled. In six more days life would slowly return to normal, for the period of mourning would vary depending on degree of kinship and friendship with the deceased. Yet Alicia was certain that her life would never be the same, her mourning never ended. A light had been taken from her world, a star from her sky.

Walking back to join the others, she wondered how she would live without Rudolpho's love. That a new tribal leader must be chosen barely entered her consciousness. Rudolpho had always been their leader since she could remember, and somehow it seemed that even in death he would still lead them. And yet she heard the voices of the men declaring that it must be done soon. They could not go on for long without a strong hand and voice to guide them.

"Todero. He is wise."

"Manolo. He is the oldest."

"Stivo. He is the son of the *phuri dai.*"

Stivo. Alicia shuddered, forgetting for only a moment her pain. No. They could not chose Stivo. No matter if he were the son of the earth goddess herself, he was no Gypsy leader. Surely they could see that. Cruelty did not prove strength nor sharp words wisdom.

"Stivo. My son should be your new leader." The voice was Jana's, the *phuri dai.* The old woman stood erect, her deeply lined face stern with determination, her silvered black hair blowing in the breeze. She looked awesome, like some ancient priestess, as she pointed a finger at them, her eyes unblinking as she demanded her way. Those eyes reminded Alicia of a reptile, and she shuddered. So distant and cold, those eyes had always stared at Alicia with malice and they did so now as the woman smiled. "I have had a vision, a dream. My son is the only one who can give us guidance. He will make us strong again, strong to oppose this Christian demon we know as Torquemada. Stivo. Stivo must be the one."

It was as if she had cast a spell. "The witch!" Alicia muttered beneath her breath. "My father's ashes are not yet cold, and already she seeks to replace him."

Opening her mouth to speak, to protest, Alicia found to her horror that her voice was lost in the cry that now came forth. "Stivo. Stivo. Stivo."

Running to the open field, assembling in unruly manner,

the Gypsies lifted Stivo up three times in the air amid loud acclamation. Stivo, the man who had shown Alicia no kindness, who had threatened her more than once and promised to possess her body one day, was now their leader.

38

Miles away from the Gypsy caravan Rafael de Villasandro stood before the black-garbed priest, a smile frozen upon his lips. In his hand he held the painting of Mary and her blessed son, an offering that would ransom many lives.

"And yet my own life is forfeit," he whispered, thinking once again, as he had for many days, about Alicia. Had Solis given the message? Would she wait for him until this bloody business was over and he could return for her?

"What did you say, my dear friend?" Juan Dorado asked, his eyes scrutinizing the painting, his tongue flicking across his lips as if he would devour the canvas.

"I was only thinking aloud," Rafael answered quickly. He must never let this man look into his heart.

"About your ordeal with the Gypsies?" Before Rafael could answer, the priest rattled on. "Heathen scum, all of them. To think that they abducted a *Christian* gentleman from his own abode! Your brother told me the entire story, and I must tell you that I was shocked."

"They didn't . . ."

The priest put up a hand in annoyance. "Say no more about it. I'm sure it is a thing you will want to forget. But let me promise you that one day I will see Castile, León, and Aragón rid of the vile heretics just as surely as we will rid ourselves of the *Conversos*. Of that you have my promise." Standing before the flickering flames of the candles, he looked like the devil himself as he scowled in anger, and for just a moment Rafael was filled with an all-consuming fear. This creature, priest or not, was evil, his soul twisted with hatred.

Putting a tight rein on his thoughts and feelings, Rafael thrust the painting forward. "Here, father. Take it. It is yours, as I promised." He had the urge to reach out and take hold of this man who claimed to do the will of God, to shake him until his teeth rattled, to tell him that it was he who was the heretic, not the Jews, the *Conversos*, or the Gypsies, but he wisely held his temper. Someday he would tell this man what he truly thought of him, but not now.

Caressing the canvas as a man might a lover, Juan Dorado relished his treasure. "Come, we must find a place of honor for it."

The radiant hues from the stained-glass windows illuminated the two men as they wound through the corridors, but the intricate designs and beauty of the windows were lost on Rafael. How could one think of beauty in the company of a man with a heart of stone whose only thought was to reach out his hand and bring death to so many?

At last they came to a small alcove lit by seven flickering candles. It was here that Juan Dorado had decided to hang his masterpiece, high above a tiny altar. "Here. Here. It is perfect, no?"

"Yes," Rafael answered, watching as the man went about his task with fanatical zeal. Rafael did not offer his help, instead he stood back and watched as the priest hung the painting, laughing all the while as if at some private joke.

"She will watch over all pious Christians from her lofty place of honor, and give her judgment on those who are enemies of the Lord, her son, for all eternity." Making the sign of the cross, Father Dorado bowed his head, then stepped back to take Rafael by the arm.

Looking up at the painting, it seemed to Rafael as if the smile of the Virgin were mocking Juan Dorado, as if she could look into his heart and soul and find him wanting. *It is he who is the enemy of our blessed Lord,* Rafael thought, choking at the thick incense that wafted to his nostrils as a breeze blew through a broken pane of glass, stirring the air of the church. It took every ounce of his strength to play upon this man's vanity and desire for friendship without betraying his disgust. And yet he felt disgust for himself as well. *Oh, Alicia, Alicia.* Looking up at the painting, his eyes widened in surprise as he envisioned her face looking down at him, her eyes, her smile. Alicia. Was she safe? Did Rudolpho watch over her even now as she went about her morning chores? And Stivo. Stivo. Thinking about the Gypsy braggart made Rafael clench his fists in wrath. If he touched one hair on Alicia's head . . .

"Are you all right? Shall we go outside? Rafael, my son, what is it?" Father Dorado touched Rafael's arm with genuine concern, belying the coldness of his heart.

"It is nothing. I just felt ill for a moment. Yes, let us go outside."

The air was crisp and fragrant outside the church, and Rafael was reminded of the early mornings he had spent with Alicia. Too often noblemen slept the early mornings away, but a flashing-eyed Gypsy girl had taught him that the riches of the earth were not to be found in gold but in more simple treasures. Alicia. She had given him so much. Would he ever be able to repay her?

"Forgive me if I say so, but, Señor de Villasandro, you do not seem to be listening to me. Something is wrong. What is it? You can tell me." Juan Dorado's voice had taken on a cold tone, and Rafael was all too aware that his musings were endangering all that he sought to accomplish.

"I am not content to be an olive farmer, to spend my days tending to my brother's olive groves," Rafael said quickly, hoping his lie would not be too obvious. He fully expected the priest to chastise him, but instead the frown on the father's face turned to a look of amusement.

"You are just as I was a few years ago. I am constantly amazed at how alike we are, you and I." Tugging at the sleeve of his black robe, he laughed. "I, too, have a brother. I understand how you feel. I, too, had to make my own way, but now it is I and not my elder sibling who is the powerful one. If you do as I tell you, if you give me your loyalty, I can make you powerful too. Then—no more olive groves."

"Loyalty?" Rafael took a step forward, trembling as he sensed that somehow, even with his bumbling, he was about to win the game after all. "Tell me what I must do."

From somewhere in the distance a drumroll sounded, a gruesome tolling for some poor soul who was about to lose his life. Would it be by hanging or burning? Juan Dorado seemed not to notice, yet as he spoke, the sound of the drum seemed to echo his words with a foreboding staccato.

"I have need of eyes and ears to aid me in finding our enemies, those who pretend to be good Christians but who, in fact, are Jews at heart, still practicing their heresies while secretly worshipping their God. I want you to inform me regarding these people."

"To spy for you?" Rafael could not help the scathing tone as he spoke.

The priest laughed. "Yes, that is exactly what I want you to do. I will arrange for the executions once I have the evidence needed to rid the country of such vermin. It will also be up to you to see that these heretics do not escape." As if fearing that they might be overheard, Juan Dorado lowered his voice to a whisper. "You are to leave tomorrow morning for León."

"León?"

"To be a guest of my father, or rather my stepfather, Philip Navarro. You see, I fear that my father has grown soft and foolish with age. Perhaps he is even sympathetic toward Jews. I need someone in León who feels as I do. I need *you*. Will you go?"

Rafael thought of Alicia. León was so far away. He

wanted to refuse, to turn his back on Castile and return to the soft arms of the woman he loved, but how could he when he might be able to save so many from the fires?

"I will be happy to go to León," he answered, forcing a smile. "No more olive groves, eh, father?"

"No more olive groves, my son. And for your loyalty, God will reward you." Raising his eyes toward the heavens, it was as if the priest expected God to add his voice with an "amen." "Tomorrow. Leave everything to me. It will all be arranged." Turning his back upon Rafael, he walked back into the church no doubt feeling as if he had won a great victory.

"Forgive me, Alicia. Forgive me," Rafael whispered. "May your *Del*, and my God as well, watch over you until I return."

39

A thundering rainstorm threw down its great tears from the heavens as if in mourning for Rudolpho's death as the caravan rolled along. The wagons formed a single file along the muddy road, struggling against the downpour. Women, children, and old ones, those men who were past their prime, were given the shelter of the wagons. All women— except for Alicia. As if to torment her, Stivo had ordered that she ride beside him.

It was not only damp but humid, and Alicia's clothing clung to her as she shivered against the cool morning air. She was tired and miserable, but as she glanced at Stivo out of the corner of her eye, she knew that she would receive no sympathy. Now he was leader and there was no one who would stand up to him, except perhaps Todero. Loyal Todero. But Alicia could not allow the gentle Gypsy to endanger himself for her, and so she suffered her misery in silence.

At last the wagons were forced to stop, as several became stuck in the mud, their high wheels half hidden by the dark brown ooze. Alicia welcomed the respite, reaching a hand behind her to rub her aching behind. This was the first time she had ever ridden so long or so far.

"Get down!" Stivo's order startled her.

"Get down?"

"I will not allow idleness, woman. You are strong. You

think yourself the equal of any man. I therefore tell you to prove your strength by giving the men a hand with the wheels." A cruel grin spread across Stivo's handsome face. "Down!"

"Bastard!" Alicia swore under her breath, sliding from her horse. She had suffered just about all she was going to by this man's hand. Wading ankle-deep in mud, slipping and sliding, she made her way to the entrapped wagon. Already the men had put sturdy poles through the wooden spokes of the wheels and were attempting to lift the wagon out of the mud. Alicia lent her weight to their efforts, pushing with all her strength. Ignoring the rain and mud that splashed in her face, Alicia felt a sense of elation as the wheel was pulled free. Laughing in triumph, she felt as if she had bested Stivo, but as she looked his way she could see the flash of his dark eyes and knew that her pleasure only angered him more.

Coming to her side, pulling her roughly down in the mud with him, it was Stivo who laughed evilly as he groped for her breast. "Fight. Fight, Alicia. It will do you no good. I will wait no longer. Tonight when we make camp you will be mine. I will take you any time I wish, and there will be no Rudolpho to stop me this time."

"Never! I will fight you with every breath, with every beat of my heart." Reaching up, Alicia sought to scratch his face, but he was too fast for her. Grabbing her hands, he held her captive.

"Fight me, I do not care. I do not want your heart, Alicia, only your body." Grinding his mouth into hers, he kissed her brutally as if to give her a sample of what awaited her.

Loathing his touch with every fiber of her being, Alicia bit down upon his hated mouth.

"Bitch!" he swore, loosening his hold and reaching a hand to his mouth to wipe away the blood. "Don't you know that I can have you banished. I am tribal leader, son of the *phuri dai.*"

"You cannot have me banished, I have done no wrong. You are no king, Stivo. You must still obey Gypsy law."

Mocking laughter answered her. "I will find a reason to have you banished. Being gorgio is reason enough."

"Gorgio?"

"Didn't you know?"

Alicia trembled. Stivo had the weapon with which to wound her, and well he knew her fear. "I knew. Rudolpho told me. But how did you know?"

"My mother has always known. After Rudolpho died she confirmed my suspicions. Gorgio. Little *gorgio* bitch!" His hands tugged at the neck of her blouse, pulling it from her breasts to expose the soft flesh there. Alicia's hands trembled violently as she reached up to slide it back upon her shoulders. Tilting her head back proudly, she defied him with her blazing eyes.

"I am more Gypsy than you will ever be, Stivo. I have honor, which is something you do not have. You thirst only for power and your own selfish desires." As he reached for her again she spat full in his face.

"I will kill you. Kill you for that!" Stivo swore between clenched teeth. He shook her violently. "No. I will not kill you, but time and time again you will wish you could die. Do you hear me, bitch? You will wish you could die." Pushing himself up out of the mud, wiping himself off, his eyes burning her like a brand, he glared at her. At last he walked away, leaving Alicia to stare after his retreating form.

He will do what he threatens and I will be powerless to stop him. If I cry out, he will harm those who come to my aid. Stivo is ruthless and now there is no one to stop him. They all fear him, fear his mother and her powers. What am I to do? Del, tell me, what am I to do? Closing her eyes on her thoughts, she said a silent prayer for guidance, opening them again as a word came to her mind. *León. León.* Rudolpho had told her that it was there she would find her roots. Had he foreseen this very day?

Alicia could hear the rain drumming on the wagons and

the sound of the children's cries as they huddled together against the chill of the weather. Could she leave her people? Did she have the courage to face the unknown? Stivo turned around, his face set in a taunting smile, and in that moment her question was answered. She could not stay a moment longer. She would leave the caravan. It was a thing that she had to do. It was a matter of survival.

But she must not be seen leaving. She would travel over the countryside alone! The thought was terrifying, and yet as Alicia mounted her horse she had only one desire, to arrive safely at her destination. León.

As she tensely awaited her chance Alicia's opportunity came as the whistle sounded, signaling the wagons to start up again. As the caravan plodded through the torrential rain, pitching and swaying, Alicia silently said her good-byes to those she had always known. Her people. Yes, they were her people. Gypsy or not, she had belonged to them.

Good-bye, Todero. I will miss you, Zuba. Before she could change her mind, Alicia nudged her horse onward, racing with the howling wind in the direction she hoped would take her to León.

40

Urging Grai onward, Alicia rode until the insides of her legs were chafed and bleeding, until her bottom ached and her eyes burned from the wind and rain. Past all logic, she was driven only by the fear that Stivo would follow her, that he would take her back to the camp and make true his threats. If only she could put as much distance as possible between them, if only she could reach León, then she would be safe. Somehow she would survive and start a new life in the lands to the north.

Looking back many times to make certain that she was not followed, Alicia pushed on until at last she was too exhausted to go farther. Sliding from her horse, collapsing on the ground, she crawled to a hiding place between two rocks and slept a sleep so deep that any who might have come upon her would have thought her dead. It was a dreamless sleep, which soothed her troubled mind and mended her bruised body. When at last she awoke it was still night, and she opened her eyes to the bright orange glow of the moon. The Gypsies regarded the moon as a mysterious power affecting their lives, and Alicia found the glowing orb a good omen.

"The mother of heaven coming over the horizon to feed her chickens," she whispered, remembering a story Rudolpho had told her so many times when she was but a child. Her eyes misted with tears at the reminder of her loss.

Slowly, she brushed off her skirt and got to her feet. He had been so good to her and now he was gone and she was alone.

Alone. The word tortured her, for always before she had known the security and love of the Gypsy band. It was so much easier to face hardship when you were with those who shared your hopes and dreams. But alone she felt her courage melting away, and she began to wonder at the wisdom of her flight. Doubts flooded her mind as she thought of what she had done. There was the danger of wild animals in this wilderness. Reaching for the knife she carried concealed in her skirt, she touched the cold blade and winced at the thought of having to defend herself from the strong jaws of a beast of prey. And there were dangers greater than the wild beasts. This rough terrain had been the death of many a man who had ventured too far from his own kind.

"I will go back." As soon as the words were past her lips she shook her head violently. No. She could not go back. Stivo. She would never let him touch her. Rudolpho had, told her the truth of her birth because he knew that she must find her own destiny. She would reach León or die trying. "This I vow."

Ignoring the sounds of the night, steeling her courage, Alicia climbed on Grai's back and set his head firmly in the direction of León.

Two

ECHOES FROM
THE PAST
León 1491-1492

"Whatsoever a man soweth, that shall he also reap."

Matthew 7:2

41

The journey to León had been a long and exhausting one, through acres of mud, over barren hills and through the narrow winding mountain passes. Alicia had traveled over gorgio fields and church-owned lands that served to remind her of her self-imposed exile and her vulnerability should she be caught unaware.

The days of intense heat had given way to cold nights, and Alicia had shivered at the paralyzing chill of the high winds that tore at her clothes. Winter was approaching, bringing rain and cold. Camping in forests and fields, frightened and alone, she had remembered Rudolpho, and somehow her fortitude had been renewed. All her life Rudolpho had given her wise counsel, therefore this, too, must be right. She had to reach León.

Even when it seemed that she could go no farther, Alicia had somehow managed to find the strength to pull herself to her feet, mount Grai, and resume her journey again. It had been so different from traveling with the caravan. She was on her own now, with only her horse as companion—no Gypsy music, no laughter. There were times when she even missed the frowns that had been cast her way; at least then she had not been so totally alone, so completely friendless. And in the end she found herself without even the horse, for while she was sleeping one night, someone took the only thing of value she owned, Grai. Forced to finish her journey on foot, Alicia had reached the city only by sheer determination. She was in the gorgio world now and it was here that she must stay.

But what a world it was, so different from what she had known. Her eyes opened wide as she took in the spires of the towering Gothic churches reaching up to the sky—slender, elegant, and celestial. It was not that she had not seen multicolored glass windows or courtyards filled with flowers before, she had seen them many times while traveling through the cities; but with the others around her she had somehow been oblivious of their beauty. Now her eyes took in every detail—the rippling fountains covered with soft moss, the marble pillars, the tile-roofed houses.

Beautiful, so beautiful, she thought, gazing at the sights as she walked along. Nor did the beauty dim for her in the hours she spent in Salamanca. She still saw the beauty of the *gorgio* world despite the ugliness of some of the inhabitants, who were anything but kind to her. Some taunted her cruelly, disturbed to find a bedraggled Gypsy in their midst, but Alicia tried her best to ignore them.

The bells from the chapel tolled six times as Alicia walked the streets of Salamanca in the province of León. Night was approaching, Alicia's first night among the gorgios. It was chilly, and as she walked along she clutched the tattered shreds of her makeshift shawl about her shoulders. Tired and hungry, she made her way through the crowded streets, looking warily at these people of the city. A few offered kindness, those down on their luck themselves—poorly dressed beggars or children. Others, however, those brightly-clothed gentlemen called *caballeros* and the full-skirted ladies, looked at her with open hostility, some even cursing her, calling her *gitana,* as if the very word were an insult. Alicia returned their stares with a frown and tossed back her hair with a shake of her head. *O Beng* could take these *jukela!*

At least the city itself greeted her with affection, sharing

with her its myriad sights, sounds, and smells. Narrow
streets wound through Salamanca like long, graceful ribbons, lined with balconied houses with red, green, or bright
blue shutters and black iron railings. There were adobe
buildings, too, which Alicia supposed housed the poorer of
the city's people. It seemed that, unlike the Gypsies, these
gorgios had not learned to share. Some had so much, while
others had so little.

Donkeys, pigs, chickens, cats, and dogs cluttered the road,
scurrying to make way for the boisterous tradesmen who
jostled through the streets and the ox-drawn wagons that
rumbled down the road. Here and there a small child
laughed as it tried to elude these carts in daring games that
caused Alicia's heart to lurch more than once. The children
reminded her of Palo and Mala, and she rushed forward
with the intention of cautioning them against such bravado
only to suffer the scathing rebuke of their mothers, who
warned her not to *steal* their children.

"Steal children? Gypsies do not steal children, Gypsies
have enough children of their own," Alicia mumbled under
her breath, hurrying on to escape the barrage of angry mut-
terings.

The plaza was crowded and Alicia elbowed her way
through the throng, watching the vendors with their wares.
The smells of fruits, vegetables, fresh baked pastries perme-
ated the air, mixed with the aroma of fish and leather.
Breathing deeply, Alicia wrinkled her nose, trying hard to
forget her hunger. It was the time she usually ate her supper, but as she reached into her small bag she found that it
was empty. Her supply of cheese, salt fish, hardtack, and
chick-peas was gone. There would be no supper tonight unless Alicia could find some way to make a few coins. She
remembered hearing one of the Gypsy woman from another
caravan tell about how she had managed to survive in the
gorgio world by dancing and fortune-telling, but Alicia was
too proud and so went without food that night. Finding a

small sheltered alcove, she tried to sleep, hoping that tomorrow would be better.

Alicia spent three nights in misery, suffering the pangs of hunger until at last she realized that dancing and palm reading were the only skills that could save her. The people of the town did not trust Gypsies for honest work. How could Alicia explain that she was not really of Gypsy blood? Would they believe her? She didn't have the chance to find out, for most doors were quickly shut in her face when those inside caught sight of her ragged attire. Besides, what did she know of gorgio ways—cleaning houses, making bread, serving wine? She would have to survive in her own way.

Alicia's grandmother had taught her a little about fortune-telling, and now Alicia was grateful to the old *phuri dai*, for such a skill would provide coins for food. Nor was it easy work. To be a good fortune-teller one needed a shrewd eye and a glib tongue, Alicia soon found. She had the former but not the latter. Being at heart much too honest, she was not skillful at telling falsehoods, and this was nearly her undoing until the gorgios' haughty ways and her own hunger inspired her to think otherwise.

From now on I will show these vain peacocks, she thought, watching as a finely dressed *caballero* avoided her path as if just the touch of her would taint his garments. Why should she be concerned about such people as these? They smiled at Gypsies only when they wished to have their fortunes read. Why not tell them that their dreams would come true, that they would become rich, be loved, or achieve great fame? If in a mesmerizing whisper she could spin fantasies to please them, why not?

The very same *caballero* who had so callously shunned her was Alicia's first customer. She promised him that he would win the heart of the woman he loved, and he in turn gave her enough coins to buy a small loaf of day-old bread. The promise to a goatherd that he would become a man of great renown brought forth a small hunk of goat's-milk cheese. For the first time since she had arrived in Salamanca, Alicia's hunger was satisfied, yet even so, her conscience chased happiness away. Rudolpho would never have approved of what she was doing. Gypsies never practiced fortune-telling among themselves. Only the *phuri dai* had the vision.

I'm sorry, Papa, she reflected, looking up at one of the stars that pulsated in the dark gray of the dusk. She remembered one of his sayings, *Eyes which see not, break no heart,* yet the star seemed to show by its vibrancy that it approved of what she was doing, and that thought made Alicia feel more at ease. Fortune-telling was a joke that was played on the gorgio to gain money. Poor, foolish gorgios, who believed so strongly in the future! Gypsies knew that the present, the now, was more important. Today. Live for now, possess the passing moment passionately, without regrets. Roms lived in the present. If the present was well lived, then one need not worry about the future, nor regret the past. And that was exactly what Alicia intended to do. She had to put aside her thoughts of what had been and live day to day. Somehow she felt Rudolpho would understand.

Salamanca had many pickpockets, hustlers, and whores loitering the street in search of victims. Luckily none of them bothered with a ragged Gypsy girl in their midst. As fiercely as the gorgios avoided her, Alicia shunned them. At least what little she made she made honestly; she could take pride in that fact. She did not ask the gorgios for any payment but took only what they offered freely. Even so, more often than not, she was ridiculed so savagely that at last she sought another means to appease her hunger in addition to palm reading.

Looking about the crowded marketplace, Alicia judged that dancing might bring her quite a few coins tonight. Milling about the street, the many finely-garbed citizens were satisfying their hunger with chunks of meat on skewers, baked vegetables, fish, or cheese that the vendors provided.

After filling their bellies, they would seek entertainment, not knowledge of the future. Always after supper it was the Gypsies' fondest wish to dance or watch the dancers around the fire. Could these gorgios be so very different? Clicking her heels furiously against the cobblestones, she decided to find out. Clapping her hands as she moved to the beat of an imaginary guitar, Alicia began to dance a flamenco.

There was a boldness in her movement, yet that boldness was tempered with an innocence, a look in her flashing green eyes that proclaimed her a lady, despite her ragged clothes.

"Look how graceful she is!" called out a portly blacksmith, stopping his labors to look at her. Slowly a crowd was gathering about Alicia as the people looked on in awe.

"She *is* graceful. Her beauty would charm even the Moors."

"Who is she?" asked a vendor.

"Where is she from?" questioned another.

"We've never seen her here before," whispered the throng of men.

The women were not as bewitched as their sons and husbands. "Gypsy slut. How dare she dance so brazenly!"

"We should shoo her away."

"No, let her stay! Gypsy or not, she enthralls all who look upon her," the men insisted.

Alicia varied her movements from a wild foot-stamping, whirling dance to another, flowing with beauty, as she swayed from side to side. In her mind she could envision Rafael and pretended to dance again for him, closing her eyes to envision his face. If only he had loved her, things might have been different, she thought. If only . . .

A cold, raspy voice shattered Alicia's mood. Looking up, she saw a black-robed figure staring at her, his dark eyes raking her over. "She dances as if possessed by the devil!" Raising his eyes to the sky, he crossed himself quickly. "All you who value your souls, leave this place of damnation lest you find yourselves consumed by the fires of hell. She is evil. This one is evil. She has no soul!"

Alicia stopped dancing, a shiver running up her spine. The name Torquemada ran through her mind. Was this one of his evil priests? He had to be. She had heard whispers that the spies of Torquemada were everywhere, watching, waiting. A slip of the tongue or an act of defiance could have dire consequences.

"The priest, he tells us true," choked an old man, taking to his heels in fear.

"Gypsies are spawns of Satan," the black-robed priest intoned, again making the sign of the cross. "Chase her away." Stepping into the shadows, he vanished as quickly as he had appeared, seemingly appeased that he had planted his seed of suspicion and fear.

"Gypsies *are* spawns of Satan. We should run this one out of town!" shrieked an old woman in outrage, echoing the priest's words.

As quickly as the people had embraced Alicia, they turned against her, murmuring in anger. Picking up a stone, one old woman cast it at Alicia, striking her on the shoulder.

"Leave us!" cried another woman, adding her stone to the onslaught that now followed. The air rained sticks and stones, the crowd had turned violent. Had Alicia not been so swift of foot, she would have suffered grieviously, but she skillfully eluded her attackers. Searching desperately for a place to hide, she sought shelter behind the thick door of one of the great stone churches, closing the door firmly behind her.

Trembling, her chest heaving as she tried to catch her breath, Alicia waited until the tumult outside had quieted before opening the door to peer out. Although they obviously did not know where she had run to, there were still people milling about. She would have to remain here at least for a time.

"Fools! Gorgio fools!" she whispered under her breath.

They were so self-rightous. Would they never change their
minds about Gypsies? She had only tried to entertain them
and in this way earn a few coins. Was that so very wrong?
Dancing was a good thing, not evil. Something so joyous
came from *o Del,* not from *o Beng;* could they not see that?
Shaking her head, she knew there was no hope for these
gorgios, nor for her. She would never be able to understand
them, much less live among them. It would be one more
night without food to give her strength. One more long,
lonely night.

Breathing a sigh, Alicia reached up to untie the scarlet
scarf from around her head. Her badge of wifehood. Strange
that she wore it even now. Running her fingers through the
tangles of her hair, she thought of the time she had spent
with Rafael. It seemed a lifetime away. So many things had
changed since then: Rudolpho's death, Stivo's appointment
as leader, Alicia's flight from the caravan, the long, tedious
trek across the Toledo Mountain range to the valley of the
province of León.

Wiping her face free of the dirt and grime that had been
flung at her, exploring her arms and shoulders for signs of
bruises or cuts, Alicia resolved once again, as she had many
times of late, not to think about Rafael. She had enough
gorgios here in this city without being tortured by memories
of another one, particularly of *him.*

Gorgios, she thought angrily. So far she had received little
kindness from any of them, and to think that Rudolpho had
told her she was one of them . . . It made her shiver in
revulsion. They were scornful and hateful; she wouldn't be
one of them, she would not!

Walking away from the door, Alicia looked about her,
deciding to just tell fortunes from now on. Dancing was
dangerous. Still, she had to do something to survive. *O Del*
would want her to live, but not to be driven from the city,
she resolved stubbornly. Winter was approaching, and
without the shelter of the city's gates, without her people,

she would die if she left. Like it or not, she could not run away again no matter how much she was tempted.

Looking about her, Alicia found a small alcove beside a wooden altar, and reaching into her pocket, took out her meager belongings, which she had hidden in the fold of her skirts lest some thief steal them from her. She examined the ribbon Todero had given her to bring her good luck, the shard of pottery from her marriage flagon, and lastly Rafael's ring. How strange that she had thought to take it from Rudolpho's hand the night of his death. She should have burned it with her father, but instead she had kept it. Why?

The truth pained her. She could not forget Rafael as easily as he had forgotten her. Forlornly she raised her head to look about her, fearing that perhaps the black-robed priest might come again to harm her; but it was quiet, and she decided that she was all alone.

Alicia had never been inside a gorgio church before. Did Rafael's God live here? Rudolpho had always told her that God was in the forest, not in a church, and yet somehow she had the feeling that *He* was here, that somehow she was not alone.

She stared wide-eyed at her surroundings, at the flickering candles on the altar, the bright mosaic inlays that formed pictures, the altar, the statues. Her eyes rested on the statue of a woman holding a child, and she was struck by the kindness on the woman's face, as if she felt Alicia's pain and wanted to help her. Who was this woman? she wondered.

Walking about as if in a trance, Alicia reached out to touch the cold stone, fully expecting it to feel warm, like living flesh, but it was just a statue and not real after all.

Another statue caught her eye, of a man bound to a tree, a cross. He was nearly naked, wearing only a loincloth, his bare feet bound together, a crown of thorns upon his head. Poor man, she thought, her eyes misting with tears. She wanted to soothe him, to take away all his pain, to lift him gently from where he was a bound prisoner and tend his wounds.

"Are you the gentle Christ? The one Rafael told me about?" she asked, as if expecting the statue to speak to her. In a way it did, for suddenly she knew in her heart that it was the Christ. The look of peace upon the motionless face mesmerized her. How could one such as Torquemada, that evil priest, worship this man and still hold such hatred and bitterness in his heart? It was difficult for Alicia to understand. Why did these gorgios listen to words of hatred? Why did they not instead look deep into the eyes and heart of the gentle Christ?

Alicia was tired, and the questions flooding through her mind saddened her. Making her way to the door with the intention of leaving, she glanced back at the statue on the cross and somehow longed to stay here within the safety of these walls. For the first time in weeks she felt at peace. Seeking a place close to the statue, she curled up into a ball and fell asleep.

42

"Who are you? What are you doing here?" The voice was soft, yet Alicia opened her eyes with a start. Seeing that it was another of the dark-robed figures that hovered over her, she put up her arms as if to ward off any abuse that this one might offer her.

"Please. Please. I was just so tired . . ." Cautiously her eyes met those of the priest to find them staring back at her, but there was no hatred written there, only concern.

"Don't be afraid, I won't harm you." Reaching out to put his hand on her shoulder, he asked again, "Who are you?"

"My name is Alicia."

"Alicia. A lovely name for a beautiful señorita." His gentle blue eyes appraised her. "You have a look of sadness about you, my child. Tell me how I can be of help to you."

Alicia's eyes swept over the man. He was short and stout of frame—one might have called him fat—with a round face and wide-toothed smile. He was jovial-looking with a kindly manner and soothing voice. She wanted to trust him, she yearned for friendship, yet she had trusted gorgios before, only to find betrayal. "I do not need help," she answered warily. "I am a Gypsy. Gypsies are strong."

He put his hands upon his bulging waist and looked at her in reproachful annoyance. "No one is strong when hungry. Why, just look at you. You are nothing but skin and bones. How long has it been since you have eaten properly?"

Alicia was too stubborn and proud to tell him of the hardships she had endured. "I ate only yesterday." Rising to her feet, she clutched the tattered wisps of her shawl about her shoulders defensively.

"Yesterday? Yesterday? Blessed Lord, you poor child. Well, we will rectify that in an instant. Come with me."

Alicia stood rooted to the spot, afraid of trusting yet somehow feeling a liking for this priest. "I do not need charity. I work for what I eat."

"Of course, of course. I'm sure that you do, my child. I will let you earn your bread, have no fear." He laughed. "I am a terrible cook, as you will see." He patted his rounded belly. "If you will fix a bit of breakfast for me, I will share the fare with you. Now is this not a fair trade?"

Alicia admitted that it was, saying mischievously, "I shall prepare you roast hedgehog." As Rafael had done once, the priest shuddered. Apparently gorgios had no fondness for such succulent meat.

"Thank the Lord we have none of those spiny creatures about. No, no. You will have to settle for roast pig, I fear." He motioned again for Alicia to follow him, past the stone altar, out of the chapel. There were people praying in small wooden stalls, and the priest bowed his head in acknowledgment as he passed.

"What are they doing?" Alicia was curious.

"They light candles and talk with God," he said in reply.

"Talk with God?" She thought about the statue of the Christ. "But He was back there." Pointing to the chapel, she gave him a questioning look.

"No, no. That was His Son, who died for our sins." They walked through the long, winding hallway and down a flight of stairs.

Alicia was silent for a time, then she asked, "And who was the woman with the child?"

"Christ's mother, Mary, with the Infant Jesus."

Now Alicia was thoroughly confused. "Jesus? Who is this Jesus?"

The priest smiled. "The Christ. In time you will understand, child." He hurried her along with a light pressure on her shoulder.

Alicia shook her head. "It is all very confusing." Matching the priest's long strides, she fought to keep up with him. These gorgios were a strange lot. Still, the memory of the compassionate face on the statue of the Christ came to her mind and she had the sudden longing to learn more. "How did he die, this Christ?"

Pausing in his stride, he answered, "He was crucified, nailed to a cross." Alicia winced and started to speak, but he silenced her. "Because of his sacrifice we who believe in him have everlasting life."

"All gorgios?"

"Those who believe." They had reached the kitchens, and Alicia saw that a fire was burning in the large oven. Sensing the direction of her eyes, he added, "Evil men are doomed to purgatory and suffering. Hell and damnation. Everlasting fire. It is their lot to be slaves of the devil."

"Of *o Beng*? What a terrible punishment." Alicia gasped. She wanted to ask more questions, but her hunger for food outweighed her hunger for knowledge, at least for the moment. A large wooden bowl was filled to overflowing with ripe fruit, and in spite of her resolve Alicia's mouth watered as she took a step forward.

"Help yourself, my child. Take what you want."

Alicia reached out to pluck a handful of grapes, stuffing them into her mouth. They were tart but she relished them, letting their succulent taste caress her mouth. Suddenly in horror she realized what she was doing. Hunger was a frightful thing, it took away one's pride.

Swallowing quickly, Alicia looked at the priest with her head held high. "I told you I would fix your breakfast and

then I would eat. That was our bargain and I will hold to it."
There was a mound of fresh bread-dough already fashioned
into a loaf, and putting it on the wooden paddle, Alicia
thrust it into the fires of the oven. Seeing the familiar white
oval shapes of hens' eggs, she broke open several, chopping
peppers and onions to blend into the mixture. It reminded
her of the day Rafael had left her, and her eyes misted with
tears before she could blink them away.

"You are sad, child. Has someone hurt you?"

Stubbornly she shook her head. "No. It is only the onions
and nothing more." Although he knew better, the priest
held his tongue. This girl had pride, courage, and spirit, and
he admired her. Somehow he would find a way to help her
before the morning was out.

"I have exhibited poor manners," the priest said, instead
of asking further questions. "I have not told you my name,
though you told me yours. My name is Father Julio." His
blue eyes twinkled with laughter. "I'm half Irish, you see,
which accounts for my red hair—what there is left of it. I
grew up in my mother's Ireland."

"Ireland?" Alicia had heard of that faraway country.
"What are you doing here in León?" She had assumed that
he was from one of the provinces of Spain like all the other
gorgios, but now she realized that he did have just a hint of
an accent.

"I was called here by God." His voice lowered as if he
were afraid for others to hear his words. "It is my intent to
be God's instrument in putting an end to these barbarous
burnings. It is not right for one man to so mistreat another."

Alicia knew at once that he was referring to the Inquisition. "Torquemada is a demon!" she hissed.

Silencing her with a finger to his lips, he nodded. "Torquemada *is* a madman. He must be stopped. But come, let us
talk no more about such gruesome matters. Tell me about
yourself instead."

Alicia talked about the Gypsy camp as she bustled about

the large kitchen. She was surprised at how easy it was to cook in a *gorgio* kitchen, one that was within stone walls.

Heaping two plates with sliced ham, fruit, and freshly baked bread, she smiled at last at Father Julio. Scooping the eggs out of the pan, she gave him the larger portion, taking a small amount for herself, curious to taste this gorgio dish of eggs. "I *am* hungry," she confessed, finding her self beginning to trust this priest at last. Taking a place by the oven, Alicia sat upon her heels in Gypsy fashion, by the fire, to eat.

Taking his place beside her, sitting upon the floor in similar fashion so as not to embarrass the young woman, Father Julio realized that because she was Gypsy Alicia was not familiar with the practice of sitting at a table to eat. Well, she would soon learn the ways of the *gorgios,* as she called them. Perhaps he could help her.

"Tell me more about yourself, Alicia." Surprisingly he found it rather comfortable upon the floor and reflected that perhaps there was more to these Gypsies than he had ever supposed. "How do you come to be in Salamanca and not with others of your kind?"

Between mouthfuls she answered all his questions, telling him about her father's death, his revelation that she was not really a Gypsy, her fear of Stivo, the journey to León, and her hope of finding out just who she was. "I do not think I want to be gorgio!"

"You poor child, I do not blame you. Certainly your own people have not shown you much kindness. And such a long journey all by yourself!" Father Julio murmured sympathetically, reaching out to pat her hand. "And to think that after all you have gone through you have met with nothing but hostility here in Salamanca. I am ashamed of my countrymen and women."

"They are wrong about Gypsies. Gypsies are an honorable people. Rudolpho, my papa, was the finest man on earth."

"I'm certain that he was, child." Wiping his mouth with

his sleeve, Father Julio looked over at the girl. He had to find
a way to help her; he couldn't turn her out upon the street,
where she might starve or come to harm. But her pride. He
knew that she would not take charity. What was he to do?

"I miss the caravan," Alicia was saying. "Particularly
Todero and Zuba. And the children, Palo and Mala."

"The children. Yes, the children." Clasping his stubby fingers together, the priest grinned at her. Alicia's words had
given him an idea. "That is the answer. Children." Casting
her an imploring look, he said, "Alicia, stay here. We need
someone to help us with the little ones, the children. Like
you, they have no one."

"The children?" Alicia's wooden plate clattered to the
floor.

"Children with no parents. The church has taken them in
to care for them, but I must confess that they have not been
given the attention they deserve. Perhaps you could . . ."
He smiled at her and she returned his smile with sincere
affection, sensing that this man was like Rudolpho in many
ways.

"I would like . . ."

"What is going on here? Father Julio, what are you doing
squatting on the ground?" The voice was deep and authori-
tative, and Alicia turned her head with a start. Standing in
the doorway was a man dressed entirely in scarlet from the
hat atop his head to the tips of his shoes. He had a large
nose that reminded Alicia of a bird's beak, and he scrutinized her with black beady eyes. "And who is this ragged
girl? Another of your foundlings, Father?"

Alicia was upon her feet in an instant, glaring defiantly at
this man. Another of the hostile nobility. Well, she would
not stay another moment under the same roof with such as
him. Gathering the ends of her shawl about her, she started
to walk toward the door. Bolting to his feet, the priest followed her.

"No, Alicia. Stay!" Father Julio said gently. "Do not listen to this man's unkind words." In anger he confronted the brightly plumed man. "Don Enrique Dorado, I am ashamed of you to so mistreat one of God's children. Your father, Don Philip Navarro, would never act so rudely."

"Ha. My *stepfather* is a fool who lavishes money upon your foolish charities until he threatens to impoverish us. I am not so simple as he." Again his eyes roamed over Alicia, this time with an appraising eye. "Ragged though she be, she is at least a beauty. Give her to me. I will feed and clothe her." The sneer on his face declared clearly what the man had in mind, and Alicia pulled the corners of her shawl about her body as if to hide it from him. He was no better than Stivo, this one. A lusting animal who thought a woman only good for one purpose.

"I would never go with you!" she snarled at him. "Never! First I would starve."

Pushing the priest out of his way, Don Enrique reached out to capture a long strand of Alicia's hair. "Spirit as well as beauty. I like that in a woman." Pulling back his thin lips, showing crooked white teeth, he laughed.

"Leave her alone. This is God's house." Stepping in front of Alicia, Father Julio bristled with anger.

"A Gypsy, from the looks of her. Haven't you heard of Torquemada's warning concerning these beggars?" For a moment the two men had forgotten Alicia's presence as they fought their own private battle. Looking from the priest to the beak-nosed man, Alicia quickly made her decision. She could not stay here, no matter how kind the priest had been to her. The plumed one was dangerous to her, she sensed it with every fiber of her being. Silently she ran to the door, pausing only for a moment to look back on the only gorgio who had smiled at her with kindness. She would remember him in her heart for a long time to come.

"I do not listen to Torquemada. I listen only to God and the Pope. I give love and charity to those in need, as my

Christ bids me do, and not you or a thousand men like you will ever . . ."

The sound of a slamming door stopped the priest in mid-sentence. Forgetting about their confrontation, the two men looked around to see that the Gypsy girl had gone.

"Alicia. No. Come back!" Father Julio picked up the long skirts of his habit to follow in pursuit, but when he reached the doorway he found that the dark-haired woman had vanished. Racing up the stairway, he said a silent prayer that he would find her, but she was gone, taking with her any hope he might have had of helping her.

43

Rafael de Villasandro paced the floor of his bedroom at the Navarro household in agitation. He had been in Salamanca for two weeks and as yet had learned very little, though he had visions of doing so much, of saving so many lives. So far nothing had been accomplished. Nothing. Had he left the woman he loved only to stay cooped up in a gilded cage like the parrots brought back as pets from the lands to the East?

But at least it was a comfortable cage! he thought in self-mockery.

The Navarro residence was a two-story stone hacienda surrounding a large tile-paved courtyard. Enclosed by a black iron grille fence, it was definitely one of the finest houses in the city. Philip Navarro was a man of great wealth.

The house was filled with art treasures—paintings, sculptures, fine hand-blown glass. It was obvious that Don Philip Navarro loved beauty. No wonder his stepson, Juan Dorado, had such a fine eye for masterpieces. In this at least he was like his stepfather, though in no other.

Rafael had been given a room on the second floor, looking down upon the garden. It was possible to enter the building unnoticed from a private entrance near the courtyard, and he could come and go at his leisure, which suited Rafael's needs. There were dozens of servants about, but Rafael had noted that before six in the morning, after eleven at night, or during the afternoon siesta the house was relatively quiet, and he could pass in and out at his leisure as if invisible.

Rafael's chamber had a high ceiling; an *estrado,* or elevated platform, covered with cushions, where he often liked to sit; a large bed; and a bed chest filled with all the belongings he had brought with him. The walls were covered with tapestries, bold in design and delicate in workmanship, that depicted woodland animals frolicking in the forest. The tapestry reminded Rafael of Alicia and the short, blissful time they had been together. So often he had been tempted to go back and look for her, to ask her to come with him, but he knew that she was safe with Rudolpho. Rafael could only offer her danger.

But someday I will *return for you, Alicia. Someday.* The thought of roaming the countryside strangely appealed to him at the moment and he understood the Gypsies' love of freedom. The last days he had spent with the caravan had been the happiest of his life. Strange that he had realized that fact only after leaving them.

There is honesty among the Gypsies, not this devious, dangerous plotting I am forced to endure among my own kind! he thought in frustration. A spy, an informer, that was what that conniving Dorado intended him to be. The very thought rankled. He wants me to keep an eye on one of the priests here, that is why he sent me. Father Julio. The name was branded on his brain, but not for the reason Juan Dorado intended.

Rafael stopped pacing only long enough to glare briefly out of the window. It was December, and the light from this northern window was hazy, the sky threatened rain. Winter was full upon them. If anything was to be done about the endangered *Conversos,* it must be done soon, before the sea storms were upon them.

So far Rafael had learned that two *Converso* families had come under suspicion, a physician by the name of Abraham Isaacson and a moneylender by the name of Noah Ravalya, to whom, Rafael suspected, Juan Dorado owed a great deal of money. By ridding himself of Ravalya, the priest's debts would be obliterated. Clever. Vile. Evil. But then it was not unusual, was it, to burn those who had financed one's debts? Queen Isabella herself had used the service of a Jewish lawyer, who had lent the impoverished queen twenty thousand sueldos for her wedding ceremony to Ferdinand. It was true that she had repaid him when she became queen, but also true that he had not been spared from the Inquisition. The Inquisition was a law unto itself, and woe to any who dared voice outrage. King Ferdinand's own physician, Ribor Altas, a baptized Jew, had been burned. No one was safe from those who derived their power from the misery of others.

Those who had converted to Christianity were endangered, but so far the Jews themselves were safe. The Inquisition's concern was not in persecuting Jews but in the apostasy of those who had become Christian by conversion. Strange, Rafael thought, that though the purpose was to convert non-Christians to Christianity, the very principles of the Inquisition rendered so-called heretics safe from prosecution as long they did *not* become baptized. Even so, Rafael feared lest Torquemada turn his attentions to the Jews. There were nearly a quarter of a million in Spain and there were rumors of Torquemada's malice toward them. Only Ferdinand's hesitation to harm them kept them safe. Yet terrible tales were being whispered about the Jews, just as there had been before his mother's death. That they tried to lure Christians into Judaism and that they sacrificed Christian children were the most recent rumors.

Such ridiculous charges. Rafael shook his head, so deep in thought that he did not hear his host come up behind him until Don Philip reached out a hand to touch his shoulder. "Don Rafael, you look worried. Is there anything that I can do?"

Whirling around, Rafael greeted his host with a forced

smile. "No, everything is perfection, Don Philip, and I appreciate your hospitality." Rafael remembered how warmly he had been greeted and welcomed into the household. Philip Navarro was a handsome man whom Rafael judged to be about fifty, though his gray hair and beard made him appear older. Impeccably dressed in black hose and gold-trimmed doublet, he was every inch the nobleman.

"I am glad. I am glad," Don Philip answered with a slight bow. His smile was sincere, and Rafael thought how much he had liked and respected this man from the moment he met him. Juan Dorado's stepfather was an honest man, a proud man, a man of honor. How could the stepson be so totally different from the man who had raised him?

For that matter, how is it that Philip Navarro is the only man of honor in this sea of barracudas? Rafael thought sourly. He had no love for Juan Dorado's brother, Enrique, either, for he was a man interested only in women, gambling, and his own well-being. Nor did Rafael like Doña Luisa, Philip's wife, the mother of Enrique, Juan, and their sister, Violetta. Despite her smiling, polite manners she appeared to Rafael to be selfish and dangerous. Philip Navarro deserved much better.

An embarrassed silence pervaded the room, and Rafael suddenly realized that he had been so intent upon his own thoughts that he had scarcely heard what Don Philip had said. Now the man awaited an answer, and Rafael could only look at him helplessly. Feeling a bit foolish, Rafael decided that truth was the only solution.

"I apologize for my rude behavior, Don Philip, but I did not hear what you asked me. I have been, I fear, in a world of my own these last days. I have lost my heart to a young woman and can hardly think of anything else."

Philip Navarro laughed, a deep, musical laugh. "I understand. Really I do." His eyes took on a faraway look. "I, too, was once very much in love."

"With Doña Luisa?"

The gray-haired man shook his head sadly. "No, my heart

belonged to another." His eyes misted with a trace of tears
as if the subject were still much too painful to speak of. "I
was married once before, long, long ago. My wife died in
childbirth, giving me a beautiful daughter."

"Daughter? Violetta?" Rafael was confused.

"No, she is my stepdaughter. My own daughter drowned
in an accident when she was but a child of three. I fear the
nurse was careless in her duties. That negligence cost me the
life of my precious daughter. I have never gotten over her
death." There was a long pause as Philip Navarro regained
his composure. "But come, let us speak no more about it.
That was many years ago. I came to ask you if you would
like to go riding with me. I have many fine horses in the
stables. Andalusians."

"It would be an honor." Bowing, Rafael followed his host
out of the door and down the flight of stairs. He was anxious to see these horses. Perhaps he could talk Don Philip
into selling two of the stallions. Imagine how surprised Alicia would be when he brought back such a magnificent animal as a present for her when he returned.

Walking through the courtyard, past the gate to the stables, Philip Navarro was interested in this young man who
was his stepson's friend. He asked Rafael many questions
about himself, ending with "Tell me about this young señorita you have become enamored of. What is her name?"

"Alicia."

Rafael smiled, but his smile was frozen on his face as he
saw Don Philip's face pale. Reaching out, he touched the
man's arm.

"I am all right. It is just that . . . that . . . the name
. . . Blessed Cristo, it was the name of my daughter! Alicia.
For a moment . . . but how foolish of me to be so unnerved by hearing you speak the name that once belonged
to my daughter. I must forget. Forget." Philip Navarro
quickened his step, motioning for Rafael to follow, and for
the moment Alicia *was* forgotten.

44

Rafael entered the elegant and spacious dining room of the Navarro household several hours after his brisk and invigorating ride. Philip Navarro's Andalusian horses were indeed magnificent, six perfectly matching jet-black stallions. Don Navarro had picked out two of the high-spirited horses for their ride, and Rafael had found the animals to have grace and speed, combined with the strength and regal beauty of their breed. Rafael had enjoyed riding beside Don Philip and soon discovered that he respected him more than he had any other man, with the exception perhaps of Rudolpho. Both were men of wisdom and honor, and Rafael reflected that had they ever met, the two men would no doubt have taken an instant liking to each other.

"Ah, Señor Rafael, how handsome you look." It was Doña Luisa Navarro who spoke, eyeing him up and down as if *he* were a prize stallion up for sale and she the prospective buyer. From the first day he had arrived, the woman had made it obvious that she fully intended to do everything in her power to marry him to her daughter, Violetta, a young woman who mirrored her mother in looks. Rafael knew that he would have to be wary.

Smiling, Luisa Navarro pointed to the empty chair beside her daughter at the dinner table, indicating that he should take his seat. Shrugging his shoulders, adjusting the high collar of his brown velvet doublet, Rafael sat down.

"Good evening, Señor de Villasandro." Violetta Dorado fluttered her eyelashes slightly and looked demurely down at her plate as aristocratic Spanish girls were taught to do in the presence of a man. Tall, slender, and large-boned, she looked somewhat foolish in her attempts to act girlish, only appearing awkward instead. Dressed in an intricately patterned gown of emerald-green and gold brocade, worn over the wooden hoops of her *verdugado,* she tended to wear too many jewels, perhaps in an effort to disguise her plain features. The colors of the gown did little to complement them; indeed the green only seemed to make her complexion look more sallow. Rafael noticed that Violetta, like her brother Enrique, was plagued with the same prominent nose. Her jet-black hair was worn at the back of her head in an unflattering style, which only seemed to add inches to the length of that nose. In spite of his resolve, Rafael found himself comparing this young woman to Alicia. Señorita Violetta was the sort of woman his father would have picked for him. Of that Rafael had no doubt, and the thought pricked his anger. Was there no room in this world for love? Were Violetta Dorado the Queen of Castile and León, he could never marry her.

Fool. I was a fool to leave Alicia, he thought in anger. *I can never marry any other woman when my heart belongs to a green-eyed Gypsy witch.* The thought tormented him that he might never see Alicia again, that when he returned for her she would be gone. If such a thing happened, could he live without her? No. No.

"Señor, is something wrong?"

Señorita Violetta had noticed his frown, and now, despite conventions, was looking up at him. Something about that look pricked Rafael's sympathies and he smiled at her. Was it her fault that Doña Luisa hovered over them like a mother hen?

"You look beautiful, Señorita Violetta," he lied.

Her answering smile was radiant. She had full lips, her

teeth were perfectly formed and as white as pearls. Clearly her mouth was her one redeeming feature. If only she would smile more often.

"Thank you for the compliment," she said softly, casting her eyes down again in the modest demeanor she had been taught so well. It was obvious to Rafael that she found him attractive, and he felt strangely sorry for the girl. He didn't want to hurt her—he was not that kind of man—and yet he knew that in the end he would wound her pride.

I cannot marry. I am married already, he mused, surprised that such a thought should enter his mind. He had married Alicia in a pagan ceremony, one not recognized by his people; yet at this moment his heart longed for her and he realized that she truly was his wife.

Fluttering over him like a bird of prey, Luisa Navarro chattered on and on throughout dinner about her daughter's accomplishments. Violetta could weave, Violetta could cook, Violetta could sew. Like many girls of her class it appeared that this one, too, had only one purpose in life: to become a wife and then a mother. Violetta would accept for her husband a man of her parents' choosing, an arranged marriage. With docility she would pledge her life to a man, whether she loved him or not, without ever questioning her own heart.

As I, too, would have done once. But not now. Never now. Oh, Alicia . . . Closing his eyes, Rafael frowned to think how stupid he had been. Happiness was as fragile as a spider's web. Had he torn that slender thread when he rode away?

"We have prepared all your favorite dishes. Are the scallops not to your liking? Do you find too much garlic in the sauce? You have hardly touched a bite." Doña Luisa had clearly misunderstood Rafael's frown.

"The food is delicious. It is just that I am not very hungry." Making another effort to please his hostess, Rafael raised the spoon to his lips.

"After our ride, I am as hungry as my horses." Don Philip

chuckled, winking in Rafael's direction. It was plain to see that Don Philip clearly understood his wife's motives and was amused. "Perhaps our guest is fearful of losing his freedom."

Violetta flushed, staring down at her plate, but Doña Luisa's gray eyes flashed fire. "Silence your tongue, husband," she hissed under her breath, recovering her composure to smile at Rafael. Despite the grimace of her mouth, there was no smile in her eyes, and Rafael found himself wondering what Philip Navarro had seen in this woman. They seemed a mismatched pair. Had this been an arranged marriage? Rafael's eyes appraised the woman. Doña Luisa wore a great deal of makeup to hide her waning looks, yet it appeared that she might have been attractive once, despite her thickening figure. Had Don Philip found her lovely?

Philip answered his wife's anger with a scowl, just barely managing to control his own ire. In silence the man and his wife fought a private duel, maintaining for others a show of flawless cordiality, yet Rafael sensed Don Philip's unhappiness. What had happened so long ago to tie him to this woman? He could only wonder.

It was a long time before Philip Navarro smiled, but when he did, it was in Rafael's direction, and Rafael was amazed by the natural camaraderie that had sprung up between them.

"So you like my horses?" Don Philip asked, smiling proudly as Rafael nodded his head in agreement. "I would have guessed that Juan . . ."

"Frey Dorado, Philip," Doña Luisa admonished, her mouth set in a grim line. "My *son* is a priest of the holy church."

"Father Dorado, my esteemed stepson," Philip corrected, his smile quickly fading. "Has he told you about our bulls, Rafael?"

"No, he has not."

"I breed fighting bulls for the arenas of Madrid. The finest bulls in all of Spain. It is a pastime of mine that has managed to become quite profitable."

Rafael raised his eyebrows in surprise. "For the bullfights?"

"Yes. We have bullfights here in Salamanca every Saturday. We must go together, you and I, and you will see for yourself what fine stock comes from my land."

"I would like that." Rafael remembered having passed by one of the corralled areas near the stables and seen the powerful horned beasts grazing there. They had appeared to be magnificent animals, and though he was not an avid fan of the bullring, he thought that he might enjoy seeing such animals pit their skills against a matador. Besides, it would be a good chance for him to move through the crowds and listen for word of Torquemada's doings.

"We shall go, then."

Doña Luisa Navarro snorted disdainfully, obviously piqued that she and her daughter were being ignored. "You and those foolish bulls," she whispered under her breath. "Sometimes I think you show them more attention than you do to me, your wife."

"If I do, woman, it is because they do not goad me with their evil tongues." Philip Navarro threw back his shoulders and held his head high. "But we will argue no more at this table. We have a guest, Doña Luisa, remember that!" Picking up his wineglass he drained it, gesturing with his hand for Rafael to do the same.

It was then that Don Enrique chose to make his entrance, sweeping into the room like a threatening rainstorm, his booming voice shattering the silence and nearly causing Rafael to spill his wine.

"That idiot priest. He has done it again!" Standing with his arms folded in front of his chest, he remained as still as one of the statues. All eyes turned in his direction.

"Done what?" Philip asked in annoyance at his stepson's

intrusion. He shot the dark-haired red-garbed man a look that boded ill as he waited for the answer.

"Taken in another beggar, or at least tried to. One would think that he fancies himself some sort of saint, while all the time it is *our* money that he so lavishly throws about. I reminded him of that."

"Not *our* money, *my* money. How many times must I remind *you* of *that*? It is not your place to interfere with Father Julio."

Doña Luisa threw down her spoon, quickly taking the side of her son against her husband. "Your money it may well be, but with all the coins you give to that fat priest, you may soon impoverish us all."

Don Philip cast Rafael an apologetic glance, embarrassed that his family should so easily forget their manners and speak so freely in front of a guest. Despite his obvious fury, he carefully controlled his voice as he spoke. "Perhaps a lesson in poverty and humility would do you and your children some good. Have you forgotten that before you married me, you, too, knew the taste of hunger? How, then, can you show such little feeling for those victims of misfortune?"

Doña Luisa was properly chastised, and now she, too, lowered her voice as she affected once again the highborn lady. "It is God's will that they suffer. They suffer for their sins. Poverty is their punishment."

"Their punishment?" Don Philip shook his head in disbelief at her words. "Were poverty the punishment for sin, there would be far more beggars in this city than there are already." His eyes met hers and held in a manner that made Rafael wonder what secrets this family shared, what bitterness hid within these walls.

Don Philip's wife did not answer. Instead she sprang to her feet and left the room with a rustle of skirts. Although her daughter looked in her direction, she did not follow, and

Rafael wondered if the young woman was not often torn between the two parents as they battled each other.

"I did not mean to anger you." Don Enrique was all smiles and pleasantries as he bowed low before his stepfather. I meant merely to advise you, Father. Charity is a worthy virtue, even our noble Queen has said so, but one must also look to the future and ensure that tomorrow we will not also be begging in the streets. I beg you to have caution, that is all. Not you, nor I, nor Father Julio can clothe and feed every beggar and tattered Gypsy who walks our streets."

At the word *Gypsy,* Rafael stiffened. Don Enrique had said the word as if it were loathsome, stirring his anger. If he had found the dark-haired eagle-nosed man irritating before, he found him doubly so now.

"I doubt that you see many Gypsies begging for their food. They are a proud and noble people who take care of their own. I think perhaps we could learn from their example."

Don Enrique turned his attentions to their guest. "And just what do you know about Gypsies?" His smile was condescending as he toyed with his mustache.

"I lived among them."

"Lived among them? How interesting. I had no idea . . ."

"A young Gypsy woman saved me from drowning and offered me kindness. Before that time I regret to admit that I suffered the same misconceptions about them as you do. But I see now that I was wrong. We could learn a great deal from them."

A derisive smile curled Don Enrique's lips. "So you, too, champion their cause. How, then, do you and my brother get along so well? I wonder. He detests Gypsies and Jews as well."

Something in his manner urged Rafael to caution. In silence he listened as Don Enrique told the story of the young Gypsy girl he had found with Father Julio. "She was, I will admit, a beauty. She ran away, much to my dismay. I would have made her earn her money. I would have had more use for her than some eunuch priest." His laugh made no secret of his meaning. "Ah, but it is just as well, since I am this very night leaving to grace Queen Isabella's court."

Rafael felt as if the walls were closing in on him as he fought with his anger. What if this were Alicia instead of some other poor unfortunate woman? Would he hold his tongue then?

I would tear him apart! he thought, thankful that Alicia was safe in Rudolpho's keeping. She was many miles from here, yet something deep within Rafael urged him to help this Gypsy girl, one of Alicia's Romany sisters. He remembered Zuba, so quiet and serene. What if this poor Gypsy girl was like her? How long could she survive? He had money. He would enlist the priest's aid in finding her, and when he did he would give her enough money to keep her out of the clutches of men like Enrique Dorado.

"On the grave of my mother, I swear that I will do all that I can," he whispered. Ignoring Violetta's questioning eyes, he rose to his feet and left the room.

45

Rafael spent a sleepless night haunted by dreams and visions. Alicia stood before him in her wedding dress, ribbons and flowers adorning her long dark hair. Smiling, she started toward him, calling his name softly, whispering words of love. He reached out to her, trying desperately to touch her, but with each step she drifted farther and farther away from him until she vanished into the early morning mist and he was left all alone.

"Alicia, come back," he mumbled, fighting against the bed linens, which in his dream he imagined to be arms holding him back. Leering faces peered down at him. Juan Dorado dressed in the black robes of his holy order, uttering the word "Gypsy" as if it were a curse; Enrique Dorado clothed all in scarlet, the color of blood, laughing, reaching out lasciviously to grab Alicia as she suddenly appeared again. Pushing them both aside, he struggled to reach her, but a man stepped directly in his path. His father! Like some demonic being his father kept him from going to Alicia, and he could only watch as her garments were slowly stripped away and she was left trembling on her hands and knees.

"Gypsy. Jew. *Marranos. Conversos.* Gypsy. Jew. Gypsy. Burn her! Burn her!" Voices in his head shouted over and over.

Tossing his head from side to side, fighting with the man who held him, Rafael was helpless as she started to scream. De Torga. Where was he? Carlos, help me. Please. Please.

Rafael awoke with a start, his heart beating wildly in his chest. He knew what the dream meant. It was his guilty conscience. Gypsies, like Jews, would be in danger soon. Already there were those who were calling the Gypsies blasphemers and threatening to cut out their tongues. Already the Supreme Council of the Inquisition was searching to find a way of ridding themselves of the Gypsies. So far no Gypsies had been arrested or punished, but what if such talk became law? He had left Alicia's side to come to the aid of people he did not even know. Was he noble or was he a fool?

"Alicia," he gasped, feeling a tightening in his chest as he spoke her name. Did she understand? He had not left her side willingly, though perhaps at first he had thought she was not good enough to be his wife, that the pagan ceremony had meant nothing. Now he realized that in every sense of the word, that in his heart and soul, she *was* his wife, as truly as if a priest had spoken words over them. He had been blind to the depth of his feelings once, but never again. The treasured memory of the passion they had shared would live forever in his heart. She was his love, his life.

Rafael heard angry voices downstairs. It was Don Philip and Doña Luisa arguing, destroying any chance they might have had for a happy marriage with each word that was spoken. He heard Don Philip inform his wife that he was riding into town, anywhere to be away from the barb of her tongue. Then the slamming of the front door reverberated through the house. Was that the kind of marriage that would have suited him? A marriage with "one of his own kind"? Putting his hands over his face, closing his eyes again, Rafael knew he wanted only Alicia. He should have brought her with him to be at his side. He was worse than a fool! But was it too late? Could he find her?

Jumping out of bed, dressing in a frenzy of excitement, he knew what he must do. He must find the Gypsy girl and send her back to Rudolpho's camp with a message begging

Alicia to forgive him and bidding her come to him. The Gypsy girl would help him. Alicia had told him many times that the Romany people were one, that all Gypsies helped one another, keeping a web of message lines so that they were always in touch with each other.

Slipping into his soft leather boots and lacing up his doublet, he scolded himself a thousand times. He had found happiness and love only to run away from it, and despite his noble reasons, his desire to save lives and become a hero, he knew now that to accomplish his mission he must have Alicia at his side. He couldn't think, couldn't function, without her. Nothing mattered to him in this life except Alicia. Seeing how unhappy Philip Navarro was had opened his heart and mind to the truth. He had glimpsed into his own future if he, like Philip, lost the woman he loved.

Making his way to the stable, he watched Philip Navarro saddle his horse and was tempted to ride into the city with him, but the expression on the man's face clearly spoke of his need to be alone, and so Rafael watched as the older man rode out, then mounted his own horse to follow the path that his heart led him to pursue.

46

Wrapping her arms tightly about her, Alicia tried desperately to keep warm beneath the small cart where she had found shelter for the night. Huddling into a small ball in an effort to hide from unfriendly eyes or from those who might harm her, she closed her eyes. Despair overwhelmed her and she fought against the urge to give up, to stop fighting so hard to survive. It would be so easy to go to sleep and never wake up again. Who really cared what happened to her? Certainly not the gorgios. Rafael had no doubt forgotten her. No one cared, no one.

Clutching at her stomach in an effort to calm the wrenching hunger pangs, she thought of how she had actually buried her pride last night to beg for a few coins to buy bread, but no one had shown her any kindness.

No one but Father Julio, she mused. He alone cared what happened to her. Just the thought of one person truly caring livened her spirits. Running her hands through her hair, she realized just how disheveled her appearance must be. She who was always so clean had not had a bath since arriving in Salamanca. She was dirty and ragged. No wonder the priest had pitied her. In shame she recalled how a small child had pointed at her as she had begged for bread and the mother's scathing words: "Don't be fooled by her. I have heard about Gypsies."

Why did they hate them so? They did not even understand Gypsy ways. No Gypsy would ever watch another human being starve to death without offering him bread. The gorgios were cruel, except for Father Julio. Father Julio. She was tempted to go back to the church to seek him out, but the memory of the man in red stopped her. The man with the countenance of a hawk and the eyes of the devil would harm her if given half a chance. No, she could not go back, but neither would she think of dying, of never waking up. Rudolpho would want her to survive. She *would* survive in spite of these gorgios.

The roosters had just started their early-morning crowing and the sound distracted her for just a moment. Rubbing the sleep out of her eyes, she rose to her knees, brushed the dirt and straw from her skirts, and peered out from beneath the wagon. The streets were deserted. Most of the townspeople were still abed.

Again the roosters crowed, and Alicia took heart. Where there were roosters there were hens. Following the sound, she envisioned her breakfast. There was no fire over which to cook a chicken, but hens meant eggs and she was hungry enough to snatch a few for her breakfast. When one was hungry perhaps even raw eggs could soothe the stomach. Even though Gypsies never ate eggs, she remembered that both Father Julio and Rafael had relished them.

Alicia found the hens in a small barn attached to a one-story wooden building down the street. Ducking into doorways, she made her way toward the barn without being seen, but as she approached the building the chickens began cackling, threatening to give her away.

"Hush, chicka. Do not carry on so or you will bring down the walls about my ears." she scolded softly, reaching her slim fingers beneath the soft underside of one hen. Taking an egg, tapping it lightly to break the shell at the top, she let the warm, sticky, slippery substance fill her mouth. Wriggling her nose in disgust at the taste, she swallowed quickly and reached for another. Strange how this one did not taste nearly as bad as the first. Was it possible to acquire a taste for them? She felt stronger now that she had eaten, though the thought of having taken something that did not belong to her bothered her soul. But there were plenty of eggs, and the chickens would surely replenish what she had eaten. So thinking, she reached for another and then another until a woman's shriek behind her startled her.

"Thief! Gypsy thief. My chickens. My chickens!" Standing in the entrance to the barn was a stout woman, her girth blocking Alicia's escape.

"No, I'm not stealing the chickens. . . ." Alicia sought to explain, but the woman's shouts frightened the birds and the hens pecked and scratched at Alicia, drawing blood before she could pull her hands away. "Please, I do not want your chickens. I was hungry. I only took a few eggs." Standing up, she met the woman nose-to-nose, her eyes pleading with her for silence. Now she knew why Rudolpho had strickly forbidden the stealing of these gorgio birds.

"Liar, I caught you red-handed. I will see you punished for this." Running to the doorway, the woman looked for a soldier to take Alicia away, but Alicia pushed her aside with a strength born of desperation. She would not let these gorgios lock her up; she was free, she was Gypsy. Fleeing down the cobblestones as two men gave chase, Alicia ran for her very life. Darting in and out among the small adobe buildings, she tripped once or twice and fell to the ground, bruising her arms and legs, only to get up again and renew her flight. In her terror, Alicia grew careless, fleeing directly into the path of a horse and rider.

"Make way for Señor Navarro, Gypsy bitch!" shouted a silver-clad soldier, but it was too late. Tripping over a loose stone, Alicia was hurled to the ground by the force of her flight. The fall knocked the breath from her body and she could only lie there waiting for death as the sound of the horse's hooves came thundering down upon her.

"Madre de Dios!" Philip Navarro saw the young woman in

his path and tried desperately to rein in his horse, but could not. Judging the distance and the speed of the animal, he knew that the only way he could save the young woman's life was by hurtling over her, risking the chance that she would be struck by the horse's flying hooves. "Blessed Cristo!" For a moment after the jump he feared to look back, but when he did, he was relieved to see that she was unharmed. Had he been a less skilled rider, the Gypsy girl would be dead, but his many years of riding and training horses had rewarded him and the young woman as well.

Dismounting from his horse, Don Philip ran back to help the young woman to her feet. "Señorita, are you all right?" She was so pale, so thin, that his heart went out to her. Was this the girl Enrique had told him about? "Here, take my handkerchief." Gentle he wiped the dirt from her face, brushing back the hair from her eyes as he did so. "I did not see you. You ran in front of my horse before I could even think . . ."

"I'm all right." Alicia's voice was barely more than a whisper as her eyes darted back and forth looking for any sign of her pursuers. "Please, let me go now." She struggled to get up, but Don Philip's hands restrained her.

"You might be injured. Let me help you up." Putting his strong arms about her, it was only then that he saw her face. "Madre de Dios!" he gasped again, staring at the girl in disbelief, as if seeing a ghost. His heart stopped for a fleeting moment, then started to beat again with a furious pounding. This Gypsy girl. She was beautiful, the most beautiful woman he had ever seen. Her hair, dark, rich brown, shining with red highlights in the early-morning sun, reminded him of hair he had once loved to touch. The nose, small and straight, the skin so smooth, all reminded him of another face; but it was the eyes, those twin emeralds that gazed back at him with such fiery pride, that were his undoing. He knew those eyes so well, they had haunted him for many years.

"Please let me go." Alicia was frightened by the way this man was looking at her.

"Catalina! Catalina!" he gasped, taking a step forward. It was as if he had gone mad. Catalina was dead. Many years had passed. Seventeen years. His wife was dead. Dead. This could not be his beloved wife and yet . . . The resemblance was astounding, leaving him trembling and torn with poignant memories.

"I must go. They are after me. Please. Please." Alicia tried desperately to pull free of the strong hands that held her, but she was exhausted from her ordeal and could only stand helpless before him.

Philip Navarro sensed the girl's fright but somehow he could not bear to part with her. It was as if she had brought back another time. "Catalina."

"My name is not Catalina." Alicia shook her head from side to side in denial.

Sadness clouded Philip Navarro's eyes. "No, of course it is not. I am sorry. It is just that you remind me of her. She was my wife. I loved her so, but she is dead and I cannot forget her no matter how hard I try."

Alicia was touched by his sadness and reached out a hand to touch his shoulder. "I'm sorry that she is dead." She was strangely drawn to this man and wondered why. He was a gorgio, a total stranger, and yet suddenly she found herself pouring out the story of the eggs and the chickens, of her innocence and her fear that she would be imprisoned. Why did she feel so gratified when his eyes told her that he believed her?

"I know you did not mean to steal the hens," he whispered, leading her to his horse. "You must come with me. I will not leave you here on these streets to suffer again from people's ignorance."

Alicia looked at this handsome face, smooth, devoid of the wrinkles that might have plagued other men of his age.

She was intrigued by him, but still she said softly, "I cannot take your charity. I am Gypsy and Gypsies must be free."

"You will be free," Philip Navarro assured her. "As free as the sparrows that fly past my windows. You may come and go as you like, but you will have food and shelter and my protection if you desire it."

"I will work for my food and shelter." As she threw back her head, her green eyes met his with firm resolve.

"If you insist. Only come with me. Please." His eyes were in such startling contrast to the tan of his face—blue eyes that held the look of kindness. Alicia studied his face; looked at his hair, gray with silver threads that shone in the morning sun. She decided that going with him was the right thing to do.

Lifting her onto his horse, Philip Navarro felt young again, as if the years had melted away.

47

Alicia held tightly to the waist of the silver-haired gorgio nobleman as they rode through the winding city streets. Ignoring the shocked faces of the people milling about, openly staring at the proud *caballero* and the ragged Gypsy girl, Alicia had an overpowering feeling that this was her destiny, that in some way *o Del* had brought this man to her.

They traveled beyond the city to the outskirts, and Alicia opened her eyes wide as a huge hacienda surrounded by an iron fence loomed in their path. Sunlight danced on the tiles of the roof, and it looked almost unreal, like a vision brought on by hunger or moon madness.

"This is my home," the man whispered with pride, and Alicia couldn't help but be awed. She stared in open fascination as her benefactor guided the horse onward.

When they arrived at their destination, the man helped her down from the horse right in front of the stables. With a snap of his fingers, he enlisted the aid of the stableman to tend the animal and the man did as he was bid while ogling Alicia as if he had never seen a woman before.

"José, mind your manners," Philip Navarro barked, motioning him away. Turning to Alicia, he smiled again. "Your beauty has mesmerized him, Señorita." Gently he took her hand. "Come."

As they walked up the cobblestoned pathway toward the hacienda, Alicia looked all about her, questioning the wis-

dom of what she had done. She didn't even know this man.
Why, then, had she come with him? What was it about him
that made her decision seem to be so right?

"You will like it here," Don Philip was saying. "I will
make certain that you are comfortable." Here and there a
circular balcony jutted out from the second floor, encased by
the same iron grillwork that fenced the entire house. Climbing up the walls was a mosslike plant that looked strangely
like the flames of a green fire.

"Beautiful." Alicia sighed as her eyes glanced upon a
white marble statue of a naked angel that stood guard over a
fountain by the front door.

"It was sculpted in Venice," Philip Navarro said proudly,
walking with the buoyant step of newfound youth as he led
her to the front door. The door was opened by a white-
turbaned young Moor, who smiled, his gleaming white
teeth contrasting sharply with the darkness of his skin.

"Hadaj, tell Juanita to prepare a plate of figs and cheese.
And have bath water sent up for this young woman. She is
to be our houseguest." The Moor bowed silently, then hurried off to obey his orders.

"Your guest?" Alicia whispered. "No. No. I cannot live
here without repaying you in some way for my food and
shelter." The old stubbornness she had shown with Father
Julio crept over her and she lifted her chin in defiance, but as
her eyes met those of the silver-haired gentleman, her heart
melted. There was such sadness in his eyes that she forgot
all about her own pride and asked, "Why do you look so sad
when you look at me? Is it because I remind you of her, of
Catalina?" Strange how that name sounded so soothing
upon her lips.

He nodded, telling her about the death of his wife after
she had borne him a daughter, about how much he had
loved them both, about his grief when he also lost the child
and how he had wanted to die when he lost them. "But God

did not answer my plea. I am still walking the earth, though my heart is dead."

Alicia felt his pain and reached out to him, touching his hand. "I understand your sadness. I, too, have lost someone I loved. My father."

"I am sorry, my child." There was a long silence before he whispered, "Perhaps together we can soothe our sorrow." He led her up a winding staircase and stood before the thick wooden door a long moment before he said, "When I saw you I felt suddenly alive again."

"You showed me kindness. You are in truth a noble man."

"No. I am not being noble in bringing you here, but selfish. Seeing you, being in your presence, enables me to pretend, if only for a moment or two, that Catalina is not dead. Forgive an old man for using you in such a way, but hearing you talk, seeing your face, your smile, has allowed me to go back in time to a happier day. I owe you a great deal for such a gift."

"But I must pay you in some way."

His fingers covered her lips, silencing her protestations. "Let us talk no more of your repaying me. If you are happy, I am rewarded threefold."

He opened the door and Alicia stepped into the room. The first thing she noticed was the fire burning in the large stone fireplace, and she quickly made her way toward its warmth to take the early morning chill from her body.

"I have ordered food and bathwater sent up. *Mi casa es su casa.*"

He left, closing the door behind him, and Alicia realized that she was alone. Looking around her at the grandeur of the room, she felt fiercely out of place. She wondered how many Gypsy wagons would fit inside. At least eight, perhaps ten. The strange high bed in the middle of the room was nearly as large as Rudolpho's wagon had been. It had a large canopy overhead, much like the one that had fluttered overhead on her wedding day as she and Rafael had taken their vows, vows that had meant nothing to him, she thought in anger. Leaving the fire and approaching the bed, she noticed the four thick posts that stood at each corner, reminding her of the trees of the forest. She could see that there were designs carved in the wood, a design of leaves and swirls. Running her fingers over them, she could not help wondering what Rudolpho would say if he could see them.

Oh, Papa, is this what you wanted for me when you told me that I was not truly Gypsy, when you whispered the word "León" while you lay dying? His spirit seemed to answer "yes" from the depths of her heart where he was entombed. She was now back among her own kind, but would she find happiness here?

Exploring the room, gazing at the handwoven rugs and the tapestries with their many colors, she was dazzled by the intricate workmanship. There were four tables with high backs beside the bed, three of them covered in thick cushions, and she wondered what they were to be used for. Surely one did not cook in such a room as this, but what else was a table for except to hold cooking supplies? As if to answer her question a small wizened old woman entered the room with a tray filled to overflowing with food. Setting it on the bare table, she motioned toward one of the cushioned tables.

"Sit down and rest yourself, Señorita, while you partake of these culinary delights," the old woman said.

Alicia filled a plate with figs, cheese, and apples, then sat upon the floor beside the cushioned table, managing only by her pride to keep from gulping the food down. Balancing the tray in one hand, she leaned the other upon the velvet cushions, looking up only when she heard an intake of breath from the woman.

"No. No. No." Her eyebrows raised, the woman's look and tone were scolding. "Sit upon the chairs, not upon the floor."

Throwing back her head, Alicia held her chin up at a

proud angle, wondering what she had done wrong. "I am comfortable where I am." Her manner was defiant, but she silently took note of the name the woman had called the strange tables. Chairs. She would remember that word and that these foolish gorgios used them to rest their bottoms.

Again she began eating, hardly tasting the food that passed between her lips, eyeing the old woman up and down, wondering if she would be friend or foe. Juanita, he had called her. Alicia decided that although she was gorgio, Juanita would show her kindness. Her eyes said as much as she regarded Alicia with motherly concern.

"Now, get out of those torn and dirty clothes," she commanded as three young boys poured buckets of steaming hot water into a large tub they had brought in and placed near the fire. "You take your bath while I find you something to wear." With a cluck of her tongue the woman was gone.

Stripping off her blouse, skirts, and soft leather shoes, Alicia edged closer to the tub. Alicia was fascinated by the sweet smell of the water. Having bathed all her life in rivers and ponds or by means of sponged stream water in winter months, she wondered just how she was supposed to bathe in this enormous bucket. Was she to stand beside it and splash the water over herself as the Gypsies might do, or stand knee-deep in the water's warmth? Deciding on the latter, she dipped in her hand, surprised to find the water too hot. Were these gorgios going to cook her? Their skin must be several layers deep to stand such scalding water.

Adding cold water from a bucket left beside the tub, Alicia at last cooled the bath and stepped inside. Although it was still a bit too hot, she soon became used to the warmth, relishing the soothing water as it enveloped her legs. Reaching down and cupping her hands with the water, she splashed it over her body, enjoying herself and the feel of being clean again until she heard a voice behind her. Juanita had returned.

"Sit down in the tub. Don't be afraid, Señorita. And use some of the soap to clean your body. Watch." Reaching for the small white object, Juanita showed Alicia how to work up a lather. The smell of the soap was like the wildflowers of the forest in spring, and Alicia spread it all over her, from the top of her hair to the tips of her toes, laughing at the bubbles that formed as she moved about in the tub, wiping her eyes and frowning as the lather stung her eyes. "I like this *soap,*" she said aloud, leaning back to let the warmth envelop her body as she closed her eyes. This, at least, this one gorgio habit, she approved of. "Someday I will tell Zuba of this and we will laugh together." Where was Zuba at this moment? she wondered wistfully. Would she really ever see her again?

At last, when the water grew cold, Alicia stood up, took a soft linen towel from Juanita's outstretched hands, and dried herself.

"I found a robe for you among Doña Violetta's things," the servant exclaimed, holding forth one made of blue brocade. Although it had obviously seen better days and was now faded and worn, Alicia thought it beautiful and stroked its designs and the threads of deep blue in fascination. "It is too large for you, but it will do until I find you a decent dress to wear."

It was too big, but it was dry and clean and Alicia was grateful.

"Thank you, Juanita," she whispered, smiling at the old woman. The smile was returned.

"I will let you rest now," the servant said, handing Alicia another linen towel to wrap around her hair. "If you need anything, just call me. Señor Navarro wants you to find comfort here." Waddling toward the door on her short legs, she looked back, hesitating before she spoke, as if she feared to be heard by other ears. "Let me warn you about Doña Luisa. Stay out of her way or you will not be happy here." With that warning spoken she left the room.

"Doña Luisa. Doña Luisa." Why does that name sound so familiar? Why does it fill me with fear? Alicia had not even met the woman and yet somehow the name was one that she imagined she had heard before. "Strange." Suddenly her newfound contentment was shadowed with a dark foreboding.

48

The doors of the church clanked shut with a resounding noise and Rafael reprimanded himself for letting his emotions goad him to show such irreverence. It was just that now, having made up his mind to send a message to Alicia, he was desperate to find the Gypsy girl. It would be like looking for a chick-pea in a wheatfield, for Salamanca was a large city, but he had to try. The logical place to begin was here in the church where Enrique had seen her.

"May I help you, my son?" Rafael whirled around to find himself looking at a smiling priest whose round face and manner reminded him of a cherub.

"You are Father Julio?" It was as if his desire to find the priest had conjured him up, for he knew without asking that the priest was that kindly churchman.

"I am."

"Then you can tell me about the Gypsy girl you gave shelter to several days ago. I must find her!" Rafael could hear his heart pounding so loudly in his ears that he was certain the priest could hear it too. "Where did she go?"

Father Julio was silent, but his expression clearly spoke of his determination to protect the girl and his fear of Rafael's intentions.

"Please, you must tell me. I swear that I mean her no harm. I only want to give her a message to give to one of her own people, another Gypsy girl, a woman that I love with all my heart." His eyes held a plea that was communicated to the dark-robed Father immediately. "I am not a man like Enrique Dorado, a simpleton whose narrow-mindedness affects his ability to see past his nose. I am not one of those who scorn the Gypsies, I have no intention of harming her. Please."

"I believe you, my son. I believe you, but I am afraid that I do not know where she went." He shook his head. "Such a pity. Such a pity. I wanted to help her. She was so thin, little more than skin and bones, yet such a proud little bird. She insisted that she would not take charity." The round face contorted with anger. "I would have convinced her to stay here with us, where she would have known only kindness, but Enrique Dorado came thundering in like the devil himself and frightened her away!"

"He told me the story. I have no doubt but that such a one as he could frighten God himself. But I came here hoping that the Gypsy girl might have come back or that you might have some idea where she might have gone." Remembering Alicia's certainty that no Gypsy would travel alone unless banished, he asked, "Have you any idea why she was separated from her caravan? Did she say anything to you about herself, anything that could help me find her? Was she banished?"

"The young woman left of her own free will after the death of her father, who was the leader of the caravan. His last words bade her come to León. Poor man. Had he only known the hostility she would meet, he would never have made such a suggestion. You see, Enrique Dorado is not the exception but the rule. We Christians talk about charity and brotherly love, but they are only words without actions of the heart to guide us." He motioned for Rafael to follow him. "Come, let us go to my quarters and find a little simple comfort. A glass of wine perhaps." As they walked Rafael could not help comparing Father Julio with that other, Juan Dorado. They were as different as winter from spring, night from the light of the sun, yet both were priests of God. The difference was ambition. Juan Dorado had chosen to take the vows of the church to further his own ends; this kindly, jovial priest to be one of God's earthly angels.

Objects of art had lined Juan Dorado's walls; shelves of books lined Father Julio's room. Making a sweeping gesture with his hand, he grinned. "These are my friends, these books. With them I can travel through time and unlock the secrets of the greatest minds. It is what distinguishes man from the animals, I believe, this ability to read the written word.

"Yet there are those who would take such a gift away and lead us back into those years when man was an ignorant creature so that man is at their mercy. I must allow myself the hope that reason will prevail, for man's intellect is his link with God." The priest gestured to an old wooden-backed chair. "Sit. Sit." After pouring Rafael a glass of wine he took his own place in a chair similar to the one Rafael sat upon. "But I will not go on and on about about my own thoughts. You were asking about this young Gypsy woman."

"I asked you if she had been banished from her tribe. I have heard that this often happens. You said that she left of her own free will after the death of her father; but knowing as I do of the fierce loyalty Gypsies have for one another, I do not understand why such a thing would cause her to leave."

"Pride. Fear. The man who took her father's place was her enemy and would have made her suffer a woman's greatest indignity. He threatened to make use of her body anytime he so chose. Was it any wonder she ran away?" Father Julio clasped his hands fervently. "There are evil men everywhere. Poor child. Poor, beautiful child. If only I might have helped her."

"Perhaps if I can find her, you will have your chance." Even though he did not know the young woman, the story of her flight to León struck a chord deep within Rafael's soul. Perhaps by his kindness to her he could atone for his foolishness in leaving Alicia. He could not help but think that save for the mercy of God, that young woman might have been Alicia. Were Rudolpho to die and Stivo to take his place, she, too, would be faced with a dangerous enemy.

"You must find her before it is too late. The day that she came to me she had barely escaped from the crowd. I have so many fears for her. I see her eyes in my dreams, those bright green eyes, begging me to help her."

"Green eyes!" Rafael felt as if someone were choking him; he could barely get the words out. A green-eyed Gypsy was, he knew, a rarity, yet what a foolish man he was to even suppose that . . . no . . . it couldn't be. Still, he found himself asking, "What was her name?"

"She had a strange name for a Gypsy, but then, I can only imagine that it was because she was not truly a Gypsy at all. Her father had adopted her. On his deathbed he revealed the truth. What a shock that must have been to her."

"Not a Gypsy!" Rafael could not help but remember Alicia's pride in her heritage.

"And then the people here in Salamanca treated her so cruelly. She told me she could never live among her own kind. Poor Alicia. Poor child, torn between two worlds."

"Alicia?" Rafael gasped, afraid to move, afraid to breathe. "No, it can't be."

"Alicia *was* her name. I remember the name, my son." Father Julio bolted from his chair and came over to Rafael to lay a hand on his shoulder. The young man was deathly pale, as if he had just seen an apparition. "Are you all right?"

"Her father . . . do you remember her father's name?"

"That I do not remember." Putting his hand to his brow, he closed his eyes to concentrate. "Ricardo . . . Ramondo . . . Rodrigo . . ."

"Rudolpho?"

"Rudolpho? Ah, yes, Rudolpho was the name. I remember thinking of the Holy Roman Emperor Rudolph at the time." He smiled sheepishly. "That is how I remember names, by linking them with historical personages. Rudolpho. Yes. Yes."

"Madre de Dios!" In his shock Rafael swore aloud, causing Father Julio to chastise him with a frown. It was *she*, his Alicia. It had to be. Still, he held a hope that it was not, for the thought of having left her to such a fate was more than he could bear. "Where was she from? Did she tell you? Did she say where her caravans came from?"

"From outside Toledo. She spoke of a forest there." Father Julio suddenly realized why Rafael was asking all the questions. "You know her. She is the one that you spoke of loving. Yet she had such sadness in her eyes. She was crying, yet she tried to tell me that it was the onions. I knew differently. I knew that her heart had been wounded. . . ." Father Julio turned his head away for only a moment. When he looked back where Rafael had been, he saw only an empty chair.

49

Rafael's head was reeling wildly as he rode through the streets of Salamanca. Alicia! He had to find her! What had he done? What had he done? The answer whispered back at him with each hiss of the wind that swirled in his ears. He had deserted the only woman he had ever loved, left her to the cruelest of fates. His proud Gypsy love, the only woman he wanted as his wife, was walking the lonely streets of Salamanca, friendless and hungry.

The demon of guilt hurried him on as all sorts of images whirled about in his head—Alicia huddled in a dark alleyway, hungry and cold from the chill of the night; Alicia suffering the taunts and wounds of an angry crowd. He had to find her!

Rudolpho dead! The thought pierced through him like a knife. That proud, wise, noble man whose only thought had been for his daughter's happiness. Dead. Gone. Poor Alicia, to have suffered such grief alone without his arms to comfort her, Rafael thought bitterly, cursing himself for ten kinds of fool. He had ridden off with his brother when he should have listened to his heart! Now Alicia's suffering was his punishment, his purgatory.

"Alicia!" His cry mingled with the howl of the wind. Had he really thought it would be so easy to find her? How many streets were there in the city? Yet he knew he must search every alleyway, every church, every house.

Rudolpho had known he was dying! The thought tormented Rafael with every thud of his horse's hooves. Little by little the Gypsy leader had been dying and that was why he had been so insistent on marrying his daughter to Rafael, to protect her from the malice and cruelty of Stivo. Rudolpho had known what would happen when he died, had read the lust in the younger Gypsy's blazing eyes, and had sought a way to keep her safe. He had trusted Rafael with his most treasured gift, and Rafael had been so blinded by his own thoughts that he had betrayed Rudolpho's faith in him. Could Alicia ever forgive him? Could he ever forgive himself?

Rafael rode, ran, and walked through the winding streets and alleys, stopping passersby, knocking on every door, daring to hope that he would find at least one person who would tell him that he had seen a Gypsy girl. He clung to the small shred of hope that he could find Alicia, no matter how fragile that possibility might be. Vendors and tradesmen did not escape his query, not did the beggars on the street; but though there were several who remembered seeing a young Gypsy woman several days ago, not one of them could give him hope that she was anywhere near the marketplace now.

At last the twilight faded into a darkness that cast long shadows on the high adobe houses and stone walls of the city, and Rafael was forced to admit defeat, at least for the moment. Yet he refused to return to the comfort and luxury of the Navarro house, nor would he give in to his hunger and use the coins in his pockets to purchase his supper. Somewhere in this city Alicia was walking about ragged and starving. How could he taste bread, knowing that she went hungry? How could he seek the solace of his soft bed while she huddled alone in an alleyway, sleeping on cold, hard stones?

The bells from from a nearby church chimed eight times as Rafael walked the streets, having stabled his horse for the night. The area that he chose was a haunt for thieves, prostitutes, soldiers down on their luck, and those whose love of wine had been their ruination—a dangerous place for a nobleman. It was the only part of town that would offer sanctuary to a Gypsy, and he held on to the hope that Alicia would come here for the night.

Skillfully dodging a foul-smelling drunk, keeping a hand on his sword all the while, Rafael scanned the area with his eyes. Dark shadows hovered about the moon like evil ghosts, blocking out all light, and at last, thirsty, hungry, and tired, Rafael found a resting place. Pillowing his head against his arm, he tried to find comfort from his thoughts, but sleep eluded him. *Alicia,* her name would be forever branded on his heart, her face a lovely dream to haunt him.

"I am a Gypsy, Gorgio," he seemed to hear her say, with that haughty tone that bespoke her pride. A Gypsy! So different from his own kind, he had thought, wild and untamed. Gypsy, the people his own people scorned. How wrong he had been, just as blinded as those who had persecuted his mother. Christian. Jew. Gypsy. Moor. What did a name matter? Living, breathing, loving, marrying, caring for their children, mourning the loss of a loved one—weren't they people after all?

Gypsy! If Alicia had been a nobleman's daughter, would he have left her behind to follow his fate into Toledo? Gypsy! It was a word he, too, had scorned in his foolishness. Yet was there any man greater than Rudolpho had been? Any woman as worthy of his love as Alicia? Gypsy! But even in this the devil had mocked him, making him a victim of his own blindness. Alicia was not a Gypsy, she was one of his own after all. What a cruel joke!

"Noooooooo!" Forgetting where he was, the danger that lurked all around, Rafael uttered a cry like that of a wounded animal. He was in danger of losing her, the most beautiful soul that had ever touched his life.

And what of Alicià, how had she felt when Rudolpho had

at last told her the truth? Had she wept? Had she raged?
Poor Alicia, to find out that she was not a Gypsy after all.

The night was cold, and in an effort to keep warm Rafael
grasped his knees, hugging them to his body as he had when
he was a small boy. Rocking back and forth, he battled the
demons that tore at his heart, but there was only one way to
exorcise them. Gone now were all thoughts of Juan Dorado,
all ideas of heroism. He resolved to stay in Salamanca until
she was found. Tomorrow at the crack of dawn he would
send a message to Don Philip to explain his absence and
hope that when he returned to that noble gentleman's house
it would be with Alicia at his side.

50

The soft light of the early-morning sun teased Alicia's closed lids, and in startled confusion she quickly opened her eyes, gazing up at the ceiling. Where was she? The memory of kind blue eyes stilled her fear as she remembered the nobleman whose house she was in. Lying on a blanket by the side of the large bed, for she had found the gorgio bed much too soft for her liking, Alicia stretched her arms and legs and looked around her. A large tapestry on one of the walls was the first thing to catch her eye, the rich woodland scene so lifelike that Alicia felt tears sting her eyes at the memory of the tranquil happiness she had once enjoyed.

But tomorrow is gone and I must live today, she thought, brushing away the tears that had escaped her eyes. *O Del* had been kind in bringing her here, away from the cold and the cruel stares of the angry gorgios. She had been given another chance for life, and more than this she could not ask.

A light tapping announced an intruder, and Alicia watched as the door opened slowly to reveal Juanita's face. "Señorita, are you awake?" The woman entered the room to gawk at Alicia sprawled on the floor. "Are you hurt? Did you fall?"

Alicia got up quickly, realizing that once again she had offended the woman with her Gypsy ways. "I did not fall," was all Alicia said, eyeing the tray that the woman was holding in her hands.

"Fresh milk and fried cakes made from bread batter dropped into boiling olive oil, sprinkled with sugar. For you."

Remembering last night's lesson, Alicia moved toward one of the chairs, easing herself down upon the cushion. It was not as uncomfortable as she would have supposed, and she smiled at Juanita as she took the tray from her hands. The sugared bread was delicious. Alicia showed her appreciation by licking the last granules of sweetness from her fingers only to find Juanita once again watching her in horrified silence.

"You must not do such a thing," the woman scolded. "There are cloths to clean the hands."

"But I only . . ." Alicia was stung by the rebuke, having only wanted to thank the woman by such a gesture. It was the *Gypsy* way.

Juanita's expression softened as she read the hurt in Alicia's eyes. "There are many things that you must learn, Señorita. I must remember to be patient. Such things will take time. Don Philip has told me that you are to be our honored guest."

Alicia was fiercely defiant, she would not take charity. "I am to be like you, a servant here. I must work for what food and shelter I receive." Her eyes scanned the room once more as she wondered just what kind of work she could do.

"Then your first task is to get dressed." Leaving the room for just a brief moment, Juanita returned with a bundle of clothes in her hands. "These will have to do until the dressmaker can make you some of your own. They are slightly out of style."

Alicia chose a bright red skirt and a separate black bodice that laced across a white chemise. She guessed that these garments, like the robe, had belonged to the woman Juanita called Doña Violetta and thought how grateful she was to the woman for giving her the use of her clothes. She must seek this woman out and give her proper Gypsy thanks for her generosity.

"These were Doña Violetta's when she was growing from child to woman." Juanita prattled on as she tugged at the snarls in Alicia's hair with a wooden comb, dividing the thick tresses into two long plaits. "She was such a sweet child until *she* poisoned her with her own cruelty. Poor Don Philip! You will soon see, Señorita, that this is not a happy household. But come, I will speak no more of it. He has asked to see you first thing this morning, and in all things do I comply."

Alicia wanted to ask Juanita so many things, about Catalina, about the silver-haired gorgio, but the woman's firm hand in the small of her back prodded her out the door and down the long stairway. Walking through a wide archway, Alicia found herself confronted by her benefactor.

"The most pleasant of mornings!" His smile was cheerful as he took her hand. "Did you rest well?" His hair and clipped beard shone with silver in the morning sun, and Alicia stared at him in unabashed fascination as he studied her with his startling blue eyes. What was it about those eyes that tugged at a corner of her brain?

"I slept most soundly, thank you."

"And the gown that Juanita found for you is most becoming, I see. You look very lovely, Cat—" He started to call her by the other woman's name but silenced himself just in time. "No. I must never again call you that; you have your own name. Forgive me." He raised one silvered eyebrow as if asking her to tell him what she would like to be called.

"Alicia," she answered quickly. Hearing her answer, he grew quite pale, and Alicia wondered why he looked at her as if he were staring at *o Beng* himself.

"No. No, it can't be. It is but a cruel jest." His voice was so soft that Alicia barely heard him, but the wounded look in his eyes brought forth her pity. "God is mocking me!

Why? I have ever been a righteous man. Why, then, does he bring forth a woman who looks the image of my dead wife and bears my daughter's name, the name of my girl child who drowned!" Reaching out to grasp her by the shoulders, he looked searchingly into her eyes. "You would not lie to me? This is not a trick? A plot? A way to torment me?" The wide innocent eyes staring back at him answered truthfully. "No, you are not the kind of woman who would consort with my wife. And if Alicia is in truth your name . . ."

Anxious to please him, Alicia reached out for his hand. "If my name brings you pain, you may call me anything you like. I would not want to be the cause of your hurt. You have been kind to me."

"Alicia!" His grasp was warm as he gripped her fingers. "Alicia. I will repeat the name until the pain within my soul lessens. Alicia. Alicia." The grimace of his frown slowly dissolved away. "If it were any other who bore that name, upon their soul I would be angry, but somehow the name suits you, child." Motioning Juanita away, he led Alicia into a huge room, his eyes studying her all the while. Nodding his head, he bade her sit down on a chair that was nearly as large as a bed. Though this one was of wood and not padded, Alicia found it to be comfortable in its way, though she would have preferred sitting on her heels on the floor. "Tell me all about yourself. Have you always been a Gypsy?"

Alicia began her tale at the beginning, telling this gorgio gentleman all about the kindness Rudolpho had always shown her, about her pride in being his daughter, her happiness in living among the members of her caravan. She talked of Zuba, of Todero, of Mala and Palo, laughing as she related the joy she had felt in being in their company, yet her eyes grew dark as she mentioned Stivo's name. As she spoke, her entire life was set before the Spanish gentleman, yet Alicia found herself telling him everything, even about the gorgio who broke her heart.

"It was because of the gorgio that Rudolpho, my papa,

died," she said bitterly. "He tried to ride after him to bring him back but his heart . . ."

"And after he died you left the tribe."

"Stivo was made their leader, and I could not stay, knowing he was my enemy. What he wished of me was unthinkable, an insult he would never have dared thrust upon a girl of Gypsy blood." Her eyes misted with tears. "But he knew that I was not born among the Gypsies, that I was not Rudolpho's true daughter, no matter how much he loved me in his heart."

Philip Navarro held his breath, his voice coming out in a choked gasp. "You are not Gypsy?"

"Rudolpho told me the story before he died, though he knew it would break my heart. It was a thing I had to know." Closing her eyes, Alicia fought the tears that threatened to flood her eyes at the memory of that tragic day. "He told me a woman had brought me to the camp, a gorgio. I had no parents to care for me and so she hoped the Gypsies would take me with them. Rudolpho told me that it was to León that I must come, to know the truth of my birth."

"The truth of your birth." Philip Navarro was staring at her, but his mind seemed to be miles away, and Alicia wondered if he had been upset by her story. "Yes, we shall soon know more about this matter and the falsehoods devised by others." At Alicia's quizzical look, his tone of voice softened. "But perhaps with your help I may chase away the demons of the past. Will you help me, Alicia? Will you bring a ray of joy into the life of an aging man?"

Nodding quickly, Alicia was pleased to see him smile. The pain faded from his blue eyes, and she thought once again what a handsome man he was, a strong and just man like Rudolpho. She listened to his avowal to make a lady of her, little realizing how great a change was about to come into her life as she fulfilled her destiny.

51

It was raining. Big drops of *o Del*'s tears splattered against the round windows, and Alicia looked toward the greenish yellow panes of glass in frustration, longing to be out of doors, feeling confined in this gorgio dwelling no matter how spacious it was. Sighing, she walked to the windows and laid her forehead against the cool glass, resigned to be patient. The weather would clear, and when it did she would be able to walk out on the terrace again. There were flowers and shrubs planted there in earthen jars, green and fragrant with the smell of life, and when the weather permitted, Alicia spent all of her free time there, savoring a last link with her Gypsy life. She would in fact have much preferred to sleep there had Don Philip permitted it, but not wanting to see him frown, she had held back the request. It was his desire, he had said, to make her a lady.

A lady, Alicia thought sullenly. She was not certain whether she was living a dream or a nightmare, for this living as the gorgios did was no easy matter. There were so many things that must *not* be done, so many rules and regulations, that she wondered that the gorgios remembered them all. Yet the wish to please the man who had shown her such kindness led her to do her very best. Just to see him smile was well worth the price she had to pay.

Pacing the room, Alicia reflected on the three days she had spent in Philip Navarro's house. He had been very kind

to her, this Alicia could not deny, though at times he made
her feel uneasy with his questions and searching looks, and
she did not understand why. It was almost as if he were
trying to make her retrieve something from the farthest recesses of her mind, yet his interrogations only gave her
headaches. She wanted to remember, but each time she
came close to piercing the veil of memory, she found herself
standing before a locked door. Perhaps *o Del* did not want
her to remember, at least not now.

Nor was she certain she could be happy in the gorgio
world no matter how she tried. There were times when Alicia wondered if she was honored guest or prisoner, though
at all times Philip Navarro was true to his promise to let her
come and go as she pleased. Still, was it any wonder that
Alicia avoided the eyes of the women of the house, who
looked at her with the same hostility as the women in Salamanca had. Heeding Juanita's advice, Alicia kept well away
from Philip Navarro's wife, sensing the woman's enmity.
Being more at ease with the cook, stable hand, and house-
maids, Alicia delighted in the servants' company. She soon
learned that Doña Luisa avoided those she considered her
inferiors. The kitchen was the one place where Alicia could
be herself, crouching upon her heels and listening to the
tales and legends of Spain. El Cid soon became her favorite,
for in so many ways his courage reminded her of
Rudolpho's. Perhaps the gorgios were not so bad after all.

The tinkling sound of the dinner bell intruded upon
Alicia's thoughts, making her scowl. That first thing that
Juanita had attacked was Alicia's habit of eating with her
hands. Thrusting two strange-looking objects at her, which
she said were to be used to carry food from the plate to her
mouth, Juanita had been insistent that Alicia mimic her as
they sat at the servants' table to eat. Such foolishness. Why
did the gorgios not eat sensibly with their fingers? Remembering the first time she had brought food to Rafael, Alicia
recalled the look of shock in his eyes when he had learned

he would have to eat with his hands. Had he felt as strange then as she did now?

"Use the fork to hold your meat securely as you cut off a small piece with the knife," Juanita had said, watching as Alicia struggled to use the strange pronged instrument to lift the smaller portion of meat to her lips. Trying to manage such a skill without allowing the food to fall into her lap sorely vexed Alicia and she cursed aloud, which only tried Juanita's patience further. Cursing was most strictly forbidden.

Must not, cannot, should not, were phrases that Alicia had heard quite often the last few days, so often that she wanted to run from the sharpness of Juanita's tongue; but once her own anger had cooled she put such thoughts aside. A Gypsy, be she one of the blood or not, would never break a promise, and she had given her word to Philip Navarro that she would stay.

Why had she given such a promise? she wondered now. Was it because she had a feeling that this silver-haired man was part of her destiny, that *o Del* in his wisdom wanted her to bring him a measure of happiness? Was that why she gave in to his wishes to make of her a gorgio lady? No physical bonds kept Alicia within these walls, but something more binding than doors or chains, an affection for this man that was growing deeper every day. Not since Rudolpho had died had she felt such a bond.

Philip Navarro would have made a good Gypsy, Alicia thought with a smile, wondering if she would dare pay him such a compliment. Would he be offended, would he take her words to be an insult when she only meant them as the highest praise? It was an interesting thought as she made her way down the stairs, pausing as Doña Luisa crossed her path, a familiar frown on her face.

Poor Don Philip, to have such a wife, Alicia mused, skillfully avoiding the woman. Was it any wonder that this house had an air of gloom? Nor was this woman's daughter any better. Philip Navarro's family sat about the table with such grim frowns that Alicia had thought they were in mourning and had naively asked Juanita who had died. Dinnertime was supposed to be a time of shared laughter, of talking and music. The Gypsies knew the proper way. The Gypsies. She would remember to speak with Don Philip about it.

The flames from the fire had burned down to embers. The tantalizing aromas from the kitchen mixing with the smell of wood-smoke reminded Alicia that she was hungry. The door to the servants' quarters was down the hall past the family's dining room, and as Alicia passed by she heard angry voices from within.

"How much longer do you intend to have that . . . that *creature* in this house?" Alicia recognized the shrill tone as Doña Luisa's.

"For a long, long time," was Don Philip's answer.

"You dare to go against my wishes in this matter?"

"Just as willingly as you always choose to go against mine. The young woman makes me happy, she delights me with her unspoiled ways. In her company I find joy."

"But she is a *Gypsy*. She will steal all that we own and make off in the night." At this insult Alicia cringed, longing to confront the woman with her lie.

"She was raised by the Gypsies, but is in fact a woman of Spanish ancestry. Perhaps her bloodlines are even more distinguished than your own, dear wife." There was a mockery in Don Philip's voice, as if he were reminding Doña Luisa of her own origins.

"You dare to so insult me. We will see what happens when Enrique returns from court. He will be just as thoroughly against your having *that* woman here as am I. He will tell you. He will make you see. I only hope that you will listen to him! *My* son, Don Enrique Dorado, is a gentleman in all ways." *Don Enrique Dorado.* The name tugged at Alicia's memory, though she could not remember where she had heard it before. Surely if he were this woman's son, he would be most unpleasant, she reasoned, not in the least anxious to incur his scorn.

"If he is a gentleman, it is because . . ." Don Philip did not finish the sentence. "But I will not argue with you. I am too content. I have come face-to-face with a ghost and find it a most pleasant confrontation. I have found, my dearest wife, not to trust the words of others who would speak falsely to achieve their own ends. Things are not always as they seem at all."

"You are talking nonsense. Nonsense! I do not understand what you mean." Doña Luisa sounded flustered.

"You will, Doña Luisa. In time you will." Alicia would have listened to more of the conversation, but seeing Juanita motion to her from the servants' entranceway, she hurried on, ashamed to have been caught eavesdropping. It was a thing strictly forbidden among Gypsies. Expecting Juanita's reprimand, she was given no such rebuke and could only assume that to gorgios such practice was accepted. Would she ever understand such strange ways? No. Yet after hearing Doña Luisa's words of scorn she was even more determined than before to try. Philip Navarro had said that she made him happy, that she gave him joy, and she would not disappoint him. She would make him proud of her and at the same time make that scowling wife of his take back her vile words. By her father's eyes she so swore.

52

Unshaven, drawn and haggard, Rafael de Villasandro did not look at all the handsome young noble he was. He looked, in fact, much like the beggars and other tattered personages crowding the dirty street, though little did he care. Overwhelmed by his sorrow, he thought little of his pride. Having searched every inch of the city, he had met only disappointment and defeat. Alicia was nowhere to be found, and he could only conclude that the worst had happened.

Two weeks had passed, a time in which he had witnessed the coming and going of the Christmas celebration and the welcoming of the new year, but had found little cause for joy. The woman he loved was gone, apparently forever. Had he been a monk or a priest, he would have scourged himself in punishment for his wrongdoing, but instead he chose a more fitting punishment, roaming the streets homeless and hungry as she had been forced to do.

But at last weakness and hunger had overwhelmed him, and being merely mortal, he was forced to seek sustenance, purchasing bread and goat's-milk cheese from one of the vendors on the street, thus keeping his body alive though his heart and soul were to him but useless things. In his misery he wanted only to be left alone. Gone now were his lofty ideals, his fierce desire to aid others.

In a shadowed tavern he sat alone, though the rough-

hewn wooden tables were crowded with people. It was a
gathering place for the poorest and most unsavory sorts, a
place he would once have avoided at all cost yet was drawn
to now in his wretchedness.

The loud din of chatter mixed with the clanking of glasses
as tall stories were swapped, gossip exchanged, and tongues
set wagging, divulging the latest tattlings. Rafael sat back in
his chair, drained his glass of wine, and tried to ignore all
the talk, but every now and then a whisper or phrase caught
his ear.

"The war in Granada is ended."

"It is about time that it should be."

"So many lives! Though at least Spain has a victory."

"So much *money*! Cristo! Would that I had but a thou-
sandth of the florins spent."

So the war was over, Rafael thought. At least that was
something to be joyous about. The last stronghold of the
Moors in Spain had been conquered. What would King Ferdinand and Queen Isabella do now? He imagined they
would have a great deal to keep them busy, for everyone
knew how the kingdom had suffered because of the war.

"I just returned from Aragon. There have been riots because of the Holy Inquisition. One inquisitor was killed. No
one favors these burnings."

Rafael could not help but give his full attention to these
mumblings, remembering Juan Dorado. It would serve that
one right if he were to find such disfavor; but as to death,
Rafael wished no one ill.

"Speak for yourself, Ramón. I for one think all infidels
should be driven from our land. What about those equally
infidel who are right in our midst? The Jews!"

"But I heard that they gave large sums of money to the
Queen to aid Spain in winning the war!"

"That only proves their wealth. They are all rich, while
men of León such as us wallow in the dirt."

"Their houses are filled with hoards of silver and gold, while we suffer."

Their evil grumblings stung Rafael to anger. Fools! Could they not see what was happening? Now that the Moors had been defeated, Torquemada was preparing to wage another kind of war. This agitation that had been sown by the officers of the Inquisition was but the first step.

"Torquemada has said that God gave the victory to Spain over the infidels so that Spain could be cleansed. Of Moors, of Jews, and of Gypsies as well."

"Drive out those cursed bastards and their evil eye!"

Like a cape before a bull, Rafael saw red. Fueled by wine and his own misery, he brandished his sword and leaped to his feet with a movement so violent that it knocked over the table.

"Spain should be cleansed of fools such as you!" he shouted. Rafael was definitely outnumbered, but he needed to lash out and cared little for the consequences. It was men such as these who had made Alicia suffer.

"Who is he?" asked one of the men, a big burly blacksmith.

"I don't know or care, but no one calls me a fool!" The man and four of his companions rose to their feet, circling Rafael menacingly. "Take back your words or suffer for your arrogance, Señor!"

Before Rafael had time to say one word, they were upon him, wielding bottles, knives, and swords, intent on drawing his blood. The air was rent with the sound of blade upon blade and the violent oaths of angry men.

"He fights like a madman!"

Whirling and lashing out, Rafael did indeed fight like one possessed, yet even the most skilled swordsman in Spain could not have held out against so many indefinitely. Slowly but surely Rafael was surrounded, and the glaring eyes of the men declared they would not be gentle. Rafael put two men on the ground and yet another took to his heels, but the other seven were now closing in for the kill.

Though Rafael had proved himself a formidable opponent, he was preparing himself for the pain that must ultimately be his when suddenly, to his surprise, he found he was not alone. "It seems you have need of help, *Signore!*" said a voice, adding his sword to Rafael's own. He proved himself to be a most able combatant, wielding his weapon with amazing agility. Though Rafael and this stranger were outnumbered, they were not outclassed and soon had sent the enemy into retreat. Only then did Rafael dare take a close look at his rescuer, and he was impressed by what he saw. At his side was an imposing man in his thirties dressed in the flamboyant Italian style, a sleeveless tunic striped in dark green, orange, and red with undertunic of darkest green and hose to match. The leg of the left hose was striped like the overtunic in orange and red, and his dark green cap was adorned with colored plumes. Thick dark hair beneath the hat showed just a touch of gray at the temples, which added to his air of distinction. Not handsome perhaps, yet a man one would never forget.

"Who are you?" Rafael asked, feeling the need to know.

The dark-haired man bowed politely. "I am Giovanni Luigi Alberdici, at your service, Signore, and you?"

"Rafael Córdoba de Villasandro." They exchanged but a glance, yet in that brief span of time each had taken the other's measure. "Why did you help me?"

"I do not like the odds against one to be so great, and I did not like what was being said. Perhaps we have given them something to think about."

"I would like to think so. I was rash, but when they spoke so of the Gypsies I had to act. I have no liking for those who would persecute others, be they Gypsy, Moor, or Jew." Bending down to pick up the table he had sent crashing to the ground, Rafael bid this Giovanni join him. "Giovanni Luigi Alberdici, your name sounds familiar to me."

"I am but a simple ship's captain. A Venetian merchant of sorts. I have several ships floating in the Bay of Biscay right now."

"The Bay of Biscay? What brings *you* so far inland?"

Giovanni's eyes were veiled for a moment with caution. "There was someone I was seeking, though I have found his fate to be a most unpleasant one. Let me say no more."

"A ship's captain. How many ships do you own?"

"Five. I am an exporter and importer. I bring into your country our fine Venetian glass and take back olives, peppers, spices, and Castilian lace."

Five ships, Rafael thought. Five ships headed for Venice. Although it was Fernando de Torga, the mapmaker and navigator who had taken it upon himself to find the ships that would take the converts to safety, Rafael could not help thinking how valuable this man's aid would be. Five ships! "Are all of your ships in the bay?"

"No. Only four: the *Fiducioso*, an older ship but one with fond memories; the *Fedele*; the *Carità*; and, last but not least, the *Onorevole*. Faith, Hope, Charity, and Honor, all things I hold dear."

"Four ships," Rafael corrected, enough to take a large number of fugitives to Rome or Constantinople. This man was honorable and couragous, but would he dare risk a fine of five hundred florins? Being a Venetian and thereby a Christian, this matter of Jews and converts was not his problem, and yet Rafael sensed that this Giovanni would be willing to help. But how could he broach the subject without risk? Torquemada's spies were everywhere, but surely this ship's captain was not one of them.

"Perhaps it is none of my concern, but I have the feeling that you have more than ships on your mind. You have the look of a troubled man. I am a good listener, *amico mio.*" The dark eyes that met Rafael's were compelling, and Rafael found himself telling this man he had just met all about

Alicia and his search for her. "And so you think that she has met a sad fate?"

"I want to believe that she is alive and that I will find her again, but I fear such thoughts are fantasies. She is gone, and I am the sorriest of men."

The Venetian captain shook his head. "Believe in your heart, not in your head. Things are not always as they seem." He took off his plumed cap and laid it on the table, preparing himself for a long stay. "My friend Stephen once lost his love and searched all of Venice to find her." He laughed. "And do you know where she was all the time, this very lovely lady?" Rafael shook his head, not even daring a guess. "She was living among the beggars of Venice on their island."

"Among the beggars?"

"As the guest of the King of Beggars himself! Stephen had given up hope, *amico mio,* but when such a love is shared between two people, things always turn out right in the end. And so will it be with you too. I know. Loving this Alicia of yours as you do, you will see her again."

Though it seemed impossible, somehow Rafael found himself believing. "I pray to God that you are right!"

"And if you cannot find her, then perhaps she will find you. That was the way it was with my Isabella, and now she has made me the happiest of men; but that is another story." Gesturing for more wine, Giovanni watched as the tall, thin tavern keeper first poured a glass for Rafael and then for himself. "And now to talk again of my ships, you seem to be quite interested in them. Are you, then, a sailor?"

"A sailor? No. I own olive groves on the lands bordering León. I only hope that I can put them to use for things other than growing olives." Rafael decided to take the chance and trust this man. "I am interested in your ships because I intend to aid those in danger from the Inquisition. Do you know a man named Fernando de Torga? He is a mapmaker, navigator, half Spanish and half Italian, Venetian, too, I believe."

"De Torga? I know him. It was this de Torga I came to Salamanca to see."

"And did you?"

Giovanni shook his head, the corners of his eyes wrinkling as he frowned. "Then you do not know."

"Know what?"

"Fernando de Torga has been arrested."

53

Rafael could hear his heart pounding in his ears. "De Torga has been arrested?"

"Keep your voice down, *amico mio*. He is being questioned, that is all. Let us hope that he does not reveal too much."

Rafael's grasp upon his glass was so fierce that he nearly broke it. "You do not know the ways of the inquisitors. They can break a man as easily as an eggshell with their tortures. Have you any idea what they do? They apply cords to the arms and twist them, tighter and tighter. But that is the kindest of the tortures. There is the torture of water, where they put a funnel down your throat and . . . Need I say more? And they call themselves *Christians*! Followers of one who preached gentleness and love."

"As for myself, I have faced greater dangers. If we use caution and move quickly . . ." Giovanni assessed Rafael. "Unless you have changed your mind."

Rafael's eyes shone with a feverish light. "Changed my mind? No! I am more determined than ever. Because of my quest, I lost the woman I loved. Let the good that I do now be her epitaph. The thought of death does not frighten me. Nothing has changed, Señor, except that now I must take upon my shoulders de Torga's task as well as my own. We will target the end of January for our first shipload of fugitives. I will give you a detailed map so you will know just where my property lies. I will take it upon myself to find out which families are in danger and bring them to my lands. There I will give them provisions and shelter."

"And I will ready the ships and aid you in smuggling our cargo through the countryside and streets of the cities." Raising his glass, he offered a toast. "To our success. May God be with us."

Rafael hesitated. "You do not fear Torquemada's wrath?"

"I do not fear this mad priest. I have no fear of any man, not even the Doge of Venice himself. But I do fear injustice and the flames that are ignited by hate." The glasses clicked, and each man let the wine caress his throat. Then, when they had drained their goblets dry, they looked at each other, smiled, and quickly detailed their plans. "There is one among the priests who is our own." Giovanni's voice was less than a whisper. "Father Julio. Do you know him?"

"Not as well as I intend. But what is his part in all of this?"

"His part is twofold. First, he will aid you in finding out who is in danger. Second, he will forge the documents needed to get our ships and human cargo out of port." Giovanni offered his hand, grasping it with strength and with the warmth of friendship. "God go with you."

"God go with *you.*"

"And may you find your Gypsy love when all is said and done." Plopping his plumed cap upon his head, he strode out of the tavern without even a backward glance. Rafael was just as anxious to leave, for now that he knew for certain of Father Julio's involvement, he was of a mind to talk to the priest. Thus he hurried to the church and, finding the door open, stepped inside.

It was dark, except for the flicker of candlelight at the altar, and Rafael found himself drawn to that sacred place. Dropping to his knees, he prayed for many things; for an end to Torquemada's madness, for the safety of those who were the victims of his wrath. He prayed for peace and tranquillity to come once again to the land. He whispered a separate prayer that God in his mercy would watch over Alicia, wherever she was, that she would be safe, that he *would* see her again. At last, when he rose to his feet, he felt free of his guilt, free of his pain. Without Alicia he would never be truly happy, yet his soul was at peace again.

"So, you have come back, my son." Father Julio's voice spoke from the back of the church, but in twelve quick strides he was at Rafael's side, breathing heavily from the exertion.

"I had to talk with you. I apologize for leaving so rashly."

"I understand."

"I had to find her."

"And did you?"

"No." Reaching out for one of the candles, Father Julio held it up to Rafael's face and recoiled from what he saw. "I feel as if I have been to purgatory and back."

"And you look it, my son. But it was so needless. So unnecessary. If you had only waited, you would have learned that God works his wisdom in mysterious ways." He reached out to touch Rafael's arm in a gesture meant to soothe him. "Your Gypsy has been found."

"Alicia? When? Where?" Pulling free of the priest's grasp, Rafael scanned the church, thinking to find her. "There is so much that I must say." Noting the priest's frown, he felt a twinge of panic. "She is not injured? Where is she?"

"She is not here. It was not to me that she came. I heard the story only yesterday. The poor child was nearly trampled in the streets, but she was saved by the most noble of men and it is at his house that she is staying."

"His house? Whose house?" In his zeal to find out, he grabbed at Father Julio's habit. "Tell me, father. You must tell me." Seeing Father Julio scowl, he dropped his arms. "Please."

"Why, Philip Navarro's. He took her there the very same day that you came to see me."

"Philip Navarro's! Philip Navarro's!" Rafael's mouth formed a perfect O in his shock.

"Yes. Philip Navarro's." Father Julio watched as Rafael threw back his head and laughed. It was an eerie sound, one that chilled his soul, and for a moment he feared that Rafael had lost his mind. "My son, please. This is a house of God."

"A lady among the beggars, a Gypsy in a nobleman's house. Giovanni was right. And I have been the biggest of fools, not once but twice!" Now Father Julio was certain that Rafael had taken leave of his senses. In wary hesitation he watched as Rafael's laughter ceased. "All the time I searched for her she was living right under my very nose. What an idiot I was. What a fool! But Giovanni was right, when such a love is shared between two people, things *do* always turn out right in the end. I have found her! It matters not where, I have found her!" Rafael hugged the priest in his exuberance, then ran from the church to see his love.

54

The moon was haloed by a haze of gold and silver, moon-beams danced down upon the tiles of the terrace, giving it a magical appearance and enchanting Alicia as she stared through the window of Don Philip Navarro's house. The trees within the courtyard whispered in the wind, and Alicia tried for a moment to pretend that she was in the forest again, but the dream was quickly shattered. That life was behind her, and this fine hacienda was her new home.

She had grown familiar with the house, for Don Philip let her wander through most of the rooms in the hope that once accustomed to the grandeur, she would feel more at home. It was built around a central courtyard, and every bedroom, including her own, had a balcony overlooking the garden.

When spring comes I will enjoy smelling the flowers blooming there, she reflected. But it was only January; spring was so far away. How long had she been in this house? she wondered, having lost track of the days. Long enough that she was no longer completely Gypsy. She had changed, caught between two worlds, trying to sit astride two horses, just as Rudolpho had warned.

Rudolpho. He would not recognize her if he saw her now, nor would any of the tribe. She looked every bit the gorgio lady, just as Philip Navarro intended. The thick mass of dark hair was braided into thick plaits, intricately coiled atop her head. Her skin was much lighter from days spent indoors away from the sun. Her cheeks still had a healthy pink glow, her lips were touched with a natural pink tint, but her eyes held a haunted, lonely look. Alicia just did not belong to this world yet, no matter how many fancy dresses she wore, and Don Philip had given her many of late.

I look like a Spanish lady, she thought, gazing at her reflection in a large mirror. Was that Alicia who stared back at her, or someone else? Gone were her blouse and many skirts and in their place was the stiff-skirted dress worn by the women of León. The one she wore today was of a brilliant red, sprinkled with flowers of gold brocade, a dress Alicia thought beautiful with its full-flowing sleeves. Worn over an underskirt that was revealed at the hem, the dress was, Don Philip told her, of a style that was the latest rage of the Spanish court. Queen Isabella herself was said to have started the trend for the laced bodice. Worn with a corset, it made the waist seem tiny in comparison to the voluminous skirt.

Corsets, she thought in annoyance, touching that instrument of torture she so detested. Like the iron fence around the house it symbolized of her loss of freedom and her estrangement from Gypsy ways.

Foolish gorgio women. How could they stand these foolish clothes? It was difficult to sit and to walk with the ridiculous wooden hoops attached to the skirts. Alicia tried for the hundredth time to make herself comfortable. *Verdugos,* the bell-shaped hoops that were sewn into the dress, were the object of her curses more often than not, and had Don Philip not insisted she wear them, Alicia would have thrown hers into the fire. But he had been so kind, and if she could please him by wearing these silly skirts, then perhaps it was not so great a price to pay.

Everything is stiff with these Spaniards, she thought irritably: *their dress, their speech, the way they hold themselves so erect, as if afraid to relax.* It had been difficult for her to admit that she was one of them, that they were of her own kind, yet she could not hide from reality any longer. They were gorgio and she was too, yet oh how she longed to be as free as she had been before! She accepted her new lot in life, but that did not mean that she would ever forget her past happiness, or could, in truth, ever forget Rafael. Rafael. She was living in his world now, just as he had once lived in hers.

"Ah, here you are, sulking in your room again." Alicia whirled around to find Doña Violetta standing in the doorway, the corners of her mouth drawn down in her usual frown. Don Philip had been kind to Alicia, but the same could not be said for this young woman or her mother, though Alicia had tried very hard to win their approval. Incensed by Don Philip's growing affection for the Gypsy girl, Violetta had shown her nothing but contempt.

"She is treated as an equal to *me*, your daughter!" Alicia had heard Violetta complain more than once. "She, a beggar from the streets."

Señor Navarro had quickly silenced her, explaining that as long as they lived in his house, both Violetta and her mother would show respect for his guests. Since then Violetta had held her tongue, giving voice to her hostility only when Don Philip was not around.

"I was not, as you call it, 'sulking,'" Alicia answered, "just thinking."

"Well, you can do your thinking downstairs! *My father* sent me up to tell you that dinner is ready." In a rustle of blue brocade, Violetta was gone. At first she had treated Alicia like a servant, for Alicia had been firm in her resolve to work for her food and shelter, but at last Don Philip had convinced her that she was doing *him* a favor by being there. And now Alicia was treated on equal terms with Don Philip's daughter. Could she really blame Doña Violetta for resenting her? Would she have been jealous if some young woman had vied with her for Rudolpho's affections? Trying to put such thoughts from her head, Alicia followed Violetta down the stairs.

The others were already seated, and as she entered the

room to take a place at the far end of the table, Alicia could feel Doña Luisa's cold eyes upon her. There was always hatred in the woman's eyes, hatred and fear, and Alicia was reminded of a slowly heating caldron that at any time might erupt and boil over. Lately those malevolent gray eyes had haunted Alicia's dreams, and though she had tried to push such foolish thoughts from her mind, she had the feeling that she had seen such eyes before. Now once again those eyes were watching her, hovering anxiously between Alicia's face and her husband's. What was it she expected him to do, to say?

"Ah, you look lovely in the red, but then I knew you would, Alicia." Don Philip's eyes were warm and gentle as he looked Alicia's way. "Come, sit. Sit."

Alicia took her place hesitantly, having little liking for the strained relations between these people seated about the table and the tension that always crackled in the air. She was so new to this matter of *manners* that always, at the back of her mind, hovered the fear that she would do something wrong, forget to use the communal napkin to wipe her hands, be unskilled in using her knife and fork, forget to say *please* and *thank you* when something was passed her way. Hearing Doña Luisa refer to her as *that heathen* when Don Philip was not around only added to her discomfort.

"Are you not hungry, *niña?*" Don Philip's expression showed concern. "Eat! Eat!"

"She was not here in time to say grace!" Violetta's eyes were mocking. "Should she not learn to come to the dinner table in time? Or does *she* not have to thank our God for her food?"

"Violetta!" Don Philip's mouth trembled with rage, setting his gray mustache dancing. "I will not warn you again. Alicia is our *guest!*"

"Forgive me, Father." Casting her eyes downward, Violetta said no more, though Doña Luisa's expression was triumphant. Alicia suspected correctly that Doña Violetta

had purposefully delayed advising her that dinner was being served in an effort to embarrass her. Why were these
two women so determined to be her enemies?

For a long while Don Philip was deep in thought, remaining silent as he ate; then he looked at Alicia and said, "Violetta has reminded me, though that was not her intent, that
it is time you learned the scriptures, my child. I will have
Father Julio counsel you." Alicia remembered the kindly
priest from the church and she smiled her assent. "Do you
know anything at all about Christian ways?"

"I know that they light candles and talk with God. And I
know about your Christ," Alicia answered proudly, remembering that day in the church. "I know that Mary was his
mother and the mother of the baby Jesus as well."

"Christ and Jesus are the same, my child. You will need to
learn that. But I am pleased that you are so well advised
already."

Taking confidence in Don Philip's praise, Alicia continued: "He was nailed to a tree so that all gorgios would live
forever. He wanted to save them from the fires of *o Beng* so
that they would not be slaves." Her eyes grew thoughtful.
"I think perhaps this Christ must have been a Gypsy, because he was poor, went wandering about the countryside,
and like the Gypsies was . . ."

"A Gypsy? Jesus, a Gypsy!" Doña Luisa was clearly outraged. "If only Juan were here to hear such talk. She is a
heretic!" The woman's gray eyes burned with ire, and for a
moment Alicia thought to find herself banished from the
table, but Don Philip as always came to her defense.

"Woman, hold your tongue! She is not a heretic but an
innocent child who needs to be schooled in the *Faith*! Had
she not been so cruelly betrayed . . ." Don Philip had not
time to say more, for it was upon this fiery scene that Rafael
de Villasandro entered the room. "Don Rafael!" Philip
Navarro was clearly stunned by his guest's unkempt appearance, but ever the gentleman, he said not a word. "I was

worried about you. The message you sent me was vague. . . ."

But Rafael was not listening to Philip Navarro; his attention was riveted upon those unforgettable eyes, which now looked back at him with anger and pain. "Alicia?" His voice was incredulous as he appraised this vision of loveliness before him. Gone was the Gypsy girl and in her place was the most beautiful Spanish lady he had ever beheld. "Alicia!"

At the sound of her name Alicia froze, Rafael's face but a blurred outline through a veil of tears. Her senses were in turmoil, yet remembering his desertion, anger hardened her heart. She couldn't think; could scarcely breathe. She felt like a trapped animal shivering beneath the intensity of his gaze.

"Alicia!" Forgetting the others, Rafael took a step forward, longing with all his heart to gather her into the security of his arms. He had been thinking about this moment of reconciliation all the way back to Don Philip's house, and was not prepared for Alicia to back away. "Alicia?"

"No!" Her voice was barely more than a whisper. "Go away!" All the hurt and resentment that had been simmering beneath the surface erupted. "I hate you. I never wanted to see you again." Turning her back, she was like a bird in flight as she fled the room.

55

"Alicia!" Rafael sought to follow her, but Don Philip blocked his path. "Let me go to her; there are so many things I must say."

"Give her time alone with her tears and her thoughts, she must cry her emotions out. That is a woman's way." Don Philip was insistent, his look giving both Violetta and Doña Luisa warning. Though she puffed up like a frog, venom gathering at her tongue, Doña Luisa for once kept silent. Rising, she gestured her daughter to follow, and both women left the room, their food scarcely touched.

"I am glad that they have left, for there is much that I would say to you, much that I would know. But come, this is not the place. Too many eyes and ears." He nodded toward the servants.

"I must see Alicia!" Once again Rafael started toward the door, but Don Philip's firm grasp on his arm restrained him. Reluctantly Rafael followed him into the library, a long, narrow book-lined room with leather chairs and a large oaken desk.

"How is it that you know Alicia?" Philip Navarro's manner was direct. "Is she the same young woman you told me about?"

"Alicia is the woman I love. She saved my life and took me to her Gypsy camp. Since that day my life has not been the same."

For once Philip Navarro laughed. "No, I suppose not. She is full of fire, yet I have never known a more gentle heart. She delights me!" Philip Navarro gestured for him to sit down. "Tell me your story and perhaps I can help you in this matter of the heart."

In a jumble of words, Rafael bared his soul. He told of taking Alicia's virtue, then leaving her, to stalk the thieves who had robbed him—unaware, as he spoke, of Don Philip's scowl. Rafael told of his fear that Alicia had been a victim of the villagers' brutal raid upon the Gypsy camp, of having searched for her in vain, only to be reunited with her when Rudolpho took it into his mind to have him abducted.

"He is a man of my own heart, this Rudolpho. Would that I had met him!"

"He was wise and strong, and I shall never forget him. He was resolved that I should marry his daughter. Alicia is my wife by Gypsy law." Reaching into a hidden pouch in his shirt, Rafael brought forth the piece of pottery that had been shattered at the marriage rite. "Once I might have scoffed at such a ceremony, but now . . . Alicia *is* my wife, no matter what the priests may say."

"Your wife?" Don Philip cocked a silvered brow, then seemed to approve of the idea. "But why was she, then, in Salamanca alone? Why did you not bring her with you?"

"Because I am a fool!" Rafael kept silent on his reasons, not for lack of trust but because he did not want to involve Don Philip in his schemes. Even a man of Don Philip's position was not totally safe from Torquemada. "But I suffered for my stupidity! Then, when your son, Don Enrique, mentioned having seen the Gypsy girl, I knew that I had to find Alicia again, that only then would I be happy. I sought out Father Julio, only to learn that Alicia was that same girl. I had thought only to find her, to give her a message for the woman I loved; instead I was thrown into the depths of despair." Raising his hand, Rafael traced the lines of his torn and dirtied garments. "That is where I have been these last weeks, searching for Alicia. When Father Julio told me that she was here, I came immediately."

"Only to be met by a tearful woman who appears to have been deeply hurt by you."

"She doesn't understand; that's why I must explain! I love Alicia, more than life itself. If I didn't know before, I know now. Having feared losing her forever, I faced the desolation being without her could bring. She *must* forgive me! She *must* love me again!" Rafael felt greatly unburdened, yet now he realized that instead of listening to Don Philip, he had babbled on and on. A sudden jealousy stung him. What if Philip Navarro's intentions were amorous too? He had fed Alicia, sheltered her, clothed her like an angel. Merely in the name of charity? He doubted it, and now he realized that he had to know this man's intent. "But you know of my feelings. What is your interest in Alicia?"

Don Philip smiled, delighting in Rafael's obvious jealousy. "I saved a young Gypsy girl only to find her the very image of my wife, of the woman I lost so long ago. I brought her here, and I must admit my motives are not entirely unselfish." Seeing Rafael's back stiffen, he hastened to add, "for she is the same age my daughter would have been."

"Your daughter?"

"It seems too good to be true, I even question the reality of it myself, yet it must be so. The name Alicia is not truly Spanish but a form of the name Alice. It was my great-grandmother's name and one I bestowed upon my daughter when she was born. I thought it the most amazing coincidence until I learned that Alicia was not truly Gypsy."

"And that is the greatest irony of all," Rafael said under his breath, thinking of his own prejudice against Alicia's supposed heritage.

"She was *taken* to the Gypsy camp! I can only suppose the reason, yet I have my suspicions."

"And you think . . . ?"

"I was told that my *niña* had met with an accident, that

when she was with her duenna she had drowned. Though I had no reason to doubt the story, her body was never recovered. Now I feel with a certainty that I was told a lie. I believe with every fiber of my being that Alicia is my daughter. I have been trying to pull aside the shroud in her mind that veils the truth, but so far I have been unsuccessful. She has been fighting the memory for so long, but it will come back to her in time. . . ."

Rafael and Philip could not know that at this very moment another shared their secret. Her ear pressed to the door, Doña Luisa could hardly believe what she was hearing. Could this young woman be the child she had taken to the Gypsies? The age, the name, the green eyes—all had added to her dismay. She was helpless to do anything yet determined that her husband should never know of her treachery. Now all that had changed. All that she had schemed and worked for would be lost if Alicia remembered. Had all her plans come to nothing? Juan, Enrique, Violetta, what of them? What of her own fate? She would never forget what poverty was like, and she would not return to that realm again!

Enrique. Enrique would know what to do. She must be patient. She must wait until he returned and then, somehow, they would rid the household of this *Gypsy girl.*

56

Standing upon the balcony of her bedroom, looking down at the rain-drenched garden, Alicia felt the mist blend with her tears. Her gown was damp, yet she scarcely noticed, preoccupied with the tumult of emotions at seeing Rafael again. Her legs were weak, her heart beating at a frantic rate, as she listened to each sound, wanting him to follow her yet at the same time fearing a second confrontation.

Afraid? No, she would not allow that unworthy emotion. Squaring her shoulders and lifting her chin, she refused to be intimidated. She was wise, she was strong, she could face any obstacle. It would be far better to deal with his unsettling presence now than to prolong her heartache. She was not a child, she could not run away again. Yet when the door to the bedroom swung open and she looked into Rafael's dark eyes, that is exactly what she was prompted to do. Only the knowledge that she had nowhere left to run kept her from taking flight.

"Alicia! I must talk with you!"

"There is nothing I want to hear, Gorgio!" Her jaws clenched as he approached her.

"Perhaps that is true, yet I intend to have my say." Seeing his determination, Alicia breathed a deep sigh and came back into the warmth and light of the room. Rafael studied her carefully, noticing the changes in her that went far beyond the garments she was wearing and the style of her hair. When they had last been together she had been as much child as woman; now she had fully matured, possessing a beauty that was startling, a loveliness that even the marks of her unhappiness could not diminish. "I love you, Alicia!"

"Love? Ah, Gorgio, you do not know the meaning of the word. Love is more than the coupling of bodies; it is a thing that comes from the heart. Whispered words are meaningless; it is deeds that speak. Your desertion told me how little you truly cared."

"But I did care, that's why I hated to leave. . . ."

"Then, why did you? We were happy. I would have reached up and plucked a star from the sky if you had wished it. You told me then that you loved me, and I wanted to believe you. But I am no longer the silly Gypsy girl who so foolishly offers her heart."

"I had my reasons. My brother came searching for me. I could not take the chance that any harm would come to you or your people." He did not dare tell her the whole story for fear of endangering her life.

"You worried about me, Gorgio, yet you left without a word of good-bye."

"You must believe me, I intended to return for you. That's why I left the ring. It was a pledge, a vow."

"The ring?" She could feel the cool hardness of metal against her skin, where the ring dangled from a piece of ribbon in the valley between her breasts. "Solis gave me this ring you speak of. She told me it was to repay me. She told me you were happy to leave."

"That lying bitch!"

"She so swore on her father's grave!"

"Even so, she lied. If she were before me now, I would make her take back her words. I loved you then and I love you now." Moving forward, he bent his head so that his lips were nearly touching her ear. The whisper of his voice sent chills down her spine and she shivered. "But you are cold, your dress damp from the rain. Let me warm you, Alicia."

Mesmerized, she started to give herself up to his embrace, but the memory of her father's death rose up like a wall between them. Rudolpho had died trying to bring Rafael back to the camp. "No! Rudolpho died because he followed after you. His heart . . . I can never forget that."

"I'm sorry that he died. He was a most noble man. But Alicia, I did not kill him! He was a dying man, that's why he was so fervent in his desire that we marry. He wanted you to have someone to take care of you when he was gone."

What he said was true, she could not really blame him for Rudolpho's death, but what of the rest? Had he left her only once, she would have been willing to forgive him. Yet Rafael had left her twice. She had forgiven him; had opened her heart to his love again, only to find him gone. There were still scars on her heart that would never heal.

"Would you have left me if I been a gorgio woman and not Gypsy?" she asked softly. Her eyes were wide as she searched his face for the truth.

"Alicia . . . !" He could not answer her; in truth he did not really know. Wasn't this the same question he had asked himself so many times?

"But I am not Gypsy now! So you think that I am worthy of your love? Is that not so?" She gasped out a string of curses, hardly aware of what she was saying as her Gypsy pride and anger took hold of her. "And do you think I can so easily forget that you scorned me? If you do, then you are a fool! I will never forgive you. Never! The day that you left, my love died! They burned my papa on the funeral pyre, and just as he was consumed by fire so was my love. It died with Rudolpho."

"Then there is nothing more that I can say. Be happy, Alicia. Like you I am a guest of Don Philip, but I will not bother you again with my pleadings." His eyes were dark pools of misery as he looked at her. A stubble of beard roughened his cheeks, and she longed to reach out and touch it, to wipe the pain from his face with her caress.

"Rafael . . ." She wanted to reveal to him that she was lying, that her love would never die; but because she was afraid of trusting him again, of opening her heart to him only to be betrayed, she merely watched as he walked toward the door.

Rafael paused, his hand on the latch. Turning back only briefly, he feasted his eyes on her beauty. "I much preferred you with your hair flying about your shoulders," he said. "*Querida*, my one and only Gypsy love." Then he was gone. Alicia felt as if the winter wind that blew across the mountains had swept over her. She longed to call him back, to tell him that she loved him too, but her voice was a soundless whisper.

The next few days were painful, for though Alicia longed to avoid Rafael and the reminder of her heartache, there was no way to avoid him. In these moments she yearned to tell him that she would forgive him, that she loved him still, only to be reminded of his betrayal. She wanted to run away, to flee, to hide. How could she hope to escape this dangerous love that she carried in her heart when she was constantly reminded of her longing by Rafael's presence? She felt like a caged bird. Trapped. And yet as painful as it was to see him, to be so close to him, the thought of never seeing his face again was even more disquieting.

Stubbornly she vowed to forget him, but the memory of the love they had shared was embedded in her heart, her soul, her mind. She did not have to look at him to know where he stood, what he wore, or the expression on his face; her senses told her, and in spite of her obstinate pride she was consumed with yearning at every beat of her heart.

The days seemed endless, yet time passed so quickly when Rafael was in the room. Then, at night, alone and aching for his arms, she succumbed to dreams. He was her first love, her only love, and the knowledge that his room

was just down the hall was the ultimate temptation. To be
with him again, to love him, to feel the burning fire of their
passion now and forever. Alicia fought a battle within herself, but pride kept her from Rafael's arms and from his bed.
He had been the one to leave, and she could only think it
was because of his shame at loving a Gypsy.

Nor did Doña Luisa's attempts to interest Rafael in Violetta soften Alicia's resolve. At breakfast and at supper Violetta was always seated by his side, her dark eyes looking
in Rafael's direction, a reminder to Alicia that Violetta Dorado was a part of Rafael's world in a way she could never
truly be. Despite her newly acquired manners and her elegant clothes, Alicia would always be a Gypsy at heart, and
each scornful glance that the young woman cast her way
reminded her of that.

Doña Luisa never missed the opportunity to compare the
two young women with the most genuine of smiles upon
her tight, thin lips. Violetta never had a hair out of place,
while Alicia's mass of dark brown tresses always seemed to
tumble from the chignon atop her head. Violetta always
seemed to know the right thing to say; she was witty and
bright, while Alicia was unpredictable and amusing with her
exotic ways. Violetta's embroidery work was flawless, while
Alicia knew that hers was a jumble of snags and tangled
threads. Violetta never raised her voice, but Alicia would
sometimes forget herself and let go with a colorful streak of
Gypsy oaths when she was angered.

This evening Alicia met Rafael's eyes as he gazed across
the dinner table, and she wanted to smile; but before her
mind could will her lips to obey, Violetta's trill of laughter
reminded Alicia of that young woman's presence, and she
hastily looked away.

Throughout the evening meal Doña Luisa was determined
that Violetta should capture Rafael's eye; and though
Rafael's expression tried to relay the message that the young

woman meant nothing to him, Alicia's hurt and jealousy knew no bounds.

Let him have the homely gorgio, she didn't care! She ate, but tasted nothing, drank too much wine, but still could not escape Rafael's haunting presence.

Violetta twittered and cooed, and though Rafael did not return her attentions, Alicia was still wounded to see him at her side. She silently cursed Violetta and Rafael as well. Violetta was his kind; he deserved the horrid gorgio woman who hovered at his elbow. *She* didn't care. Still, as soon as Alicia found an excuse to leave the table and escape to her room, she felt the aching, scalding flood of her tears.

57

Like a dark-cloaked stranger, danger stalked Rafael. Spies of Torquemada were everywhere. Suffering from the sting of Alicia's rejection, he was foolishly brave, and in that brazen fearlessness, successful. Working closely with Father Julio, he was able to keep one step ahead of the secret emissaries of the fanatical Juan Dorado, and in this way gather together a group of *Conversos* who without his help would have faced not only torture but the fires of the Inquisition as well.

Rich men, poor men, merchants, nobles and peasants alike were in danger, and Rafael could not help but feel bitter revulsion for those willing to bring such agony upon their neighbors with their accusing tongues. All that need be mentioned was that a converted Christian refused to eat pork or rabbit, celebrated a Jewish holy day, or was seen reading the Torah, to bring about arrest and questioning. Once a man was suspected, his entire family was in jeopardy, as the officers of the Inquisition sought evidence and testimony in the most brutal ways. There was no mercy except death, no end to the torture but through confession, no verdict but the fires for those found guilty.

Isaac Eli Diego, a physician of great renown whose family had been converted to the Christian faith thirty-five before, was one of those suspected. It was rumored that he was practicing Judaism secretly, and he was denounced to the

Inquisition. Rafael suspected a rival physician, a man of less skill and intellect, to be his accuser, and he damned the man silently for his malice. Isaac Diego and his wife, two sons, and a daughter were saved, but his brother had already been taken by the inquisitors and could not be rescued. Nor was he the only victim. Much to Rafael's sorrow it seemed that for every two accused *Conversos* he saved, at least one was beyond help.

"I should have moved more swiftly!" Rafael said to Father Julio now as they watched the arrest of a spice merchant, one of the unfortunate victims they had been unable to help escape.

"I am as much to blame as you. Do not punish yourself with recriminations. Who could have known? Who could have guessed?" Father Julio's eyes were sad. "He was denounced by a man who owed him a goodly sum of money. A most treacherous way to escape a debt."

"And now his wife must suffer as well!" Rafael shaded his eyes against the sun and watched the barefoot prisoners being marched through the winding streets of the city to the ominous beat of a drum. The merchant was a prosperous young man in his twenties, known throughout the city for his honesty. Now he was to die, condemned to burn at the stake, and Rafael could not help but think that but for the grace of God, that merchant could very well have been he. All it took was enemies. "Father Julio, is there any way . . . ?"

"Of helping them now? No, my son. No! Get such foolish notions out of your head. Any attempt would only ensure your own untimely death."

Rafael knew in his heart that Father Julio was right, but as he listened to the steady beat of the drum, saw the pale faces and frightened eyes of the merchant and his wife, his mind was filled with daring thoughts. How he would like to snatch these hapless victims from under the noses of the inquisitors.

"Heartless bastards!" he swore beneath his breath. Though no other ears heard his oath, Father Julio did, and was quick to caution him with a frown.

There were ten prisoners in all in the procession, dressed in yellow sacklike garments adorned with images of devils and hell flames at the hems. Walking with downcast eyes, each carried an unlighted candle. Rafael knew well what lay ahead: stakes driven into the ground to which each prisoner would be tied and burned alive.

Merciful God, why? Rafael could not understand the religious fervor that could lead a man to take the life of his own kind. God was God. What difference did it make how He was worshipped? He could never understand Torquemada's fanatical zeal. He had expressed such thoughts to Father Julio and had been given his answer: he did not understand because he was a reasonable, rational man.

Sitting in Father Julio's library, they had indulged themselves in theological discussion, feeling safe within the stone walls. Rafael had begun by asking the priest why so many of the converts risked so much to practice Jewish custom and law, for many had, in truth, faced punishment and death to keep to their former faith.

"Many Jews see Christians as men who say one thing and do another; men who worship Jesus, who preached charity and selflessness, who are yet driven by greed. While there are those who starve in our streets, we clothe ourselves in finery and jewels. We talk of chastity, while many of our priests, monks, and bishops indulge themselves with mistresses and lovers. One Pope, Rodrigo Borgia, known as Pope Alexander VI, flaunted his bastards. We must seem to some to be wanting in godliness indeed."

"But to die for their beliefs?" Rafael had thought of his grandparents, who had been willing to face the fires yet who had so fortunately escaped.

"I honor those with such courage. I can only hope that some day all that is wrong with our faith will be corrected, that we will once again be a faith of brotherly love. Perhaps one day when this madness of the fires is over . . ."

This madness of the fires, Rafael thought sadly. He wondered what Alicia thought of the Christian teachings she was now learning and felt suddenly saddened. There was such innocent beauty in what her people believed. Would she understand this mission he had undertaken? If he told her his secret, his decision to help the converts, would she approve? Would she forgive him if he told her about Giovanni, de Torga, and the ships waiting in the bay? He had been tempted to tell her so many times, only to let caution silence his tongue. He could not put Alicia in danger even at the risk of her scorn. And so these last few weeks he had managed to lose himself in work, trying to forget his pain. Would she ever love him again? He could only hope. Two ships of fugitives had sailed for Rome, two ships still waited in the bay, and Rafael vowed that when the last of these ships had left Spain his mission would be over. When the danger had passed he would tell Alicia and hope that a small spark of love still burned within her breast.

"May God have mercy on his soul, for I fear that I cannot find it in my heart to grant him forgiveness." Father Julio's whispered avowal brought Rafael back to the present, and he focused his eyes on the subject of the priest's scornful words. The procession was coming much closer now, and Rafael could see that Father Julio's eyes were riveted upon the priest at the head of the crowd, carrying the green cross of the Inquisition draped in its black crepe shroud.

"Father Julio, who is that man?" Rafael already knew the answer, and a sense of imminent danger overwhelmed him. In self-seeking vanity the black-clad priest reached up to remove his hood, erasing any shadow of doubt. Juan Dorado had come from Toledo and was now in Salamanca, and Rafael could only guess at the reason.

58

It did not take Rafael long to find out why *Frey* Juan Dorado was in Salamanca, for he learned it from the priest's own mouth. Having firmly ensconced himself in Father Julio's church, using that kindly priest's library as his own office, Torquemada's inquisitor and fellow officer of the auto-da-fe summoned Rafael to his presence.

The night was cold and the ring around the moon looked ominous as Rafael made his way through the side streets, past the now deserted stalls of the vendors, heading for the unwelcome interview. All sorts of fears ran through his head: that somehow Juan Dorado had found out about the ships; that de Torga had mentioned his name with the last breath of his confession; that Giovanni, the daring ship's captain, had been captured; that the ships had been intercepted; that somehow the wily priest had found out about his Jewish blood and his mother's execution. The acrid smell of smoke still lingered in the air, a bitter and macabre reminder of today's burnings and a prophecy of his own fate should he be caught. Yet, remembering the agonized cries of those who had died, knowing that he had saved others from such a blaze, quickened Rafael's heart with resolve. He did not regret what he had done, only that he had broken Alicia's heart in the process. Alicia. She would be all that he would regret leaving if it was his destiny to face his own punishment.

The rhythmic pounding of horses' hooves echoed in the night, and Rafael nervously glanced behind him, well expecting to see the dark-clothed members of the *Militia Christi*, the Inquisition's secret police, following after him. But instead it was merely some young *caballeros* out for a night ride and, judging by the cocky grins on their faces, proposing to do some mischief. With a sigh of relief he crossed the street and hurried toward the church, anxious to get this confrontation over with.

Illuminated by sputtering candles, Juan Dorado's face was just as pale, his eyes just as beady, his lips just as thin and mocking, as Rafael had remembered. Surrounded by a stack of documents, he seemed to be smiling as he scanned the contents of one parchment. So intent was he that for a moment Rafael thought that the priest had not heard him enter, but he raised one thinly arched eyebrow and murmured "Come in" before Rafael could make a sound.

"You summoned me, Your Grace." It kindled a spark of ire in Rafael to be quite so obsequious, but caution was necessary.

Casting the papers aside, Frey Dorado looked up with an impassive face that hid his mood. "Sit down." The cold eyes that scrutinized Rafael were hard. "I had expected to hear from you, but you have remained disappointingly silent."

"I apologize. My only excuse is that I have been preoccupied. Your father is a most interesting man."

"My *stepfather*. I know very well how he occupies his time. Those foolish bulls! But your duty is to aid me no matter what the distraction. It was our agreement, was it not?"

"I have been diligent in my assignment; it is just that I have nothing to report."

Juan Dorado's eyes squinted dangerously. "Nothing? Are you telling me that there is not one word of gossip in all of Salamanca, not one convert, not one Jew, whose activities would be of interest to me? Am I to deduce from this that Salamanca is a perfect city, a veritable paradise of devout

Christians?" He slammed his fist down upon the table, sending the documents flying. "Bah! Were that true, I would not have witnessed the burnings today. How is it that you were not the one to advise me of such transgressions?"

Rafael trembled inwardly from suppressed rage, yet he managed his most ingratiating smile. "I am sorry, truly sorry. I will be more diligent in the future."

"And did you not know about the merchant? I was told that you had dealt with him not once but twice."

"He seemed to me the most devout of men, but then I lack your perception, Your Grace."

Juan Dorado forced a smile. "I know by just a glance what lingers in the heart of a man. As for you, I have heard that you are a man whose heart is within the grasp of a beautiful woman. Perhaps I cannot blame you for your frailties this time."

Rafael caught his breath. Had this sly weasel somehow learned about Alicia? The thought was not a pleasant one, for Rafael wished to keep Alicia away from this one's eye, even though she lived beneath his stepfather's roof. "A woman?" He affected innocence of the matter.

"Do not worry so, I fully approve of your attentions to my sister. Violetta will bring a high dowry and has been instructed to be the most docile of wives."

"Violetta?" The very thought was ludicrous, but Rafael quickly attuned himself to the game. "I hoped to keep my feelings secret, but knowing that you will smile upon my attentions to your sister, I am well relieved." Remembering Doña Luisa's ministrations, her obvious attempts to maneuver his attentions to her daughter, Rafael knew well where Juan Dorado's information had come from. Were he not careful, he would find himself with a most unwelcome wife. *Wife,* he thought, *only Alicia can ever be my bride!* Were she to shun him, then he knew that he would live alone for the rest of his life. But never Violetta! Better all alone than she.

Much better the tonsure and habit of a priest! She was too much her mother's daughter.

Juan Dorado seemed in a more jovial mood, perhaps confident that at last he had found a suitor for his sister, and he talked freely of many things. That he was fond of his mother and Violetta was apparent in his every word, his every smile. He confided to Rafael that he had always been his mother's favorite, that they were in many ways of like mind. His devotion, however, did not extend to Don Philip, whom he spoke of in anger, annoyed because Philip Navarro held so tightly to the purse strings. His own lack of fortune had sent Juan Dorado into the priesthood, but now he had no regrets. Frey Tomás de Torquemada's family had been lesser than Juan Dorado's own. Torquemada had been poor but exhibited the zeal for perfection and the fanatical ambition to purify all Spain for Christ. Now as Grand Inquisitor he had come a long way, and Juan Dorado clearly hoped that his own ambition would make him as fortunate.

"Of course, Frey Torquemada was confessor to the young Isabella before she married Ferdinand, but I, too, seem to have caught the Queen's eye, and with the help of Torquemada himself . . ." Feigning humility, he shrugged his shoulders. "A worthy vocation for the son of a woman who married a very rich widower." He seemed to tire of idle chatter, and with a flick of his wrist picked up one of the documents and turned again to more serious matters.

"Have you any idea what it is that I hold in my hand?" Rafael assured him that he had not. "The tool by which we can rid Spain of all danger."

"Have the *Conversos* ceased to be a danger?"

Juan Dorado's laugh was menacing. "The converts are no longer important. It is a bigger fish that must be caught, and now that the hated war with the Moors is at an end, it can be baited." His voice lowered to a whisper as if he feared someone might hear. "The Jews themselves."

"The Jews?" Rafael turned pale. He had heard the rumors

—fierce bigotry sparked by other wagging tongues—but he could not believe that even Torquemada would dare to openly attack those who were among Spain's most loyal subjects. The tribunal of the Inquisition had been established to deal with those who apostatized from the Christian church, not the Jewish population in general. Yet he knew the Jews were resented because, in spite of all the laws and rules controlling what they wore, what trades they might pursue, and where they could live, they had somehow prospered. Such prosperity caused envy, which was easily fanned and kindled into hatred. He had even heard foolish prattle that Christian blood was a darker red, as if blood could suddenly change color when baptized into a different faith.

"The triumph of the Cross will never be complete in this land as long as Jews continue to be numbered among Spain's inhabitants."

"What are you saying?" Rafael was finding it more difficult all the time to control his emotions.

"We will demand they convert or face imprisonment. It is no wonder the *Conversos* are so easily swayed when they see how leniently we treat these Jews. The evils of the Jews are notorious and unconquerable. In spite of the measures taken to keep Christian and Jew apart, despite the Inquisition, that evil persists. The Jews try maliciously to convert new Christians back to their own. They have seduced many back to error, and the fires of the Inquisition cannot burn them all! I hold a first draft of an edict of banishment in my hand. It needs only the monarch's approval and it will become law.

Banishment! The word pounded through Rafael's brain. To be exiled from one's own country would be the greatest of injustices.

"The sovereigns have postponed decision on this matter, despite Frey Torquemada's pleadings, yet it is my opinion that Torquemada holds them in the palm of his hand. They will act in accordance with his counsel."

"But they have proved their loyalty!"

Juan Dorado squinted his eyes dangerously. "Jewish gold was needed for the war with the Moors, but now the war is over." His eyes glittered evilly. "Though the Jews sense Torquemada's intent and have argued most eloquently in their appeals, reminding Isabella and Ferdinand that it was they who supplied the money for the campaign against the enemies of the cross, Torquemada will be the victor."

No! Rafael thought. *It could not be.* Isabella and Ferdinand could not be so cruel as to turn their backs on such loyalty, nor be so blind to the truth.

"They will be forced to look the matter in the face. Torquemada will give them no peace. It is only a matter of time. And that is why I have called you forth. To prepare for Torquemada's victory. When the Edict of Banishment is signed, I will be prepared with your help."

Slowly Rafael rose to his feet, keeping his eyes on Juan Dorado's face all the while. "What would you have me do?"

"I want you to compile a list of all the Jews in Salamanca and a list of their properties. I would know the value of their wealth so that we will be prepared."

So that you can seize it for yourself, Rafael thought vehemently. He wanted to tell Juan Dorado *no,* to spit in his sneering face, but he kept his silence, hoping to turn adversity into triumph. Somehow he would do all within his power to thwart Torquemada and this serpent who did his every bidding. He would make a list of the Jews, but not for the reason Juan Dorado imagined. Rafael needed to warn the Jews of the city that a storm was about to break so that they could find shelter from the malevolent gale. Perhaps if the Jewish leaders were warned, they could make a successful plea for their cause. Rafael could not believe that any country could imprison so large a number of its people. It was against all the laws of mankind and God. And if Torquemada did indeed have his way, who then was safe from his malice?

Torquemada had to be stopped, but if that proved impossible, if indeed the Jews were imperiled, he knew he must do everything in his power to give them the same aid he had given the converts. He had two ships waiting. Two ships. He could only pray to God they would not be needed, that Torquemada and his ambitious inquisitor would in some way be stopped.

59

The streets outside Salamanca were crowded, and Alicia elbowed her way through the throng of people, hurrying to catch up with Philip Navarro. Today he had offered her a special treat, a chance to attend the bullfight and watch one of his prize bulls match its strength and grace against a *torero*, one of the most skillful bullfighters in all León.

"Señor Navarro!" A young man, face downy with his very first beard, bowed low to Don Philip and swung open the narrow gateway to the wooden-fenced bullring. Alicia found herself amid an excited populace, howling and shouting *olé* so enthusiastically that she thought the bullfight had already begun. In confusion she stood near the gate, but Don Philip smiled reassuringly and motioned her on.

"Señor Feroz is perhaps the greatest *torero* in all Spain, but I think my Diablo will be a match for him." Don Philip put a protective arm about Alicia's waist and maneuvered her through the crowd, which reminded Alicia of nothing less than a stampeding herd of animals. The fearful thought that were anyone to stumble he would be trampled eased somewhat when Don Philip showed her to a benchlike chair on a raised platform from which they would view the action.

The loud sound of horns startled Alicia, and she saw that a procession had begun at one end of the bullring composed of men on horseback followed by others on foot, all as brightly garbed as birds in full plumage. Dark blue, bright yellow, brilliant green. A gasp of awe and anticipation passed through the crowd like a gust of wind as the procession advanced to the middle of the ring. With the grace of dancers, the bullfighters moved forward, bowing to the crowd amid shouts of *"Torero! Torero!"* But it was one figure alone that drew the greatest response as the throng rose to their feet. Dressed in the deepest, richest red from hose to cape, the man Alicia knew at once to be Feroz took off his cap and threw it as a token to the crowd.

"Bravo! Bravo! Torero! Torero! Feroz! Feroz!" For the moment, this greatest of bullfighters was as a king to the onlookers, and Alicia could not suppress the thrill of anticipation that flooded over her. Surely this fighting of bulls must be a glorious thing for everyone to be so excited. Even Don Philip, usually so calm, added his shouts to the crowd. Sitting up stiffly on the edge of her seat, Alicia held her breath, not really knowing what to expect. Just how would a man fight a bull? She remembered the time Rudolpho had tended an injured cow. The animal had been nearly mad with pain, and he had wrestled it to the ground. She expected this bullfighting would be much the same.

When the initial noise had died down, Philip Navarro smiled and said, "I am glad I asked you to accompany me today. It is the first time in weeks I have seen you without a frown." His eyes were questioning as he glanced her way. "Something has been deeply troubling you, and I would like to help you if I can."

"It is nothing!" Alicia's eyes could not mask her pain as easily as her lips whispered the lie.

"That nothing is eating you up inside. It will make a bitter woman of you. Tell me, Alicia. Have I not proven to be your friend?" He had wanted to tell her so many times that he was certain she was his daughter, yet a small voice still urged him to wait. He would tell her in time. "Who has made you unhappy? Doña Luisa?"

Alicia's expression answered for her. "She is not kind. I

have tried in every way to please her, for she is mistress of the house, and Juanita has schooled me very well in this matter of manners. But . . . but . . ."

"She is constantly deriding your skills. I have noticed and cautioned her many times. She is jealous, *niña*. You must not listen to her barbed tongue." A fleeting look of sorrow touched his face, to be replaced by anger. "I have grown so used to her turbulent ways that it is just like water off a gander's back, but I will not have you a victim of her petty anger. You are like a fresh summer breeze, a gurgling spring, refreshing my tired heart with your innocent smile. You have given me renewed interest in life and I am grateful, Alicia. Give no more thought to the bad manners of my *wife!*"

Alicia started to tell more, for Doña Luisa was only a part of her trouble, yet, uncertain how to tell him of her longing for Rafael, she kept her silence, watching the procession as it paraded by. Strange how she imagined Rafael's face, his smile, on every man who approached. Even far away from him she could not hide from her desire, and she cursed the weakness in her that this gorgio nobleman inspired. Rafael! Rafael! Rafael and Violetta. It sounded a death knell in her heart.

Even thinking of Rafael brought her pain, the pain of unfulfilled longing. She had never known that just the thought of a man could cause such sorrow, and yet it did as she mourned over and over the loss of their love.

Before leaving for the bullring, Alicia had overheard Doña Luisa's insistent words to her daughter. Nor was it the first time the woman had espoused Rafael de Villasandro's eligibility and charm. "It would be an ideal arrangement to have a marriage between you and Juan's wealthy friend," Doña Luisa had said. "He is a landowner. Olive groves. He would be most suitable, most suitable indeed."

"And he is handsome. . . ." Violetta's voice had reminded Alicia of the moo of a lovesick cow. She was not blind to what was going on, nor was she without ears. The very thought of Rafael and Violetta . . .

"He is *my* husband! *Mine*," she had wanted to say, feeling the shard of pottery brush against her skin, the final proof of their vows. Only by the greatest effort had she checked her jealousy. She knew that Rafael did not recognize their marriage. He was free, at least in his own eyes, and yet he had said that he loved her. So many times she had wanted to flee to his arms. Should she? Was it too late? The staccato beat of a drum echoed her heartbeat, and turning her attention once more to the arena, she saw that the bullfighters were gone. In their place stood their opponent, one lone bull.

"Is that Diablo?" Don Philip shook his head and showed his disdain for the puny animal. The beast with its menacing horns and powerful legs looked wicked to Alicia's eyes nevertheless. Watching the torero, resplendent in green and black, spreading his cape wide as the bull pawed the ground, she thought it to be a strange amusement. Suddenly the bull charged and Alicia could not stop the scream that arose in her throat. She seemed to remember another such time from the depths of her mind, and instinctively she shouted, "He will be killed. Oh, please, do something, *cariñoso Papá!*"

"*Cariñoso Papá.*" Don Philip whispered the words shakily, remembering the small child who had called him that. Affectionate father, his daughter's name for him. If there had been any doubts as to Alicia's identity, he had none now. "It will be all right. The bull will not kill him." Giving in to his impulse of protection, he gathered her into his arms. "Oh, Alicia, Alicia, I cannot doubt you now." Her large questioning eyes bored into his soul, wondering at the words she had just spoken, words that seemed to come from another time and place beyond memory. "Have you not guessed, do you not know? Alicia, I am your father!" In those words his soul found relief.

Shouts of *bravo* and *olé* from the crowd drowned out her

reply, yet Don Philip could see from Alicia's expression that she was shocked by his revelation. He had wanted to tell her for so long! He just couldn't keep the secret any longer.

"Alicia! Alicia!" Her silence worried him. "All these years I thought you were dead. She told me that you had drowned. But as in so many other matters, she lied to me!"

"You are my father?" Alicia let that thought settle in her mind. "My father!" Reaching out, she tangled her fingers in the silver of his beard and smiled. So many times she had compared Don Philip to Rudolpho and had found that in all ways he measured up very well, as well as any *gorgio* could. Rudolpho would have been pleased, this she knew instinctively, and that knowledge soothed her. "I feel in my heart that what you say is true, but Rudolpho . . ."

"Will always have a very special place in your heart. I understand and would never want to do anything to compete with his memory. He gave you the love that I was unable to bestow, and for that I will always be grateful."

Alicia watched the bullfight through a haze of tears, relieved that Don Philip had not lied and that the torero always managed to avoid the great horns with a sweep of his cape. The action in the arena moved in a blur as she tried to gather her thoughts. Her father! Philip Navarro was her father. She was not alone anymore, and that thought brought her joy. Was it possible, then, that right from the first she had sensed that there was something special about the silver-haired gorgio? Was that why she had accompanied him to his house without fear? Reaching out and taking his arm, she gave free vent to her affection. He had been so kind, how could she help but love him? But there was so much she needed to ask, so much she needed to know. Remembering his questions, she tried to piece together in her mind the fragments of what he had told her. His daughter had been taken from him when she was a child of four. Hadn't Rudolpho told her that she had been the same age when she had come to him? Putting her hand to her brow, she tried

desperately to remember, but all she could see in her mind
was those cold gray eyes. Gray eyes! Eyes like Doña Luisa's!

"No!" She couldn't believe it! What woman would be so
wicked as to take a child from its father? And yet . . .
Right from the first, the woman's very presence had unnerved her. Somehow she had to remember, for only then
would she truly be free from the vague memories that
haunted her.

"Alicia, look, it is Diablo. That fierce black animal is *my*
bull!" Heeding Don Philip's words, she looked up to see the
magnificent animal enter the bullring, to be matched with
the torero, now elegantly dressed in red. Alicia had been
horrified to learn that the bulls' reward for skill and bravery
was death by a thrust of the torero's sword. Instinctively she
squeezed Don Philip's hand. "It is up to the crowd, Alicia.
Let us hope that they will allow Diablo to be spared."

The crowd was poised on the edge of their seats. Those
who had not been fortunate enough to find benches stood
up on tiptoe, straining for a glimpse of the drama. Pawing
the ground, snorting his disdain, this bull was a crafty one,
not so easily baited. Instead he stalked the torero, matching
him thrust for thrust. Head low, horns glittering in the sunlight, the bull at last lunged, drawing the torero's blood.
Burying her face in Don Philip's shoulder, Alicia could not
bear to look. She had wanted the animal to be spared, but
not at the expense of the bullfighter!

"*Toro! Toro!*" Once so devoted to the bullfighter, now the
crowd cheered the bull, and Alicia cursed the ruthless
throng, who seemed to hunger for the sight of blood, human
blood. This bullfighting was more brutal than she could ever
have believed! She was certain that the man in red would be
killed, yet this time when the bull lunged forward the torero
moved quickly aside, showing no sign of his pain. All that
was caught was the hem of his cape.

It was a strenuous duel, fought by man and beast, a pendulum that swung back and forth as first one then the other

was victor. The crowd was roaring in response, *"Torero! Toro!"* Echoing the shifting balance of power with thunderous cries.

Only when the crowd grew silent did Alicia dare open her eyes, but it was not the bull or the bullfighter that loomed before her. A face she remembered only too well hovered but a few feet from her own, smiling a wide-toothed grin. Seeing him again made her shiver. In sudden fear she tried to hide behind Don Philip's large frame.

"Alicia, what is wrong?"

"That man, the one who is looking this way. Who is he?" She remembered Gypsy stories of the evil eye, remembered how she had laughed at such a thought. Now she held her hands up before her face as if to ward off this man's evil. "I remember him. He is the man I fled from at the church."

"I know." Don Philip's revulsion showed frankly upon his face. Regretfully he answered her inquiry. "The man is Enrique Dorado, Alicia. But have no fear, I will not allow him to harm you."

"Enrique Dorado?"

"Doña Luisa's son, my stepson. May God in his mercy protect us, he has come back from King Ferdinand and Queen Isabella's court."

"Your stepson?" Alicia watched as Enrique Dorado came closer, managing only by the greatest effort not to run away. Don Philip would protect her, he had promised. The approaching man turned his attention toward the arena, holding his thumbs up like the others in the crowd to give a sign that Diablo should be spared. Alicia could not help wondering if this Enrique Dorado would show as much mercy toward her.

60

As closely as the torero had stalked the bull, Enrique Dorado stalked Alicia, his eyes following her every move. His gaze was fierce, predatory, and sly, reminding her of a vulture as he glanced Don Philip's way. As fearful as Alicia was of his doing her harm, she feared for the man who had professed to be her father even more. She had no doubt but that Enrique Dorado lay in wait, longing for the time he could pick his stepfather's very bones. Such a thought brought a silent vow to her lips: Just as Philip Navarro had sworn to protect her, so would she guard him. Enrique Dorado, beware!

"Diablo was the crowning glory of the day! I am glad that he was spared. You are a true master of the bulls." Don Enrique's smile was ingratiating as he looked his stepfather's way. Without being invited he took a seat beside Alicia, purposefully brushing her leg with his thigh. "But it is much more than bulls that interests me now. Who is this fair señorita that graces your arm?"

"This is Alicia María Navarro, my esteemed relative and a most honored guest of mine." Don Philip's expression was fiercely protective, warning Don Enrique to avoid any further show of familiarity.

"Alicia Navarro? A distant cousin perhaps." He captured Alicia's fingers in his hand, bringing them up to his mouth for a kiss of greeting. "Then you are my relative as well—by

marriage, that is." His appraising glance clearly proved that
he did not remember Alicia; did not envision her as the
ragged Gypsy but as a noblewoman of high degree. For the
moment all thought of the bullfight was forgotten as the
wily courtier tried to ensnare Alicia with his false charm.
His attentions continued on the way back to Don Philip's
house, intensifying dramatically as the family sat around
the dinner table. Enrique Dorado made no attempt to hide
his attraction to Alicia, much to Rafael's dismay.

*If that vain buffoon dares to touch her, he will see the proof of my
anger,* Rafael thought irritably. Even though he doubted Alicia would ever have any interest, the man's attraction to
Alicia ignited his jealousy. Though she returned his glance
with cool disdain, Rafael could not keep from looking at
her. She was so beautiful!

The candlelight cast a glow across her creamy bosom,
teasingly displayed by the fashion of the day, and he longed
to reach out and touch that soft skin. He remembered the
texture of her flesh, the warmth of her, the taste of her
beneath his mouth, and a painful surge of desire flooded
through him. Her hair was highlighted by the candles'
flames, wound tightly in a coronet of braids, and he wanted
to loosen it and run his fingers through its silky softness.
Alluring as she was in her new mode of dress, Rafael longed
to have his *Gypsy* back.

Never had time stretched out so dismally as it did now
that Rafael was victim to Enrique Dorado's chatter. He
wanted to take Alicia by the hand, to escape with her to the
garden and there tell her of his love, win her affection again;
but he was helpless to do anything but caress her with his
eyes. Alicia! Alicia! Did she know how her scorn wounded
him? Was she aware of his pain? His bold stare questioned
her, and for just a moment he dared hope, for just a heartbeat of time, that he saw love reflected in her eyes. But then
Alicia looked away and Rafael's illusion was shattered.

He looks so sad, Alicia thought, *as if the weight of the world were upon his shoulders.* From deep within her heart the seed of forgiveness blossomed, and when her eyes met Rafael's again she smiled—a smile that inflamed his dreams. Somehow he would find a way to be alone with her, and when he did, he would dare all to win back her love. Enrique Dorado be damned!

"Don Rafael! Don Rafael!" In spite of the fact that he had ignored her throughout supper, Doña Luisa spoke up, demanding Rafael's attention. "I don't believe you heard a word my son had to say. Are you not interested in what is happening at court?" Without waiting for Rafael's reply she chattered on, repeating word for word what her son had revealed. "How sad, how alarming, that the sovereigns' daughter has lost her husband. Enrique has said that she is truly heartbroken. Poor Alfonso, to fall from a horse and die. And what is your opinion of this sea captain?"

"Sea captain?" Rafael was harshly jostled back into reality. Thinking for a moment she was speaking of Giovanni, he pretended surprise. "Sea captain? I know of no sea captain."

"But all Spain has heard of Christopher Columbus. Even I have given him money for his foolish venture. Imagine his daring to come before Ferdinand and Isabella espousing his need for *three* ships capable of braving a voyage of two months or more. *Madre de Dios!* And he has asked to be made admiral and requests a royal commission." Enrique was eager to continue the story that his mother had begun.

"And what did their majesties say?" Rafael was intrigued, wondering if there was any chance that perhaps these ships and supplies could be used for his own needs.

"They have denied him, but I suspect that in the end he will have his way. Queen Isabella is clearly impressed with the man, Italian though he be. He has insisted that he must set sail no later than August. We shall see, we shall see. But it is this other problem that concerns our dear sovereigns at the moment, the problem of the Jews!"

"The Jews? What do you know of them?" For the first time Rafael was genuinely interested in what Enrique had to say.

"What do I know?" Enrique Dorado smiled, prolonging his tale, relishing the opportunity of being once again the center of attention. Ignoring Rafael, he directed his words to Alicia as if she were the only one in the room. He spoke of absurdities, stories Rafael had heard before, circulated by those whose purpose was to discredit the Jews and increase Torquemada's power. He told falsehoods—of Jews trying to sacrifice Christian children, of sacrilege being done to the cross. It was even alleged that the illness of the young Prince Don Juan was the result of Hebrew infamy. Enrique revealed that a letter from the Jews of Constantinople to the Jews of Toledo instructed them to use deceit against the Christians in their vocations as merchants, physicians, and clerics. "It is known that a Jewish physician in Toledo carries poison in his fingernails so that when he touches the tongues of patients they will die."

"I do not believe one word!" Before Rafael could speak up Don Philip issued his protest. "These stories are malicious misrepresentations fostered by envy and ignorance. I am surprised that you, Enrique, lower yourself to utter them. What makes it worse is that such ridiculous whisperings are considered saintly zeal."

"My brother has himself testified to such things!" Enrique defended himself and his brother Juan as well.

"It is a good thing that Ferdinand has not the power in León and Castile that our sweet Queen has. At least Isabella will bow to reason, else our Jewish neighbors will be in peril," Don Philip said confidently, rebuking his stepson with a stern look.

"Isabella herself has finally agreed to Torquemada's demands," Enrique continued. "How can she argue against the truth? The Jews refuse to accept Christ as God, they have intruded into Christian lands, they rob, steal, and kill Christians, even children. They are still insolent, though the age-long suffering God has put upon them proves his scorn for them."

"Or his love," Rafael muttered, loathing this popinjay as much as his brother.

"Enough! Enough! I will not hear such slander in my house. The Jews are citizens of León, Castile, all of Spain, and my neighbors. . . ."

"They will be your neighbors no more." Enrique looked like the cat that had eaten the sparrow. "Torquemada and Juan are right, there will be no united Spain as long as they are on our shores. Spain must be Christian throughout!" His eyes flashed with ire, yet there was a secretive grin on his face. "But then, you will not know what has happened if you silence me. . . ."

"Don Philip, please let him speak." Rafael had to know what was happening.

"*I* was there that day the Jews pleaded their cause, sniveling about what they had done for Spain, promising to keep to their ghettos and have no more dealings with Christians. Their spokesmen were Abraham Seneor and Isaac Abarbanel." Rafael knew them to be the two Jews who had undertaken and so admirably effected the equipping of the Castilian army for the campaign against Granada. "They pledged thirty thousand ducats toward expenses incurred in the war. Thirty thousand ducats. Enough to tempt any man, even a king, but Torquemada himself was there to thwart such temptation. Learning what was afoot, he thrust himself into their Highnesses' presence to denounce such a proposition!"

Rafael could imagine the scene that had enfolded; knew the persuasiveness of this cold, hateful man, spreading his poisonous opinions and lies. He would seem a little pale, a little breathless in his excitement and the anger by which he would undoubtedly be possessed. His deep-set eyes would glow somberly with the fever of fanatical zeal and indignation. He would draw his lean old frame erect, holding in his shriveled, sinewy old hands the cross.

"Judas once sold the Son of God for thirty pieces of silver. Your Highnesses think to sell him again for thirty thousand? Sell him, then, but acquit me of all share in the transaction!" Enrique's voice boomed as if for the moment he had become Torquemada himself. "And with that he crashed the crucifix upon the table before their startled Highnesses and abruptly left the chamber." Enrique's smile was smug. "And so the edict of expulsion was signed."

"Expulsion? It is to be banishment, then." Rafael was too filled with sympathy to be enraged. So, it had come to this. He damned the Torquemadas of this world and the Juan Dorados as well. Hatred and prejudice had brought a sad ending to those who did not deserve it. He knew the sovereigns would never have issued such a decree had it not been for Torquemada's fanatical malice.

Torquemada. The name brought fear to Alicia's heart as well. It was well known that he scorned the Jews, but she knew he hated the Gypsies too. *Banishment.* Her heart wept for these Jews and she prayed that *o Del*, their own God, and the gentle Christ would watch over them. This matter of faith puzzled her, for it was so contradictory. Jesus spoke of love and living together as brothers. Why then did this priest of Christ provoke such hate? She would have to ask Father Julio that question when she next saw him.

"What about the Gypsies?" She had asked the question before she could silence her tongue.

"The Gypsies? The Gypsies?" Enrique threw back his head and laughed. "We will rid ourselves of them as well. Like the Jews they are to be banished from these shores!"

61

As swiftly as a shooting star, Alicia flew out of the dining room, through the solar, running down the long corridors in her anxiety to be alone. Pausing at the the doors opening out into the garden only long enough to catch her breath, she quickly looked behind her and, satisfied that no one was close behind, pushed at the final barriers to the outside.

It was chilly, a stiff March wind whipped at Alicia's face and hair, yet her shivering was caused not by the fierce breeze but by what she had heard Enrique Dorado say: *Banishment.* The word implied far more than mere exile. It meant a renewal of hatred and violence toward people who had been resented since the first day they had set foot on Spanish soil. Todero, Zuba, and the others, what would happen to them? Where could they go? Drawing the corners of her shawl around her, Alicia closed her eyes as a feeling of helplessness swept over her. She didn't even know where they were. How could she help them? Was there nothing she could do?

Anxiously she turned her gaze toward the sky as if the pulsating stars could give her an answer. A star for everyone on earth, which one was Zuba's star? Which one was her own? Did she even believe that Gypsy fable anymore? In truth she did not know what to believe, nor to whom she should offer up her prayers. Father Julio spoke of a loving God, the Christian God, yet she could not turn her face away from *o Del*. Weren't they one and the same? One God but with different names? Was he not the Jewish God as well? "Help them all. Oh, please help them! Father Julio says you are merciful. Then show your mercy. Please, dear God. Don't let *o Beng* have his way. Are we not *all* your children?" Father Julio had spoken of Christ's followers as sheep in need of their shepherd, and she could only hope that at this very moment *He* was standing guard to keep Torquemada away from his flock.

Alicia walked along the garden path trying to sort out her thoughts. So much had happened today that she scarcely knew how to cope with it all. The appearance of Enrique Dorado, a man who frightened her with his menacing eyes and his news of the banishment, was a deep cause of worry. Then, too, Don Philip's avowal that she was his daughter was another matter Alicia needed time to think upon. And Rafael. She loved him, there could be no denying that; and tonight, when their eyes had met, she knew that he loved her too. Was she a fool to let her pride stand between them? She was Don Philip's daughter. Deep in her heart she sensed it was the truth. Her blood was just as noble as Señorita Violetta's. Did it matter that Rafael would think her worthy of him now when he had scorned her before? Could she stand aside and watch Doña Luisa have her way? Was she so staunch in her vow that she would remain silent and let Violetta marry the man she loved? No! Pride was a lonely bedfellow, hadn't she found that out by now?

The snap of a twig alerted Alicia to the fact that she was not alone, and she turned in the direction of the sound. A figure stood half hidden by the foliage that encircled the courtyard, and thinking it to be Rafael, Alicia hurried forward.

"Rafael?" The figure did not turn around, nor was there any answer. "Rafael?" Cautiously Alicia slowed her steps, searching the darkness with her eyes. "Who is it? Who are you?"

With every nerve in her body Alicia could sense piercing eyes upon her, appraising her body. It was not Rafael, of this she could be certain. Nor was it Don Philip. Hadaj always wore white, and this man wore a dark doublet and hose.

There was no escape. Like a wolf stalking its prey, Enrique Dorado had carefully positioned himself between Alicia and the patio door. "It is a lovely evening, is it not, Señorita?" The sharp lines of his profile were clearly revealed in the moonlight as he stepped out of the shadows.

"Very lovely, Señor, but a bit too cold. I think that now I will go back inside." Keeping a careful distance from him, she tried to walk by, but his long arm reached out to capture her.

"Do not be so hasty to depart, beautiful one. We should become better acquainted." He pulled her roughly into his arms, making his intentions only too clear.

"Let me go!" Alicia struggled, but he was insistent.

His only answer was laughter as he dragged her to the shelter of a row of bushes. Startled, terrified by his sudden advance, Alicia fought as violently for her honor as she had with Stivo. Her hair, pulled free of its confinement, blew in wild disarray about her shoulders, her eyes challenged him. No man would take her without her consent, gorgio or Gypsy. This one talked of being a gentleman, but he was no better than Stivo! Then, just as Stivo had, he would feel her sting.

"Let me go!" One last time she warned him, but Enrique Dorado would not be swayed. Thinking her too frightened to flee, he loosened his hold. It was just the chance that Alicia needed. In deference to her Gypsy ways, she still kept her knife hidden beneath the folds of her skirt. Now she was thankful for its protection.

"Philip thought that just by his command I would stay away from you, but I will show him that I always take what I want. And I want you."

"But you will not have me, Gorgio!" Her blue brocade gown was snagged and torn from the scuffle, exposing part of her breasts as they heaved in anger. Holding up her arms, Alicia prepared to defend herself.

"Gorgio?" Enrique Dorado was obviously baffled. How many defenseless young women had fallen victim to his bold lechery, Alicia wondered? Had they all been so easily conquered, then? Well, not she! Never she! The point of her knife glittered in the light and Enrique widened his eyes. "*Dios*, what is that?"

"A knife, Gorgio. If you take one more step, you will feel how sharp it is." He ignored her warning. "I will use it! Beware! I do not want to harm you, but I will."

"You are but a woman, I am not afraid. Put it down. There are other things that I would have you hold with your hand." His dark eyes leered at her and he grinned. That he meant to ravish her she had no doubt, and as he lunged at her Alicia struck out. "Ahhh . . . you have wounded me!" Instead of taking it as a warning, Enrique was only angered. "I was going to be gentle, but *Dios*, I will make you sorry for what you have just done!" He tore at her skirts, bringing her again within his grasp, and Alicia found to her horror that her foolish hoops and skirts hindered her. Dodging to one side, away from the knife, Enrique caught hold of her wrist, and only by the greatest effort was Alicia able to keep hold of her weapon. Looking wildly about, she searched for any sign of the other members of the household. Surely someone would hear the commotion. Sensing her thoughts, Enrique Dorado laughed cruelly. "They are all immersed in their theological discussion. No one will hear."

"Then I will have to fight you all by myself!" Taking advantage of his arrogant conceit, Alicia struck out with a violence that stunned him. Blood gushed from his wounded arm, and Enrique stared at the spreading deep red stain.

"I didn't want to harm you! But I had to! I had to!"

"Who are you? What are you?" Enrique's eyes squinted

with fury and pain, recognizing her at last. "Father Julio. The Gypsy whore! A Gypsy! A filthy Gypsy! What are you doing here?"

"I am not a Gypsy, though I wish I were. I am Philip Navarro's daughter." Outrage had made her confess what she should never have revealed.

"His daughter?" Enrique looked at her with disbelief. "His *daughter*? He has a stepdaughter!" He didn't even want to contemplate what such a truth would mean. "But whoever you are, I warn you. You have made an enemy of me. No one sheds Enrique Dorado's blood, much less a woman. You will regret what you have done. With every breath that you take you will be sorry. I will see that you are repaid."

62

Only one candle lit the room. The flame flickered and danced about, stirred by the whispers of the man and woman who stood face-to-face. Enrique Dorado and his mother, Doña Luisa, were hastening to conspire, and the tone of their conversation was both angry and frightened.

"Then she speaks the truth. That same Gypsy whore who attacked me is the old man's daughter. *Madre de Dios!* We are ruined!"

"No we are not! I have not worked and planned for all these years to assure you of an inheritance only to be pushed aside by the appearance of that little . . . *Cuidado,* I hear a noise!"

"It is only the howl of the wind. All in the household are asleep." Just to make certain, Enrique pushed the door of the library aside and looked out. Satisfied that no one was about, he returned to the matter at hand. "But how did he find her again?"

"She came to him."

"Father Julio's Gypsy?" Seeing her nod, he swore. "Damn him for his meddling. Had I known that day who she was, she would never have had a chance to interfere in our lives."

"But she *is* here and Philip knows. . . ."

"You should have gotten rid of her much sooner."

"I could not take such a chance. What was I to do, poison

her?" There was a long-drawn-out silence. "I could never do such a thing. I am not evil, nor am I a murderer, Enrique."

"Yet if you had used a more permanent method of ridding us of her presense, we would not be bothered with her now! Such a stupid thing to do, taking her to the Gypsies. Had I not been just a child, *I* would have thought of a much better plan."

"You are ungrateful! It was I who thought only of my children in sending her away. I never wanted you to suffer as I had. That was why, when Philip's wife died, I did everything that I could to convince him to marry me. I was successful. How was I to know that he intended to leave everything to his daughter when he died?"

"He has not yet changed his will?"

"No. Not yet! He has not even confided in me, yet he knows. I heard him tell Rafael de Villasandro. And if *she* ever remembers that I was with her that day, we will all be sent packing. Philip must never know what I did."

"You do not think he suspects?"

"Suspects, but does not know for certain. I have been a very fortunate woman, for Alicia does not seem to remember anything about her past." Her laugh was scornful. "She is Gypsy through and through!"

"Gypsy!"

"I waited until you came back, hoping you would know what can be done. We cannot arouse suspicion by openly harming her. Philip guards her day and night as if she were a precious jewel, and our guest, Señor de Villasandro, is always watching her as well. And Juanita. Ha! One would think she were her mother the way she hovers near. If we but raise a finger to harm her . . . No, it is too dangerous."

"Then *we* will not harm her." The fire of the candle was extinguished by his exclamation, leaving the room in total darkness. "She is, as you say, a Gypsy!"

"She is Philip's daughter. Any fool can see that. I took her to the Gypsies myself. I know. . . ."

"But others do not! She is a *Gypsy*! How can your idiot husband prove otherwise? By your own lips you tell me that the girl does not remember."

"And the Gypsies have been banished! *Dios,* what a plan."

"She is a blasphemer, a heathen, and one of those that Torquemada chooses to exile from our shores. Need I say more?" The room was filled with their ominous laughter. "You need have no further worry. When the Jews and the Gypsies are exiled, she will be among them, of this you have my word!"

63

Rafael paced his room like a caged bear, watching as the candle in the wall sconce burned lower and lower, marking the passing hour. He couldn't sleep, but then, had he really expected to after what he had learned at dinner tonight? Enrique Dorado, the very name made Rafael seethe as he remembered the way he had devoured Alicia with his eyes. She was not safe in this house with such a one about.

Enrique Dorado! The more he saw of the man the more he detested him. In his way he was just as dangerous as his brother. And what of Alicia? Had Enrique recognized her as the Gypsy girl he had frightened away? No. He had treated her with the greatest deference, though the lust in his eyes could not be hidden.

The sound of footsteps in the hall alarmed him anew. Who else was up at this hour? Curious, he peered through a crack in the door to see that it was Enrique himself stalking about. He saw him pause for a moment outside Alicia's door, his hand poised on the latch, but before Rafael could give vent to his rage, Enrique moved on down the hallway and vanished into his own room.

Rafael had kept away from Alicia, remaining true to his promise not to beg her forgiveness, yet now he knew that he had to see her, talk to her, warn her. Alicia, who was so innocent of deceit, he had to make her understand the evil of the Dorado men.

Moving quickly to her room, he fumbled at the latch only to find, as Enrique Dorado had also discovered, that it was locked. But having made his decision, he was stubborn in his resolve. "Alicia! Alicia! Open the door, I must speak with you!" His voice was an urgent whisper. "Alicia, it is Rafael."

"Rafael!" The sound of his voice was the sweetest sound in the world to Alicia at that moment. Forgetting all else but the need to feel the strength of his arms, she opened the door.

Rafael strode quickly inside, closing and locking the door behind him lest Enrique decide to return. Turning around, he was unnerved by the fear he read in Alicia's eyes. Was it of him? "Alicia, I am not here to harm you. I must warn you. I didn't mean to frighten you. Perhaps I should leave."

"No!" She was shaking all over and without hesitation Rafael gathered her into his arms.

"Alicia, what is it? Why are you trembling so?" He felt her body draw close to him, and he pulled the whole soft, supple length of her against him, breathing in the fragrance of her hair. "Alicia?"

"Enrique . . . tonight . . . in the garden." Tears sprang to her eyes and she clung to him fiercely. "He is such a one as Stivo."

"Dorado? I will kill him!" The muscles of his arms stiffened, his jaw clenched with anger, yet his embrace soon calmed her. Alicia at last stepped away, regretting for a moment her weakness, remembering her pride. "Did he touch you?"

Rafael's question was answered by a derisive laugh. "I would not let a man like him degrade me in such fashion. Ha! He soon felt the sting of my knife!"

"Your knife?" Rafael could well imagine the scene, and despite the seriousness of the situation he laughed, imagining Dorado's surprise to find his victim not as helpless as he had supposed.

"You laugh, Gorgio!" All the weeks of schooling and learning had vanished, and Alicia was once more just as he had remembered her, loved her. Once more she was his fiery Gypsy.

"I am merely relishing my delight to have my lovely Gypsy back in my arms again." She was wearing a simple gown of white linen, her feet were bare, the long dark tresses of her hair were unbound, flowing free. He couldn't resist the temptation to run his fingers through her hair as he had so longed to do these past few weeks. "You will never know how much I have missed her. Doña Alicia is a lovely Spanish lady, but even she can not take *my* Alicia's place!" His gaze slid slowly over her slim body, lingering on the rise and fall of her full bosom.

Aware of his prolonged stare, Alicia lifted her chin, her eyes blazing defiance; yet seeing the love written so clearly in his eyes, any words of scorn she might have said died in her throat. She was aware only of a flutter in the region of her stomach, beating gently like the wings of a butterfly. Unsettled and confused by the contradictory emotions he aroused within her, she was strangely silent.

"I love you, Alicia. I have said that many times before, yet I say it again." His mouth tightened into a grim line, the tiny lines around his eyes deepened. "I came here tonight to warn you about Enrique Dorado, and now I can see that my warning came too late. He is dangerous. All the Dorados are. I fear we find ourselves in a nest of vipers. How I wish that I could take you away."

"Take me away?" She wasn't certain what she longed for, yet she searched his face intently. Did he mean what he said? Dressed only in dark blue hose and white linen shirt, he looked undeniably handsome, and she found her eyes roaming over him with infinite care. His features were intensely masculine, but it was his mouth that captured her attention. Oh, how she wished to feel the taste of his lips again.

"Would you go with me, Alicia?" Adding to the turmoil within her, Rafael took her hand and pressed the warmth of his mouth against her fingers.

At that moment Alicia knew that in spite of everything she would always love him. "Yes, I would go, Rafael." All the barriers of her prideful defense were down, and she only knew how much she wanted him, how much she needed him. A lock of his dark hair had fallen across his forehead, and without even thinking, Alicia reached out to smooth it back.

The new harmony between them was fragile, and Rafael was cautious lest he break it. He had dreamed of being with her, her bewitching smile beckoning him toward remembered delights, the curves of her body driving him half mad with longing. Even so, he moved slowly to take her in his arms. Alicia's eyes were huge, the color on her cheeks high, as they stood clinging to each other. His mouth was only inches from hers, yet Alicia did not pull away. All that mattered to her was that she was in his arms again. He had chosen her and not Violetta! He loved the Gypsy after all and not the lady!

Gently at first, his lips came down on hers, and the touch of his warm mouth engulfed Alicia in the maelstrom of bewildering, intoxicating sensations that she remembered so well. Ah, it was sweet to have him kiss her again, to be once again in his arms, to feel his heart beating against her own. She let out a soft moan as her arms crept around his neck, her breasts pressed against his chest, and her legs strained against his. She was aware only that she had wanted this despite her anger, despite her pain.

At Alicia's surrender Rafael forgot everything but the soft body of the woman he loved in his arms. All the hungry desires that had been kept so tightly under control for so long now sprang free. His arms tightened about her with fierce intensity.

"Alicia!" Whispering her name, his mouth blistered hers

with its heat. His was a fierce, insatiable thirst that could
never be quenched. His lips were everywhere, at her ear, on
her brow, caressing her throat, then back on her mouth
again. Bodies molded to each other, arms entwined, they
were fused as if into one being, and Alicia knew that whatever happened, she could never deny Rafael again. They had
wasted so much precious time, so many valuable moments
when they might have been together. It didn't matter that
he might leave her again. She knew that the currents that
drew them together would always bring him back to her
arms. She would wait for him if it took forever. Hadn't she
known that she would always belong to him that first night
beneath the stars? No other man would ever possess her.
She loved Rafael, and for her there would never be another.

Feverishly she arched up against him, her body aflame
with desire. She ached to be naked against him, to lie by his
side in the moonlight. He was her husband by all the laws
and vows she cherished; consummating their love was only
right. Though she had denied it by her words, she had
wanted him to come to her, wanted him to love her. That
was why she offered no protest when he picked her up in
his arms and carried across the room, setting her down
gently on the huge bed.

"You know that I want to make love to you, Alicia, but I
will leave right this moment if that is what you wish." His
breathing was ragged, his eyes bright with desire, yet Alicia
knew that were she to bid him, he would do as she asked.

"Don't leave. Oh, Rafael, I wanted you to come to me. I
thought that it was the skinny gorgio woman . . ."

"Violetta?" He could not mask his smile. "Loving you,
Alicia, my eyes are blind to any other woman, though Doña
Luisa is most adamant. She wants a husband for her daughter, but she is unwise to choose a man who already has a
wife." His knowing lips moved with tender urgency across
hers, as if sealing their vow once again. Slowly, languor-
ously, his fingers moved over her body, drawing down the

bodice of her nightgown to expose the ripe fullness of her breasts. Seeing the shard of pottery that she wore around her neck, he touched it reverently. "I have been the greatest of fools, Alicia. Can you forgive me?"

"I forgave you long ago, no matter what words passed my lips. I belong to you, Rafael. Now and for ever more." Still, as she watched him bring forth his own piece of their marriage vessel from a pouch within his shirt, tears filled her eyes. She had thought the Gypsy ceremony had meant nothing to him, and yet he, too, had kept the token of their union near his heart.

Alicia looked at Rafael for a long, lingering moment. It was as if they were seeing each other for the first time, as if they had never met before yet had known each other forever. She felt a flow of tenderness for him, a love more fierce than before stirring her body and heart.

The touch of his hand upon her breast made her tremble, her pulse quickened at the passion that burned in his eyes. Closing her arms around his neck, she offered her lips, wanting him to kiss her again. Wrapped in each other's arms, they explored each other gently, giving vent to emotions too long denied. With impatient hands they undressed each other, and with a groan Rafael covered her body with his own, his legs entwined with hers.

Passion exploded between them with a wild abandon as they joined in body, soul, heart, and mind. Like the currents of the river, her body drew his in a sensuous rhythm, her long legs tightening around his hips, possessing him as fully as he possessed her. Her body was a vessel of sweetness consumed by his warmth and love, filled with sweet, fierce fire. Ecstasy erupted hotly between them, plunging them into an abyss of aching pleasure. There was nothing but the desire and need that possessed them, molding them forever into one being, binding their hearts together for all time.

"I love you, Alicia. I will always love you. No matter what happens, no matter how it may appear, you must always

remember that. I'm asking you to believe in me, trust me."
Rafael gazed down upon her face, gently brushing back the
tangled hair from her eyes. "There is a mission I have undertaken that must be accomplished before we can be together."

"I will trust you." Snuggling up against him, she buried
her face in the warmth of his chest, feeling safe and happy.
For a moment the lovers were untouched by the world's
cruelty and evil, knowing only their contentment. And Rafael felt himself charmed by her innocence. For that fleeting
moment he was able to forget all his worries. There was no
Torquemada, no Inquisition, no hatred, no violence, only
love.

They spent the rest of the night together, their bodies
entwined, each unwilling to be the first to break the won-
drous spell that had been so intricately woven around them.
They made love once more, gently, without fierce intensity
but ultimately as sweetly. Alicia didn't want to sleep, not
now, but as Rafael caressed her back, tracing his fingers
along her spine, she drifted off to delightful dreams.

"Rafael?" Opening her eyes to greet the morning, she
found herself alone, and for one brief moment she feared
that it had been only a dream after all. A dream! A shattering wave of disappointment flooded over her, but as her
hand reached out she discovered what he had left behind—
his shard of pottery beside her own. A token that he would
return, that their love would forever join them together just
as surely as their wedding vows had foretold.

64

Certain now of Rafael's love, Alicia viewed the world through different eyes. She was content, secure, and felt truly alive. The world was beautiful! Not even Doña Luisa's persistent efforts to match Violetta with Rafael could spoil her happiness. What had once caused Alicia pain now proved to be merely comical, for though the young woman favored Rafael with her most scintillating smiles, though Doña Luisa catalogued her daughter's skills relentlessly, Alicia knew now that Rafael would never choose Violetta as his bride. How could he, when by his own admission he already belonged to Alicia? With each night that descended he gave proof of that love.

Alicia found, however, that happiness was a fragile thing. Alicia and Rafael could not shut out the rest of the world indefinitely. A storm was about to break, and Rafael found himself at the heart of the gale. Alicia could read his anxiety in his eyes, but though she begged him to confide in her, he maintained his silence, fearing to involve her in the danger. In the weeks that followed he spent extended periods of time away from Don Philip's house. Alicia would have been consumed by worry had she not remembered her promise to trust him, her new awareness that love and trust must go hand in hand. The thought reassured her. Rafael would come back.

Of course there was a great deal to keep Alicia occupied.

Her father was always the most attentive of men, and the
bond between them had grown much stronger now that she
knew that he *was* her father. Although it disappointed him
that she could not remember her early years, he did not
mention it. Don Philip was a patient man. Fearful of fanning
the flames of Enrique's hatred toward him, Alicia did not tell
her father of the attack in the garden, but she never again
walked among the flowers alone, always carried her knife
hidden in the folds of her gown, stayed in the company of at
least one of the servants, and kept her bedroom door carefully locked and bolted. Even so, Enrique Dorado's eyes unnerved her. She had made an enemy and she could not allow
herself to forget that fact. It was as if Enrique Dorado
watched and waited, but for what, Alicia did not know.

Summer hovered in the air, teasing the senses with its
promise of the beauty to come. Though Alicia yearned to be
outdoors, she carefully avoided the garden. Following the
example of the other women of the household, she attended
to her stitchery despite the fact that she was constantly
frustrated by the prick of the needle. Gorgio foolishness, she
called it, receiving Juanita's stern rebuke and a lecture on
women's duties. Still, no matter how hard Alicia tried, she
could not master embroidery, and though the other women
seemed to enjoy it, she found it hard to give it her full
attention. Thus she was only too happy when her father
invited her to come with him into the city. Ignoring Doña
Luisa's reproving eyes and condescending remarks, Alicia
escaped from the house as happily as a once-caged bird.

The crowded streets were hung with banners and flowers,
creating a jubilant mood, and Alicia was caught up in the
gaiety. A woman in love was like a bright, shining star,
radiating light. Don Philip could not help but notice, and he
was pleased.

"Rafael de Villasandro is a fine man, a gentleman. I am
glad that he has brought a smile to your lips of late."

Remembering their passion-filled nights, Alicia blushed,

wondering what her father would think if he knew. "I love him, Father, and now I know that he truly loves me! He told me so."

"And did you doubt it? I never did. Why, I remember that right from the very first moment he saw you, his face was radiant with his love. He had told me several months ago of his love for a young Gypsy woman that he longed to find. I am glad that at last he has."

Troubadours and minstrels clad in bright colors, lutes and harps flung over their backs, mingled with the throng, always ready to trill a song for a coin or two. Alicia caught the eye of more than just one who poured forth his admiration in melodious poetry, Don Philip made a great show of protecting his daughter, scolding several of the young men, yet softening his words with a wink of his eye. One young man, however, was afforded his smile and a most enthusiastic handshake.

"That handsome auburn-haired *caballero* comes from a neighboring family. Alfonso Suárez is his name. Long ago he cast his eyes in Violetta's direction, but Doña Luisa thought him unsuitable."

"Why?"

"He was but a fifth son. With no fortune, no lands, and no hope of ever attaining riches, he adopted the wandering life of a troubadour. *Dios*, it is a pity. I fear my unhappy stepdaughter will remain forever a señorita."

"Then I am sorry for her not to know what love is."

The loud clang of a bell announced the hour, adding its voice to the laughter and singing of the throng, and Alicia learned from her father that many of the revelers were on their way to a jousting tournament. Though such events were not as popular as they had been a hundred years ago, they were still attended by a goodly crowd, and Alicia was filled with avid curiosity.

"Is this jousting like a bullfight?"

Don Philip smiled. "In many ways similar, but in other

ways different. In jousting, two men battle in mock combat
in order to win fame and display their skills. Perhaps in
many ways facing another human being is much more dangerous than facing a bull. I do not know." Gently he
touched her shoulder. "Come, I will show you." He led her
to the area that had been set aside as a tiltyard, tiered with
benches set beneath canopies. "When you were a child you
loved to accompany me, though I'm certain you did not
fully understand all that was going on."

Alicia tried hard to remember, but as with many other
things her mind was a blank. Still, the sight of the brightly
colored pavilions and the young men in armor delighted her.
Raising the hem of her long skirt to make walking easier,
she kept pace with Don Philip.

Like the streets of Salamanca themselves, the pavilions
had a festive air, yet there was an undertone of tension.
Everywhere people whispered about the edict of expulsion,
and as they came closer to the tiltyard, two men were nois-
ily voicing their opinions.

"By this edict all Jews of any age, be they male or female,
who refuse to receive baptism must leave Spain within one
month and never return upon pain of death."

"Spain is well rid of them, I say, as well as of those thieving Gypsies!"

"Gypsies are not thieves!" Alicia could not keep her silence.

"What do you know about it, woman. I say they are!"

"They are not!" Only Don Philip's firm hand on her arm
kept her from arguing the matter any further. With a strong
but gentle hand he led her to a bench sheltered from the
sun, and here they watched the helmeted men on horseback
buffet each other with their swords and lances.

It was a blazing-hot day, and Alicia soon grew thirsty.
She had merely to gaze at the long tables laid out with fresh
fruits and refreshments to bring her wish to Don Philip's
notice. Eliciting a promise that she would not move from her

seat, he pulled forth his coin pouch and walked toward the tables. Alicia's gaze was following him when her eye glimpsed a familiar figure in the shadows between the tables and the pavilion. Rafael! He was here. Anxious to be at his side, and forgetting her promise to her father, Alicia rushed toward him. But as she came closer, she realized that he was not alone. A tall dark-haired man with a brightly plumed cap stood beside him, and they were deep in conversation. Succumbing to her curiosity, she inched a little closer.

"We must move and move quickly, Giovanni," she heard Rafael say.

"The boats will be ready. I only await your cargo, *amico mio.*" Innocent words, and yet Alicia was not fooled into thinking them harmless. Rafael's all too frequent absences told her that something was going on, and her intuition whispered that Rafael was in danger. He had spoken to her about a mission. What could it be? If she hoped for an answer, she was to be disappointed, for as she approached, the two men stilled their talk and she was met by a tense silence.

"Alicia? What are you doing here?" Rafael's exasperated look told her that she had intruded.

"Father brought me. I've never seen a joust before. Rafael . . . ?"

"Ah, so this is the fair Alicia you have told me about." The man named Giovanni swept her a courteous bow. *"Bella! Bella!* No wonder she has won your heart. Now I know why you searched the streets of Salamanca so feverishly for her."

Alicia blushed under the scrutiny of his gaze. There was something she instinctively liked about this Giovanni and, impulsively, she returned his smile.

"But I must introduce myself. Giovanni is my name."

"Giovanni. I will remember."

"Giovanni is a sailor, a ship's captain, Alicia, though he is a long way from the sea here in Salamanca. He wishes to trade Venetian glass for olives and Leonese beef."

"Olives? Beef?" There were many questions she wanted to ask, but Rafael's manner, though courteous, clearly informed her that this was not the time, and his air of secrecy only alarmed her further. She doubted that he had told her the truth, yet she had no time to ponder the matter, for just a short distance away she saw Don Philip returning to their seats and craning his neck to catch sight of her. Regretfully taking her leave, murmuring a hasty good-bye, she left the two men and hurried away.

Rafael watched her walk away, longing to call her back. Whenever he was near her he was drawn to her, remembering the curtain of her dark hair flowing about him, her warm body lying beside him, offering him the purity of her love. Now every muscle in his body ached to hold her again.

"You have not told her?" It was more statement than question.

"No. It would be dangerous if she knew."

"It could be more dangerous if she does not." Giovanni raised one brow. "But come, we must not arouse suspicion by lingering. Let us return to our seats and make a great show of watching this tourney. I am told one of the jousters is from Venice. Would you be interested in a wager on his prowess?"

Neither man realized that they were being watched, yet two pairs of eyes followed as they walked away. "The woman that greeted him is the one that I told you about, Juan. She is staying now at our stepfather's house."

"Alicia!"

"Our *Gypsy.*"

"I suspect that Rafael de Villasandro is her lover."

"Her lover?"

"You seem to find that disturbing."

"He is a man in whom I have placed my trust. If he is involved with this *woman,* there could be most unpleasant consequences. Let us hope that I have not been foolish."

"He seemed disturbed when I told him about the edict. Could it be that he is a wolf in sheep's clothing?"

"Perhaps. He should be more carefully watched, Enrique." Juan Dorado steeled himself to the matters at hand, adding Rafael de Villasandro's name to the list of those who would merit the attention of his spies.

65

It was late when Rafael returned to the Navarro house, yet in spite of the hour he longed to find solace in Alicia's arms. Perhaps there he could forget what he had seen today. The Jews of Salamanca were preparing for their exodus.

Christian charity! Rafael thought bitterly. He had heard of Jews giving their house in return for a donkey or selling a vineyard for a piece of cloth. Knowing that the Jews were being forced to dispose of all their property, that they must take the proceeds with them in merchandise or in bills of exchange, the noble Christians of the city were driving ruthless bargains. They consoled their consciences by saying that a greater injury would have been done to these *neighbors* if their property had been confiscated outright; yet wasn't that exactly what was being done? They were banished from the country that had been the home of their ancestors for centuries, compelled to dispose of all that they owned quickly; and there were many who were eager to take advantage of these forced sales, Juan Dorado among them.

All that Rafael had been able to do was to promise them passage on a ship, and he knew in his heart that this was not enough. Still, were it to be discovered that he had aided them, he had no doubt that there would be retribution. It had been decreed that no Christian could befriend or assist them, give them food or shelter, under pain of being called to account as an abettor of heretics.

Nor had Torquemada been content to end the matter there. In his great zeal he forbade anyone to help the Jews along the roads, hoping that if their misery was great enough, they would see the error of their ways and agree to conversion. Upon this campaign he had now sent forth his army of Dominicans. With royal sanction an edict had been published that exhorted the Israelites to receive baptism. It stressed the fact that those who did so before the appointed three months had come for their emigration would be entitled to remain. Remain and be burned at the stake as *Conversos*? Did he really think that those who had not abandoned their own faith by now would be prepared to do so under such dire threat? The man was either mad or a fool.

Rafael had arrived in the city before the gates were opened, before the merchants had set up their stalls. He had been appalled to see that the black-and-white-robed Dominicans were already there, exhorting the Jews to receive the waters of baptism. They had been as bold as any street vendor, and Rafael had been sickened by the spectacle. It seemed that no place was sacred. In their zeal they had penetrated into the very synagogues. Even Jews weeping over the graves of their dead, grieved by the thought of the dead they were abandoning, were approached by Torquemada's friars and priests. A few converted, but the majority did not. Those whom Rafael was able to contact had been taken from Salamanca to Madrigal, from Medina del Campo to La Mota, and thereby to Portugal and Giovanni's waiting ships. Venice and Italy were their final destinations. An interlocking chain of sympathizers had been found along the route, as loyal in their aid as Rafael himself. Some Christians still felt bound by the laws of brotherhood.

But Rafael did not want to think about it anymore. For just a moment he wanted to put it out of his mind. He wanted the sweet oblivion from pain that he always found in Alicia's arms. Alicia. He had nearly given himself away today when he found himself staring into her lovely face.

Did she sensed his turmoil? Did she suspect something was wrong? He had met Giovanni near the pavilions for safety's sake. It was dangerous to be seen conversing in the shadows, but to be amid a riotous crowd seemed innocent enough, or so he and Giovanni had reasoned. He had never thought to see Alicia there.

The entire house was in darkness as Rafael pushed open the door. Not even one candle illuminated his way, yet he knew by heart the path to Alicia's room. Quickly and soundlessly he made his way to her door, tapping upon the thick wood with the knock that would tell her it was he. Though he feared she would already be asleep, he was pleasantly surprised to hear the door open.

"Rafael!" Stepping inside, he held her tightly in his arms, silencing her words with his kiss. Her long dark hair was unbound, entangled in their embrace, and Rafael cherished the glory of those silken tresses. *Dios,* how he ached for her.

Only the soft glow of moonlight illuminated the room. Gazing down at her face, Rafael read worry there, woven with the love she never attempted to hide. She was so beautiful, he mused, his eyes moving lovingly over her face. She seemed innocent, untouched by the world's cruelty, a tantalizing haven of comfort and sanity in a world gone mad. For a long while he was content just to hold her, then he swept her up in his arms and carried her to the bed. With a sweeping movement he tugged at the covers, laying her down upon the linen, drawing her down upon the softness. He kissed her again, molding his lips to hers as his tongue explored the recesses of her mouth with the greatest tenderness. Caressing her, kissing her, he left no part of her untouched, and she responded with a passion as wild and untamed as her heart.

"I love you, Alicia!"

Staring up into the mesmerizing depths of his eyes, Alicia felt an aching tenderness for him. Reaching up her arms, she clung to him, drawing in his strength and giving hers in return. She could feel his heart pounding and knew that hers beat in matching rhythm. Reaching out, she explored his body as he had done hers. His flesh was warm to her touch, pulsating with the strength of his maleness. For the first time, it was Alicia who was the aggressor, soothing Rafael with her gentle love, taking away all the pain that ached in his heart. She was his, he belonged to her, and Alicia gloried in their mutual possession. There was nothing in the world but this man filling her, loving her. The fierce and beautiful sweetness of their joining filled them both.

"Alicia, sweet Alicia. I pray to God that I will never bring you any more pain."

"The only pain I would ever have is being without you!" She pressed closer to him, entwining her legs and arms around him as if in that way she could hold him to her forever. "Oh, Rafael, I sense that you are in danger. That man, Giovanni . . ."

"Is friend, not foe. He is helping me. More than this I cannot and will not tell you. I cannot take the risk."

"Rafael . . . !"

"Shhh, love." Gently his lips caressed hers, silencing her questions, driving all worries and doubts from her mind. For the moment there was silence, except for the beating of their hearts, the whisper of their sighs, as sweet, hot desire fused their bodies, bringing peace and delight before the fury that was to come.

66

Summer was in full flower, bringing hot sunny days and warm sleepless nights. It was a time that Alicia would remember as the month of her greatest happiness and the time of impending sorrow.

The month of June was ushered in with festivals, music, and revelry. It seemed a time when any excuse was appropriate for celebrating. For the first time in her life Alicia was completely ruled by her emotions, giving herself up to the contagious mood that abounded. Only Rafael's frequent spells of melancholy threatened her complete happiness, but though she questioned him continually, he maintained his silence. Even so, the times when she was in his arms brought her the greatest contentment. Sheltered within the protective cocoon that Philip Navarro had woven around her, she was unaware of the intrigue that seethed within the very walls of the hacienda.

On this evening Don Philip had planned a fiesta, one in which he planned to acknowledge Alicia as his daughter, or so he told her. Alicia María Navarro, his daughter and his heir. Alicia had listened to him with a mixture of elation and apprehension. She was proud to be his daughter yet could not help but wonder what such a declaration would do to Violetta's pride. Though the sullen young woman had shown her nothing but hostility, Alicia did in fact feel sorry for her, wishing they might have been friends. And what of

Doña Luisa? Though the woman had made an attempt to show Alicia the utmost courtesy, enmity still flickered in her eyes.

Stars glittered brightly in the black sky overhead, a breeze wafted the faint scent of roses from the garden below, and as Alicia stood on her balcony she breathed in the fragrance of the warm night air. The garden had been strung with lanterns and the soft strumming of a lute accompanied the song of the minstrel who was striding about the pathways. Alicia recognized him as Alfonso Suárez and smiled. When a woman was in love, she longed for others around her to know such blissful passion, and Alicia could not help but wonder if this man might yet make Violetta smile. If her stepsister were a happy woman, she would have no need to be envious of others.

> "The face of my love is as white as a rose,
> the wing of a raven is black as her hair."

Stopping beneath Violetta's balcony, the minstrel made no secret of the fact that he was singing his ballad for her. Glimpsing Violetta from her perch above the garden, the scarlet-clad Alfonso showed clearly by his expression that he had not forgotten her. The flame of passion he had once felt was still there.

"Alfonso! Quiet, you will bring my mother's wrath down upon both our heads. Have you forgotten how fierce her temper can be?" Violetta's voice was only a whisper as she looked hastily over her shoulder.

"Let her be angry! I never should have left you, Violetta. You are the only woman I will ever love."

"Alfonso!" Violetta's protestation could not hide the joy his words brought, and Alicia was surprised how lovely the dark-haired young woman could be when she smiled.

"Come away with me!" A discordant strum on the lute accompanied his plea.

"I cannot. Oh, Alfonso, my mother wants me to marry another."

"Do you love him?"

"He is very handsome, and my mother says . . ."

"Do you love him?"

"I don't think so. But I could not bear to break his heart."

"Yet you break mine."

"Don't talk that way."

"Then give me proof of your love. A token, that is all I ask." Alicia watched as Violetta plucked the rose she wore in her hair and threw it at the minstrel's feet. "A red rose, perfect and fair, yet it blushes in envy of your lips."

"Alfonso, you must not talk that way. I am soon to be married. My mother . . ." Alicia stepped hurriedly inside. Though she was sure of Rafael's love, Violetta's words stung her heart. Closing the door, she gave the minstrel and his lady love their privacy. Slowly she made her way downstairs.

The solar was filled with people Alicia did not know, gentlemen dressed in brightly colored hose and doublets, ladies in many-hued gowns as brilliant as the petals of the flowers that grew in the garden. They reminded Alicia of the gorgios that had scorned her in the city when she first arrived, and she felt suddenly nervous and shy. She didn't want to meet them, she just wanted to run away.

"Alicia, there you are!" Don Philip greeted his daughter warmly, kissing her on the cheek. "Today is a day I have long treasured in my dreams, a time that brings me happiness as well as pain. Eighteen years ago today you were born. I thought it a most fitting time to introduce you to my friends."

"The day I was born. My grandmother would have said it was a good day for the stars."

"The sign of the twins. Had your mother lived to see this day, she would have been very proud." Taking her arm, he wove in and out of the groups of guests, obviously well pleased with himself and showing himself by his smile to be the proudest of men. He introduced Alicia at such a furious pace that she knew she could never remember all the names. There were tall men, fat men, men clean-shaven and bearded. Some ladies were small, some were stout; there were those whose hair was tinted reddish gold, some were dark-haired, and there were others whose hair was touched with gray. Alicia was greeted with warm enthusiasm by some of the very people who had stoned her in the street, though she knew they did not recognize her. Father Julio had told her that forgiveness was a blessing, and with a sigh Alicia tried to banish all misgivings from her mind. If these were her father's friends, she would somehow learn to like them.

Alicia sought out Rafael, and seeing him enter the room, she felt her heart quicken. From across the room their eyes met, and she was aware of his sorrow. Her only thought was to reach out and touch him, but the presence of her father's guests was a human barrier that kept them apart.

Conversation was exchanged, music was played, and wine was served as the hours passed by. At last Rafael managed to maneuver himself to Alicia's side. "Don Philip tells me that it is your birthday. I told him long ago that we were married, Alicia."

"You told him? He knows?"

"He wants very much for us to say our vows again before a priest. Does that idea upset you? Will you become my wife once again?" She felt the warmth of his breath as he whispered in her ear, "I love you, my lovely Gypsy wife."

Alicia could not find the right words to say, but her smile answered for her. She had been waiting for him to ask her to marry him according to the Christian laws, knowing that such vows would please the gentle Christ. Father Julio had been adamant in stressing the importance of such a ceremony. Now she would be bound to Rafael by Gypsy law *and* by Christian law. It was good. It was right. Rudolpho himself would have been pleased. Together they made their way

to where Philip Navarro stood to get his blessing, one Alicia
knew would be forthcoming.

"Father . . ." Alicia's words were drowned by a furious
shriek. Having gone to her daughter's room, Doña Luisa had
returned without Violetta, bearing a note in her hand.
"What is it? What is wrong?" Fearing the worst, Alicia followed Rafael and Don Philip as they hurried to the dis-
traught woman's side.

"What has happened? Stop your crying, woman, and tell
me?" Don Philip took the message from his wife's hands,
but instead of crying he broke out into a smile. "Violetta.
She has eloped. She has run away with that minstrel, Alfonso Suárez." He winked at Rafael. "She says to tell you
that she is very sorry that she must break your heart. She
wants you to try to forget her."

"*I* will never forgive her. To elope with that . . .
that . . ." Wringing her hands, Doña Luisa hurried away,
overcome by a storm of frustrated tears. Though Alicia
hated to see anyone cry, she felt laughter bubble up from
her throat. She was delighted for Violetta's happiness and
relieved that the young woman would no longer hover
about Rafael. It seemed that all had turned out very well.

Alicia basked in the glow of her happiness. She had found
her father, she was loved by Rafael, what more could she
possibly want? Though the room was brimming with people, it was as if she and Rafael were all alone. Even Enrique
Dorado's leer could not ruin her happiness. Her eyes were so
filled with the sight of Rafael that she hardly noticed the
entrance of the black-robed priest until the others in the
room looked his way.

"You have come to join in the festivities, Frey Dorado?"
Don Philip's tone was cold, though he bowed his head
slightly in a sign of respect.

"I have come on God's business!" Cold, cruel eyes scrutinized Rafael. "There is an enemy in our midst." A gasp
echoed his words as all within the room turned their eyes

Juan Dorado's way. From out of the shadows seven special officers of the Inquisition came into the room.

"You dare to invade my home!" Don Philip was not afraid of his stepson, yet he was unable to stop the armed men as they surrounded Rafael de Villasandro.

"This man is under arrest." At Juan Dorado's signal, two of the men grabbed Rafael's arms.

"Under arrest? What am I charged with?"

"It is not the policy of the Holy Office to inform a prisoner of the charges against him. It is only for us to bring about your confession."

Alicia was a wild creature, pushing her way to Rafael. "No! You can't take him away. You can't!" Brutally she was shoved aside, watching in helpless outrage as Rafael was dragged away, a prisoner of Juan Dorado's hatred.

67

"Rafael!" Alicia's mournful cry was lost in the shouting and the tumult his arrest had unleashed. She tried to follow, but her father blocked her way. "I must go to him! Father, please!"

"No, Alicia. We must be calm. We must use caution. Hysteria will only serve Rafael's enemies. To run after him at this moment would not help him and only endanger you as well. Do you understand me?" Alicia nodded, weeping helplessly against his chest. Stroking her hair, he tried to comfort her. "It must all be a mistake. Rafael is the noblest of men." He turned his eyes toward his wife in anger. "Your son has gone mad, woman. He has turned against the very man he sent here as his guest. Why? Is he so poisoned by his power?"

"Perhaps this Rafael is not as noble as you believe." Turning her back, she stalked away but kept her eyes riveted upon her husband and his daughter, hoping that in some way events could be turned to her own advantage. Meeting Enrique's eye, she communicated her thoughts in the intensity of her gaze.

Alicia's sobs tore at Don Philip's heart, and unaware of his wife's intent, he sought to quiet his daughter's anguish with a hasty promise. "I will go to my stepson right this moment. I will make him rescind this mockery. Within the hour I will have Rafael back within the haven of your arms." Escorting his daughter to the safety of her bedroom, he bade her stay inside, and through the mist of her tears Alicia promised to obey him. Watching from her balcony, she saw her father leave the house, heard the sound of his horse's hoofbeats as he rode away. Her father had told her to wait, but how could she? Rafael was her love, her life! She ran to the door with determination only to have reason flood back into her mind. Don Philip was wise, just as Rudolpho had been, and if he had told her to remain here, he had very good reason for such counsel.

It was quiet in her room, a haven from the turbulence below, a peaceful retreat where Alicia now struggled to sort out her thoughts. She would give her father time to help Rafael before she let her own emotions goad her on. And yet the thought that Rafael might really be guilty terrified her. She had heard him talking with the ship's captain about cargo; knew of his secrecy, his determination to hide what he was doing even from her. Should she seek out this Giovanni and find out the truth? No. Love meant trusting, and she knew deep within her heart that Rafael would never do anything to harm others. She had to be patient. Her father would return as he had promised, and when he did, Rafael would be with him.

Alicia sat down upon her bed, closing her eyes, trying to still the thudding of her heart, willing herself to be calm. Patience was not so easily achieved. "Oh, God, please send Rafael back to me!" she whispered, remembering Father Julio's teachings, his assurance that the God of the Christians answered prayers. Would he hear her? In desperation she repeated the prayer, saying it much louder this time, so loudly that at first she did not hear the knocking.

"Alicia! Alicia!" Doña Luisa's voice sounded outside the door, accompanied by the rhythmic beat of her hand. "Alicia, let me in. I have received a message from your father."

"My father!" Without pause Alicia ran to the door. "What has happened?"

"Open the door and I will tell you," came the reply.
Though Alicia had no reason to fear Doña Luisa, still her
hand paused on the latch, not wishing to confront the woman's scorn. "If you do not open the door this instant, I will
go away. I am a busy woman. The fate of Rafael de Villasandro is no concern of mine!"

Silently, slowly, Alicia opened the door to her night visi-
tor. "My father. Rafael . . ." Her heart froze as she saw
instantly that Doña Luisa was not alone. At her side, smiling
ominously, was her son, Enrique. "No!" Alicia threw her
body against the door, but Doña Luisa quickly wedged her
foot in the opening. "What is going on? Why . . . ?" From
the darkest recesses of her mind Alicia seemed to remember
another such confrontation.

"You are to come with me, with *us*. We are going to take
you to your father. He is asking for you." Doña Luisa's
smile was as hard and cold as ice, yet her voice was soft and
amiable.

"No! My father told me to stay here." Green eyes met
gray eyes in a silent duel, one Alicia knew had been fought
once before, a long, long time ago. It was as if she were
reliving an old dream, a nightmare, as the woman reached
out to grab her and hold her captive.

"There is no time to argue. Come along. *Date prisa!*" She
tugged at Alicia's arm, but Alicia was no longer a small,
innocent child who obeyed. The hard life of the Gypsy had
made Alicia strong, and now with a violence born of her
anger she pulled free. "Enrique! Quickly. Catch her before
she gets away."

Malevolently Enrique stared at her, daring her to try to
run past him, but Alicia was not so easily cornered. Bolting
toward the balcony, she fully intended to jump, but strong
arms reached out from behind to halt her in her flight. "Not
so fast. You will not escape me this time, *Gypsy!*"

Struggling, Alicia attempted to cry out, to scream, but he
covered her mouth with his hand, smiling all the while at

his mother. *The knife,* Alicia thought. *My knife!* Somehow she had to retrieve it!

"Silence her quickly or she will bring the servants!" Enrique obeyed his mother's request with a torn piece of Alicia's shawl. "The guests have all left, the servants have retired. It will be quiet downstairs, but we must hurry before Philip returns." She cast a triumphant glance at Alicia. "I tried to rid this house of you once before, but you came back to haunt me. This time you will not return. I will tell your father that you were so bereaved by the fate of Don Rafael that you disobeyed his advice and ran away. With so many dangers at night, who could say what tragedy befell you?"

"We will take her to Juan. He will know what to do. Is he not expert in ridding our city of unwanted *Gypsies* and Jews?" A tense silence, deadly and dangerous, followed Enrique's words, and the enormity of what had been planned stunned Alicia. An icy, sickly feeling of despair overwhelmed her. They would take her away and she would never see Rafael or her father again. No! She wouldn't allow such a thing to happen. Rafael needed her! Her knife, it was her only chance to escape. Her knife, it was her only thought as she was dragged along.

"There is a wagon outside, already harnessed. If we are careful, no one will ever suspect . . ." A gasp of surprise cut off Doña Luisa's words as the door was thrown open. Standing in the doorway like an avenging angel was none other than Philip Navarro.

"What is going on here?" His eyes gleamed with anger as he reached for his sword.

"We caught her stealing, husband! When I attempted to scold her, she came at me with a knife. Had it not been for Enrique . . ."

"Liar! Bitch! Do you take me for a fool! Once you might have been clever with your story of how Alicia ran away from her nurse and fell in the river. I did not know the

depths of your treachery then, but now I am much wiser.
Unhand my daughter or you both will feel the bite of my
sword!" Philip Navarro did not have to repeat his threat.
With a growl of frustration Enrique pushed her roughly
from his arms.

"Papa! Papa! I remember now. She came up to my room
just as she did now. She grabbed me. She told me that you
wanted to see me, but it was a lie. She took me to the Gypsy
camp!" Fumbling in the folds of her gown, she brought
forth her knife, holding it up threateningly just in case Enrique Dorado had any thoughts of violence.

"No, Philip, not I. Not I! The child has gone mad!"

"Has she, Luisa? Did you think I had not suspected? I
truly hoped you were innocent. I gave you the benefit of the
doubt, thinking perhaps the nurse had meant to profit from
the abduction of my child, but tonight you have given yourself away and forced my hand. I want you and this vile
creature you have spawned out of my house tonight!"

"No!" Burying her pride, Luisa Teresa Dorado Navarro
slumped to her knees, her arms outstretched in supplication.
"I did not mean any harm. Forgive me! Forgive me! It is just
that I loved you so that I was jealous of the child." Her eyes
were wild as she looked toward Alicia. "I am sorry. I will
never do anything, say anything, to you again. Only do not
throw me out into the streets!"

"I will not see you starve. I am an honorable man. But I
wish never to see your face again, do you hear?" Don Philip
shook his head in disgust. "Now leave me, both of you,
before I change my mind. I tremble to think what would
have happened tonight if I had not been in time. May God
forgive you for the years of misery you cost me, for I know
that I cannot." Anger furrowed his brow as he watched
Doña Luisa and Enrique leave, but the frown melted away
as he gathered his daughter into his arms. At last Alicia
really did belong to him.

"Where is Rafael, Papa?" Her heart froze as she sensed his answer. "They would not let you see him!"

"He is being fiercely guarded, may God damn Juan Dorado to hell! But he has not won! My stepson has not been victorious. I will send Father Julio to the pope, if need be, to hear Rafael's case. No matter what must be done, you will have the man that you love by your side again. In God's name I so swear."

68

The passage to the dungeons was dark and eerie, made more so by the flickering flames of the torches the dark-robed men held aloft. The steps were steep, and once or twice Rafael was certain that he would stumble and fall to the bottom. Only the strong arms of his jailors kept him from falling.

"Why am I being taken to this filthy place? I am a citizen of Castile. You have no right to treat me in this manner!" Rafael asked the question, though he knew that he might never be told. Such was the way of the Inquisition, and yet Juan Dorado seemed eager to reveal his intentions.

"For aiding and abetting Jews for one thing. For crimes against the church. For being yourself a *Converso.*"

"A convert? That is a ridiculous charge and you know it! I am no convert but a loyal Christian."

Juan Dorado's answer was laughter, chilling and cruel. In the glow of the torchlight his face looked as if it were molded in wax—pale, expressionless, only the eyes mirroring his malice. "Loyal Christian? That is hardly the term used for one who is accused of transporting fugitives and Judaizing."

Rafael did not have a chance to answer the charge, for as quickly as he had spoken, Juan Dorado grew silent again, giving a signal to his henchmen to lead Rafael down a long, poorly lit corridor that was the entranceway to a dozen or more tiny cells. Very little air circulated in the windowless area and the smell was foul. Rafael wondered if he would ever be able to accustom himself to such a stench, but that was the least of his worries now.

"Agh . . ." The shriek of a man in the throes of agony shattered the stillness, and Rafael could not help but cringe. He knew he was trapped, with no hope of escape. Even so, all he could think of was Alicia. She must not be involved in any of this! He could only pray to God that Don Philip would protect her.

"Put him inside the second cell!" Juan Dorado's voice was emphatic. "I will show him what happens to those who have betrayed my friendship!" Selecting a key from the ring he carried, he made a mocking bow of gallantry. "Let us hope these accommodations will be suitable."

Rafael heard the lock click in the door and felt a hand push him inside. For just a moment he was free of constraint and he lunged at the hated priest. With the agility of a cat, Juan Dorado moved aside.

"Chain him!" Three guards came forward to hold him.

"No!" Rafael struggled, but he was outnumbered, and they managed to subdue him easily. Shoving him into the tiny cubicle, they pushed his wrists into manacles that were attached to chains in the wall.

"That will cool his temper!" one of the guards exclaimed.

"Only a sincere and open confession of all that you have done will save you from further harm." That Juan Dorado meant torture, Rafael well knew, yet he refused to show fear. "Give me the names of those who aided you."

"Go to the devil!"

Juan Dorado pretended concern, his voice taking on a hushed tone. "Your only chance for salvation is a full and open confession of what you have done. Who are your accomplices? Who?"

"No one. I have done *nothing* and I did *that* all alone!" He would never betray Giovanni or the others, never. "There is nothing to tell."

"Then I am sorry for you, Señor, for yours will be the most miserable of lives until you cooperate." For a long while Juan Dorado questioned Rafael, until his ears buzzed and his head began to ache. Questions. Ridiculous questions. "Do you ever eat pork?"

Rafael laughed. "Yes, when it is cooked just right it is one of my favorite meats."

"You eat pork though you are a *Converso*?"

"I am *not* a *Converso*. I am a Christian, though you have not given me cause to be proud of my faith. Men like you mock God."

"Silence, else I charge you with blasphemy as well." He paraded back and forth in front of Rafael, his tiny eyes studying him avidly. Lowering his voice, he confided, "I know that you are no convert, but it will be your secret and mine. For no matter what a man has done, one need only accuse him of being a convert to see that punishment is meted out freely."

"You know and yet you would watch me suffer. What kind of man are you?"

"A man who does what must be done. But I need not explain myself to you, a man who bears the stigma of Jewish blood!" Seeing Rafael's look of surprise, he added, "I have found out about your mother and your secret shame."

"My mother was a beautiful woman, an honorable woman, a woman of whom I am proud. There is no shame in having come from her womb, but I am not a Jew."

Juan Dorado trembled in rage. "By the laws of the Jews themselves, any child that is born of a Jewish woman is a *Jew*! I have vowed to purge all Spain of anyone whose blood is so tainted!"

"The Jews were in Spain long before the Christians. If I were a practicing Jew, I would be proud of it." He dared not say more for fear of Juan Dorado's reprisal.

"So you reveal your true feelings at last. What a pity there was no notary here to take down your confession, but I will remember." Wrathfully he summoned the guards again. "He will soon give us the information we desire."

Rafael was unchained and led down the hall into a larger room. Accustoming his eyes to the light, he scanned the room, and seeing the instruments of torture, cringed at the ghoulish display.

"Frey Dorado's toys," quipped the jailor, smiling to show his missing front teeth. "I think, Señor, that it will not be long until we hear you beg for mercy."

It was the usual procedure to show the prisoner the instruments of torture, to let them consider the consequences of failing to "confess." "I am generous." Juan Dorado grinned. "We will give the accused two weeks to think over his sins. Two weeks, then we will continue the examination."

Two weeks, Rafael thought. He was trapped with no hope of escape. Damned if he confessed and damned if he did not. Denial of guilt would only bring the agony, the rack, the strappado, or the water torture. Admitting guilt would assure him of being burned at the stake.

"I must confess, say what you want to hear, to escape suffering. Isn't that what you *holy* people expect?" Rafael's eyes were scathing in his contempt.

"You must give us the information we desire." Juan Dorado grinned. "By the way, Señor de Villasandro, that lovely painting you gave me, I have added another such work to my collection. One that belonged to your brother!"

"My brother?" Rafael's face paled at the thought of Carlos and his family in the hands of this demon. Frey Dorado read the fear in his heart, and like a beast of prey, moved in for the kill. "He is also a prisoner in Toledo. His wife has told us some very interesting tales."

Dios! That a man or woman would confess to anything under torture, Rafael knew. Poor María. Poor, gentle, loving

María. What must they have done to her! "I am neither Jew nor convert. My brother and his children and myself, as well, are loyal Christians. How many times must I tell you?"

"Nor a Gypsy?" Again the blood-chilling smile. "Am I to suppose that you do not know the woman who lives at the Navarro house?"

"She has nothing to do with this!" Rafael had the furious need to protect Alicia even at the cost of his own life. He could bear any torture if he knew that she was safe.

"We shall see. We shall see." It was then that he informed Rafael of his plans. Within two weeks Rafael was to be taken back to Toledo to stand trial, a trial to be attended by none other than Frey Tomás de Torquemada himself.

Three

DESIRE AND DESTINY
Castile, Summer 1492

All for Love, or the World Well Lost.

Dryden, Title of play on theme of
ANTONY and CLEOPATRA

69

The first rays of dawn sparkled over the horizon, lighting the pathway of the party of riders who made their way toward Toledo. Alicia had traveled this route once before. Then she had been alone, now she was accompanied by her father, ten of his servants and retainers, and the ship's captain, Giovanni. Having learned of Rafael's whereabouts, it was their intent to free him, be it by royal pardon, trickery, or force.

"We should disguise ourselves as monks and snatch Rafael out from beneath their very noses!" Giovanni was bold, and his presence was a balm to Alicia's tortured soul. Despite the peril, he persisted in believing all would be well.

Alicia tried to share his optimism and wondered if she dared tell him about the *mulengi dori*. The piece of ribbon that Todero had used to measure Rudolpho's coffin was said to have magical properties and could be used just once—to aid one who was imprisoned or in danger. Now she would use it to free Rafael.

"I would dress as one of God's angels if I thought it would get Rafael past the guards. But first we must seek an audience with their Highnesses. Isabella is at heart a just woman who is loyal to those who have served her. Despite the hold this toad Torquemada has over her, I believe that she will listen to me. When I was a young man I fought for Isabella's right to rule against Henry IV's mad daughter, Juana, and

since that day the Queen has listened to my advice." Philip
Navarro and the Venetian sea captain had quickly established a mutual respect for each other, and at the Spanish
nobleman's declaration Giovanni nodded his head. "I must
make her see the wisdom of setting Rafael free."

Alicia regarded her father with a twinge of guilt. She had
not told him all she had learned from Giovanni. He didn't
know that Rafael and Giovanni were more than pleasant
acquaintances. She herself had learned only recently of
Rafael's brave stand against Juan Dorado and the real purpose of the ships that were to carry those in danger to
safety. She had thought he had betrayed her; the truth made
her heart ache with love. To her eyes Rafael was a hero, but
how would the Queen view his deeds? Alicia could only
wonder.

Now that it was daylight they rode at a furious pace, and
Alicia was grateful to be dressed as a boy. The leather boots
and the long-sleeved doublet and hose were much more
comfortable than she had ever supposed. From a distance
one might have mistaken her for a young man, for her hair
was carefully tucked up in a cap, but a closer look at her
long-lashed eyes and the soft swell of her breasts gave her
away.

"How long before we reach this Toledo of yours?" Giovanni's voice was tinged with pain, and Alicia suspected he
was not used to traveling on horseback. Along the road to
Castile he had talked vibrantly of Venice, where the streets
were made of water, and Alicia supposed there would not be
many horses there. Clearly he was more comfortable on water than on land.

"Only a few more miles, Señor," Don Philip answered,
pointing up ahead to where the dirt road merged with the
cobbled streets of the city. From the distance they could see
the soft glow of twilight illuminating the high stone walls of
a castle, and Alicia could not help wondering if Rafael was
there. Just the thought of him made her heart flutter in an-

ticipation. She had vowed that if he was condemned to die, she would die with him. In this world or the next, they would be together.

The last three miles seemed as thirty to the weary travelers. Alicia's eyes were red-rimmed from looking at the sun, and when she first saw the crowds of people swarming out of the city, she thought she was seeing things. Rubbing her eyes, she knew at once that they were all too real.

"They are Jews, the people that Rafael was trying to help," Giovanni said sadly. "Look at them and remember the sight of man's inhumanity to man."

On foot, on donkeys, on horseback, in carts, young and old, able-bodied and feeble, they formed a forlorn procession. The exodus from Spain had begun. Toiling onward in the heat and dust of the July morning, they presented a spectacle so desolate and lonely that even the most hardhearted of onlookers viewed the scene with pity.

A swarm of inquisitors came after, driving the human wall of fugitives before them. Southward to the sea, westward to Portugal, eastward to Navarre, they headed, fleeing as their ancestors had done so long ago. Alicia remembered Father Julio's story of the Hebrews' flight from Egypt, and she could only hope that God would part the ocean for them again.

The grief and agony she saw in their eyes tore at Alicia's soul, and she damned Torquemada again and again. What would happen to these people? Her father had told her of the Grand Inquisitor's decree forbidding any to help them. Rafael had ignored that decree, and the thought of what he had done made Alicia fearful yet proud. Courage like his would be rewarded, she had to believe that. Father Julio had said the same.

The closer they came to the city, the sparser the crowds became, and it was only then that Don Philip lost his temper. "Fools! Isabella and Ferdinand both! Spain is banishing her merchants and financiers. I have no doubt but that the

Moors will soon follow, our finest artisans and agriculturists. We are our own worst enemies, and all because of men like Juan Dorado and Torquemada. If I were a man of the sea, I would have requisitioned all my ships to aid these poor wretches." His eyes met Giovanni's in a flash of understanding. "That was what Rafael was doing! And you . . . ?"

"Yes, Signore. I am glad that you know. Rafael is the bravest of men. I cannot let myself believe that a man such as he could meet such a sad fate as the stake."

"You risk your own life if you are caught."

"That is the chance I must take. There are too few men like Signore de Villasandro. I could not live with myself if I did not stand by him. Giovanni has never deserted a friend!" He urged his horse at a faster pace, showing his gleaming white teeth in a challenging smile. "Come, we must not linger here. If I have my way, Rafael will feel the warmth of Alicia's arms before the day is out."

"You well may have your way. Let us pray to God that Isabella shows her mercy, for I fear that Torquemada will not."

70

It was dark in the prison cell, dark and silent. The only reality that Rafael knew was the tiny six-by-seven-foot cell and a pallet of straw that was his bed. Denied a window, he was never completely certain about the hour of the day, but at least here in Toledo he was not chained to the wall. Smiling ruefully, he counted his meager blessings.

Lying flat on his back, he stared up at the ceiling, envisioning Alicia's face. Thoughts and memories of her were all that saved his sanity, and he wondered if she even knew where he was. Poor Alicia, what anguish she must be going through now, but at least she was far from the Grand Inquisitor's clutches. Just the thought of her safety gave him reason to be thankful.

Closing his eyes, he tried to sleep. Sleep was his only recreation, dreams his only escape from the dank, putrid cell; yet there were times when even that was denied him. They woke him at random intervals both day and night, trying to unnerve him and make him more pliable to their demands. Was it any surprise that he was always exhausted or that his head ached? Hunger, too, kept him awake. All that he was given to eat was stale bread and a watery soup, and that just once a day, barely enough to keep him alive. Juan Dorado would not want death to cheat him out of a victim! Still, with all his misery Rafael could be truly thankful that he *was* alive. As long as there was life there was hope. Hope, the ultimate gift of faith, an emotion that separated a human from an animal.

Rafael had been in Juan Dorado's prison for four days before he was thrown into a heavily guarded wagon, his arms and legs chained together. It had been a rough, torturous ride to Toledo, made more so by the thought of never seeing Alicia again and fear of the unknown. Each time he awoke he expected to find it all a terrible nightmare only to realize that he was indeed Juan Dorado's prisoner, another victim of the Inquisition. Strange that even though he had seen others suffer, though he was actively involved in helping others escape, he had never truly thought this could happen to *him*!

Opening his eyes, Rafael reached out to touch the notches he had made on the cold stone floor, calculating roughly the time he had been incarcerated in this gloomy cell. Not quite three weeks. His jailors were prolonging the suspense, hoping the anticipation would bring him fear. Mental torture. All the while they had held over his head the threat of the rack. Nor was it an idle threat. From the screams and groans he heard all about him, he knew that the instruments of torture were being used quite frequently. Soon it would be his turn.

Juan Dorado. Juan Dorado. The name echoed through his brain, and he fought desperately against the hatred that threatened to choke him. Hatred was a base emotion bringing only evil in its wake. He would rise above men like Torquemada and his right-hand man, Juan Dorado. Torquemada. How many days before he would find himself face-to-face with that carnivorous man? Had he any hope of finding mercy here? Would the Grand Inquisitor spare him? Rafael had heard of prisoners who had been kept in prison for years before being brought to trial; and it was the possibility of this, more than the immediate threat of death, that agonized him. To waste away in this hellhole! Complete isolation was threatening to drive him mad. Even the jailor's face was a relief as he opened the door with a jangle of his keys. "You are to come with me!"

"And just where am I going?"

The guard growled, "Just wait and see!"

Once Rafael would have been more than a match for this tall, skinny man. It had taken several guards to subdue him the first time he had been thrown into a cell. Now, however, after being inactive for so long, deprived of proper nourishment, he was as weak as a newborn calf. Rubbing his arms and legs in an attempt to bring the circulation back, he nearly succumbed to a wave of dizziness that swept over him. There would be no subduing his enemy now. Juan Dorado had seen to that!

Expecting to be led to the torture chamber, gritting his teeth to resign himself to his fate, Rafael was surprised to find himself instead in the audience chamber of the Holy Office. It was a court composed of inquisitors delegated by Torquemada, including Juan Dorado, whose thin-lipped smile told Rafael he would find little mercy here. Seated about a table upon which stood a tall crucifix between two candles were several monks and two priests, one a notary and the other the fiscal advocate. Holding forth the Gospels upon which the accused was to be sworn, they asked Rafael his name, birthplace, the particulars of his family, and the diocese in which he had been raised. Rafael answered each question curtly, staring Juan Dorado directly in the eye to issue a silent challenge.

"Do you know of what you are accused?"

"Of heeding Christ's counsel to aid my neighbor and show brotherly love," Rafael answered. His reply brought a rush of blood to Juan Dorado's face, causing the pale flesh to turn nearly purple with rage.

"You lie. You aided the Jews, the killers of Christ. You helped them. I have proof that you provided ships!"

"Torquemada issued an edict to exile the Jews out of Spain. I merely eased the speed and comfort of their flight.

With so much violence there were few places left for them to run."

"You aided Jews!"

"Was not Jesus himself a Jew?"

"He was the Son of God! The Son of God himself established the Christian church!" Rising from his seat, he pounded upon the table. "Thus God wishes all nations to be Christian. Heretics, Jews, and Gypsies are a crass insult to God's intent!" His manner was condescending, like a father to an errant child. "Heresy must merit eternal punishment. In snuffing out a heretic each of us is saving his potential converts and the man himself from everlasting Hell and damnation! Thus must I save you."

"I am not a heretic!"

"And yet you lived among Gypsies. Deny that if you can! I have the written testimony of one who watched you, one who witnessed you murder his companion." Rafael knew at once that this was José, the man who had tried to kill him by throwing him in the river. This was the repayment he got for sparing the man's life. Now to be accused of Manuel's murder was the greatest travesty of justice.

"I have never in my life murdered an innocent man!" Rafael watched as every word he said was set down on parchment by the scribe, whose quill moved quickly across the page. "You are heeding the word of a thief! The evidence he gives is false."

"You call him a liar?"

"I do!"

"Enough! It is you who are on trial here and not this other man." Juan Dorado squinted his eyes, taking another line of attack. "Your sister-in-law has preceded you in this office, and your brother as well. She told us many interesting tales. She said that while you were living in her husband's house she observed Jewish rites with her own eyes, that you changed your linen on Saturday, never ate pork, and bathed Friday nights to prepare for your Jewish Sabbath. You were

heard to mumble Hebrew prayers, swaying back and forth."
It was a lie, as Juan Dorado very well knew.

"You are a bearer of false witness or a fool, Frey Dorado. I
am not a Jew! To marry my father, my mother accepted
baptism. I was born a Christian of Christian parents. I was
myself baptized into the Christian faith." Rafael turned toward the other robed men in the room. "Jews wear a beard.
Do you see such facial hair on me?" He brushed the stubble
of his unshaven face. "Only the lack of a razor marks my
face with shadow. Jews have been forbidden to ride horses,
yet I have spent a great deal of my time on horseback. Jews
are not allowed to bear weapons, and yet until you took it
away from me, my sword was my companion!"

"Do you recite the Kiddush, the Jewish prayer of faith in
God?"

"I do not!"

"Do you keep the Pesach Feast, the Passover? Have you
ever studied the Torah?" In his attempt to incriminate Rafael, Juan Dorado was nearly incoherent. Even his own
counselors seemed impressed by Rafael's answers. "Do you
believe that the bible was dictated by the word of God?"
Like one possessed, Juan Dorado moved forward to shake
his fist in Rafael's face. Babbling his questions, he moved
the matter on to the *Conversos,* openly accusing Rafael of
crimes against Spain by aiding such fugitives. Fearing lest
Rafael redeem himself with his answers, Juan Dorado hurried through his accusations without giving Rafael time to
reply. "Confess the truth to me, because, you see, I already
know of the whole affair. Tell me of others who were involved so that I may save their souls. Do not fear to confess
all."

"There is nothing to confess!"

"He is a strong man!" A short, paunchy monk seemed by
his expression to admire Rafael.

"Not so strong that I cannot break him. I can see that I
will need Torquemada's help after all!" His smile was ruth-

less. "It is usual to allow prisoners time to consider the consequences of withholding their confessions. Thus, in my infinite mercy, I will give Rafael de Villasandro one more day to contemplate his sins. We will return here tomorrow morning to continue the examination, and this time he will not escape." Standing up, he waved the others away, watching as they filed through the door. Only when they were gone did he turn to Rafael again. "Think about what I have said. You have heard of the strappado? The rack? The torture of the water? All these will be your fate if you do not give me what I ask. Tomorrow the torture begins."

71

~~~

The large hall of the palace sparkled with a hundred candles and torches, and Alicia's chest constricted with emotion as she heard the pages call out her father's name. Would his plea for Rafael be successful? Touching the *mulengi dori* that was tucked inside her bodice, Alicia felt confident that it would. Surely the Gentle Christ himself would work *His* magic, too, to free Rafael. How, then, could all not be well?

As they marched the long distance to the dais, where the King and Queen were seated on their high-backed chairs, Alicia looked at the two men at her side and the splendid picture they made. Her father was dressed in a long, flowing green velvet gown, open at the front to reveal its gold lining, a striped tunic beneath, gold hose, and black cap. Giovanni was garbed more flamboyantly, in his gown of red velvet, a feather nestled in his hat. Clothed in black and gold, holding up her long skirts, Alicia walked in between. As they reached the thrones she followed their example and swept down in a bow. A chattering hum from others gathered in the room greeted their entrance, a noise that was silenced at once by Isabella's upraised hand.

"Your Majesties," Don Philip greeted.

"Rise, Don Philip." Queen Isabella was all smiles, welcoming the man who had been her most loyal subject and her friend. "It has been a long time since I have seen you, too long. Ah, but with the war in Granada and the other matters that occupied my mind, I have let time be my master."

"And yet it has not marred your beauty. You are as beautiful as ever. Perhaps even more so."

"And you are the same charming *hidalgo* that I remember."

Alicia raised her eyes to look at this woman who was Queen, the woman who held Rafael's fate in her hand, and decided that she liked her. Don Philip had told her that in her youth Isabella was said by her courtiers to be beautiful, and though the Queen was in her fortieth year, Alicia could glimpse that loveliness even now. Of medium stature, her figure verging on plump, Isabella had deep-blue eyes and hair the color of chestnuts, hair now winged and silvered with touches of gray. Meeting those blue eyes, Alicia smiled.

"Who is this pretty young woman with you, Don Philip? Have you taken another wife?" The chattering in the huge room began again, only to hush at the Queen's stern rebuke. "Rise, child." Her eyes lit on Giovanni. "And who are you?"

"I am Giovanni Luigi Alberdici, Venetian merchant and ship's captain."

"Another sailor!" The Queen seemed delighted, but the King, who sat at her side, merely grumbled, making his thoughts on Giovanni's vocation known. "I have made the acquaintance of another navigator and captain from your land. Cristoforo Colombo."

"I have heard of him. He is, however, from Genoa and not from Venice. I have heard he seeks a new route to the East."

"And do you think by going west he can reach the Indies?"

Giovanni smiled. "I believe that anything is possible, Your Majesty."

His answer was the right one, for Isabella smiled once again, a triumphant gleam in her eye. Looking toward her husband, the King, she thrust back her shoulders with pride, as if perhaps they had quarreled on the subject. Only then did Alicia notice the King, for he was overshadowed by the Queen's bright personage. Heavy of jowl, dark of hair, stocky in build, Ferdinand was not a man who smiled often, Alicia mused. Sensing her gaze, his dark eyes assessed her avidly in a look that made her flush. Hastily she turned her eyes away.

"Who is this fair flower?" The King at last made his presence known and his interests as well.

"This is my daughter, Alicia María Navarro. God has seen fit to give her back to me. And it is on her behalf that I have come. Within the walls of the city the man she loves is jailed, wrongly accused by my stepson. I beg that he be offered mercy and released into freedom." Don Philip's words were met by silence, interrupted only by the pounding of Alicia's heart as she looked anxiously first at the Queen and then at the King.

At last Isabella broke the silence. "Your stepson is Juan Dorado, priest and inquisitor. If he has spoken out against this man, it is a matter of faith and not of government. Why, then, have you come to me?"

Don Philip bowed humbly before his sovereign. "Because I know that Your Majesties keep detailed watch over the operations of the Inquisition and that appeal can be made to you from its decisions. I am thus appealing!"

Rising from her throne, Isabella paced the length of the dais, the hem of her deep-red gown brushing the floor as she walked. Her husband's eyes followed her, and Alicia felt a flash of fear, seeing Ferdinand's unrelenting expression. Don Philip had told her that the King himself profited from the confiscated property of the condemned. Would he, then, not be in favor of Rafael's ruination?

"I would speak with Frey Dorado. Bring him forth!" Isabella's command thundered through the hall, to be instantly carried out. Striding up to the dais, dressed in his robes of black, Juan Dorado's eyes blazed with malice as he faced his stepfather.

"You dare to meddle in matters of God?" he asked, crossing himself to impress the Queen with his piety.

"You seek to do injury to an innocent man to serve your own ends. I seek justice." Philip Navarro could not disguise his loathing for his stepson.

"Don Philip has come on behalf of his daughter. He seeks the release of . . ."

Juan Dorado did not give the Queen time to finish her words. Cruel mocking laughter issued forth from his lips. Holding up his cross, he waved it about. "His daughter! His daughter! The ravings of a demented man. This is not his *daughter*, Your Majesty, but a Gypsy. A heathen. A sorceress to so befuddle his mind!"

"No!" Alicia was horrified. "I am his daughter!"

"Don Philip Navarro's daughter died when she was just a child! She drowned! Are you, then, to say that like our blessed savior Jesus you came back from the dead?"

"No, I . . ." Alicia was confused, not knowing what she should say.

"She is my daughter!"

"I say that this she could not be. I have witnesses, those who will testify that the child in question was neglected by her nurse, fell in the water, and was swept away."

"She is my daughter!"

"Of that you have no proof! *No* proof!" Reaching for the neckline of his cowl, he tugged at at it frantically, as if he might be strangling. "She is unbaptized. A Gypsy! If you but let me question her, I will prove the truth of my accusations by her own confession. My stepfather is a fool. He comes to plead for the life of a relapsed Jew at the pleadings of a Gypsy! But God himself will lend his verdict. Take her away."

Hurling himself at Juan Dorado, Philip Navarro struggled frantically to keep Alicia away from the hands of the guards, who were acting to obey Juan Dorado's instruction. "No. You cannot harm her. I will not lose the daughter I so recently found. No! Your Majesty, I beg you." His plea to Isabella did no good, or so it appeared.

"I will go, Father. I will be brave." Alicia threw back her shoulders and held her head high in a show of dignity. "If Rafael must be sacrificed, then I am prepared to die by his side if need be." Her eyes met the Queen's as she was pushed along, her piercing gaze delving into that woman's soul. "Father Julio has taught me about the love and forgiveness of the gentle Christ. How is it, then, that his followers show no such love to each other? Why do they show no mercy? I think in my heart that God looks down from the sky and cries at such hardness of heart." She could not say anything more, for she was brutally dragged away, herself a victim of Juan Dorado's treachery.

72

The door of Rafael's cell was flung open and he was unceremoniously escorted by two guards down a steep flight of steps to an underground chamber. "Hurry! Hurry! The Grand Inquisitor himself is prepared to see you." The guard emphasized his command with a jab into Rafael's side.

"Torquemada?" In answer, the door to the chamber was opened and Rafael found himself face-to-face with the man who had made all of Spain bend its knees. Rafael had seen him several times before; but even so, the sight of him now made his hands tremble. It was like staring into the face of Satan himself. Surely even that fallen angel could not have been so fierce.

"You are Rafael Córdoba de Villasandro?" Torquemada was tall and gaunt, his tonsured hair the lightest shade of gray. The eyes that bored into Rafael were deep-set, sunken, yet even now filled with the fire of a fanatic. His body was bent and stooped with advancing age, yet even that could not detract from the power he displayed. This man knew well how to thrive on the emotions of others. "Need I repeat my question?" The cruel mouth beneath the large nose barely moved as he spoke.

"I am he."

"He is Rafael Córdoba de Villasandro. Let us get on with this matter." Juan Dorado stepped from behind the other man's shadow. He seemed agitated, determined to hurry the proceedings. "We have sifted through the evidence with care, we have questioned him. He has been shown the torture chamber yet has refused to confess or name his associates in the crime."

"What evidence have you?" Torquemada's voice was but a rasp.

"I ordered the questioning of some sailors on the coast bordering Spain and Portugal, as well as seeking out many of the fishermen in that area. My emissaries have documented my reports. I have further information about this man's mother. She was burned as a *Conversa* several years ago."

"My mother was a Christian of Jewish descent who was wrongly convicted."

"She was burned as a *Conversa*?"

"She was innocent. Of her memory I am proud." Again the scribe sat at a small round wooden table, setting down in writing Rafael's every word.

"He will not recant, his arrogance is too strong. We must use torture in this matter!" Heeding Juan Dorado's admonishment, the guards stretched Rafael out upon a wooden table and bound him down by ropes. Strong cords were tied about his wrists and ankles, tightened mercilessly until they cut through his flesh. All the while Juan Dorado poured forth his questions and demands. Through hours of agony Rafael resisted giving in to his pain. Nothing in this world would loosen his tongue and bring any other man to this end. Giovanni was his friend and the others men of courage. Better to die himself than have their agony upon his conscience. Thus he suffered in silence until the blessed darkness of unconsciousness swept over him.

"Douse him with water so we may bring him to and start our interrogation again." A guard reached for a bucket of brackish water and did as he was bid. With a moan Rafael stirred and opened his eyes. "There, look how he glares his defiance at me. This method is too mild; we must use the garrucha, the strappado."

"It is not our intent to kill him," Torquemada said in rebuke.

"The physician will attend him. I know this man. It is the only way to save his soul and that of the others as well."

Rafael felt confident that he could conquer the pain of this torture just as he had the first. It seemed, after all, a harmless machine, consisting of no more than a rope running through a pulley attached to the ceiling of the torture chamber. Stripped of his clothing, standing naked but defiant, Rafael felt the pinch of his torturers' hands as his arms were pinioned behind him. One end of the rope was bound about his wrists, the other end threaded through the pulley on the ceiling.

"Think. Think, my son. You are hungry, tired, naked, and bound. Tell us what we want and you will be spared." Torquemada's voice was nearly compassionate, yet his eyes flashed zealous flames. He made great show of pious concern, but Rafael's silence enraged him. "Then, so be it."

Slowly two of the robed men drew upon the free end of the rope, gradually raising Rafael's arms behind him as far as they would go. Backward. Upward. Continuing until they brought him up on tiptoe, then raising him slowly off the ground altogether until the whole weight of his body was thrown upon his straining arms. Rafael in all his life had never felt such pain. Against his own wishes he uttered a scream, only to be pulled even higher until his body was dangling high above the heads of the Inquisitor and the other robed men.

"Tell us what you know. Who aided in the escape of the *Conversos*? Was it your Gypsy lover who purloined the ships with her sorcery?"

"No! I do not know any Gypsy!" Rafael said the lie through his clenched teeth. He had to protect Alicia. Juan Dorado was capable of anything.

Angry with his denial, Juan Dorado ordered that Rafael be hoisted even higher toward the ceiling, then allowed to drop a few feet, his fall being broken by a jerk that threatened to pull his arms from their sockets. "He protects this Gypsy, this witch!" He glared at Rafael. "Tell me what I want to know. One more time will I ask you, de Villasandro."

"I have nothing to say to you!" Rafael was again dropped, cringing at the excruciating pain, yet holding back his screams. When he reached the ground without confessing, weights were attached to his feet, increasing the severity of the torture, which was instantly resumed.

"Who were your accomplices?"

"There were none. I have done nothing wrong. Nor do I know any Gypsies." Rafael felt pain shoot through his arms and his shoulders but smothered his screams yet again. He would die rather than endanger Alicia. She was Philip Navarro's daughter! He would protect her. All would be well if Rafael could only maintain his silence. A little while longer, just a little while. Ignore the pain. Biting his lips to muffle his yells, he tasted the warmth of his own blood.

"Bring him down. Satan himself must be in league with him. I have seen few men conquer their suffering so." Torquemada eyed Rafael with profound interest. "We will suspend the torture for today."

Feeling blessed relief as the ropes binding his wrists were torn away, Rafael clenched and unclenched his fists to bring the blood flow back into his numb wrists and fingers. "Thank you, Your Grace." He was sore and shaken, but at least there was no permanent damage done to his body. At least his arms were still in their sockets.

Torquemada held up his hand, but before he could offer any comments Juan Dorado whispered in one hooded man's ear, sending him hurriedly away. "He says that he has done nothing wrong. He denies knowledge of any Gypsies. I will prove now that he lies. I have four Gypsies within my grasp and I will bring one of them forth right now."

Rafael cringed, fearing that somehow Juan Dorado had managed to get some of the members of Alicia's band into his power. Who would it be? Solis? He had a score to settle with her for her lies. Still, he would not want even Solis to face such punishment. Stivo? Were he to find himself face-to-face with him, he would lose all self-control. Zuba? Todero? Nothing on earth could have prepared him for the moment when Juan Dorado opened the door and pushed Alicia inside.

"Alicia! *Madre de Dios!*"

"Rafael! Oh, Rafael." She ran to him, burrowing her head in the naked flesh of his chest, winding her arms around him. "They have Zuba and Todero. Stivo and the others. Oh, what are we going to do? We can't let my people die!" By her innocent words Alicia had condemned not only herself but Rafael as well. Before Torquemada's eyes he was branded a liar.

"If he lies about one thing, then he is false in his other words as well." Like a spider Juan Dorado was weaving his treacherous web. "I will prove that everything he says is a falsehood. He is a *Converso* who aided other *Conversos* and Jews. One who is in league with Gypsies and blasphemers. To the fires with him! To the fires with them both!"

"Do with them what you must." Without even a backward glance at the prisoners, Torquemada swept out of the room, leaving Rafael and Alicia to Juan Dorado's justice.

"She is innocent. But *I* am guilty. I will confess all if you spare her. Promise me that you will set her free, and I will be prepared to spit in the eye of Satan himself."

"No, Rafael! No!" Alicia shook her head violently. She would not allow him to sacrifice himself for her. She would not let him face his torment alone.

"If I free her, then you will confess all?" Juan Dorado's usually frowning lips curved upward in a smile. He had no intention of freeing Philip Navarro's daughter, but this he did not say.

"I want to be with him, please." Alicia's eyes were wide with pleading.

"Let me spend just one night in her arms and I will do anything you ask of me. I will sign my name to your document." Rafael felt as if he were bargaining with the devil himself. Perhaps in a way he was.

"Why not? It is but one small thing to ask." Juan Dorado's acquiescence aroused Rafael's suspicions. Even so, the thought of one night in Alicia's arms tempted him beyond his endurance, and he was willing to take the risk. Besides, he could not put from his mind the chance of escape. Thus, with his arms wound about Alicia's waist, he walked in his naked splendor back to his cell. Somehow he would think of a way to save Alicia. It was his last thought as he heard the door close behind them, but this time he welcomed the darkness.

73

Hearing the heavy door close behind them, Alicia struggled to accustom herself to the dim light of the cell. "Rafael?" Feeling the touch of his hand upon her shoulder, she
gave herself up to the strength of his arms.

"I thought I would die when I saw you enter that cell.
Dios, Alicia, how do you come to be here? All this time I
thought you were safe in Salamanca. That was my only
comfort, knowing that you were safe and far from here."

"My father brought me here at my insistence. He told me
that he intended to plead your case before the Queen and
King. All would have been well if not for that evil priest!"

He held her away from him, and she could see the look of
fear in his eyes. Fear for her. "Listen to me, Alicia. You must
think very hard and remember all that Father Julio has
taught you. You must not mention *o Del* or anything at all
about your Gypsy ways. To do so will mean danger. Do you
understand?"

"Yes, I know what you are saying. That I must deny the
people that I love, the things that I was taught since I was a
child, just to save my own life. I must act as if I never knew
Rudolpho, the wisest man I have ever known. Am I to deny
loving you as well?"

"Yes, if by so doing you will be spared. I am a doomed
man, Alicia. I thought that I could fight against injustice,

and in so doing I have forfeited that which I hold most dear. You!"

"You have not lost me, Rafael. You will never lose my love. Perhaps now that I know of what you have done, I love you even more. All the time I thought you had deserted me, you were being the most noble of men in aiding those in danger." She touched his face, tracing his profile with gentle, loving fingers.

Rafael drew away, warring with his emotions. "I am a condemned prisoner, an outcast, scorned by my own people, in danger of losing my life. Somehow we must prove Juan Dorado a liar. There must be some way for Don Philip to prove that you are his daughter. Then at least you will be safe!"

"It doesn't matter, Rafael. I am prepared to die with you if I must. In truth I *am* more Gypsy than gorgio, no matter if I am Don Philip's daughter. I will always carry Rudolpho's teachings in my heart." She reached inside her bodice and pulled forth the piece of ribbon that had measured Rudolpho's coffin. "This is known to give aid to one who is in danger or imprisoned. I brought it for you. It will free you."

Rafael silenced her words with his hand. "Hush, Alicia. Such talk sparks of blasphemy. Were anyone to hear you, you would be as doomed to the fires as I. Put all such thoughts from your mind."

Her eyes sparkled with tears. "I cannot. I am what I am, Rafael. Father Julio has taught me many things about your Christian ways that I believe, but there is much about Gypsy beliefs that I hold in my heart as well. In some ways I am confused, yet one thing I do understand. *O Del* and your Christian God are the same. It is not what we call him, but how we treat others that matters. The gentle Christ talked of brotherly love, and the Gypsies believe in it as well. Are we so very different, then? Enough so to take our lives or chase us from this land? It is loving one another that is important; why cannot this frowning priest see that?"

"Because he is not as wise as you." He kissed her then, a kiss that spoke of his love, the caress of his mouth arousing them both to hunger. Alicia moved against him in a manner that wrenched a groan from his throat. "You must not die, Alicia. You must live for me. You have your entire life before you. You must marry and raise the children we have been denied, with a man who will protect you as I am helpless to do now." The very thought of her in another man's arms, bearing his babies, tore at his soul, but Rafael was determined to think only of Alicia's well-being.

"I will never bear another man's child. I want no other man. I want only you, Rafael. Give me your child. Tonight!" Rafael was completely naked, and the stroke of her fingers upon the bare flesh of his chest and abdomen set him on fire. "Love, me Rafael! Love me!"

His hands stroked her hair. In her innocence she had given him a way to save her. A pregnant woman would be free of the threat of torture and death, at least until her baby was born. It would take several months for the child to be formed. Time, precious time. Respite from the danger. Enough time perhaps for Don Philip to find a way to save Alicia. Even Isabella could not be so hard of heart as not to give mercy to a woman expecting a baby. And he would be leaving behind a part of himself; in that way he would not fully die. A baby, born of his love for Alicia.

"I will love you, Alicia. With all my heart I will always love you." He had been weak, but her love made him strong, soothing away all the hurt and pain of the last few weeks. What once had been only a pallet now became a lovers' bower. Reaching down, Alicia pushed the bodice of her gown from about her shoulders, baring her breasts to his gaze and to his touch.

"Beautiful. So beautiful." He cupped her full breast in his

hand, imagining his child suckling it. Now *he* would taste of its sweetness.

Their hands explored each other, their mouths meeting again and again as they gave themselves up to the power of their love, basking in its warmth. If they had only tonight to be together, if the future looked bleak, the flame they lit tonight would blaze fiercer than any the Inquisition could ignite.

Alicia had been accused of being a Gypsy, a sorceress, yet it was Rafael who worked a powerful magic, he who was the weaver of spells. She felt as if she were floating, hurtling away from the earth and back again. Her insides turned to molten fire at his kisses and her desire raged like an inferno. Burning with passion, she flung her arms around him, holding him close as her mouth returned his kisses with frantic urgency. All the days of anguish, of searching, of wanting, all questions in her mind, drifted into oblivion as he made love to her. He was gentle yet urgent, bringing her to a fever pitch before he covered her body with his own. She was like a blossoming flower, opening to him, sheathing him inside her softness. Clinging to him, her arms about his neck, she answered his movements with a fluid motion of her own.

In the beauty of their joining, the darkness of the outside world was forgotten and only the magic of the moment was real. Lying entwined, they sealed their vows of love and knew at that moment that whatever happened, their love could never be destroyed. And somewhere deep within her heart, Alicia knew that she would bear Rafael a child.

74

Nestled in Rafael's arms, Alicia dozed peacefully in the aftermath of their love. Dressed only in her chemise, she looked somewhat like an angel as she slumbered, and even the black-robed monk who peered through the slits in the door was moved by the sight. He had been instructed by Juan Dorado last night to eavesdrop and listen to any conversation that might be used against them, but Brother Rodrigo had not had the heart to obey such a request and had left the two lovers alone. If that brought forth Juan Dorado's wrath, then so be it.

Fearing to startle them, yet knowing that their time together had come to an end, Brother Rodrigo coughed and cleared his throat, waking the sleeping lovers. Seeking the warmth and security of Rafael's arms, Alicia clung to him as if their love would keep him from harm.

"Don't take him away!"

Rafael gently pulled free of her arms, his gaze intent, as if memorizing her face forever. "I made a bargain, and this morning I must pay. Juan Dorado will only have one victim!" Rising to his feet, clothing himself, he prepared to face Juan Dorado and Torquemada. "Take me to your priests."

With deep sympathy written in his eyes, the monk opened the door. "If it means anything at all to you, Señor, I must let you know that I at least believe that you are innocent of evil. How I wish that I could help you. Juan Dorado pretends to be a saintly man. Torquemada has brought suffering, but his quest is to bring religious unity to Spain. What Frey Dorado does, he does in his own interest."

"I know that you could never have spoken in my behalf, but I appreciate your compassion. At all costs Alicia must not be harmed. If that means sacrificing myself, then I am willing." Rafael's voice lowered to a hush as he saw the familiar hated form of Juan Dorado coming down the long, winding hall. He looked pleased with himself, relishing his supposed victory. The parchment he carried in his hands Rafael rightly supposed to be for his confession. He had only to sign his name to secure his death by fire. His death. Of all things on earth, never seeing Alicia again brought the greatest ache to his heart.

Bear me a son or a daughter, my love, he thought, meeting her eye. *Know that I loved you and that you brought me the greatest joy.* As if sensing his thoughts, Alicia paused in donning her garments to put her fingers to her lips in a final gesture of goodbye.

"I have in my hands the transcripts of your interrogation. I have taken the liberty of composing your statements." Juan Dorado did not even try to hide his smile. "Ah, when I remember our first meeting, how you so completely fooled me with your fawning ways. I know that it will be a long while before your soul is free of its purgatory. I could have used you. . . ."

"As you have used everyone you have come in contact with? I think you are even using Frey Torquemada for your own gain." A blow across the face silenced Rafael's talk, yet his thoughts were his own. If only he could let Torquemada and the King and Queen know of Frey Dorado's perfidy, of all the funds that had crossed his palm and never come to the Queen's and King's coffers. Juan Dorado had used the Jews' misery to enrich himself, but who would believe Rafael's testimony? Who would even hear him? Frey Dorado made great show of his piety. He never ate meat, his bed was a plank, his flesh never knew contact with linen, his garments were of the roughest spun wool. Even his servants whispered among themselves of the priest's strict discipline. Yet Rafael knew the truth. Juan Dorado had asked him to make careful, detailed account of the exiled Jews' property, and Rafael knew that it was, in some way, to benefit Juan Dorado himself.

"Excuse me, Your Grace!" A young monk who had taken his turn as guard in the middle of the night appeared before Frey Dorado. Juan Dorado made a point of ignoring him, focusing his attention on the parchment.

"You will never know how I have longed for your ruination," he rasped. "Since the day I first found out that you had betrayed me. Seeing you with Philip Navarro's whelp was my first hint of the mischief you intended. I remember that day at the tournament very well. You did not know that I saw you talking with a certain sea captain." Rafael's limbs grew weak. Had Giovanni's involvement also been found out? "Oh, that I could put him to the rack, that interfering foreigner!"

"Your Grace." The young, timid monk tapped lightly at Frey Dorado's shoulder.

"For the love of God, what is it?" Turning his head, Juan Dorado's expression was much the same as that of one glimpsing an insect on his arm. The unfortunate monk stood silent, gathering his courage to speak again.

"The Queen. The King. You have been summoned to bring your prisoner and the girl and come to the hall right away."

For the first time since his incarceration Rafael felt a ray of hope that he would have a chance to be heard, a hope encouraged by the look of surprise and dismay on the priest's face. Whispering a prayer in his heart, he followed Juan Dorado, four monks, and Alicia up the long, twisting stairs and toward the hall. Entering that spacious room, he found an assembly waiting that included Philip Navarro and Giovanni.

"Your Majesties have summoned me?" Fidgeting with the transcript, Juan Dorado seemed nervous. "I was about to get my prisoner's confession."

"Through torture and threats?" Philip Navarro's comment was received by a dour look from the Queen. Ignoring her rebuke, he gathered Alicia into his arms, holding her in a fiercely protective grasp.

"A special delegation was sent to Pope Innocent, our most Holy Father, in regard to Señor de Villasandro's arrest. Father Julio has sent a message instructing us that there are to be no more *interrogations* until further notice." Rafael listened to the Queen's statement in relief. At least for the moment he was saved. "Our pontiff has been stricken with a fever. Most unfortunate. We will pray for his recovery."

"But Your Majesty, I have but to obtain Rafael de Villasandro's signature and we may have our auto-da-fé! And what of this matter of the Gypsy girl?"

Queen Isabella's eyes touched upon Alicia gently. "The *Gypsy girl,* if indeed she is a Gypsy, has impressed me with her words on the subject of mercy. Too many times we are hard of heart in such matters. I wish to show her that I can grant mercy just as willingly as the gentle Christ, whose words I heed. Therefore I abrogate the prior judgments that have been made and will myself assume jurisdiction over this proceeding."

"You?" Clearly Juan Dorado was incensed yet dared not argue.

"Don Philip has ever been my trusted adviser and my friend. I heed his counsel in this matter. You have laid forth the charge that this young woman is not his daughter but a Gypsy. He calls you a liar and has made accusations as to your loyalty. Don Philip himself, who paid for your education in canon law, charges that you are unfit for the high office that you bear. He puts forth the opinion that your struggle for power is to satisfy your own ambition and not to spread the word of God. He further charges that you milk the revenues due both church and the sovereignty. A most serious charge!"

"I am loyal to God first and my Majesties second! He is wrong. He is jealous of my success, of my calling. He is a foolish old man. Why do you listen to him?"

"In all ways I find that Don Philip is wise." Queen Isabella gave Philip Navarro permission to speak.

"Ambition is your only loyalty!" He challenged his stepson to say otherwise. It was then that Rafael saw his chance to corroborate Philip Navarro's sentiment. Moving forward, he revealed Juan Dorado's command to record the value of the properties of all condemned personages.

"If you will but scrutinize his ledgers, I think you will find that this cleric is nothing but a pirate and a rogue who has betrayed your trust, Your Majesty." Rafael forced himself to bow, despite the ache in his body from the agony that the priest had inflicted upon him. "Collected taxes went into his coffers and not your own. He took a painting from my hand as a gift, then confiscated another such work of art from my brother, after he had him charged with an untruthful crime. He has collected lands, livestock, and all means of goods. All titled in his name!"

"A serious charge!" Isabella raised one eyebrow in surprise.

"One that is not true," Juan Dorado hissed.

"I will let God be the judge!" Turning her head from side to side, looking first at one, then the other, Queen Isabella thought of a plan that could reveal the truth to her, one used for several generations before that was still used occasionally. "Trial by combat! It is an appeal under royal judicial sanction and control, to the judgment of God. That will settle the matter. I will allow you, Frey Dorado, to choose from among Castile's champions, for you are of the cloth and not able with weapons. Señor de Villasandro, however, appeals to the romantic side of my nature. Not only will he fight for his own honor and freedom, but for his lady as well. If he is successful, he and all those he requests will go free. I will take it as a sign that he and all whom he seeks to protect are innocent in God's eyes."

"Surely not all, Your Majesty!" Juan Dorado's face was flushed with suppressed anger.

"All! It will be the will of God who is the victor. In Him I place my faith."

75

The combat was to be held in a place similar to the field in Salamanca where Alicia had watched young men joust for pride and glory, yet now more than pride was at stake. If Rafael lost the match, it would be seen by Queen Isabella as a sign from God. It would signify not only his guilt but that of others as well. Foolish gorgios, Alicia thought. If Rafael lost, it would be because he was tired and half starved, driven beyond his endurance, overpowered by a stronger opponent, one who had not faced the peril of tortures. And yet it was a chance!

Don Philip had given her a finely wrought gold cross, and now she clutched that tightly in her right hand and the *mulengi dori* in her left, still torn in her beliefs. Would God protect Rafael? Would her prayers be answered? How she longed for Father Julio's presence. There were so many questions she needed to ask.

The grounds were decorated with banners, the colors reflecting the loyalties of the onlookers, and Alicia was shocked to see such display. This was not an amusement but a matter of great importance; how, then, could there be laughter? She even heard wagering going on, men in the crowd deciding a winner and placing coins on their heartless bets. Did they think that God would approve of such a thing, that he would aid one of the combatants so that they would be the richer? Just the thought made her shiver.

A howl of excitement rose from the crowd, drawing Alicia's attention to the field as Rafael and his opponent took their places. Unlike the jousting tournaments, Rafael and the challenger were on foot and wore no armor, and Alicia was all too aware that this battle might very well be to the death.

"God be with him!" Alicia whispered aloud, clutching the arm of her father, who sat beside her.

"He will, Alicia. Of that I have no doubt. Had I no faith in God's judgment, I would have tried to stop this combat. I feel certain Rafael will prevail." It was a sentiment Giovanni echoed.

Their words calmed her, and she was able to relax somewhat as the two men came forward. They were dressed in hose and long tunics, Rafael in yellow with red flames emblazoned on his chest, the emblem of those charged by the Inquisition; the other man in a white tunic with red cross, a symbol similar to that worn by those who had traveled afar on the Crusades, in deference to Juan Dorado.

Reaching the end of the field, Rafael turned toward Alicia, and bowing, saluted her with his sword in acknowledgment that she was his lady and that he was to fight for her. Such a gesture brought applause and cheers from the crowd that wished for Rafael's success and boos from those who hoped to see him fall.

"Their Majesties have arrived," Don Philip exclaimed, pointing to a separate row of seats that were decorated with the sovereigns' coat of arms, castles and lions. "Now the combat can and will begin." Alicia watched as the Queen herself beckoned to Rafael and Juan Dorado's champion. Holding forth a huge golden cross, she bade each man kiss the crucifix as the audience roared its approval.

"Rafael has chosen to use a sword. He has chosen well." Giovanni mumbled his approval. "The ax is cumbersome." Alicia was relieved to see that Juan Dorado's champion had chosen the sword too. The battle-ax looked awesome and more able to maim.

Be safe, Rafael. Be safe, my love, Alicia thought as she watched him prepare for the battle. *Live for yourself, for me, and for the unborn children we have yet to conceive. I want to give you many children!*

Rafael saw Alicia's eyes upon him and felt the depth of her love strengthen the resolve of his abused body. He had to win! He had to win! The thought of never seeing her again, of the danger to her, was too painful to contemplate. Warily he eyed his opponent, a short, burly man bulging with muscular strength. Brawn would be this one's advantage, but Rafael knew that cunning and agility would be in *his* favor.

The piercing shriek of a trumpet silenced thought as the two adversaries advanced, swords leveled. Clutching their shields, they prepared for what was to come. Now Rafael would be forced to fight while babbling onlookers craned their necks to watch the spectacle.

It was a brutal fight, sword against sword, shield against shield. Controlling his breathing, ignoring the pounding of his heart, Rafael was aware that the short, stocky figure would try to catch him unaware. Grasping his sword with determination, gripping the hard hilt as his opponent struck out, Rafael had just enough time to parry the blow; yet it was fierce, the power behind the sword enough to send Rafael to the ground. As the crowd gasped, he rolled away from another strike, which was thrust into the soft soil just inches from his head.

"You won't escape me so easily next time." Disappointed that his weapon had not drawn blood, Rafael's foe threw himself upon him. Locked together in combat, the two men rolled upon the ground as the crowd roared with excitement.

Freeing himself at last from the large man's grip, Rafael

stood back. "I don't want to kill you. My quarrel is not with you, Señor. My intent is only to prove my innocence."

"That is a thing that you will not do, for I am anxious to shed your blood. I have no liking for those who go against God!" With a grunt the man lunged again, his sword upraised, his eyes shining with the thirst for victory. Once again Rafael parried the blow just in time.

The sound of sword on sword rent the air as the two men fought their furious battle, a test of strength, courage, and skill. Again and again the large man lunged, his anger at being so easily thwarted making him careless. His senses honed by danger, his sword arm swinging forward, Rafael blocked each thrust until, with a sudden burst of strength, he knocked his enemy's sword from his hand. The crowd roared, their cries, voicing their thirst for blood. They did not want to be cheated of this spectacle.

The King, himself able with a sword, leaned forward in his seat, angry at the outcome of the match. In a loud voice he urged Juan Dorado's champion to pick up his sword, a request that was quickly heeded as the man took advantage of the King's interruption.

The onlookers waited tensely as the two men prepared to fight again. Rafael cursed his own sense of honor that had not allowed him to strike an unarmed man. Pray to God that it would not mean his own end. Days of little food and rest now took their toll. He was dizzy, his arms not fully recovered from the strappado, ached in their sockets. While he might have been able to withstand a short battle, he feared that as the time wore on he would tire. His body could endure just so much, even for honor and love.

Rafael's aching eyes seemed to imagine three men hurtling toward him, lunging, striking. Shaking his head, he sought to clear his vision as his opponent suddenly lunged out like a beast of prey. Pain pierced his shoulder as the blade of the sword struck him. The warmth of his own blood seeped from his wound down his arm.

"Rafael!" He could hear Alicia's wail even from a distance. His tunic whipped about his legs, the wind tugged at the hem, as he fought against the agony of his injury. The crowd was on its feet awaiting his certain defeat, but he was equally determined that despite the blow he would win.

With a bellow of rage his opponent lunged for the death blow, his sword whistling through the air. Rafael ducked just in time, his outstretched leg proving to be the other man's woe. Hurtling to the ground by force of his own pursuit, the man let anger blind him. No longer thinking clearly, he was charging wildly like a madman, and Rafael used this to his advantage. Aiming a strike quickly and carefully, he felt the thrust of his sword blocked by the other man's flesh.

"*Dios*, you have killed me!" Curling up like a babe inside its mother's womb, the man grew silent, the bright splash of crimson proving that Rafael's aim had been true.

Closing his eyes, whispering a prayer for the man's soul, Rafael heard the shouts and cheers from the crowd. A man lay dying and they were shouting. The very thought chilled Rafael's soul. He had won, but the price had been another man's life. Anxiously he watched as the physicians rushed across the field, expecting the pronouncement that he had struck a mortal blow. Instead he was relieved to hear the physicians proclaim that if he were bled in time, the man would live.

Rafael heard the sound of trumpets shrill again and saw the onlookers turn their heads in the direction of the Queen. As if through a fog, he heard her pronounce him innocent by virtue of his victory, but it was only Alicia's face that he sought, her arms that he wanted now. His heart was soaring with the knowledge that with the help of God, right had triumphed. It was his only thought as he slumped to the ground.

76

Rafael opened his eyes to the gray mists that swirled before him. Where was he? "Alicia?"

"I'm here, my love." She grasped his hand and held it to her breast. "God was with you and with all of us as well." Her face hovered over him with tender concern. "The Queen and King have judged you innocent, and I have been named my father's daughter as well as his heir. Zuba, Todero, Stivo, and the others have been promised safe conduct until they can reach the shores of Portugal. So you see, all is well!"

"Where are we?" He reached out one arm to draw her closer, bringing her head onto his chest, wincing slightly as she brushed his injured arm.

"In that place where we first met. Your victory caused such a stir that Father sought a place of safety from those who meant well but whose exuberance might have harmed you. Perhaps he also knew that we would want to be alone." The fog in his brain had not quite cleared yet, but as he looked around him he knew instantly that they were in the spot that once had been the Gypsy camp. The roar of the river mingled with the whisper of the wind.

"The *mulengi dori*, where is it?"

"In the river where it belongs. I know that it was God's will and not any magic that kept you safe for me. Father

Julio has always told me that right overpowers wrong, and now I know that he told true."

"Father Julio is in all ways a wise man. I hope that he will hurry back from Rome. I have need of a priest." He laughed at her worried look. "It is time that we were married and I would have no other marry us." He kissed the soft dark hair that tickled his face, pulling her down to lie beside him. Don Rafael's cloak had been spread upon the ground to act as a bed, and Rafael asked, "Where is your father?"

"He and Giovanni have it in mind to watch over us, but we are well out of sight of their eyes. Are you rested enough, my love, to . . ." In answer Rafael enfolded Alicia in his arms, his mouth closing hungrily over hers, blazing a path to her throat. They had their entire lifetime to be together, many sunsets, many dawns, rain and sunshine, beneath the sun and beneath the stars. Love truly had conquered all.

Don't miss next month's tempestuous historical romance, EVERY TIME I LOVE YOU by Heather Graham.

Williamsburg, Virginia
July 1774

Dusk had fallen. He waited for her by the corral, hidden in the dying light by the leaves of an old shade elm. Curious, he fingered the note again and again. He smiled, and brought the fine vellum paper to his face to inhale the violet fragrance that scented her stationery.

Meet me at the corral. At dusk. Katrina.

That simple a missive. No kind or tender words, no hesitance, it was almost abrupt. It didn't matter. He didn't know her game, but he would play it. Since he had touched her he had known that he would move heaven and earth to have her. And though she could run from him, she could never flee from the thing that simmered and sizzled and flamed between them. A man could not love so quickly, he told himself; but he did. Everything else in his life had been child's play. The dances, the reels, the flirtations, the lessons learned from the whores and the chambermaids, and even a refined but lonely widow or two. A touch, a kiss, a flirtation, an affair; nothing compared with this. Nothing had so taken his heart and mind, so distracted him from thought and reason.

James had warned him that it would be a trick. The British already had arrest warrants out for a number of men in Boston. This wasn't Massachusetts, Percy argued. If and when the Colonies chose the path of separation, Virginia would stand hard and firm—it would be the British who would run, the Tories who would be called traitors.

That time had not yet come, James had told him.

Percy idly crossed one ankle over the other and leaned back against the bark of the tree. A wistful smile touched his features and the night breeze blew a lock of ebony-dark hair across his forehead.

None of it mattered, Percy knew. If she brought with her the sure promise of hell and damnation, he would be here still, waiting for her.

There seemed to be a sudden whisper in the wind, a rustling in the foliage. Percy quickly slipped beyond the tree and waited, his heart pounding. Someone in a dark cape and hood moved about in the darkness.

Katrina had not known that it would be quite so frightening. At night, with the darkness growing and the trees seeming to wave and weave ominously, the town itself seemed very far away. Moving from doorway to doorway, tree to tree, trying to blend with the darkness, she had thought again and again that she should leave. She should run, she should disappear.

There would be nowhere to run. Nowhere far enough to run. She had wanted to come closer to Percy Ainsworth. She had wanted to touch him. Like a moth, she'd had to kiss the flame, and now she was doomed to pay. It was a bitter irony.

A nightbird shrieked suddenly out in the darkness, and she nearly cried. She could barely see the horses in the corral. She could hear the pale strains of conversation and laughter coming from the tavern. Inside, she knew, small bands of men met. They talked and they talked, and they toiled, wrote, and planned. Rebellion. They were traitors. They were all traitors. And Percy was one of them. She had to remember that.

She could not see him. The sun had fallen completely; the moon—a half crescent—was making a slow ascent into the night sky. Katrina swallowed briefly, remembering all the old tales she had heard about Indian raids. There were no Indians around here now. They were long gone. She was still afraid of the darkness, of the whisper of the wind, of the skeletal fingers of the trees.

"Percy?"

She whispered his name and stepped into the clearing. A sound came from behind her and a hand clamped over her face. She tried to scream, but the hand was too tight, and she was dizzy and weak with the terror of it.

"Shh! It's me!" She heard his voice, quiet and commanding. He didn't release her, though, not until he had taken her back into the shadow of the elms. When they were there, he tossed back the hood to her cape, and he stared down into her eyes.

They were cobalt by night. A tempest of emotion. He mustn't be fooled, he warned himself. "You are alone?" he asked her.

She nodded.

"What are you doing here? You ran rather briskly before, if I do recall correctly. You swore that you hated me, and you ran."

She tried to lower her head; he caught her chin and raised her eyes back to his. "I am alone!" She told him. "And—and I do not hate you."

Her heart seemed to hammer and slam against her chest. She could not go through with this. They were fools; they did not know him. They had not accosted ebony eyes that could sparkle with laughter and darken like the devil's own with suspicion and mistrust. He was young, with the passion and aggression of youth, yet full grown to power, and through the fascination the fear remained.

"Why have you come, Katrina?" His voice was harsh, uncompromising. Tonight he was not the man who had whispered so eloquently of love.

"I wished to see you."

"Why?"

She stared at him, then tore from him, spiraling like a

dancer to catch the fence and stare out into the darkness of the corral. "Mr. Ainsworth," she said softly, "surely you've room for some compassion and mercy in your heart!"

He came beside her. "Don't play the flirtatious little coquette with me anymore, Katrina. I am not one of your brother's fool lackeys in a red coat or high court, macaroni fashion. We have played this game too long. You know that I love you, and you know that I want you. So tell, simply, why are you here?"

He caught her shoulders. He slowly turned her around. He ground his jaw down hard, fiercely reminding himself that in more ways than one she was the sister of Henry Seymour. She was a well-bred young lady from a sheltered home. He had moved too quickly with her. He could not bear her playing the flirt, but neither would he tread anything but gently with her. He would take care when he touched her. He would recall the innocence of her eyes and the angel's pale gold of her hair, and stem the flow of urgency that came from the seductive feel of a woman's form within his arms. And still, he would have the truth from her now.

He lowered his voice but spoke still with a ruthless command. "Why, Katrina?"

"Because I am sorry," she whispered.

He looked down at her for several long moments. He smoothed his thumbs over her cheeks tenderly. He thought that her skin was like silk. She was so very young and beautiful.

He looked from her to the darkness of the road beyond them, then he gazed across the corral and pasture to the door of the barn. He looked around them both again and saw nothing but the darkness of the night and the shapes and the forms of the horses and the trees, and, in the far distance, the rolling landscape.

"Come on," he told her. He slipped the hood back up about her head and face and set his arm around her shoulders. Quickly he led her across the open space to the barn.

Inside, he closed and bolted the door, then fumbled in the darkness to find the lantern. He lit it, and raised it high, setting it into the bracket by the door. He wandered on into the barn. In the center of it he paused, drawing his frockcoat from his shoulders, folding it neatly over the gate of a stall. He turned back to Katrina, who still hovered in the doorway.

He bowed to her. "May I take your cloak, milady?"

She shook her head nervously, remaining where she was. Percy did not come to her. He was different tonight. He taunted her, he took what he wanted, but always he was eloquent, and somehow gentle. Tonight he seemed to prowl with vibrant energy. The air was charged around them, and she wondered at herself incredulously that she had come here with him, alone.

She knew what he wanted of her. Once she had been so haughty, and now she doubted her own ability to resist him, for his kisses were a narcotic that robbed her of strength; his touch was a drug that set fire to her very soul.

But he did not touch her then. Perhaps he knew her treachery. She feared him if he did.

He walked on farther, then sat against the high pile of hay stashed in the corner, stretching out his long legs, grinning to her as he selected a piece of the stuff to chew upon.

"The accommodations are not much, I must admit. But do have a seat."

She smiled, and he loved her smile. She was shy and nervous here, but it came so quickly to her lips. She stepped into the room, not far yet, but closer. At last she paused where he had done so, and she untied her hooded cloak at the throat. It fell gracefully from her, and she laid it with his coat upon the stall gate. She was so, so beautiful, he thought. Her hair was down, no ties to bind it this night. It was a golden wave that cascaded about her, and he could not help but imagine it spread beneath her, or wound around his naked flesh.

Fool, he warned himself, do not think such thoughts. He

could imagine himself going to Lord Henry Seymour—and asking for his sister's hand in marriage. Lord Seymour might well have apoplexy.

He patted the hay beside him. "Come. Sit. I promise, I am no wolf. I will not bite you."

"Ah, but dear sir! I believe that I have been bitten." She grinned quickly, with a flash of sultry humor touching her eyes, and he wondered fleetingly what she was thinking. He was convinced of her innocence—but maybe all women were born with the ability to seduce.

Or maybe just a few . . .

She set a hand upon the structural pole and swirled around it. "It is dangerous to come too close."

He shrugged, chewing idly on the hay but watching her more carefully. "Dangerous, Katrina, for which one of us, I wonder?"

She stood silent, and he thought again that she was so beautiful. She was like a young doe. It seemed that she would bolt again, when she had just come.

"Katrina!"

She turned to him.

"It is done," he warned her. "The games are over. The teasing and the flirting, they are done. If you have come to taunt me again, I warn you, run now."

She lowered her head. "If I have taunted you, I am sorry. But you, Percy, are as guilty as I, for you were first to drag me here."

"Aye. But you see, I always knew that I loved you."

She looked up, startled at the tenderness in his tone.

Percy stood, pushing himself up from the hay. He came over to her and took her hands in his own. He wanted to tell her that she must choose her side, and that her choice must lie with him, for he did love her. He looked at her, and all he saw was the beauty of her eyes and the shining, rosy moisture of her slightly parted lips.

He kissed her.

He held her fragile chin in his hand, and he kissed her.

Her lips were parted and she offered him no protest, and he filled her mouth more fully with the taste and texture of his own, sweeping each sweet crevice with the seduction of his tongue. Her arms were around him too. Hesitantly she returned the kiss. Her hands fell upon his shoulders, then she grew bolder, and her fingertips raked through his hair. She darted the pink tip of her tongue against his lips and over his teeth.

He swept his arms around her hard, and he brought her to the hay, still kissing her. And when they fell there, his lips continued to know her, to seek, to devour, to savor and taste. He stroked her throat with the brush of his fingers and he kissed it. Her breasts—high, young, firm, beautiful—were pressed full against her bodice, and he buried his face within their shadowed seduction. He felt her tremble, and he rose above her and saw that her breath came fast and shallow, that her eyes, wide and dilated, were upon him with the cornflower color of a cloudless day, innocent, and beautiful. . . .

And trusting.

His own hands trembled.

He set them against her bodice, pulling upon the ribbons there, and the ties and the binds. Her breasts spilled free to him, and his caress upon them was the most tender touch he had ever dealt, and then tenderness was lost, because a passion unlike any he had ever known seized hold of him, and he meant to seduce her quickly, and with no mercy.

Tease him, Henry had ordered her. Flirt and cajole, and play the haughty minx, my dear, as you are so very fond of doing. Laugh and smile and bat your lashes, for the fool is falling in love with you. Talk to him, and bring me names and dates and places.

Talk to him . . .

Her brother's words left her mind as quickly as they had come, for Henry was the fool. Percy was different.

And she was the fool, for she was falling in love with him. She could not flirt; she could not cajole. Henry did not understand; this was no boy, but a man. She could do nothing but follow his lead, and where he led, she ached to go.

She moistened her lips, staring up at him. She had to stop this now. "Percy!" Her voice was breathless. "No! We mustn't—"

"Why did you come?" he demanded harshly, his eyes nearly black.

"Because . . ."

"Why?" The single word was snapped so abruptly, she felt as if she had been physically struck.

"Not for this—"

"So you do play the tease, the whore—"

She slapped him with all her strength. Startled, he brought his hand to his face. Katrina shoved against him, struggling from beneath him. "Don't you ever—"

"No!" She was upon her knees; he caught her wrists. He dragged her back to him, holding her close. "Damn you, Katrina Seymour! It is over, haven't you understood? If you come to me as a woman, then so help me, I will have you as one!"

"Damn you!" She cried out to him. "Damn you for being a bastard and a traitor!" She was close to tears. Her breasts were bare and forced against his chest, and the air sizzled with the fierce tension in her words.

"Let me go!" she demanded. She could feel him with her bare flesh, and she longed to tear away his shirt. She wanted to run, yet with an ever-growing desire she wanted this to go on, to go on forever and ever. She wanted to discover the path where he would take her. "Let me go!" she pleaded again. "I swear that I hate you!"

"Bitch!" he swore. But his fingers threaded into her hair. Harshly he lowered his face to hers, and he kissed her. He kissed her until her lips were swollen, until they were both breathless. Until the sizzling tension taken from the air entered into them and began a molten fire that swept through their limbs.

He moved his lips just slightly from hers. "I love you,

Katrina Seymour. Deny that you love me too, and I will let you leave."

She opened her mouth. She wanted to deny him. No words came to her. She shook her head desperately.

He pressed her back into the hay. He kissed her lips, and her forehead, and her throat. Then his mouth fell against her breasts. He laved and sucked and grazed his teeth over her nipples, and the wildfire seized her. She clutched his head against her, and she whispered to him, and she didn't know what she said herself.

He stared at her then, watching her eyes as he removed her shoes and her stockings. His fingers teased her abdomen as he worked at the drawstrings of her pantalettes and petticoats. She began a tremendous trembling as she felt his fingers against her bare abdomen.

He kissed her again, and then maneuvered her to free her hooks, to pull her muslin gown over her head. He tossed aside her stays and laces, and she suddenly realized that she lay before him, completely naked in the hay.

With a soft cry she came to him, needing his arms around her to hide that nakedness. "No," he whispered to her, and he laid her back in the hay and spread her hair against it.

Upon his knees, he hastily shed his waistcoat and his shirt. Supple muscle rippled in the darkness. He shifted to free himself of his boots and hose, and then his breeches. She closed her eyes and then opened them, and she shivered, but even as she did so, her eyes widened and she thought that he was beautiful. Truly beautiful.

His hands scorched a stroke of silk and fire against her flesh; he kissed her and kissed her, and was so fevered himself that should she speak, he could probably give no mind to her. . . .

He was glorious. As fine and sleek as a puma, as muscled and powerful as a bear, as sure and swift as a hawk. Mindlessly she touched his shoulders and luxuriated in the ripple of sinew and tendon and muscle. His belly was drum taut, and the same ebony hair that crowned his head and dusted his chest created a rich nest for that forbidden part of his body that so fascinated her now. It pulsed; it lived; it was his fire. She shouldn't be there; it was wrong, no decent young woman would dare to do as he said, dare to stretch out her fingers and touch, and wind them around him. . . .

And no decent woman would let him touch her as he did. But oh, there was no denying him. His kisses were surely depraved, but she could not halt them, she could not force herself to want to halt them, she could not command her own body. She could only feel. . . .

"Oh, Percy! This is—not right!" she cried to him once.

But he told her, "Nay, sweet, for when it is love that brings us together, then God has commanded that a man should worship his woman, and, sweet Jesus, I do love you."

She believed him . . . she believed that he loved her, and she believed that anything so intense, so intimate, and so natural between a man and a woman had to be right. Her fingers curled around his, and his lips touched upon hers. His touch . . . her head began to thrash against the hay. She whimpered as he moved upon her; she gasped, then nearly screamed out as the first sudden burst of ecstasy exploded within her. Percy caught her cry with a kiss, murmuring against her lips. "Shh! Love, take care. . . ."

She could not care about the rest of the world. Damp and delirious, she twisted into his arms and her word formed against his cheek. "Oh, Percy . . ."

He chuckled softly, rakishly, and promised her, "We've just begun, love, we've just begun." He went on to fill her with himself, with sweet burning flames that engulfed and consumed her, and brought her again and again to a shuddering awe. Then he kissed her again, held her again . . . and kept her close, close to his heart. She loved that as much, nuzzling against the damp hair on his chest, feeling the protective tenderness in him as he kissed her forehead, and smoothed back the curling wet tendrils of her hair that clung there.

Only then did she feel the hay beneath her back and become aware of the flickering light of the lantern upon her circumstances. She had never meant to give herself so completely—even if Henry had not cared how she sought her information. She had cared herself. But this had not been for Henry. None of it had been for Henry. She had been falling in love with Percy since she had first set eyes on him.

And this had been brewing between them since that very first time.

She should be sorry now. She was "ruined"—as they would say; fallen, lost. She should feel the shame and the horror of it, but she did not. She bowed her head against him and he held her tighter, and he whispered to her, "I love you."

"Percy . . . I love you too."

"Come away with me."

"I cannot. My brother would have us followed—and you hanged."

"Your brother be damned."

Feeling troubled, she rolled around, looking deeply into his eyes. She pressed her fingers against his lips. "Don't say that! He has power. He would have no difficulty calling you a traitor."

"Bah!" He was decidedly angry, but perhaps that was part of his charisma, that very boldness and passion, his dead-set belief in his glorious cause. "I swear to you, Katrina, in a year or so it will be Henry Seymour who runs!"

"That may well be so, my love, but now they are writing out arrest warrants for such men as Hancock and Adams."

"That is Massachusetts, this is Virginia."

"Pardon me! Percy, Percy! Please, take care! Do you think that the King's men will care about such distinctions? They will shortly declare the Commonwealth of Massachusetts in rebellion; blood will flow—"

"Aye," he interrupted softly. "Blood will flow." He leaned upon an elbow then, and stroked her cheek. "Trust me, love, the tide will ebb my way!" Excitedly, he went on to tell her about the secret liaisons being carried on with important men in Boston.

Men who would soon have nooses strung about their necks, Katrina thought.

"Percy, don't tell me all this—"

He laughed and hugged her, his dark eyes alive and vibrant with youth and determination. "My love, I have to tell you these things; I have to make you see the error of your ways."

His enthusiasm was so great that she could not help but smile. But then there was a soft knock upon the barn door. Katrina let out a soft cry of horror and groped about for what remnants of her clothing she could find.

"Percy?"

The hushed whisper came with another, louder, rapping on the door.

"'Tis only James," Percy assured Katrina.

"And who is James?" she murmured worriedly, struggling with her corset and chemise and petticoats.

He sensed her panic and helped her with her stays and ties before hurriedly slipping into his own breeches. Tucking his shirt into his pants, he walked quickly to the door. "James?" He glanced back; Katrina was just smoothing her gown over her petticoats. He smiled, thinking of how he loved her. She needed to relax, though, he thought with tender amusement—any man would know from the guilty expression on her delicate face exactly what they had been about in the barn. He smiled at her reassuringly.

"Aye, Percy, 'tis James."

Percy opened the door. A handsome young man his own age stepped in, nodded a polite acknowledgment to Katrina, and warned Percy, "It's late. They're saying that Seymour is at Chowning's, looking for his sister."

A knot caught in Katrina's throat. "I—I've got to go."

Percy came to her, agile and quick, running across the barn on his bare feet. He caught her hands. "Run away with me. We'll ignore this ogre of a kinsman. All of them be damned."

Katrina looked at James with horror. "Percy! Cease this foolishness! What of your great and glorious cause? My brother would see that you were hanged."

"Percy." James strode to them and caught Percy's shoulders. "Have you lost your senses, man? She's right. He's her legal guardian; you can do nothing but lose your life!"

"Percy! I must go!"

Aye, she had to leave, and quickly. If she did not, Henry would close in upon them right then. She had to play the game, and play it well.

He held her hands, then pulled her close and kissed her deeply. James cleared his throat. "I'll check the way," he said, and disappeared outside. Percy released Katrina at last. "I must see you again, soon."

She swallowed. "I'll get word to you."

"I love you."

"And I, you."

He smoothed her hair and slipped her cloak back around her shoulders.

" 'Tis clear!" James called to them.

At the door Percy pulled her back into his arms one more time. "Soon!" he urged against her lips.

"I swear," she promised, and he held her briefly close against him so that she felt his breath against her hair and the pounding of his heart beneath his shirt.

Nearly sobbing, she pulled away from him and ran.

She was able to slip in without Elizabeth's being aware that she had returned. She was relieved. She needed time, moments alone to treasure the night and her love until it had to be marred by Henry's sly intrusion. She washed her face, dressed in a nightgown, and lay down in her bed in the darkness, hugging her pillow to her. She relived every beautiful second of the night in her memory, and marveled again and again at the depth of her love for Percy.

Then the door opened.

Henry held a candle high and stepped into her room without so much as a by-your-leave. She closed her eyes and prayed that he would go away, but, of course, he did not.

"Sit up. I know you are not asleep."

He spoke so confidently, she was afraid that he would touch her. She sat up, scowling at him.

He set the candle down and perched at the side of her bed. "You saw him?"

"I did." Her heart pounded with bitterness; aye, brother, I played your loathsome game, and it is my soul at stake.

"And?"

"And what?" she murmured disdainfully.

"I let it be known that I looked for you, a timely intrusion, I hope, if you were in difficulty."

She laughed mirthlessly. "What difficulty? He is a perfect gentleman. And you know full well that his manners mean nothing to you, all that you want is to hang him and all his friends."

Henry ignored that. "He is wild and brash. What did he say? Did you learn anything? Did he believe in you?"

She sighed and lowered her head, hoping he would not see the color that flooded to her cheeks. "He believed in me. Oh, aye, he believed in me." She looked up, blue fire burning in her eyes. "But there is nothing to learn, Henry. He told me nothing that is not common knowledge."

"What about these secret meetings between the Colonies?"

She shook her head. "All that I could discover is common knowledge."

Henry's eyes narrowed. "You will find out more."

She smoothed a ripple in her bed sheet with her fingertips. "Henry, he comes and goes—"

"When he is here, he will come to you."

"I found out nothing!" she cried.

"Nor did you find out anything the last time you saw him, at the ball. You must be more charming. In time he will trust you."

"There is nothing to be found out!" she insisted. "Henry, there are few who can believe now that it will not come to war—"

"Yes." He smiled icily. "It will come to war. And you will be my eyes and my ears when I cannot be there to see and hear. You will do this for me, or else I will see you wed immediately to Palmer. Or worse." He smiled. "I am your guardian, and I promise you, Katrina, I can find you a truly loathsome husband. Or I can see that Percy is arrested and hanged immediately for some trumped-up charge."

"You are a loathsome creature, Henry."

"Thank you, sister dear. And thank you for your services. I am sure that they will improve."

He smiled again and left her. The door closed. She could no longer relish the sweet memories of her secret love.

She sobbed softly, for in truth, tonight she had lost her innocence.

Experience the Passion and the Ecstasy